Searchingly honest, achingly real, THE CHEERLEADER recalls all the joy, excitement, and pain of crossing the bridge from childhood to young womanhood in a bittersweet world where sex was still a mystery and goals were clearly defined— perhaps for the last time.

Across the nation the critics cheer
THE CHEERLEADER

"It's heartbreaking at times, hilarious at others, and she's got it all down beautifully."

—PHILADELPHIA INQUIRER

"In earlier novels Ruth Doan MacDougall has shown that if you bring an uncommon mind and talent to the commonplace what you are likely to get is not the commonplace but the uncommon. Now she has used that mind and talent to deal with one of the major communal democratic experiences shared by Americans—going to high school ... I can't recall a novel in which high-school-age youngsters appear which seems to reproduce so naturally their way of talking and in fact their whole demeanor and style of living. Nor have I recently encountered a more appealing young heroine than Snowy."

—KANSAS CITY STAR

"The author has captured firsthand the standards and traditions of the Fifties ... You will be terrifically entertained."

—CHATTANOOGA TIMES

"A quite remarkable novel ... Pinpoints so accurately the personal trauma of teenage girls growing up."

—CAMDEN, N.J., COURIER-POST

"The first love affair is neatly and sensitively handled, the dialogue absolutely right, the adolescents are as they have always been."

—CLEVELAND PLAIN DEALER

"Great nostalgic touches."

—CHICAGO TRIBUNE

"No one who was there could fault her—MacDougall holds a mirror up to the Fifties and comes away with a true reflection."

—FORT WORTH STAR-TELEGRAM

# BY THE SAME AUTHOR

The Lilting House
The Cost of Living
One Minus One
Wife and Mother
Aunt Pleasantine
The Flowers of the Forest
A Lovely Time Was Had by All
Snowy (a sequel to The Cheerleader)

*With Daniel Doan*

50 Hikes in the White Mountains, Fifth Edition
50 More Hikes in New Hampshire, Fourth Edition

*Editor*

Indian Stream Republic: Settling a New England Frontier,
1785-1842, *by Daniel Doan*

# The CHEERLEADER

## Ruth Doan MacDougall

THERE IS NO FRIGATE LIKE A BOOK
*Emily Dickinson*

FRIGATE BOOKS

Visit the author's web site at:
http://www.ruthdoanmacdougall.com

Reprinted by Frigate Books 1998

PRINTING HISTORY:
*G.P. Putnam edition published 1973*
*A Book-of-the-Month Club selection*
*Bantam edition published 1974, 1975, 1976*

*"The White Cliffs of Dover" by Alice Duer Miller, reprinted by permission of Coward, McCann & Geoghegan, Inc. Copyright 1940 by Alice Duer Miller. Copyright renewed 1967 by Dennig Miller.*

*Cover design by Judith Kazdym Leeds*

*Library of Congress Cataloging-in-Publication Data*
*MacDougall, Ruth Doan.*
       *The cheerleader / Ruth Doan MacDougall.*
          *p. cm.*
     *ISBN 0-9663352-0-1*
     *1. Women—New Hampshire—Fiction.*
*I. Title.*
*PS 3563.A292C5 1998*
*813'.54—dc20*                           *98-92550*
                                         *CIP*

3 4 5    02 01 00

# FOREWORD

IN 1975, when I was seventeen, I read, and reread, *The Cheerleader*, the story of a girl's high-school years in the fictional town of Gunthwaite, New Hampshire, during the 1950s. It turned out to be one of those books from youth that stayed with me, whose wisdom I understood through my own life and desires. In my eagerness to share this wonderful novel I lost my copy, and began a long, fruitless search to find another.

In 1996, I was an English professor in New Hampshire when I wrote to Ruth Doan MacDougall, describing my love for *The Cheerleader* and my hunt for a copy, and asking if she had one I could buy. She replied that *The Cheerleader* was out of print, though fans had been clamoring for years to see it back, and that she had written a sequel, *Snowy*, partly to satisfy their curiosity. Hence I discovered, with surprised delight, that my experience had been common to many. *The Cheerleader* had sold over 300,000 copies and received rave reviews, and had even been optioned by Twentieth Century–Fox and made into a television pilot. The novel was now a classic, with its own web site (www.ruthdoanmacdougall.com) created by ardent fans. I understood why I hadn't been able to find any available copies; they were all bought, or stolen, by devotees.

*The Cheerleader* inspires such dedication for myriad reasons. Perhaps most obviously, it is the proverbial "good read," with an absorbing plot and fully rounded, very real characters who are portrayed with humor and empathy even in their worst moments. MacDougall has a genius for realistically depicted scenes, fresh, natural dialogue, and subtle sensory details that evoke worlds, as the opening scene demonstrates: "The gym was darkened now, and sawdust-wax had been sprinkled on the floor, but the smell of hot sweat from the basketball game still lingered. Down the darkness echoed record-player music." Snowy's expanding awareness of beauty is lyrically rendered, in language as spare and delicate as her tenuous knowledge: "Above her in the trees the buds were a pale haze thickening to green."

MacDougall catches the world of adolescents better than any writer I have read, portraying equally the exaggerated importance they award certain rituals and the earthy bald humor that exists even in the midst of their cruelest competitions. The hilarious drunken swim made by Puddles during a wild party exactly transmits the exuberance of unchaperoned teenagers using an adult house for adult pleasures. The heart-stopping terror of cheerleading tryouts shows the fateful significance of such high-school contests that come to symbolize larger successes or failures. Perhaps most effectively, *The Cheerleader* frankly describes sexual initiation, its mix of cold calculation, awkwardness, sensuality, and confusion. Yet MacDougall also captures the wonder of first love, which happens in a world apart and in ways that lovers find they cannot always control: "[Tom] prided himself on his trick of unhooking a bra one-handed, and he got Snowy's unhooked before she knew what was happening, but then her worries dissolved in the wonder of his mouth on her breast."

*The Cheerleader* has all the hallmarks of a classic *bildungsroman*, the novel of education or formation that shows the growth of a protagonist's mind and character as she passes from childhood to maturity and finally recognizes her identity and role in the world. Snowy, the American cheerleader whose destiny would seem to be humble compared to, say, that of Stephen Daedalus in *A Portrait of the Artist as a Young Man*, in fact struggles to fly past comparable nets, and encounters a hypocritical social hierarchy much as Pip does in the more loftily titled *Great Expectations*. The very humility of the title *The Cheerleader*, with its unmistakable connotation of shallowness, at first might put off "serious" readers, but this is in fact part of its point. Snowy's world is a microcosm of the forces that shape the lives of all young people.

The social reality of conformist, conservative Gunthwaite frames Snowy's ambitious school career, and initially she sets out to play by every rule to win every prize. Yet Snowy's rote academic grind begins to include her genuine curiosity, and she alternates between complete immersion in Gunthwaite High, where there "was no outside," and her "brief surprised vision of the school balanced on a larger sphere spinning lopsided circles in space." As Snowy grows in mind and heart, she realizes she must develop her own self. That this realization happens in a small town in the 1950s to a cheerleader, symbol of a girl's simultaneous success and subordination, makes it all the more powerful. *The Cheerleader* transcends its setting to portray a young person's timeless yearning for a full and satisfying life.

Ruth Doan MacDougall grew up in Laconia, New Hampshire, and explains that Snowy's life and world mirror many aspects of her own high-school experience. But unlike Snowy, MacDougall knew from age six that she was a writer, inheriting the life and the craft from her father, Daniel Doan, a novelist and author of two classic New Hampshire hiking guides. Following her father's advice to "write about what you know," she published three novels in the 1960s and early 1970s that contained portraits of her New England upbringing. *The Cheerleader*, her fourth novel, originated with an editor who suggested she write about high school in the 1950s; MacDougall recalls, "In a flash I saw the book in my head."

Here it is again. We fans can only hope now for the next installment: Snowy at sixty. I for one can hardly wait.

ANN V. NORTON

Saint Anselm College

*To Donald Keith MacDougall*

# I.

THE dance had begun. The gym was darkened now, and sawdust-wax had been sprinkled on the floor, but the smell of hot sweat from the basketball game still lingered. Down the darkness echoed record-player music.

Henrietta Snow, known as Snowy, stood with another of the JV cheerleaders in the doorway. She was fifteen years old. She wore dungarees and her white cheerleading blouse, its collar turned up and its starch softened, and she wore her long dark-blond hair brushed into a ponytail that looked like an upside-down question mark. She said, "How disgusting!"

But Jean Pond, who was known as Puddles and also known for saying out loud what everyone else was thinking, said, "Maybe we should've been bawling in there, too. Maybe it's our last game, too."

Snowy felt sharply sick. "Shut up," she said. "Please shut up." She glanced at her left hand, where today's date had been stamped by the boy at the desk outside the gym. March 4, the stamp said clearly. Soon it would begin to smudge. March 4, 1955.

The JV cheerleaders had changed out of their uniforms during the Varsity game. They couldn't take showers; the visiting basketball team was using the girls' locker room, and they changed in the girls' gym office and clogged their sweat with

Cashmere Bouquet talcum powder. So they had no real excuse for being in the gym office again after the Varsity game, but sensing drama, they all had wandered back. They were rewarded. The last basketball game of the year, and the Varsity cheerleaders were weeping, hugging each other, sobbing. There were six seniors on the Varsity squad; they wept for the end of glory. And the two juniors, who would be Varsity cheerleaders again next year and probably co-captains, wept partly for the end of this squad but mostly because they were expected to. The JV's sympathized, and the JV captain, a senior, burst into tears, and so did the twin who was very emotional. The gym office was a little room jammed with megaphones, lockers, the gym teachers' desks, square-dancing records, basketballs, volleyballs, and a bulletin board of game schedules, clippings, and jokes. A full-length mirror reflected the clinging group of girls, the Varsity in short green jumpers, the JV's in their dungarees and white blouses, Snowy standing wide-eyed watching.

Now in the gym the record player sang: "Earth angel, earth angel,/Will you be mine?/My darling dear,/Love you all the time."

"Well," Snowy said, and she and Puddles strolled casually over to the bleachers, but they didn't sit down because this would make them seem too obviously waiting for somebody to ask them to dance. They stood half-turned from the dance floor, as if they didn't care, as if they were on the brink of dashing off to something far more exciting. There was, however, nothing in their world more exciting than this.

The gym, in the basement of the main school building, was a sunken place, deeper than the basement classrooms surrounding it on three sides. The indoor windows high above were observation posts where kids out in the corridor would lean to watch gym classes or cheerleaders practicing or games or dances. A deep dark-brown sunken place.

But to Snowy, it was where love might find her.

She stood small and vulnerable there, her heart-shaped face tilted, listening to Puddles.

"Six," Puddles said, looking fierce, surprisingly so, because her features were very delicate. Her brown hair, not quite shoulder-length, curled at its tips like soft snails. She was taller than Snowy and fragile, but her round bottom was packed as tightly into her dungarees as Snowy's was, and her blouse had more of a shelf. "Okay," she said, once again beginning to calculate openings on the Varsity cheerleading squad, "we've got two juniors on JV's, and us five sophomores, that's seven trying for six vacancies. Somebody's got to go, and it'll be one of us sophomores. They'll move up the juniors; I can see no reason why they wouldn't move up the juniors."

"They" were the two women gym teachers, Miss Gilson who coached Varsity and Miss Jones who coached JV's. Gilly and Jonesy.

Snowy said, "They never moved up Maureen."

Puddles said, "With her looks?" Maureen, the JV captain, was plump and good-natured, a mother hen. Puddles added, "Rita and Nutty have *got* to make Varsity; Nutty is such a brown-noser, and Rita's the only one of us who can do a split."

Snowy turned and scanned the dance floor. "I don't see Rita and Tom here yet, do you?"

"Nope. Maybe they've skipped the dance and gone parking right away."

"Oh, Puddles!"

It was a time when goals shone clear, and Snowy's goal was glittering success, and success included love. Love meant Tom Forbes. Tom was a junior and one of the biggest catches in Gunthwaite High School, but so far no one had caught him except her best friend, Beverly Colby, and Bev had caught him only briefly; yet lately he'd been going out with Rita Beaupre as regularly as if they were going steady. Every Monday morning before homeroom, Snowy walked past Rita's chattering group of junior girls to see whether or not Rita had got her hands on his little gold football over the weekend.

"Hey," Puddles said, "there goes New Boy making a beeline for Linda. Isn't he a doll?"

Puddles herself had once been a New Girl, arriving in the middle of eighth grade when her family moved here to Gunthwaite, New Hampshire, from Portland, Maine. The homeroom teacher asked Snowy to take care of her. Puddles, Snowy discovered, didn't really need taking care of.

New Boy had appeared in their algebra class this week. The teacher assigned him to the desk behind Puddles', and today he'd begun what Puddles considered overtures, shoving her chair forward with his feet until she was almost squashed against her desk, then yanking it back. But now he and Linda Littlefield walked together to the dance floor as the record player yelled "Shake, rattle and roll!"

The kids jitterbugged smoothly, gazing past each other with distant bemused expressions.

Snowy strove to conform, to wear the same clothes as the popular girls, to wear her hair fashionably, to carry her books and speak the slang and know the hit songs all absolutely correctly. She had worn an anklet when anklets over socks were fashionable; she had bleached her bangs; she had dotted her *i*'s with circles; and because she was quick, she'd always been one of the first to sense a change in styles and change herself. But one thing neither she nor Bev had been able to learn properly was jitterbugging. Puddles tried to teach them, to the record player in her living room; Snowy and Bev would giggle so much she didn't succeed.

"You'll never do nothing/To save your doggone soul!/I said, shake, rattle and roll!"

Snowy watched Bev dancing with Roger Lambert and noted that Bev had certainly improved, taught by Roger. The co-captain of the basketball team, he was tall and coolly jaunty, and he terrified Snowy because he was a senior and so suave.

Then she saw Tom coming in, his arm around Rita's shoulders.

Puddles said, "Well, at least they're not parking."

"Not yet," Snowy said, miserable. Tom hadn't been at the JV game, but during the Varsity he had sat in the bleachers with some of the other football players, and Gunthwaite could have lost instead of won for all the attention Snowy paid to the game. Looking at Tom, she had prayed that he would come to the dance alone. (She'd refused to go to church anymore, the Methodist church, when she was in the sixth grade; she'd decided it was nonsense, so her praying was a combination of knocking on wood and wishing on a star.) He was wearing chinos and a plaid wool shirt, tails out, collar and cuffs turned up, and his horn-rimmed glasses, and Snowy thought him incredibly handsome. He grinned down at Rita.

"He doesn't want me/But I'll never never never never let him go—"

"Oh, murder," Puddles said, "here comes Norm, where can I hide?"

And Norm Noyes would ask Puddles to dance, Snowy knew, and it would be the nightmare. Last night she had dreamed that she was at a prom, and she was the only girl who hadn't been asked to dance. Ed Cormier had wandered up and inquired interestedly, "Why don't you cry, Snowy?" He kept saying it over and over, until finally he'd danced all night with her himself.

She could have avoided the risk of this humiliation by going straight home after the game. But she had a stubborn faith in the miracles of movies and romantic novels, so to each dance she brought her hope that Tom Forbes would notice her.

Norm said, "Got your *Silas Marner* with you, Puddles? How about reading us some?"

"Ha-ha," Puddles said, "aren't you a scream?" and her pale skin flushed.

When they were reading *Silas Marner* aloud in English class today, the section Puddles was called on to read had many references to Godfrey's wife's "bosom," and all the boys whispered and snickered while the girls sat scarlet with embarrassment.

Norm asked, "Want to dance?" His Adam's apple jiggled whenever he spoke.

"Well," Puddles said, deliberately rude, although this never discouraged him, "I guess I haven't got anything better to do."

Snowy's nightmare. And Ed Cormier approaching.

He didn't, however, say, "Why don't you cry, Snowy?" He said, "How's about a dance, for old times' sake?"

It was like last year again to them when he put his arm around her waist and took her hand, her hand curled up in his. He leaned down as they danced, with his cheek against her bangs. His breath smelled of Juicy Fruit gum.

They had gone steady most of their freshman year. He was big and dark and hearty, and he had been new and mysterious then, not somebody she'd been through grammar school and junior high with, but one of the strangers from St. Mary's, the parochial grammar and junior high school. She'd tried to ignore how when he kissed her his lips were too full and soft. From movies and books she had created an ideal boyfriend, a handsome crew-cut composite who was desired by every girl but who would pursue *her*; poor dumb Ed, like her earlier boyfriends, was far from ideal. Yet going steady with him had guaranteed she would always have a date, she would be able to go to all the movies, all the dances. It also guaranteed that she would begin to learn about Getting Fresh, and this scared her. So she broke up with him at the end of school.

She had got her bearings her freshman year. That summer she made a list of the goals ahead of her in her sophomore year:

1. Varsity
2. Tom
3. Keep my marks up
4. Join more clubs and do more in them

She had accomplished the last two, but the Varsity cheerleading tryouts weren't until the end of March, and Tom still didn't seem to know she was alive. It had been a long bleak year of dates with boys who were no more desired than Ed, of sometimes no date at all and the humiliation of baby-sitting alone watching *Your Hit Parade* and George Gobel on strange sofas in strange living rooms cluttered with unfamiliar ashtrays and tattered toys.

Dancing past, Bev made a horrible face at Snowy. Bev was tall, with short thick auburn hair worn in what was called a DA, a duck's ass, brushed back into a ridge rising upward to a curl. Her hair was naturally curly. She looked older, more finished, than the other girls in their class. And she was green-eyed and beautiful, but she loved to make faces. This one meant, "Ed? Ughy-pew," one of her favorite terms. Snowy made a helpless face.

"Sincerely,/'Cause I love you so dearly,/Please say you'll be mine."

The song ended. Snowy said, "I've got to be leaving," and disengaged herself from Ed before they could begin dancing to the next record.

He said, "Walk you home?"

She hesitated. What she had liked about Ed had been his admiration of her which made her feel very pretty and popular, and her ego was in need of a lift. But she sensed that if she let him walk her home, everything would begin all over again and she'd be right back where she was last year at this time. The walk home would be a walk backward. "Thanks," she said, "I have a ride." She hadn't. She hurried through the couples close together in the darkness, turned for a last glimpse of Tom, and Puddles called, "Hey, Snowy, wait!"

Snowy waited. Tom was clowning, dancing in swooping waltz time with Rita.

Puddles said, "I've got a great idea."

"You have?" Snowy said, wary. Puddles, when in the mood, did the wildest things. It was acknowledged that Puddles was crazy, and nothing except boys embarrassed her.

Puddles said, "We're going to drown our sorrows."

"We're going to what?"

"Well, you are, actually, since you have the big appetite."

Snowy's small size was deceptive; she could eat like a horse.

Puddles dragged her up the stairway. "Come on, let's grab our jackets and go to Hooper's. How much money have you got?"

"Seventy-five cents."

"Not enough. I'll loan you fifteen cents."

The basement corridor was brightly lighted, and they blinked. Below, the record-player music groaned after them from its subterranean depth.

"For what?" Snowy said.

"For three Awful-Awfuls."

The corridor smelled of paints from the art room they were walking past, then of sneakers as they passed the boys' locker room.

Snowy said, "You're kidding."

"Nope," Puddles said.

They went past the tunnel entrance of the Practical Arts building. The entrance was a sacred place to Snowy. Tom had his traffic post here. During school, she arranged her routes so she'd go past him as much as possible, and she treasured each of the times he said hi to her, she treasured his startling smile that made girls whisper, "Isn't he *cute!*" and when once he had tugged her ponytail, she had walked around dazed the rest of the day.

Puddles said, "I don't know why I didn't think of it sooner. You're the only one of us who can do it. Our champion!"

"And you're out of your mind," Snowy said.

Awful-Awfuls were the new frappe drink sold at Hooper's Dairy Bar. Anyone who could drink three at one sitting got his name on a plaque on the wall. So far there were only a half dozen names, boys'.

They went up the stairway to the first floor, where the junior high classrooms were, and on up the stairway to the second floor. The narrow corridors, dark even in daytime, were eerie now. In the silence, drinking fountains dribbled.

Puddles halted at one of the tall green wooden lockers which lined the corridors. They had the same homeroom, so they shared this locker. Puddles unlocked it and took out their jackets, just alike, the jackets most of the girls wore these past couple of years, woolen, blue with gray stripes down the sleeves. "Oh, come on," she said. "For chucks."

"Sit there and make a spectacle of myself?"

"The dance isn't over, nobody'll be there. Hey," Puddles added, an impresario gleam in her eye, "maybe we ought to wait till the dance ends, then all the kids will be there; you'll have an audience cheering you on."

"No," Snowy said.

Puddles snapped her jacket. "Then you'll do it in solitary splendor. Perhaps that's better, more dignified."

"Three of those things?" Snowy said, for the first time really considering the challenge. "When you drink just one of them, you think when you stand up you're going to drop to your knees."

"I wouldn't know," Puddles said airily. A fussy eater since she was a child and allergic to cow's milk, she had styled for herself a very peculiar appetite, sometimes eating nothing at meals but one odd thing like junket or olives, to the despair of her mother, who, because Puddles was anemic, tried to stuff her with liver.

"But," Puddles said, "I'm certain if any girl can do it, you're the girl."

"I ate supper," Snowy said as they started back along the corridor. "Maybe I'd better wait till some other time and not eat beforehand."

"You'll have something when you get home, won't you?"

Snowy thought of the raspberry-jam and marshmallow-fluff sandwich she was planning on.

Puddles said, "So, instead, you'll have the Awful-Awfuls, that's all."

It occurred to Snowy that if she could drink them, she might become famous. She'd be the first girl. *That* ought to make Tom notice her.

But, worried, she said, "Do you think a girl ought to try? Drinking three Awful-Awfuls isn't exactly what you could call being dainty."

"So what?"

They went down the stairs to the first floor, and Puddles pushed open the side door.

"Well," Snowy said, "I'll have one and see how I feel."

"Okay."

"I'm not promising anything, you understand."

The night was cold. They walked around to the front of the school and glanced back. Two brick buildings beyond a snow-covered lawn. Gunthwaite High School. Their world.

Jacket collars turned up, hands shoved in pockets, they walked along State Avenue toward downtown. The shrunken snowbanks looked like heaps of frozen ashes.

Puddles said, "It's one of us, you know. Either me or you or Linda won't make Varsity."

"I know," Snowy said starkly.

"The twins will. They'd make it if they both fell flat on their asses during their cartwheels at tryouts. Twins. So cute. I could strangle them."

Next to the school grounds there had been a restaurant to which their gang of girls, the Gang, would go for hot dogs when the cafeteria menu revolted them. (Snowy secretly loved every meal, even American chop suey and hamburg gravy on mashed potatoes and Chinese pie, but she complained as loudly as the other kids.) The restaurant had been dark inside, with deep leathery booths, the waitress resigned to giggling girls. They'd felt extremely sophisticated. Snowy hadn't been able to believe her eyes when the restaurant was torn down, was actually demolished. It was the first thing in her history to disappear. A supermarket took its place, and on the day of the grand opening they came over during their lunch period to explore the shining aisles. They all chipped in to buy a box of jelly doughnuts, and they nearly didn't get back to school in time for the next class because Puddles was so fascinated with the automatic doors, a brand-new experience, that she went in and out and in and out until one of the clerks told her to scram.

After the supermarket, they had to walk past a gas station, Varney's, very dangerous territory. Snowy put her chin up and stared straight ahead, ignoring it. This was where almost all the high school boys who mattered hung out, sometimes pumping gas or tinkering with their cars, but mostly just lounging around drinking Cokes and whistling at girls. Tom worked here and hung around, but he wasn't a whistler. Going to and from school, Snowy would look for him, discreetly, a sidelong peek.

Only a night-light glowed inside. Varney's was closed, so they got by safely, which was rather disappointing. They walked on past the Congregational church and a grocery store. The sidewalk was clear, plowed by the little horse-drawn snowplows Snowy had always wanted to ride on. There was a short bridge railing where a black brook between gray snowbanks disappeared under the street, and when Snowy was younger, she'd pause to lean over to see how the brook was doing, but she thought she was too old for such dawdling now, at least in public, and besides, it was cold.

Puddles said, still brooding, "Or maybe even a couple of us might get left behind, they could choose someone entirely different."

"Has that ever been done?"

"I don't know. When we start teaching cheering, we'll have to keep an eye peeled for any freshmen who are good or any sophomores who've got better than last year."

"If we find any, that'll just make matters worse."

Gloomily they trudged along, the sky far and dark above them.

Across the street was Trask's, a big factory of weathered brick where Snowy's father worked as the foreman of the lathe department. He'd explained to her what the factory made, but she, scorning it, never listened and understood only that it made the machines that made something else. Puddles' father was a foreman at the shoe factory on the other side of town.

State Avenue became abruptly residential. Behind glass curtains, rooms in the houses they passed were warm and golden, and Snowy would usually glance in for a glimpse of veiled lives, but tonight she didn't.

And then, after a Catholic church and a corner grocery store, they reached Main Street.

Surrounded by mountains, Gunthwaite was a valley through which a river flowed to a lake. The river twisted into town, crashed over a waterfall at the textile mill, and, swirling, foaming, crossed beneath Main Street. Here Snowy and Puddles did pause on the bridge.

Puddles said, "If I don't make Varsity, I'll throw myself in."

They watched a chunk of ice, still spinning from the waterfall, vanish beneath them, and Snowy almost started running across the street to see it appear on the other side, but she remembered her dignity, and Puddles said, "Let's go, it's colder than a witch's tit."

There were no shopping plazas then, no shopping malls, no discount department stores or McDonald's or Dunkin' Donuts sprawling out from the town. There was just Main Street. Downtown. Gunthwaite's population of fifteen thousand shopped at these stores that faced each other across the narrow street. The windows were dim in the ornate stone buildings and crooked wooden buildings, yet the stores were so familiar to Snowy and Puddles that they saw each display as clearly as during daytime, the rain slickers in Dunlap's Department Store, the sheet music of hit songs like "Melody of Love" and "Let Me Go, Lover" in the music store, the chocolate boxes in the drugstore, the pastel spring dresses in Yvonne's Apparel, the oranges and last summer's drive-in theater placards in the window of the fruit store.

Then there was a gas station, and then Hooper's which wasn't dim but whitely lighted, a clapboard oasis.

Snowy stopped. "It's not empty."

"Of course not," Puddles said, "it's never *empty*. Come on, we walked all the way here, you can't chicken out now." She gave Snowy a shove, and they crossed the parking lot to the small low building.

Everyone came to Hooper's. Whenever there wasn't anything to do, people went to Hooper's, and kids always went there on a date. Businessmen lunched here, parents with flocks of children bought ice-cream cones on weekend afternoons, but weekend evenings Hooper's belonged to the teen-agers. Snowy had been happy here; she'd been wretched.

She hesitated again, Puddles opened the door, and they went in.

A horseshoe-shaped counter trapped the waitresses, who whisked down the line of ice-cream cases in its middle, bending, scooping. Snowy knew that this summer after her sixteenth birthday she too would be a waitress somewhere, so for years she had been studying them and their equipment, the frappe machines, milk tank, syrup dispensers, vats of hot fudge and hot butterscotch, and the grill on which a hamburger spluttered. Snowy always did her homework well.

Some kids were sitting at the counter, and when Puddles started to sit down near them, Snowy said, "No," because even if they were only junior high kids who didn't count, they were still an audience, and she walked on around the horseshoe and chose a stool where she'd be somewhat screened by the equipment in the middle, positioning herself behind a tier of pies.

She said, "This is ridiculous."

Puddles said to the waitress, an older high school girl wearing a white uniform and a chocolate-smeared apron, "One Awful-Awful, please."

"What flavor? Vanilla, chocolate, coffee, or strawberry?"

Snowy reflected. The other one she'd had was vanilla, and maybe another kind would be better. "Strawberry, please."

"Anything else?"

"No," Puddles said, and then, "Wait, I guess I'll have a ginger ale, can't let my friend here drink alone."

"You're a riot," Snowy said, and opened the coin pocket of her wallet. The blue wallet was fat, not with money but with photographs. She took out thirty cents, her hands suddenly nervous, and unsnapped her jacket and settled herself on the stool, trying to be calm. She said, "I told you, I'll just try one and see how I feel."

"Sure," Puddles said. She pointed at the plaque on the wall. "Think of it, though. Fame! Your name in lights!"

Snowy started to giggle. "Don't get me going."

The Awful-Awful arrived. It was so thick that the straw stood straight up in it.

"God," Puddles said.

"It's your idea," Snowy said, and took a sip. Pink sludge. "What do you suppose they put in it in that machine to make it different from a frappe?"

"I can't bear to think. Let me have a taste—no, that'd be against the rules, wouldn't it. Fun, huh?" she asked brightly, watching as Snowy began steadily to drink.

Some more kids, nobody important, came in.

Puddles said, "Did you get your Latin done in study, or did you bring your book home?"

Snowy swallowed and said, "I got it done."

"Damn, I meant to ask to borrow the book tomorrow."

"You can borrow it first period Monday, if that isn't cutting it too close."

Snowy's Latin II book was much in demand. When the books were handed out last September, it had been her luck to get the most battered copy, her bad luck she'd thought until she discovered that the binding was so broken she could take out the vocabulary and rules section at the end and work with it while she translated the passages up front, instead of having to flip back and forth like everyone else.

Puddles said, "I don't have a study first period, I've got biology."

"Oh, that's right."

This was the only way their schedules differed, since Snowy had avoided biology, fearing she'd faint during dissecting. Puddles wasn't afraid of anything, Bev was afraid of summer moths that bumped against screen doors, and Snowy was afraid of dead things. So she had chosen instead a course called Modern European History, a small elective class in which she was one of only three sophomores, the rest upperclassmen, and all the dead were safely inside books. Bev took biology. Snowy felt superior after first worrying that she was being too different.

Puddles said, "Are you sure you should be drinking it that fast? I mean, maybe you should pace yourself."

"I'm drinking it slowly, for me."

"Well, it's almost gone. How do you feel?"

"Full." Yet Snowy was certain from past experience that although full, she could always eat more. She couldn't remember ever being so full she absolutely had to stop eating, not even at Thanksgiving. Her mother fretted about her appetite, wondering if she had been deprived by rationing during the war and was now making up for it. Maybe she was, but Snowy considered this just another typical example of her mother's reasoning: scatty.

"Our Snowy full?" Puddles said. "Never!" She waved at the waitress.

Snowy looked up at the plaque and thought of Tom Forbes.

Last year she had not supposed him attainable. Other older boys gradually began dating some of the freshman girls, like Bev and the twins, but she hadn't dreamed Tom would bother with them. And then one day last spring, at the end of May, she had seen him leaning against a locker talking to Bev after school. She and Puddles waited at their locker until Bev rushed up and said, "Tom Forbes asked me out, we're going to the movies with Sam Page and Joanne Carter, in Tom's *car!*" and they gasped and congratulated, and Snowy hated herself for being so jealous. At the movies with Ed, she watched Bev and Tom sitting close together, and later at Hooper's she saw them fooling around and laughing, Tom grabbing at Bev's little red silk scarf which then was fashionable for the girls to wear tucked into the back pocket of their dungarees. Tom was wearing a white shirt, collar and cuffs up, and chinos, and sneakers. (The girls wore moccasins that year, shuffle shuffle along the school corridors.) Snowy, her spoon moving automatically from a tall tulip dish of butterscotch sundae to her mouth, had watched and had made him a goal.

"Okay," she said, determined. "I don't know if I can face another strawberry, though. I guess I'll have a chocolate."

Puddles said, "Are you sure you should mix your drinks?"

"Ha-ha," Snowy said.

"One chocolate Awful-Awful, please," Puddles told the waitress.

More kids came in. The dance was nearly over. Each time the door opened, a clear whiff of winter lifted the smell of hot grease.

"Look at them," Snowy said. "They're on dates, they're not just doing something stupid like this."

"It's better than nothing."

"On the night of the last basketball game, something wonderful should happen."

"Yeah," Puddles said. "I know."

The waitress put the Awful-Awful down in front of Puddles, and Puddles said, "Not for me, it's for our champion here," and slid the glass to Snowy.

"Oh," the waitress said, and laughed. "So that's what's up." She left the empty glass in front of Snowy, as a tally, and Snowy wished she hadn't because this announced to everyone what she was doing.

It was sinful of her to choose chocolate. Ever since the sixth grade her mother had told her not to eat chocolate, and she obeyed, as frightened as her mother was about acne. And her complexion remained fine, except for one pimple (Snowy and Bev disliked the word and used "blemish") each month during her period. But she felt that this was an emergency, and she tasted, and the chocolate was better.

Puddles began giggling. "I'm sure I don't know why they didn't use my suggestion for the dance."

"Puddles, don't get me going."

In sophomore homerooms today, pieces of paper had been passed out so everyone could write suggestions for the name of the Sophomore Dance. The theme was Outer Space. Puddles' suggestion was "The Bars on Mars." The kids found this, like other references to booze, enormously daring and funny, but after school they learned that the committee had chosen "Solar Serenade."

Puddles said, "And after I spent all day thinking up some more. The Saturn Stomp. The Pluto Bark. Stardustrag. And"— she lowered her voice—"the Venus Penis."

Snowy choked. "Stop it, stop it."

"What I should've been spending my time doing is thinking up a way to get out of going with Norm; he's bound to ask me. What a fate!" she said, cracking her knuckles. Her fingers were long and slender, but she could crack her knuckles like a boy. Bev could bend her thumbs over backward, sickeningly. Snowy could do neither, but after much practice in front of mirrors she had learned to raise one eyebrow.

Her main accomplishment, though, was her appetite, and now, aghast, she realized she felt ill. Only half the Awful-Awful was gone. She inserted the straw into her mouth again and forced herself onward, half hearing Puddles, watching for Tom as more kids came in, trying to think of anything but food. She wondered who would ask her to the Sophomore Dance. Probably Joe Spencer or Frankie Richardson. Or if Ed's pride had healed enough for him to dance with her tonight, maybe he would ask her, and what would she do if it was a choice of going with him or sitting home? The thought of Ed made her think of food: when she would come here Friday nights with him, she'd order a hot dog, and Ed, forgetting, would order one too, and she'd only remind him that it was Friday after the hot dogs arrived, so she could eat both, while Ed ordered a tuna fish roll.

She swallowed very slowly. She was sweating.

Puddles said, "Every time I see Norm in the corridors, I could run for our locker and hide, but what do I do in class? Crawl in my desk?"

Snowy took off her jacket and laid it on the stool beside her.

"Hot?" Puddles asked clinically. Puddles' ambition was to be a nurse. "Your face is bright red. Maybe we should go outdoors; I could walk you up and down."

Snowy didn't answer. She looked at the Awful-Awful, reached again for the straw, and leaned over the glass, her face intent. She was praying.

Then some more kids came in, and they were Jack O'Brien and Butch Knowles, with the twins, Charlene and Darlene Fecteau. Snowy scrunched down, but Puddles stood up and waved.

"Snowy!" the twins cried. They both were clutchers, and they darted at her, clutching at her, brunette and quick, identical hectic faces, identical dark DA's. Snowy longed to be a twin, the nucleus of the Gang, assured of attention and popularity and never alone. "Snowy, you're not really!"

Jack observed the empty glass and the nearly empty glass and said, "Only one to go, huh? Think you'll make it?" and Butch moved her jacket, and they all sat down on the stools on either side of her and Puddles. Jack and Butch were juniors and Varsity football players, like Tom; that this was the first time they'd ever shown any interest in her convinced Snowy the Awful-Awfuls would be her salvation.

She sucked up the last of the chocolate.

"I'm her manager!" Puddles said. "Next stop, Hollywood!" She opened her wallet and added a nickel and dime to Snowy's remaining fifteen cents. "What flavor do you want this time?"

Anything but strawberry or chocolate. "Coffee," she said.

"Good idea," Puddles said. "Sober you up."

Word had got around; all the kids in the place knew what was happening, they were talking and watching, and more and more kids were coming in. If Tom came in with Rita, there Snowy would be, the center of attention but bright red and sweating and sick as a dog.

The jukebox pounded out the same songs the record player in the gym had sung.

The waitress set the coffee Awful-Awful before her, and the waitress too watched as Snowy took the first sip. It didn't go down very far; she could feel it at the back of her throat. She saw herself completely filled with Awful-Awfuls from her toes to her throat, and where was there room for this one?

The jukebox pounded.

She was going to throw up.

And the moment she realized this, Jack remarked, "When Bill drank his three, he puked right out there in the parking lot, he didn't even make it to his car."

Snowy stood up and heard her voice say, "I think I'd better splash some water on my face."

"You okay?" Puddles asked, worried now. "Want me to come?"

"I'm okay." She walked toward the rest rooms' doorway, holding carefully straight her body full of Awful-Awfuls. In all the years she'd eaten at Hooper's, she had never gone to the rest room. Other girls would say they were going to comb their hair, but even this embarrassed Snowy, and she knew their dates knew what else they were going to do. She wanted to die whenever Ed or her other dates went. Although she could find bathroom jokes funny with Bev and Puddles, boys and bathrooms were still disgusting to her because the love she knew about only from movies and books was so far removed from toilets. She could not believe that movie stars ever went.

LADIES. She pushed open the door, locked it behind her, ran to the toilet, and knelt.

Snowy, who had brought her hope like a flower to the dance after the last basketball game, vomited in the ladies' room of Hooper's Dairy Bar, vomited and vomited until she was weeping.

Then she got to her feet, flushed the toilet, and paced the

room, the mirror and washbasin and glass ball of liquid soap a blur around her. When she was certain she wouldn't throw up again, she went to the basin and splashed water on her face and cupped water in her hand and sloshed some in her mouth. She spat. She looked at herself in the mirror and, exhausted, wondered how she was going to walk out there and say she was disqualified.

She leaned against the wall, her hot face against the cold tiles. The idea of cheating dawned.

She had never cheated, except when it was acceptable, such as checking homework or consulting kids who'd earlier had a test she was about to take.

She splashed more water on her face, leaving lots of droplets, and walked back out into the noise. Tom wasn't here yet. Bev and Roger were, Bev subdued and sad because this had been the last time, except for alumni games, she would sit in the bleachers and watch Roger play basketball.

Snowy sat down. Puddles whispered, "You been puking?"

"Of course not," she said, and began to drink. The kids surrounded her, yelling, and then they were chanting, "Three-fourths to go, one-half to go," and Bev roused herself and joined in, "One-fourth to go, one-eighth—" and Snowy slurped up the last pale gob.

Puddles and Bev screamed and hugged her, the twins clutched her, and Butch said, "I won the bet, you owe me a quarter, Jack," and the waitress arrived to present her with a plastic medal and—"Oh, Jesus Christ!" Puddles said—a card which entitled her to one free Awful-Awful in the flavor of her choice.

Chalk dust, scuffed varnish, ink. In the two brick buildings the schoolday progressed, bells rang, and the kids moved along dark corridors into dark classrooms. There was no outside. The cold gray sky was the skin of the tall windows. But Snowy, gazing out a window from her desk, had once had a brief surprised vision of the school balanced on a larger sphere spinning lopsided circles in space.

Hers was the last lunch period, 4C, and she preferred this because it made the afternoon shorter. On Mondays, she had gym during 4A and 4B; today basketball was over for the gym classes and square dancing had begun. She hated gym-class dancing. At a signal from the coach, the boys charged across the gym toward the girls, who were chattering lightheartedly to cover their anxiety, and Snowy always feared that when the dust cleared, she'd find herself stuck with a creep. But today she'd danced with Dudley Washburn and Frankie Richardson. And Ed Cormier. They, like everyone else, joked about the Awful-Awfuls and congratulated her.

Afterward, in the locker room, she combed her bangs and ponytail and put on fresh lipstick. She was wearing an outfit she'd chosen very carefully, for Tom: a small pale-blue scarf tied over the elastic around her ponytail, a long-sleeved pale-yellow oxford-cloth blouse, collar turned up, a full blue-and-yellow plaid wool skirt, with beneath it her best white crinoline petticoat making it stick out flouncingly. The skirt was mid-shin length. Just a few inches of leg showed above her straight white socks and buff-colored loafers.

Puddles, combing her brown snail curls, was wearing a red jumper that made her look more pale than ever. The second bell rang, the other girls swarmed out of the locker room, and Puddles yelled, "Hurry up, Bev! I've got to borrow Snowy's algebra!"

Bev came out of the lav. She wore a striped blouse and a wide leather belt and, unfortunately, a straight skirt which had caused her great difficulties during dancing. It was wise to wear a full skirt, but Bev had forgotten that square dancing was beginning today. Unlike Snowy, who was conscientious, and Puddles, who

was methodical in her own way, Bev forgot many things, notebooks, club meetings, gym suit, sometimes causing such crises as
the morning they had to catch the bus that was taking the
Gunthwaite High School kids to the prize-speaking contest in
Durham, and Bev, having packed her overnight bag and spent
the night at Snowy's house, discovered one of her nylons had a
run and she'd forgotten her garter belt.

Bev also wore, on a thin gold chain around her neck, Roger's
gold basketball and, over her blouse and skirt, Roger's letter
sweater. The sweater, worn open and unbuttoned, had a green
G and green-and-white stars sewn on its loose white knit, and it
was sloppily but fashionably big on Bev, the shoulders drooping
below her shoulders, the bottom below her bottom. Bev and
Roger had been going steady since Christmas.

Bev adjusted her skirt and pulled up her socks and said,
"Honor your partner, honor your corner, allemande left, and
away we go."

"It's about time," Puddles said crossly. "I thought you'd fallen
in."

Snowy said, "Don't forget, now. Mention the Awful-Awfuls
when you're chitchatting with Tom." Although Bev and Tom
had broken up after going steady only a month, they still flirted
with each other, tantalized by a memory of intimacy.

"Hurry!" Puddles said, and she and Bev and Snowy left the
locker room, walking together, their books stacked on their
notebooks cocked against their hipbones, their matching pocketbooks dangling over the side.

The smell of the cafeteria lunch had been seeping through the
school since morning. As usual, it had a special smell of its own,
totally unlike the smell of home cooking, yet the result, instead
of a gastronomic surprise, was always just something like
chipped beef and sick peas. Snowy would have enjoyed even
that, but this year she and Bev had found their allowances didn't
match their expenses and they had to skip lunch and save their

lunch money. Their allowances were a dollar fifty, and the week's lunch money came to another dollar fifty. To double their money was worth the sacrifice. They did not, however, starve. They spent a dime on ice cream, and most of the time they ate the lunch lovingly packed by Puddles' mother, who knew that Puddles wouldn't eat the hot lunch and so made sandwiches, believing that in this way she could be sure Puddles did eat something.

They walked past the stairs to the gym, past the art room and the boys' locker room, and Snowy's heart beat faster and faster as, inside the crowd of kids, they neared the tunnel entrance.

The tunnel was a frantic place. The flow of traffic in the corridors had to be compressed into single lines coming and going, so the principal always assigned this post to someone like Tom. He wasn't tall, but he was thickset and rugged, and he stood solidly there at the head of the three steps down into the tunnel, and his presence did bring order.

"Hi," he said to Bev. The tunnel was a chorus of hi's, kids greeting each other. Bev could do what Snowy considered a hilarious imitation of Rita Beaupre coming through the tunnel, for Rita's voice was somewhat shrill, and Bev would pipe, "Hi hi hi hi hi," louder and louder until she reached the climax, an ear-splitting *"HI!"* which was Rita greeting Tom at the head of the tunnel.

Today he was wearing his blue V-necked sweater, almost the same color as Snowy's scarf, and she wondered if this was a good sign. The V showed a triangle of his white T-shirt, and dark hairs curled over the rim. Seeing them, she went shaky with the urge to touch; he said hi to her, but she just smiled and looked quickly at her feet, concentrating on getting down these three perilous steps without falling.

The cafeteria smell increased to overpowering in the tunnel. Ahead of her, Bev walked her famous walk, hips smoothly swinging, a walk so renowned throughout the school that Snowy had never tried walking that way because everyone would know she was copying Bev. When kidded about the walk, Bev claimed it came naturally, but Snowy, who had been best friends with Bev since second grade, had observed that it had come naturally quite suddenly, in eighth grade.

At the end of the tunnel there was a stairway going up into the Practical Arts building, foreign territory the College Prep kids had never been in since junior high home ec and shop, and straight ahead, in the basement, was the cafeteria, its cement walls painted, as Puddles once said, "puke green and babyshit brown." The long wooden tables with metal stork legs were green, too, and the metal chairs were brown. In one corner was a cluster of miniature tables and chairs where kids from the grammar schools, transported by buses, ate the hot lunch. Back during grammar school Snowy had walked home for lunch, but one week, when her mother was in the hospital after a miscarriage, her father had given her the money for the school lunches so her grandmother or Bev's mother wouldn't have to be bothered, and she had come here, scared on the bus and awed in this strange place. In her little plaid jumper and her white blouse-slip, her thin legs in kneelengths that became above the knees long flesh-colored stockings gartered to her underpants, she had sat on one of the tiny chairs and watched the big kids and wondered if it was possible she'd really grow up and go to school here and be like them.

"Algebra," Puddles said, plunking her books down. "Quick, your algebra, quick."

The part of the Gang that had C lunch always sat at the same table, the first table in the middle row of tables, directly below the platform on which stood a teachers' desk used by teachers overseeing the cafeteria study halls and, during lunch, by student proctors. Tom was a proctor.

Snowy said, "Okay, hold your horses," and opened her algebra book and took out her paper. "Heaven only knows, Puddles, they're probably all wrong."

"Bull," Puddles said and sat down, pulled her own paper out of her book, and went to work.

Other kids were sitting down, plates rattling on their metal trays. Today the lunch was a dead hamburger and three potato chips and fruit cocktail without a cherry.

"Well," Bev said, "shall we go?"

Snowy picked up her pocketbook, on the strap of which she'd pinned the Awful-Awful medal. She said, "What if this doesn't work? It'll all have been for nothing." She and Bev, both only-children, nearly sisters, told each other almost everything, and she had told Bev about the cheating; when Bev just laughed, she'd felt better about it.

Bev looked at her frightened face. "It'll work. Come along, come along."

As they walked to the ice-cream counter, into the cafeteria strolled Tom. Happy-go-lucky on the surface, he was aloof and unique beneath. He lazed through his school years, choosing always the easiest path, for school was not to him, as it was to Snowy, an upward struggle to the summit of success; it was a place he had to be, so he might as well take it easy. He'd given up College Prep after his freshman year, tried the business course, and this year had settled on the shop course. It amused him to excel in shop, but he was also secretly proud of his talent. And he broke tradition. He had as many College Prep friends as football-playing buddies. In the caste system, there were the very few boys like Roger who excelled in sports and in school, there were the athletes, there were the good students, and there were the boys nobody noticed. With the girls, there was the lofty elite of the cheerleaders, both College Prep and General, above the popular, the good students, the cheap, the sad. And there was the basic division between College Prep and General;

a special gang of kids who'd all been together in junior high and had absorbed some parochial school kids their freshman year, would, by their sophomore year, begin to separate into two gangs. But Tom belonged to both.

At the ice-cream counter, Bev looked back and reported, "Here comes Tom. Now he is stepping onto the platform. Now he is sitting down at the desk. And now Diane Morrissette just happens to stroll up to the platform to put some paper in the wastebasket, and she just happens to say something to Tom."

Snowy, nervous, didn't look around. "What's he do?"

"Flirt, what else? Now Diane, all aglow, is trotting back to her chair. The coast is clear."

They paid for their ice-cream push-ups and turned. Walking back, Snowy kept her eyes down, apparently very busy un-wrapping her ice cream. Her skirt and petticoat swayed at each step that brought her closer to him.

Tom said, "Roger was looking for you last period, and I can't believe I heard him right, but it was something about Peter Pan."

Bev laughed, and so did Snowy, still fussing with the ice cream, and she didn't politely leave them now as she usually did.

"Absolutely correct," Bev said. "A-plus."

"Peter Pan?" Tom said incredulously.

His face was square, his nose short and straight, his mouth thin-lipped, and behind his horn-rimmed glasses his eyes were blue. Bev, looking at him, reminded herself that he was simply a challenge in strategy, not the Tom she'd been in love with last spring, but she tried to remember why they had broken up. At the time, her joke about it had been that she couldn't wear heels with him or they'd be the same height, five nine. But they had really broken up because Bev believed in having moods with boys, to make herself mysterious, and Tom wouldn't cater to moodiness.

She said to Snowy, "Shall we tell him, or shall we keep him in suspense?"

Snowy dropped the ice-cream wrapper in the wastebasket. "Go ahead, put him out of his misery."

"*Producer's Showcase*," Bev said. "On television tonight, they're doing *Peter Pan* with guess who playing the title role?"

Tom said, "Marlon Brando?"

Snowy laughed, then bit into her ice cream. Vanilla, swirled with strawberry. She always gave Bev and Puddles shivers by eating ice cream instead of licking.

Bev said, "That just goes to show how much you know about drama." Bev was very involved in the Dramatics Club, more so than Snowy or Puddles. "Peter Pan must be played by a woman."

Snowy swallowed and spoke up. "Not in the Disney movie."

Bev said, "That was a car*toon.*"

Tom said, "But the voice was a real boy's." He gestured at their ice cream. "How can you eat those things?"

An opportunity, and Bev seized it. "Snowy can eat anything, she can drink anything, haven't you heard? She's the first and probably the only girl to drink three Awful-Awfuls in one sitting!"

"I'll be damned," Tom said, impressed. He stared at Snowy. When he'd been going steady with Bev, Snowy had been simply Bev's little friend, Bev's shadow, and when this year he'd considered the freshman-turned-sophomore girls, he had dismissed her, mistaking shyness for snottiness. Her quick hi's at the traffic post, sometimes no hi at all but just a self-conscious smile, and her leaving when he was kidding around with Bev, and the way she was so starched and ironed, all her clothes appearing new, the way she looked as if someone touched her she'd get wrinkled, the way she walked with her chin up gave her such an air of hauteur that he figured she wasn't worth any bother. Tom had no use for snobs. He said, "Last Friday night? I heard something about some girl, but I didn't know it'd been you."

His attention was worth the throwing up and the cheating.

Snowy groped for something to say to hold him. "The rewards are stupendous," she said. "Can you guess my prizes?"

"Well," he began, and Bev murmured, "I've got homework," and walked her walk away, and he forgot to watch. He said, "There's a plaque, isn't there?"

"My name in lights!" she said, stealing from Puddles, but all's fair, she knew, in love and war. "There's even more."

He spotted the medal. "What's that?"

She held up her pocketbook, and he leaned down. The top of his short dark crew cut was as flat and soft-looking as a baby brush. She could smell Old Spice after-shave lotion.

He read, " 'I Drank Three Awful-Awfuls,' " and grinned.

She said, "It should say, 'I Led Three Lives.' "

He laughed. She couldn't believe it. She had made him laugh.

She said, "But best of all, there's this," and opened the pocketbook, took out her wallet, and slid out the free Awful-Awful card. She handed it to him, and he laughed again.

She said, "I'm thinking of auctioning it off. Care to make a bid?"

"Now, Snowy," he said, teasing. "I'm hurt. How come you don't offer to share it, two straws and I'll give you a head start—"

And just at that moment Mr. Nelson, the shop teacher, came up, said, "Excuse me," and began asking Tom about the finish on a hope chest.

Snowy put the card and wallet into her pocketbook and walked hurriedly to the table. She sat down in the saved chair between Puddles and Bev and said, "*God damn it!*"

Bev said, "How far did you get?"

"He was saying we could share my free Awful-Awful. *Damn it!*"

Bev licked her ice cream. "You can still pick him up on it, don't let it rest."

Snowy shook her head violently. She didn't dare; it was too

forward; she'd never even dared ask him to a Sadie Hawkins Dance. "Mr. Nelson was saying something about a hope chest. It's probably for Rita."

"Snowy, they're not even going steady."

Puddles, scribbling away, said, "I'm not going to get them done, can I keep your paper during my study next period, I promise I won't let the teacher see me."

"Okay, but be careful."

"I'll meet you at the fountain near Mr. Dodge's room and sneak it back to you."

Nancy Gordon said, "Hey, is that Snowy's algebra, could I check my answers?" and Carol Tucker said, "Don't be such a hog with it, Puddles."

"I got here first," Puddles said. "Tough."

Last year during Algebra I, Puddles was the one whose papers everyone checked with, but in Algebra II this year Snowy, to her own surprise, had come to the forefront, and now the long phone calls in the evenings were Puddles consulting her about algebra problems, instead of the other way 'round, as well as other kids consulting her about Latin and English, too. Snowy had got four A's her first quarter this year, and during the second she'd got her usual, three A's and a B. The B was in Modern European History, and the teacher had written on her report card, "Henrietta's classwork could improve, and also her knowledge of world affairs," so Snowy had begun trying to talk more in class, despite her fright in front of the upperclassmen, and had dutifully begun listening to news on the radio and reading *Time* and *U.S. News and World Report.* She found it all very boring, none of it so important as the affairs of Gunthwaite High School.

Bev said, "Mr. Nelson isn't going to chat with him forever, you could put your push-up stick in the wastebasket and—"

"I don't dare, I don't dare." She saw Puddles' lunch bag forgotten on the table. "Puddles, what kind of sandwiches did your mother make today?"

"God knows. Liverwurst, I fear. Help yourselves."

Snowy investigated, unwrapping waxed paper, peeking inside a sandwich. "Yum, liverwurst it is," she said, and bit in. Mrs. Pond made sandwiches that had taught Snowy there was more than peanut butter in the world, though she still had simple favorites. Mrs. Pond even cut the crusts off.

Bev said, "You want the banana?" and Puddles said, "It's all yours." Bev unpeeled it, looked up at the platform, and said, "Okay, there goes Mr. Nelson, now's your chance. Go on up and say—"

"Oh, Bev," she said, "he was probably just kidding," and her Monday headache, which had been building up all morning, struck. She opened her pocketbook, dug out the little tin of aspirin, looked around for liquid, and said to Dudley Washburn across the table, "Could I have a sip of your milk?"

"Be my guest," he said, glancing up from the map he was lettering for next period. There was a jumble of colored pencils around his sandwiches. He was in her history class, and he did the best maps, even if he finished them at the last minute. Snowy had done her map yesterday, painstakingly, but as always it didn't turn out half so trim as his.

He was the person she enjoyed most, besides Bev and Puddles, although she'd never considered him as a boyfriend because she'd known him forever, ever since they had played together in the sandbox at nursery school. It still astonished her how tall he'd grown. Tall and awkward, blond and rosy-cheeked. In grammar school, he'd wanted to be both a major-league baseball star and President of the United States, but now he had decided to be first a lawyer, then a Senator, and then the President.

For a start, he was president of their class, reelected each year since junior high.

"Honestly," Puddles said, glaring at the algebra paper, "what is it going to matter ten years from now whether or not I know what X equals?"

Dudley said, "Just this morning during Latin, I said to myself is it necessary to my future life that I memorize ablative absolute rule number two thousand one hundred eighty-six point five note three?"

Snowy giggled, but she had a strictly pragmatic view of these things: they had to be learned so she could get into college. And she not only had to learn them but also had to get very high marks, because she must have a scholarship. She'd made the college decision one Sunday morning in seventh grade. She had spent the night at Bev's house and, an early riser, had wandered downstairs to the messy living room and begun looking through the bookshelves for something to read while she waited for Bev to wake up. The books on the shelves were real, not the Reader's Digest Condensed Books which her folks bought and she scorned. On a lower shelf she had discovered Bev's mother's Mount Holyoke yearbook, and she sat down on the thin worn Oriental carpet and studied it. Bev's mother was the only woman she knew, besides teachers, who had gone to college. Bev's mother was different, and Snowy loved and admired and was in awe of her. When Bev came downstairs and they were in the kitchen making Postum and toast, Snowy said, "I'm going to college." Bev said, "I'm not. I'm going to marry a millionaire."

Bev's stepfather, Fred Miller, worked at the bank. Bev's father had been killed during the war, in the third wave at Iwo Jima. Despite all the war movies she'd seen, Bev visualized it as an enormous dark tidal wave engulfing him.

Snowy didn't mention to her folks that she wanted to take College Prep until the end of eighth grade, the time to choose her high school course. They were stunned. Her mother, who hoped Snowy would be popular and marry a nice boy, didn't understand at all, and her father said he'd always wanted to go to UNH, and Snowy dropped the second bombshell: she wanted to go to a women's college, Mount Holyoke—or Smith or Radcliffe, other schools Bev's mother had talked of when she asked her. Snowy's mother had never heard of them; her father had. When he recovered, he said he'd do all he could, he would remortgage the house if necessary (he said this so solemnly she didn't dare ask what it meant), but she would have to help by getting a scholarship.

And Snowy, who'd been an average bored student in grammar school, who in junior high had mostly got B's, with an occasional A in English, in high school hit her stride. But the pace terrified her, as did her parents' pride in her.

She looked at the proctor's desk. Tom was gone. Bleakness settled down.

Bev was saying, "Roger's coming over tonight to watch *Peter Pan*, it's really lucky his folks don't have a TV so we can have a weekday date, but I never thought Roger of all people would be dying to see *Peter Pan*—"

Behind them Tom said, "We have to keep on the good side of Snowy now, Bev. She's worth a free Awful-Awful."

Bev nudged her, and she turned to look up at him and say all in a rush—

The first bell rang. Tom said, "Back to the salt mines," and started for the door, because traffic officers had to leave at the first bell to be at their posts in time.

Snowy sat still while everybody scrambled. Chairs clanged, voices yelled. Somewhere a milk bottle smashed. The second bell rang, and Puddles and Bev scooped up their books, and in a trance Snowy picked up hers and walked with them into the madhouse of the rush for the tunnel.

Through the noise, Bev said, "He's hooked, I think he's hooked. Now you have to start reeling him in."

As Snowy walked in line along the tunnel, she racked her brains for something to say to him, but she couldn't think of anything, and then anyway when she got to him, he was busy grabbing at some junior high brats sneaking out of line, so he didn't notice her at all.


After school, Snowy and Puddles, with the other girls in the Girls' Athletic Association, the GAA, played volleyball in the gym. Snowy was not athletic, but she had joined last year and suffered field hockey, basketball, bowling, volleyball, and softball, because it was the thing to do and because she wanted to become extracurricular chummy with those cheerleading powers, Gilly and Jonesy. To distract from her lack of skill, she learned to clown, howling in terror when she was a field hockey goalie, curtsying with her little gym-suit skirt when she had to walk to first base, flinching from ferocious basketball forwards she was supposed to guard, and complaining to Jonesy at the bowling alley, "My ball just creeps down the alley looking forlornly over its shoulder at me!" Bev, who was ladylike during sports, and Puddles, who was quick and bold, encouraged her, and the other girls enjoyed her, but she was never sure how amused Gilly and Jonesy were.

After volleyball, she and Puddles started walking home together. Their coats were long and heavy, Snowy's pink-gray tweed, Puddles' navy blue, and their pull-on mid-shin rubber boots were black. The bulkiness of the coats caused them to carry their books and notebooks not on their hips but hugged against their chests. Just as Snowy saw that Tom's car wasn't at Varney's gas station, Puddles said, "Look, there goes New Boy, that *is* his car, isn't it sexy!"

It was a red MGA, and Linda Littlefield was in it.

Snowy said, "Is Linda driving? She can't be."

"No, I peeked into it once in the parking lot, the steering wheel's on the wrong side, awful confusing."

"For heaven's sake."

"It's English. I didn't see him watching us in the gym windows, did you, but he must've been waiting around for Linda. I wish I'd bounced the ball right off her head."

They turned and walked along Chestnut Street. In the tall old houses, lighted windows warmed the dreary afternoon, but they only made Snowy feel colder and sadder. Puddles lived on Gowen Street, and at the corner they said good-bye. Usually Bev was with them, and Bev usually walked the rest of the way with Snowy to wait at Snowy's house for her stepfather to pick her up when he got out of work, but Bev's rehearsals of *Our Town* now conflicted with GAA and recently were lasting so late Fred picked her up at school. Snowy walked on alone.

This walk was too familiar to her, and without Bev the boredom of it throbbed like her headache. She could only dimly remember the other place she'd lived, an apartment on a nearby street, a smell of bibs and orange juice the earliest memory, the food-and-wood smell of her highchair. She remembered Christmas mornings when she stood in the doorway of her bedroom and saw in the living room the wonder of the Christmas tree heaped with Santa Claus presents; she remembered her father's going to work wearing a button that fascinated her, a button that was his picture to identify him at the factory during the war; and there was a memory of afternoon naps when sunlight against drawn shades made the room hazy and just as she was falling asleep goblins seemed to dance on her blanket. After she and her parents moved, whenever she went past that old apartment house she would stare at it and study it to try to learn who she had been when she lived there.

But she was beginning to understand that you never know at any time what you are like, and looking back, you can't remember. She walked past the yellow house where Bev had lived from second to sixth grade, and she couldn't remember who she had been when they played Sergeant Preston of the Yukon on the snowbanks, or played dolls, or pasted pictures of movie stars in scrapbooks, or to their horror got their periods.

She turned at the Emery Street corner, and her headache lessened. The street ran alongside the river, and across the river were warehouses and the backs of Main Street stores. Her mother was ashamed of this slummy view, but Snowy found it exciting. In the summertime she'd cross the street to the riverbank, and down in the trees she'd sit, sometimes reading but mostly watching the view and the river and the ducks. Occasionally she saw a sea gull. She had only seen the sea itself once, when years ago her grandfather decided she ought to and had taken her and her grandmother to the seacoast one autumn day; she had feared it wouldn't be as impressive as the movies, but there were wind and salt, the dark sea stretched high into green waves that crashed, there was a great roar and rattle of pebbles as the waves receded, and this time reality met her hopes. So she'd sit on the riverbank and watch for a sea gull, and the longing for something, she didn't know what, was as intense as pain.

Hers was the big square white house with black shutters, on a rise overlooking the river. When her parents bought it in 1946, neglect had made it shabby, and fixing it up became their obsession. Snowy at first had been happy to follow the improvements, the paint, the new sink, the new furnace, but as she grew older and eventually everything seemed to be done and her parents started over again, repainting and rewallpapering, she began to sense how their lives were spiraling smaller and smaller to this pinpoint, this house, and she began to hate it. Summer evenings, her parents would stand on the front lawn and look at the house, not at the river.

She walked up the driveway and along the shoveled path around to the back door. Her parents didn't bother about the little backyard because it couldn't be seen from the front, and now there was just a snowbank, and in the summer just bushes. Once

Snowy had planted some nasturtiums, but black bugs ruined them.

Indoors, her dog began to bark. "Silly Laurie," Snowy said, "silly powder puff," and opened the storm door and the inside door into the kitchen and crouched to receive Annie Laurie hurtling at her. When Snowy had announced she wanted a dog for her twelfth birthday, a collie like Lassie, her parents said a collie was too large and suggested a cocker spaniel; Snowy outwitted them by going to the library, getting a dog book, and discovering small Shetland collies. Laurie had a pert foxy face and soft golden fur, and Snowy chose her name from a piano songbook.

"Biscuit?" she asked, standing up. Laurie danced in ecstasy.

Snowy turned on the overhead light. It was a crisply clean kitchen, with white-and-red dotted Swiss curtains, white-painted wooden cupboards, dark-red linoleum waxed shiny, and geometric white shapes of refrigerator, stove, sink, and washing machine, but it was not cozy. There was no kitchen table, no place to sit down, because her father insisted on all meals in the dining room. There were, however, roosters. Her mother was very fond of roosters and had collected ceramic roosters, wrought-iron rooster towel racks, turkish rooster towels, a rooster memo pad, and a rooster cookie jar. Snowy hated them.

She toed off her boots and dropped her coat on the washing machine. Her mother had always used a wringer one until four years ago, when this automatic was bought; the day it arrived, her mother and father had stood and watched it go through every cycle. Snowy crossed to the cupboards and got Laurie a dog biscuit. Laurie barked for outdoors, and she let her out.

Now she was alone in the house. When Snowy started high school, her mother had gone back to work in the office of the shoe factory. Snowy didn't mind, she preferred being alone to being with her folks, but she wished Bev were here. She turned

on the burner under the little stove-top oven used for baking potatoes, and while she waited for it to heat she ate three fig New-
tons and looked at the lunch dishes in the dish drainer and again
wondered what her folks talked about alone together, because if
they talked just of their work and the house and her accomplishments and what to buy next, as they did when she was there, she
didn't see why they didn't go crazy.

On the counter were the potatoes and a can of corned beef
hash and a can of peas. She sighed. For supper there used to be
beef stew or macaroni and cheese or chicken and dumplings, but
since her mother had gone back to work, there was more and
more canned food, more and more hamburg.

She put in the potatoes, picked up her books and coat, and
went into the dining room. Three blue woven place mats were
laid on the maple table which stood on the rug her grandmother
had braided, and in the maple hutch was displayed the good
china, with its blue Currier and Ives scenes. The dining room
had recently been repapered, and her parents had discussed wallpaper patterns until she thought she would scream. Finally they
chose blue grapes. She went into the living room, and patted Kit,
the old black-and-white cat, who was sleeping in her father's
overstuffed chair. Here the wallpaper was green herringbone, and
there were more braided rugs on the polished wood floor, her
mother's rocker, and the sofa that her mother had begun talking
about a new slipcover for. Ruffly white organdy curtains were
looped across the windows. On the piano a lesson book was
open, as if Snowy at any moment might sit down and play a
Bach chorale, but in junior high Snowy had talked her parents
into allowing her to quit her lessons, and now she only fooled
around on her own, picking out hit songs.

All the rooms were as crisp as the kitchen, as on display as the
good china.

She hung her coat in the coat closet and went upstairs and
along the hallway of small braided rugs to her room, a sanctuary

where she hid in the evenings, although her parents always wondered aloud why she couldn't come down and sit with them while she studied. In this pink-and-white room, childhood blended into girlhood. Her dolls still sat around in doll chairs; a teen-age collection of stuffed toy animals was heaped on the pink chenille bedspread. In her white bookcase were the Five Little Peppers and Bobbsey Twins and Honeybunches and Maidas and Nancy Drews, but there were also more recent birthday-and-Christmas-requested books, *Rebecca, Seventeenth Summer, Gone with the Wind, A Date with Marcy, Showboat,* and books she herself had bought, paperback Agatha Christies and a paperback anthology of poetry, and there was a stack of *Seventeen* magazines on the lowest shelf. On her white bureau were her lipsticks and a big bottle of White Lilac cologne and her jewelry box and two perfume wick lamps, and a beloved Kewpie doll. And on the rosebud-papered walls there were still two illustrations of Little Bo Peep and Little Boy Blue bereft of their respective flocks, as well as big glossy photographs of the actors in last year's *Hansel and Gretel,* Bev as the Witch and herself as the Crybaby, the kids looking vivid in makeup, and this year's production of *Alice in Wonderland,* in which Bev was the Duchess, Puddles was a lobster, and she was an oyster.

She dumped her books on the mahogany veneer desk and sat down, but she didn't open her algebra book. She opened a bottom drawer. Bev kept a Roger Scrapbook of clippings about his successes, basketball and prize-speaking and debate, and Snowy had this drawer in which she had accumulated souvenirs, but, once important, they all seemed stupid to her now, grubby misspelled notes passed in class by boyfriends, three pressed corsages, some movie ticket stubs, some school pictures, and the ribbon from the present Ed had given her on her birthday last year. The present was a white angora sweater, and her mother had been rather taken aback by it because it wasn't flowers or candy. The etiquette which confused Snowy was whether or not she should keep wearing it after she broke up with Ed, but she didn't have many sweaters, so she did.

There was nothing in the drawer from Tom.

She slammed it shut and worked on her algebra until it was time to go downstairs. The kitchen smelled snugly of baked potatoes. She turned them and opened a cupboard and took down the everyday china, thick white with maroon-flowered borders, and carried it into the dining room and set the table.

Laurie barked. Snowy let her in and consulted the clock. Five fifteen. They'd be on their way home. She turned on a burner and got the butter dish out of the refrigerator. One of her mother's sayings was: "You can always tell what kind of housekeeper a woman is by looking at her butter dish." And her mother washed the dish after each stick of margarine was used up. Snowy wanted to call this another of her mother's scatty ideas, but she had to admit to herself that Bev's mother just put in another stick and soon the dish was smeary and lumpy and greasy, and Bev's mother was not house-proud.

She dropped some margarine into the frying pan and opened the can of corned beef hash with the wall can opener. She pried the stuff out. It looked like dog food, as usual, so she added a can of beets to make it red-flannel hash, and then it looked like pink dog food.

"I'm starving," she said to Laurie. "How about an hors d'oeuvre?" That word she had learned from Bev's mother. She found the rat-trap cheese behind a bowl of Jello in the refrigerator and put a slice on a pilot cracker. Laurie thumped her tail. "Here you go," Snowy said, breaking off a bit of cracker.

She leaned against the counter and glumly chewed. Every calendar they were given by the milkman, insurance company, grocery store, gas station, her mother hung up in the kitchen, unable to resist the pictures of sleighs, apple blossoms, sweet brown-and-white cows, so Snowy was surrounded by calendars which, below their kite-flying March scenes (calendars always showed spring earlier than New Hampshire weather did), told her there were just three more weeks until cheerleading tryouts.

Ever since junior high, she had wanted to be a Varsity cheerleader. It was her clear-cut ambition. Puddles did too, but Puddles also had a definite career ambition. Snowy's career ambition was a sun shining through mist; beyond the goal of a glamorous women's college was the goal of fame. She wanted to be famous because she knew someday she was going to die, and even when she was still attending Sunday school, she knew that death was the end. She would lie awake at night imagining herself gone. Bev's awareness of death caused Bev to want to have lots of fun along the way. Snowy wanted to be famous so she would live forever.

And she believed that the stepping-stones to fame began here, although she hadn't yet figured out at what she would one day be famous.

She had seen her first cheerleaders when she went to her first football game, in seventh grade. She and the junior high gang that was beginning to emerge out of the various grammar school gangs, Charl and Darl and Bev and Betty Jane Owen and Shirley Blanchard and Carol Tucker and Patty Nichols and Linda Littlefield and Dotty Mooney and Nancy Gordon, all dressed identically in gray sweat shirts over white blouses and blue dungarees with the cuffs rolled up, had sat high in the bleachers, and the autumn night was cool, and none of them paid much attention to the game but instead flirted with the boys sitting behind them—until each time the cheerleaders down below jumped up to do a cheer. And then every single girl in the Gang was riveted, studying the cheerleaders, making wisecracks about them, jealous, unable to believe that in a few years this glory could be theirs and yet anxious for the time of trial.

It had come.

Last year she and Puddles and Bev and the rest of the Gang had gone out for cheering, going to the sessions at which the cheerleaders taught cheers and jumps and cartwheels. But after a couple of sessions, Bev quit. Snowy still wondered why. Bev had said the pain was too much torture, but this didn't seem a reason to Snowy, who, so lame she could hardly walk, all her muscles screaming, would for a chance at cheerleading willingly have suffered the rack.

And the lameness passed, and the first tryouts came. They were held on the stage of the auditorium, with the judges, Gilly and Jonesy and the Varsity cheerleaders, watching from the first row, and many other kids sitting in the audience behind the rows of girls waiting to try out. The girls wore their short-sleeved short-skirted green cotton gym suits and white socks and sneakers. For once, the girls were not giggling; they sat very quiet.

They had to go up by twos, so Snowy and Puddles went together, tense and solemn with fright. They did the three cheers they had practiced and practiced, "Abnaki Locomotive," "Forward and Backward," and "Fight, Team, Fight." The Gunthwaite cheerleading style was feminine but vigorous, and everyone in the audience knew exactly how Snowy and Puddles should look. And it was fragile Puddles who had learned the trick; she cheered as easily as she danced, and by the last cheer she had forgotten her fright and was enjoying herself. Snowy looked awkward.

Then they each had to do a cartwheel. Puddles spun over lightly. Waiting her turn, Snowy wanted to disappear, to flee someplace where cheering didn't matter, where it wouldn't be so absolutely necessary for her to be up on this stage in her gym suit, sweating, sick. Her turn. Blind now, just wanting to get it over with, she ran, flipped, and her legs were straight as she cartwheeled over, and she didn't fall, she came up standing.

Then she and Puddles sat in the audience and watched the rest of the girls go up by twos.

"God," Puddles said. "Everyone and her grandmother is out for cheering."

After all the girls had tried out, Gilly, the Varsity coach, vaulted athletically onto the stage and consulted her clipboard for a few moments while the girls held their breaths. Gilly was a tall, brawny, homely woman, but when she was running down the hockey field or basketball court, she seemed briefly beautiful. In a dress or skirt she looked imprisoned, but now as she stood above them she was wearing her short green jumper and white blouse and her whistle, and she looked almighty.

Gilly liked suspense and power. "The semifinals list," she said, "will be posted on the gym office door tomorrow morning. That's all for now; you can go home."

There were groans of disappointment.

It was the cruelest night Snowy ever had to endure. It was far worse than nights after a test, waiting to find out her mark. The semifinals list would announce the girls allowed to try out for Varsity and would indicate those being considered for JV's. The next morning, when Fred dropped Bev off at the house on his way to work and she and Bev walked to school together, she was trembling so much she was afraid she'd spill her books.

Usually on winter mornings the Gang sat talking in the auditorium balcony until the homeroom bell rang, but that morning they and most of the other girls in the school were down in front of the gym office. The corridor was packed. As Snowy and Bev came down the stairs, Snowy saw them all there, chattering excitedly or standing blank, and she realized she would have to push through them and have them watch her when she read the list. Bev looked at her and said, "Want me to?" and she said, "No," and forced herself into the crowd. The list was alphabetical. One S. It was a Smith. Not Snow.

In shock, she read the list slowly. The twins' names were on it. And Pond, Jean. Puddles.

And then Puddles was grabbing her and saying, "It doesn't matter, you know it doesn't matter, you don't have to be on the list to go out for JV's, and JV's is all we're hoping for this year, Snowy, it's *okay*."

"No," she said. Her drive to be best suddenly would not let her make another humiliating attempt when she was one of the girls who had already been eliminated. "No. I'm not going out."

She sat stunned through her first period class.

But Puddles kept hounding her all day. And Bev, to atone for a flash of joy when Snowy's name wasn't on the list, said, "I really think you ought to try out," which surprised and confused Snowy because she'd supposed Bev would think she ought to forget about being a cheerleader as Bev had. "No," Snowy said.

The Varsity tryouts were held that afternoon. She wasn't going to go, she wanted to seem superior to it, but Bev said, "We've got to be there to give Puddles moral support." So, in her school clothes, not in her gym suit, she sat with Bev in the audience and watched the chosen girls.

Afterward, walking in silence to her house with Bev, she hugged her books to her chest and vowed that she would at least become the best student in the whole school.

It was her folks' anniversary. She hadn't told them about tryouts, not wanting to see their disappointment if she didn't make it, wanting to give the news to them as a present if she did. Now she could only give them the set of Libbey juice glasses. They all went out to dinner, and she sat at the Gunthwaite Inn with her napkin on her lap, looked at the grown-ups around her, and repeated to herself that cheerleading did not matter.

But that night in bed she had sobbed and sobbed until Laurie was so frantic with worry she stopped by stuffing her pillow into her mouth.

The next morning the Varsity results were posted. Puddles didn't make it; none of the freshmen did, not even the twins.

"I hadn't really hoped," Puddles said, "it's hardly ever that a freshman makes Varsity," but her eyes shone with tears. "I don't really hope for JV's either. I don't hope for anything."

And Snowy, tremulous with sympathy which overcame her pride, said, "Okay, let's go out for JV's together. Just for chucks."

The next day she'd almost succeeded in convincing herself it was just for chuckles. Calm came from fatigue; her emotions were as lame as her muscles had been. She sat through Latin I, a study, History of Civilization, Algebra I, lunch, and then in fifth period, English, she began to get nervous. During sixth period, the last period, she had a study, and she worked doggedly at her algebra, but every time she paused, in rushed the foreboding of failure, and her stomach went sick.

Once again, she and Puddles sat pale and taut in the auditorium, waiting their turn.

"Next!" Gilly yelled.

Puddles' hands were icy cold. "That's us."

They ran up the steps to the stage. The dusty wine-red curtains, drawn back, framed them. They seemed very small as they stood together in the stance so automatic to them now, left fists on hips, right arms straight down at their sides. The scuffed floor stretched away behind them to the Hansel and Gretel flats of a childlike painted forest.

Then they yelled, "Abnaki Locomotive!" and began. Afterward Snowy couldn't remember the cheerleading at all, but desperation had inspired her. Gilly and Jonesy looked surprised.

She didn't fall during her cartwheel.

When the last of the girls had tried out, the judges conferred in the gym office. The girls waited. Snowy and Puddles sat on the hard auditorium seats, and neither of them said a word. Looking up, Snowy saw Ed and some other guys leaning in the upstairs window, watching. And Bev, with some other girls in the balcony, waved, showing that all her fingers were crossed.

Then the judges returned, and Jonesy called, "We want to see a few of you do 'T-E-A-M.' " Jonesy was young and sturdy and an object of the girls' envy because she had an engagement ring. She glanced at her clipboard. "Linda Littlefield! Jean Pond!"

Snowy sat stiff, her face as flushed and stinging as if she'd been slapped. She watched them do the cheer and tried to prepare herself for congratulating Puddles.

Jonesy called, "Charlene and Darlene Fecteau!"

The twins did "T-E-A-M." Puddles and Snowy watched.

"Carol Tucker! Nancy Gordon!"

Puddles cracked her knuckles.

Jonesy called, "Diane Morrissette! Henrietta Snow!"

Puddles said, "Go on. Give it everything you've got."

Chin up, Snowy stood on the stage and looked out at Gilly and Jonesy and the Varsity cheerleaders who would decide her fate.

"T-E-A-M!"

Her jump was spectacular, arms outstretched, head flung back so far her ponytail brushed her sneakers.

Then there was more waiting. The girls understood that Jonesy was more compassionate than Gilly, and the rumor spread that Jonesy would announce the results this afternoon instead of tomorrow. Bev came down to say she had to leave to get a ride home with Fred. More waiting. Snowy and Puddles sat with their hands folded on their bare knees.

Puddles said, "I can't stand this, let's go change our clothes," so they and the twins and some of the other girls went downstairs to the girls' locker room and changed back into their skirts and blouses.

They went upstairs, and they waited.

Jonesy came out on the auditorium stage and said, "The list is posted on the gym office door."

There was a mad stampede, but Snowy said, "We must do this with dignity," and Puddles obeyed. They walked slowly out of the auditorium, past classrooms, an endless walk down the stairs and toward the gym office, and Carol Tucker ran past, tears streaming, and yelled, "You made it!" Snowy's heart stopped. Which one of them? Both? They started running. The throng around the door was hands grabbing, voices congratulating, and Snowy realized they were congratulating *her*, her and Puddles, but she didn't believe it until she pushed through the girls and finally got to the list.

> Beaupre, Rita
> Demers, Maureen
> Fecteau, Charlene
> Fecteau, Darlene
> Littlefield, Linda
> Nutter, Marjorie
> Pond, Jean
> Snow, Henrietta

Delirium. She didn't notice the girls who were leaving silently, some of them crying. She babbled and babbled with Puddles and Linda and the twins, and it was quarter of six when she got home. Her mother, in a kitchen tizzy trying to decide about the overdone carrots and wrinkled baked potatoes and dried-up hamburgers, was furious. Then Snowy gasped her news, and her mother actually screamed with delight, and when Snowy's father came into the kitchen to find out where in God's name she'd been, her mother told him even before Snowy could.

Snowy phoned Bev that evening, and Ed phoned to find out the results and congratulated her. The next morning, when Snowy came downstairs, Bev had arrived and was standing in the living room holding a little pad of paper. Suddenly Bev started tearing pieces of it off and running around and around throwing them in the air and yelling, "Rah! Rah! Rah!" Snowy picked up a handful and saw that each piece had "Rah" written on it, and she began to giggle. Only later, thinking about it in

Latin class, did she wonder if Bev had been making fun of her.
Or was Bev jealous?

But throughout the day, instead of saying hi, the kids said,
"Congratulations!" and it was the most blissful day of her life.

Yet she knew then, and had known all year, that she would
have to go through it all over again.

Nobody cared much about JV football, so Jonesy didn't
allow them to cheer at these games; Jonesy concentrated on getting them ready for basketball season. The JV's thought this un-
fair, they longed to be out on the vast field like the Varsity
cheerleaders, but they conceded they'd look pretty silly trying
to get yells from empty bleachers. When basketball season came,
there wasn't enough money to transport them to many of the
away games, so they gained most of their experience right in the
GHS gym. The games came just before the Varsity games, and
by the end a big crowd was there, and Snowy learned that success meant the heady exhilaration of cheering on the polished
gym floor, the yells seeming to swing the bright hot gym up and
out into the night.

And so her want was intensified. She wanted to be one of
those fabulous Varsity cheerleaders cheering at a game that mattered, for the boys who mattered, the crowd caring passionately,
and she herself one of those who led them.

She gave Laurie another piece of cracker and tried, like Puddles, to figure the angles. If she didn't make it this year, she
might be a JV captain or co-captain. But that was not success.
She could try out again her junior year for Varsity, but still she
would know and everyone would know that this meant she was
second-best. And what if she didn't make it next year? Would
she end up like dumpy Maureen Demers, a senior JV captain, a
joke? A failure?

After supper, she and her headache finished her homework
and then took a bath. When she had dried herself, put on her pajamas, untwisted the elastic around her ponytail and brushed and

brushed her hair smooth, she patted Noxzema on her face. Hair down, she looked at herself in the mirror, counting all the things she considered handicaps. Her forehead was high; she hid it with bangs. Her neck, she'd decided, was too long, but she could hide this also, with the turned-up collar fashion, except when she wore a sweater. Ski-jump nose, no way to hide that, or her eyes, which weren't a clear blue like Tom's but a denim blue. And unless a miracle happened pretty soon, she was going to go through life wearing 32A bras.

So would Bev. They continued to be amazed that Puddles was the one out of their triumvirate who was developing satisfactory breasts. (Snowy and Bev hated words like "breasts" and "bust," but when Puddles arrived talking about them as "bubbies," they found this word so funny they adopted it.)

Downstairs, her parents were in the living room, her mother reading the local paper, the Gunthwaite *Herald*, and her father reading the statewide Manchester *Union*, a very right-wing conservative paper. Snowy was ashamed of him for reading it; Bev's mother wouldn't allow it in the house.

When they sat here in the evenings, her parents appeared to be posing themselves for a portrait of family life. But something was missing.

Her mother, Charlotte Snow, had grown up in Gunthwaite, in a house just a few streets away, and had never traveled any farther than Manchester. A bit plump, her brown hair beginning to gray, she looked placid, but always inside she was fretting, even when she was working or listening to conversation or reading; she was always worrying about whether or not Snowy was popular, whether or not to buy that new dress at Yvonne's, whether or not she really liked the new wallpaper. Snowy's father, Hank, was slight and gray-haired. His father had died of drink, and his mother had died of the struggle to bring him and his sisters up alone, in Manchester, and as a young man he'd resolved to have a perfect family life of his own, complete with every meal in the dining room. He had a vision of a long table, himself at the head of it, a pretty little wife at the foot, and between them the rosy faces of their children turned to watch him carve the turkey and to listen to him speak. The vision had not come true, but it was necessary to him, and he pretended.

So they posed, and Snowy stood at the foot of the stairs and asked, "Could I watch TV? *Peter Pan* is on, with Mary Martin."

He always weighed his decisions. "Your homework's done?"

"Of course, Daddy."

Her mother said, "I don't see why you can't do some of your studying down here with us."

Her father said, "How late will it last?"

"Until nine thirty."

He lit a Camel, and Snowy waited, not looking at him, accustomed to this but wondering what could be unwholesome about Peter Pan.

"Well," he said. "All right."

She turned on the television. During the past few years when everyone else was buying televisions and she kept pleading for one, her father would dismiss her arguments with "I'm still not sure radio is here to stay." She'd never been quite certain how much of that was humor, and when the TV was unveiled the Christmas before last, she'd been flabbergasted.

Laurie and Kit beside her, she settled down on the sofa to watch the show. Her mother put away her newspaper and watched too, and eventually so did her father. Snowy sat rapt, twisting and twisting a strand of hair, leaving Never-Never Land only once, to slap together a fast marshmallow-fluff and raspberry-jam sandwich.

And then, when Tinkerbell drank Peter's poisoned medicine and began dying, and Peter asked everyone who believed in fairies to clap, she burst into tears, as she had while reading the book and seeing the movie. Oblivious of her startled parents, she sat clapping and crying, but this time it wasn't only Tinkerbell for whom she wept.

Thursday, and Snowy in her 4AB study, her *Silas Marner* open on her desk, stared at an illustration of little Eppie and brooded. The study was in an upstairs classroom where General students had English. Above the high dark wainscoting, the walls were an exhausted beige; on one was a murky picture of Washington Crossing the Delaware, and on another the wooden clock that trapped each class.

Tom had this study hall, too, and she'd been hoping he'd be in it today. But, as he usually did, he came in at the beginning, wearing coveralls that made him seem from an alien world, and gave an excuse slip to Miss Thayer, who was so fat she had to go up stairs one at a time, gripping the banister, a wheezing white-haired woman always wearing crepe dresses which were shiny across the enormous swell of her bosom. She was a kindly teacher, and because she was hard of hearing, the kids talked to each other throughout her classes and study halls; her discipline was nearly gone. She smiled at Tom, and he waved at a couple of guys as he left to go work in the shop.

Snowy was upset because Bev and Puddles had been silly all morning, a secret sort of silly in which she couldn't join, and this had never happened before. When one of their three got irritated with another, it was Puddles mad at Bev or Bev catty to Puddles, and Snowy was the one in the middle trying to bring about a reconciliation. She wondered if they were fed up with her because she didn't have the guts to approach Tom.

She glanced up at the clock hand. It obligingly jumped forward, and the first bell rang. She stacked her books on her notebook, and when the second bell rang, she hurried with the other kids out into the corridor, around traffic officers, down the stairs to the first floor and down to the basement.

On Thursdays, the kids wore pink, an odd custom because if you wore pink on Thursday, you were a queer. But they did. So today Snowy was wearing her pink blouse and pink kneelengths disappearing under the hem of her gray woolen straight skirt, and at his traffic post Tom was wearing a pink oxford-cloth shirt with the latest style in chinos that had a buckle in the back. "Hi," he said. "Hi," she said, got down the steps without falling, and was rushed along into the cafeteria smell of the tunnel.

Bev and Puddles had study halls in classrooms nearer the cafeteria, so they always arrived here first, but when she entered, she couldn't see them. She put her books down on their table and scanned the place, and spotted them already over at the ice-cream counter. She looked up at the desk on the platform. She wished she dared. Yet during the lunchtimes since Monday she had sat at the table and talked homework with the Gang, while up on the platform Tom as usual had been busy kidding around with upperclassmen girls and boys, and Bev, and even with Diane Morrissette, who, unlike Snowy, didn't have any qualms about forcing herself on him.

Snowy started toward Bev and Puddles, but Dudley Washburn stopped her, asking about the history assignment, and Linda Littlefield was asking her about the English test tomorrow, and there were kids around her, jokes about how the English teacher always wore a black suit when he was going to give a test, jokes about how many times the Latin teacher's bra and slip straps had fallen down in class, and through the kids she saw Tom come in talking to Sam Page. He climbed up on the platform, surveyed the cafeteria, and sat down at the desk.

"Here," Puddles said to her, squirming into the cluster of kids, "we knew you'd be starving, so we got you your ice cream, too."

"Thanks, I'll pay you back," Snowy said, and took the little carton and sat down.

Bev and Puddles sat on either side of her. Fleetingly Snowy wondered why the kids were still standing around instead of waiting in the lunch line or sitting down eating. Bev said, "We chose sundaes today, for a change, strawberry ones," and Snowy, indeed starving, unwrapped the little wooden spoon and peeled the lid off the carton. There was a brown thing lying on top of the ice cream. She thought it was a piece of gum, Bev and Puddles being funny, and she picked it up.

She screamed.

It was a frog's leg.

Bev and Puddles had correctly judged her reaction. She went mad. She jumped up and dropped the carton and screamed and screamed, "Get it out of here! *Get it out of here!*" while the kids around her began laughing and everyone in the cafeteria stood up to see what the commotion was, and Snowy kept screaming.

Tom sprang off the platform and grabbed her. "What the hell's the matter?"

She clutched at him, just like a twin. "*Get it out of here!*"

Bev said, "Oh, Tom, we're sorry, we played a joke—"

"Snowy," he said, "calm down, calm down."

Bev said, "Come, Puddles, let's go buy her a nice bottle of milk," and picked up the sundae and frog's leg and tossed them in the wastebasket as she and Puddles paraded away.

Snowy's face was pressed against Tom's pink shirt. He said, "All right, everybody, it's over, eat your lunch." He pulled out a chair, and Snowy flopped into it.

He said, "Are you okay?" He sat down beside her, and looked at her. Starched Snowy was flushed and trembling, and her nape tendrils had escaped from her elastic, soft and flyaway.

She nodded.

He said, "What was that thing?"

"A frog's leg." And when she said it, she knew that Bev and Puddles had planned this to give her another chance at Tom. She reached for her pocketbook and took out her hanky and wiped her sweaty hands. Her heart was still thumping wildly. She could still smell his clean shirt and his Old Spice.

She said, "I should have guessed. I heard somebody say something about dissecting this morning in biology. I should have guessed they'd try to be funny."

"They're a regular Martin and Lewis."

"I've got to think up a way to get even. I could tell Norm Noyes that Puddles is dying to have him ask her to the Sophomore Dance. Or would that be too mean?"

"I'm not sure who Norm Noyes is."

"I could swipe Bev's pen tomorrow before the English test, and she'll think she's lost it and have cats."

He saw her small hands and grinned. "You could use another pen. Yours must leak like mad."

It did, and her fingers were inky, the sweat smeared blue on her handkerchief. She tried to hide them, but he reached forward and touched her wrist, and because when kids who had little in common except the same school and the same town tried to make conversation, they seized any small joke between them and kept harping on it, he said, "Maybe I ought to buy that Awful-Awful card after all, and you should charge enough to buy yourself a new pen."

All the girls at the table were covertly watching.

Snowy said, very fast, "I've got a birthday coming up, I'll get a pen with my birthday money and still have the card. Did you promise me a head start?"

"I sure did." Then he said, "How about the movies, before Hooper's?"

She nearly shouted with joy. She nearly leaped up on the table and did a cartwheel right down it through the sandwiches and books and American chop suey.

She said, "That sounds like a fair deal."

"Tomorrow night?"

"Fine."

"Quarter of seven okay? You still live in the same place?" He knew where she lived because he'd picked up and brought Bev home there a number of times last spring.

"Yes," Snowy said, "the same place."

Bev set a bottle of milk and a straw in front of her. "Have you recovered?"

Tom stood up and said, kidding, "Another stunt like that and I'll have to haul you off to the principal's office."

Snowy sat smiling at the milk.

Then Tom stepped back onto the platform, and Bev and Puddles sat down and whispered, "Did it work? Did it work?"

"It worked."

"I knew it!" Bev said. "It was my idea, I take full credit."

"Oh, no, you don't," Puddles said. "I was the one who dissected the frog while you were gagging, Beverly Colby, I was the one who lugged the leg around in my pocketbook all morning."

Bev said, "But it was my brainstorm. I had it Monday night when I was shaving my legs."

Puddles said, "So that's why you insisted on a leg. I," she told Snowy, "wanted to use an eyeball. More subtle."

"Oh, God," Snowy said.

Bev said, "You see why we couldn't tell you, don't you? We wanted you to give an authentic performance."

Puddles said, "And, boy, you certainly did."

Snowy realized for the first time what she must have looked like screaming her head off, and she was very embarrassed. She had made up a romantic fantasy about Tom which she acted out each night in her imagination before she fell asleep; it took place at some splendid prom, and she'd costumed herself from movies, she was gorgeous in a swirling strapless gown, and Tom walked right through the clamoring girls straight to her and danced with her all night.

Reality once again had failed her.

But she had a date with him at last. She said, "It's not just the Awful-Awful, either. We're going to the movies, too, tomorrow night. Why do you suppose he hasn't already got a date with Rita?"

Before Bev and Puddles could begin speculating, the first bell rang, Tom left, and the other girls fell on Snowy, shrieking, "What happened? Did he ask you out? Isn't he *cute!*" and Puddles said, "Some people have all the luck. Who am I stuck with tomorrow night? Norm Noyes. He doesn't even have a license, much less a car; he has to walk me home like we were still kids."

But as the second bell rang, and Snowy saw Puddles' unopened lunch bag and remembered she hadn't eaten anything, Puddles picked up her books and began triumphantly to sing the song from the Lobster Quadrille in *Alice in Wonderland*, "Will you won't you will you won't you will you join the dance?"


"This is Tom Forbes," Snowy said, holding Laurie, who barked and wriggled. "My mother and father. Shush, Laurie, you remember him."

Her parents were doing their family-life pose in the living room, and although they'd met him when he picked up Bev, they didn't remember him any more than Laurie did, because then he hadn't been dating Snowy and was of no importance to them. Now, as Snowy dumped Laurie on the sofa and went to the closet for her jacket, they studied him.

Her father stood up and shook hands. "Nice weather today."

Tom said, "Maybe spring's coming."

Her father said, "I wouldn't bet on it."

Tom turned to Snowy and said, "Here, let me," and helped

her on with her jacket. He himself was wearing his green football jacket.

Her mother watched approvingly.

Snowy picked up her overnight case. "I'm sleeping over at Bev's," she explained to him, and Tom took the case, and she started edging toward the dining room.

Her mother said, "Have you got your toothbrush?"

Snowy considered matricide. "Yes."

Introducing boyfriends to her parents was always agony for her. She simply didn't want the boys—and especially Tom—to know that she had parents or that she lived in a house or that she had eaten the supper he could smell in the rooms. She wanted to be free of all domestic details. This obsession made her behave strangely. When Ed had said he liked her perfume and asked what it was, she had been so embarrassed she couldn't answer, which bewildered Ed. She'd wanted him to think she naturally smelled of lilacs. When she was downtown in the shoe store buying silver flats for the Christmas dance, she had seen Ed walking past and had ducked behind a display of slippers so he wouldn't see her if he happened to look in. She'd wanted him to think she just existed with silver shoes. She had read about Athena springing in full armor from the temple of Zeus, and this was the way she wanted to be. She could have done without Zeus, too.

Laurie jumped off the sofa, and Snowy picked her up and said, "No, you can't come."

Her father said, "Remember it's midnight at Bev's, same as here."

Her mother said, "Have a good time."

Tom said, "Glad to meet you again."

In the kitchen, Snowy gave Laurie a dog biscuit, set her down, and Tom opened the door. He already knew this detail, that the back door was used, not the front.

Outdoors, they walked along the path between the house and garage to the driveway, and Snowy stopped for a moment, apparently to snap her jacket but really to admire the car. It was admired by all the girls because it was a convertible, and it was known to the boys as the Cunt-Wagon. It was old but still elegant, a 1949 cream-colored Chevy with a black top, a continental tire on the trunk. Tom had saved his odd-job and summer-job money toward this goal, a car, and had bought the Chevy the day he got his driver's license last May. At Varney's, he nursed it tenderly through its various ailments.

He opened the door for her, and she slid in.

As he walked around to his door, she sniffed the car-heater smell mixed with cigarette smoke and snuggled into the red upholstery. Then she remembered Bev had said last year what a lovely car it was to go parking in, and she thought of the other girls who had sat here and gone parking with Tom, Rita Beaupre and Brenda Dutile and Ellen Hatch and Adele Roberge and all the others; she saw them as a multitude, their hair disheveled, their lipstick smeared, but the ache of jealousy was pierced by fear: she was afraid he wouldn't like her and wouldn't take her parking; she was afraid he would take her parking and she wouldn't know what to do because she'd only gone parking on double dates before, in somebody's back seat.

He started the car, and the radio came on. He backed out of the driveway and headed toward downtown, and they were alone together for the first time.

She tried to think of something to say, but she was tongue-tied.

He said, "You look very nice."

He meant that she looked soft, not starched.

She gulped. "Thank you."

She had conferred with Bev about what to wear tonight, a momentous decision, and Bev chose slacks instead of a skirt, to be casual. After school Snowy had washed her hair and then leaned over her bedroom register, curling the tips with her hands until it dried with enough wave to be brushed up into her question-mark ponytail. After supper she had taken a long bath, carefully shaving her armpits and legs. She rubbed Pacquin's Hand Cream into her legs, bottom, arms, hands, and patted on some Mum cream deodorant, which stung. Back in her bedroom, she splashed a discreet amount of White Lilac behind her ears and inside her elbows. Then she selected her best white nylon underpants, her newest bra and white wool socks, and dressed herself in these and her brown wool slacks and the yellow short-sleeved pullover she'd washed last night. She put on her buff-colored loafers. She applied red lipstick and the mascara her parents had given her in her Christmas stocking. She fastened a gold clamp around her ponytail elastic, and her gold charm bracelet around her wrist. She had been ready a half hour before he came, she and the butterflies in her stomach.

And all the while she had been wondering, as she and Bev and Puddles had endlessly discussed, why Tom didn't have a date with Rita Beaupre.

The radio sang: "Did you say I've got a lot to learn?/Well, don't think I'm trying not to learn./Since this is the perfect spot to learn—/Teach me tonight."

Today's warm sunny weather had begun melting Wednesday's snowfall, but now the cold night had frozen the snow crust into a glaze. Beneath the streetlights, the lawns were shiny white.

Tom lit a Lucky Strike, and she watched. She'd never been out with a boy who smoked. He said, "That Puddles friend of yours is a sketch, isn't she? I saw her walking home after school and gave her a lift, and all she could talk about was how dissecting frogs is kid stuff and what she really wants to get her hands on is a fetal pig."

Jealousy flared. So Puddles too had sat in this seat. Snowy had stayed later at school than Puddles, to work with Priscilla Morgan, a junior, on a column for the April Fool issue of the school newspaper. They'd been assigned an advice-to-the-lovelorn column, and Snowy considered a column a great honor, even if it was only April Fool. Amid much giggling, she and Priscilla named themselves Lily Lovelorn and began to invent. Snowy's contribution was:

> DEAR LILY,
> I have been sick almost to death over this problem! I can't hide it any longer! Please help me!
> I have been going steady with a boy for two years. He is a dreamboat, but when we are alone, he gets down on all fours and barks. In three minutes he has grown hair all over his body and starts chasing the cat. As soon as someone comes home, he immediately switches back to normal. No one knows but me. I love him enough to marry him when he's normal, but heaven knows what would come of it. What do you advise?
> DESPERATE

> DEAR DESPERATE,
> You do have a problem, but I'm afraid I can't cope with it. My previous seven husbands have all gone to the dogs.
> LILY LOVELORN

"And then," Tom said, "Puddles asked me to drop her off at Woolworth's so she could buy some malt balls for supper. I said, you must be kidding, for *supper*, but she turned red and jumped out of the car and yelled thanks and ran like hell into the store. Is she crazy, or what?"

"Her mother'll kill her when she gets them home. She goes on these binges and sometimes it's malt"—Snowy realized why Puddles had blushed. Snowy suspected the reason Puddles loved malt balls was they gave her a chance to say "balls," and she would say it so loudly when she was ordering them at the candy counter that Bev and Snowy would hide behind the yard goods, but saying it in front of a boy was an entirely different matter. Now Snowy was faced with the same problem, and she hastily substituted —"candy, she'll refuse to eat anything but this candy, and her poor mother has an awful fit."

Snowy wasn't too sure what balls were. Puddles was an authority, having two younger brothers, but they were no longer babies, they were in the seventh grade and the sixth grade, so they couldn't be used for demonstration. Puddles made do with short-haired dogs and shouted and pointed whenever she saw one, which of course embarrassed Snowy so much she couldn't look. When she'd got her period, her mother had told her the Facts of Life but hadn't mentioned balls, and Snowy might almost have thought Puddles was kidding her if she hadn't also heard about them in dirty jokes. Bev could have enlightened her, and Snowy guessed this, yet they never discussed anything more advanced than Getting Fresh with breasts; Bev's fear and shame and Snowy's shyness made it one of their few taboo subjects. Snowy couldn't really believe that Tom sitting here beside her had balls, as well as that other mysterious thing that she'd peeked at in one of Bev's mother's art books. She had only Puddles' information to go by, and Puddles claimed it got big and stood up, and once when Puddles was changing her younger brother's diapers, Puddles said it pissed in her eye.

Snowy herself blushed.

Tom said, "I asked Roger about a double date, but he's working tonight."

"Yes, he's working after school and Friday nights now that basketball season's over." Roger worked at his uncle's grocery store, Lambert's Market. "He's just going to drop by Bev's when he's through."

Then it occurred to her that if Tom had thought of a double date, he might not want to be alone with her. But Tom's only reason was that he'd learned first dates were easier if double.

On Main Street, the stores were open, and the neon signs were brilliant above the snowbanks. There was a feeling of excitement downtown on Friday nights. The stores seemed to promise more; the purchases seemed special; even the coffee at Sweetland seemed to taste better. Despite the cold, people stopped and talked to each other.

Tom snuffed his cigarette in the ashtray and said, "These damn parking meters," and drove down a side street where the town hadn't yet installed any. He parked in front of a jewelry store. When they were downtown, Snowy and Bev and Puddles would stand gazing in its window at the diamond engagement rings, wondering if they ever would be given one. Tom noticed that a snowbank blocked her door. "You'd better get out my side."

So she slid across the seat, and he took her hand as she stepped out. Together they climbed the snowbank.

Side by side, she and Tom walked around the corner, past a barbershop and a hat store, and under the theater marquee on which a border of blinking golden lights fled around and around the big words so THIS IS PARIS.

The lobby was long and chilly, the gray floor sloping slowly upward, as if to paradise. Behind a brass railing, a line of boys moved past the maroon-curtained ticket window. Tom joined the line, and Snowy went over to where the girls were waiting, talking and reading the posters of coming attractions. She saw that *Twenty Thousand Leagues Under the Sea* was coming, and—

"Hi, Snowy," Rita Beaupre said flatly.

Rita was small and dark, her short black hair sleek except for pincurl-created fluffy bangs and eartip curves like little wings. She was wearing black ski pants and a red jacket that matched her lipstick, and she was very cute. She was also very angry.

"Hi," Snowy said, feeling so pallid that she feared if Tom looked over and saw them together, she'd be invisible. She'd had this feeling before with Rita; they were the same height, so they were partners on the squad. Puddles' partner was Linda Littlefield.

Rita glanced from Snowy to Tom and back, her eyes onyx. Because Tom knew she'd always be available for him, he was offhand about arranging dates. This annoyed Rita, but she accepted it, and all through school today she'd been waiting for his last-minute invitation, all afternoon she waited, and by supper-time she was angry enough to consider going to the movies with the girls, to see if he was there and with whom. So when Wally Smith, who had heard Tom mention a date with Snowy and realized he might at last have a chance at Rita, phoned to ask her out, she'd said yes even though he was the sort of boy girls accepted only when nobody better presented himself. Wally always got his girlfriends on the rebound.

Rita said, "Out with Tom, are you?"

"Um, yes," Snowy said, rigid with embarrassment.

"He's a hunk, isn't he?"

"Um, yes."

"When did he ask you out?"

"Yesterday."

Rita repeated, "Yesterday." She didn't have C lunch, but Joanne Carter, one of the Varsity cheerleaders and a pal of Tom's since grammar school, did have it, and Rita suddenly remembered yesterday Joanne had said, laughing, "What a brawl in lunch, something scared that little Snowy, and she went ape, she practically screamed the cafeteria down, Tom had to shut her up." Rita had just been thrilled by Tom's authority as a proctor; she hadn't dreamed Snowy could be a threat.

Snowy tried to change the subject. "When we start teaching cheering next week, it's going to be funny seeing the other girls hobbling around lame while we—"

Wally Smith, holding tickets, walked over and said, "Hi, Snowy." He was a senior, but he knew her because they'd sat near each other in study halls. Alphabetically, she always came after hordes of Smiths. He said, "All set, Rita?" and Rita said bitterly to Snowy, "Have fun," and went with him into the theater.

Snowy was reading the *Twenty Thousand Leagues* poster and trying to recover, trying again to figure out why Rita wasn't with Tom, when Tom tapped her on the shoulder and said, "Is somebody going to give you an exam on that poster?" and she jerked around, then laughed.

They walked up the slope. He handed the tickets to the usher-ette at the door, pocketed the stubs, and they were in the carpeted anteroom where the food was sold. The smell of pop-corn prevailed, hot and thirsty.

Tom said, "Popcorn?"

"Okay."

They walked over to the long glass candy counter, a dentist's delight of Necco wafers, Oh Henrys, caramels, gum, Milky Ways, M&M's, and Good-and-Plentys, and, at the end, a glass case of popcorn. Tom bought two boxes. "There," he said, giv-ing her one. "Will that be enough? Should I get a wheelbarrow full?"

She giggled.

The theater was dark; the cartoon had started. When Snowy was younger, the theater had seemed to her a palace, its chande-liers and gold scrollwork and dark-red curtain and plush seats so rich and wonderful that she couldn't believe she was allowed in for just twelve cents, and although now it cost seventy-five cents and she saw its shabbiness, she still retained some of that feeling and tonight the awe was mixed with the trembly excite-ment of being here with Tom.

They followed the usherette's flashlight down the right-hand aisle. Snowy had read in a magazine's Etiquette Tips for Teens that the boy was supposed to go first if there was no usher, and the girl should go first if there was, and she always tried to obey this, which sometimes resulted in stumbling and confusion. Tom hadn't read the tip, but his courtesy was instinctive. He followed Snowy as she followed the usherette, a senior girl, and he watched Snowy's ponytail sway.

He said, "Here's fine, Claire." They began to slide past knees, and the usherette smiled at him and said, "Now you behave yourself, Tom, so I don't have to kick you out," and Snowy thought indignantly that girls older than Tom ought not flirt with him, the other girls were quite enough competition. He said hi to some kids, and then they sat down at the far end of the row, a very fashionable spot even though they had to watch the movie from an angle.

The fashionable spots changed. In grammar school, you sat in the balcony, when the balcony was open. In junior high, you sat in the middle row of the middle seats. In high school, when you were with the girls, you sat way down in the right-hand side, the boys behind you. Once Snowy and Puddles had sat alone in the left-hand side, just to see what it was like, and they'd discovered it was extremely dangerous because the wilder bunch of older boys sat there, and Puddles said she and Snowy were lucky to escape with their virginity intact. On dates, you sat farther back on the right-hand side—but not the back row, which was reserved for couples who had been going steady so long they didn't mind the jokes about back rows.

Both Snowy and Tom saw Rita, in the row in front of them, turn and pinpoint them. This was the first time Tom had noticed Rita tonight, and he was amused to see her here with Wally, yet he knew how she must have waited, and he felt guilty as well as irritated at himself for the guilt. He realized that because of laziness, he had taken her out too often, too steadily, these past few months; the date with Snowy was a way of proclaiming to Rita that he was still free. But Rita was built like a brick shit-house, and she allowed a mouthful of breast in the steamed-up car, and what else would she allow if he handed over his gold football? Rita almost had him trapped. If only, he thought, she didn't talk so much, chatter chatter chatter. Boobs and chatter. Frustrated, he munched popcorn.

The first movie was a Western with Zachary Scott. Tom and Snowy had each seen so many Westerns, from childhood Saturday matinees of Roy Rogers, Gene Autry, and Hopalong

Cassidy to the latest on television (*Range Rider* was one of
Snowy's favorite programs), that the violent stories were as
soothingly familiar as nursery rhymes, and they usually watched
them with cozy anticipation of the stagecoach chase, the
fistfights, the leap from the hotel roof into the saddle, the posse,
the box canyon, the ambush, the wild riding, the gunfight, the
sunset, and because they'd grown up listening to the radio, they
enjoyed the sounds as much as the scenes, the clip-clop of horses,
the bang of six-guns, the silence and slap of poker games, the
chink and glug of whiskey.

Tonight, however, they were too aware of each other to concentrate on the movie. Snowy was trying to do everything right,
sitting in the proper movie-watching style, on the end of her
spine with her knees up against the back of the seat in front of
her. She was eating her popcorn one piece at a time, her hand
moving mechanically as she stared unseeing at the screen. Tom
glanced sideways at her. Small-breasted. At least she didn't chatter.

But he felt that he wasn't being very friendly, not saying
anything at all, so he said, "Somebody a couple of rows down
just turned around to check up on us. Guess who."

The somebody turned again. It was Puddles, keeping tabs on
them and on Linda Littlefield and New Boy. Snowy said,
"That's Norm Noyes with her."

"From the back of his head, he doesn't look bad enough for
your revenge."

"I've relented. You know how that quote really goes? 'Revenge is—' " She stopped. Girls were still warned that brainy
women scared off men.

He said, " 'Revenge is sweet'?"

She didn't answer. She had finished her popcorn, and she put
the empty box on the floor.

He said, "It's something else?"

"Well, it's 'Revenge is sweeter than life, so think fools.' "

"I'll be damned," he said. "I never knew that."

She sat silent, so upset about her blunder that he sensed her misery and figured yes, he hadn't been friendly enough, and he took her hand.

Snowy saw the rest of the movie in a happy daze, all her sensations in that one hand enclosed in his. His palm was hard, his fingertips calloused.

Then, when the lights came on, she saw that Wally had his arm around Rita.

She looked at Tom and was puzzled by his half-smile. He said, "I guess I'll go have a smoke, will you be okay? Want anything? Candy? Coke?"

"No, thanks." If she had a Coke, she might have to go to the bathroom.

She watched him move past the kids standing and stretching, and at the end of the row he paused for Puddles, who was coming up the aisle, and he said something to her, and she giggled.

Then Snowy watched him walk up the aisle. She wondered if he was going to the men's room, as well as the lobby, and was astonished that the idea was not disgusting; it was, in fact, mysterious and sexy.

Puddles beckoned urgently to her from the end of the row. Snowy scrambled past the kids, and Puddles said, "Let's go to the ladies' room, my back teeth are floating."

Snowy looked up the aisle, but Tom had disappeared, and if she returned to her seat before him, he wouldn't know she'd gone. "Okay," she said, glad that the worry of bathroom would be taken care of.

The ladies' room had once attempted to be as impressive as the theater, but now its boudoir gaudiness of blue wallpaper and gold mirrors was raddled, and the toilets were apt to clog during the intermission rush. It was busy, and Snowy and Puddles had to wait, Puddles hopping up and down, until they could take turns at one. When Snowy came out, Puddles was combing her hair in front of a streaked mirror and saying to Linda Littlefield, "If I had any sense, I'd walk right out of here and go home; why do I want to stick around for another stupid movie and be pawed by Norm Noyes? He thinks I think he's just got his arm around me, but I can feel that damn hand creeping down down down."

Snowy smiled. She'd observed that Puddles was wearing her tightest sweater, the brown pullover they kidded her about.

Linda Littlefield was demurely pretty, she had dimples, her eyes were gray, and she wore her pale-blond hair in a short bouncy ponytail, but her voice was cool, like crushed ice. She knew from gossip that Puddles was interested in New Boy, and she said, "Well, why don't you leave?"

Puddles, comb raised, looked at Linda in the mirror. "I haven't finished my popcorn."

Tension pulsed between them.

Then Linda laughed and left.

"Bitch," Puddles said.

Snowy washed her hands and said, "Let's go," and as they walked out, along the wide aisle behind the rows of seats, she wished Puddles would tell her what Tom had said, so she wouldn't feel that she was prying, but Puddles was brooding about Linda, and Snowy had to ask, "What did Tom say to you just now?"

"He wanted to know if I enjoyed my supper. He gave me a lift after school and I got out at Woolworth's for some malt—"

Snowy said hurriedly, forestalling the balls, "Oh. Did you see Rita here? What do you think?"

"With Wally Smith? It was either that or sit home."

"He asked her out at the last minute? She didn't already have a date with him so Tom asked me?"

"Honestly, Snowy, would you go out with Wally if there was any chance at all Tom would ask you? And for Rita, it wasn't a chance, it was a certainty, ha-ha. I'll brownnose her, though; I'll find out. Look, there's Linda smiling sweetly at New Boy. Isn't he a doll! Oops, the lights."

Snowy identified her row by Rita in the row in front, and slid along to her seat identified by her jacket beside Tom's and tried to look as if she'd never left it. The previews began.

Tom, coming along the row, couldn't resist giving Rita's wing curls a tug. Rita ignored him, and luckily Snowy was so busy pretending to be engrossed in the *Twenty Thousand Leagues* preview that she didn't see. He sat down beside her and held out a paper cup of Coke. "Want some?"

Their hands touched as Snowy took a sip. She said, "Thank you."

He said, "I guess we're off to Paris now."

They were, with Tony Curtis and Gloria DeHaven and Gene Nelson and Corinne Calvert. But again neither could concentrate. They sat together deep in the seats, their knees up side by side, chino and wool, and Snowy was hoping he'd hold her hand again, and Tom was wondering why he was bothering with a first date and the tedium of preliminary moves. Yet her strangeness, her long hair, her different perfume itched at him. Halfway through the movie, he sat up straighter and put his arm along the back of her seat.

Snowy almost stopped breathing.

If she sat up, his arm would be around her shoulders. But she didn't dare. She remained low, knees up, aware of nothing but his white oxford-cloth-covered arm.

And then, just before the movie ended, she felt his hand on her hair. He was stroking her ponytail.

It was the most romantic moment of her life.


The movie ended. Sudden chandelier lights jolted the kids back from make-believe. Downtown, quiet after the stores closed at nine, awakened as they came out of the theater in warm cocky packs who jostled and called to each other. Cars roared, and exhaust bloomed white along the gray street.

In Tom's car, the radio played: "Danger! Heartbreak ahead,/ Look out, little fool, you're not wise,/Not wise to love so completely,/Or to fall for that look in his eyes."

When Snowy and Tom walked into Hooper's, into the noise of the kids and the smell of milk and grease, Tom said, "This I've got to see," and stopped in front of the plaque on the wall. The six boys' names were now followed by HENRIETTA SNOW.

Snowy looked at it, shocked. She hadn't earned it, but there it was, and every time she came here she would see it.

"Henrietta?" Tom said. "My God, I thought your first name was—well, I don't know what I thought. Henrietta?"

Embarrassed, she said, "All right, don't rub it in, I get enough remarks from Bev and Puddles."

"Rub it in? Me?" They sat down at the counter. "Just to show you, I'll confess. My middle name is Brandon."

She smiled and tried it out. Thomas Brandon Forbes. (Mrs. Thomas Brandon Forbes.) She said, "I've been Snowy forever, I don't know when it started, back in grammar school sometime. It drives my folks crazy," she added, and then could have throttled herself for mentioning her parents when she was trying to be Athena.

"I'll bet." He looked around as Sam Page yelled at him, yelled back, then said to her, "There's something else I'd better confess."

She panicked.

He said, "Now that we're here, I don't really think I can face even part of that Awful-Awful."

She laughed with relief. "Me neither." But she wondered if she could say something about a raincheck, to circumvent the moment she was dreading, the moment when he'd either ask her out again or wouldn't.

The waitress set glasses of water in front of them, said, "Hi, Tom," and, pad and pencil poised, inspected Snowy.

Tom said, "I guess I'll have an English muffin and black coffee; what about you, Snowy?"

It sounded very grown-up to her. "The same, thank you." She had never drunk coffee before.

The jukebox sang about Davy Crockett: "Born on a mountaintop in Tennessee,/The greenest state in the land of the free,/Raised in the woods so he knew every tree,/Killed him a b'ar when he was only three!"

Puddles always sang that line as "Built him a bar when he was only three."

The twins and Jack and Butch were sitting at the bend of the horseshoe. Snowy noticed Darl gesturing discreetly toward the door, and emotional Charl looked apprehensive, and she turned and saw Rita and Wally coming in. She made a quick Bev face at the twins, the "oh, horrors!" face, and then Rita passing behind said shrilly, "Hi, Tom! Hi, Snowy!"

Tom winced and said, "Hi, there, Rita. Wally." Snowy, nerves ajangle, grabbed at her glass of water and nearly choked swallowing.

Rita led Wally around the bend to stools opposite Tom and Snowy, where she could watch them across the hot fudge vat.

Tom began talking to Bill LeHoullier beside him about his valves. Snowy tried to look as if she were listening intelligently, but she was glad when the waitress brought the coffees and English muffins and she had something to do with her hands. The taste of coffee startled her; she'd thought it would be more like Postum. She looked at the sugar bowl but decided she should drink it as Tom drank it.

Tom said, "Here comes your peculiar friend."

Puddles had hiked Norm right along, so she wouldn't miss anything. She nudged Snowy and said, "Rah!"

Tom said, "What did that mean?"

Snowy shrugged extravagantly.

When Puddles passed New Boy and Linda, who were drinking frappes, Puddles all at once pretended fascination with Norm and clung to his arm, laughing vivaciously. She spotted two empty stools beside Rita, sat down beside her, and smirked across the hot fudge at Snowy.

Tom said, "You know, I have the damnedest feeling she's up to something."

Snowy didn't tell him that Puddles was being a Secret Agent. Puddles and Rita had never particularly got along together on the cheering squad—one time Puddles informed Rita they'd all be better off if Rita pulled her megaphone down over her head so the rest of them could finally be heard through her screeching —but there was Puddles brightly talking with her, while Rita looked suspicious, and Norm, ignored again, read the list of ice-cream flavors on the wall.

Snowy would interrogate Puddles tomorrow.

"Well," Tom said, finishing his coffee. "How's that appetite of yours?"

She wiped buttery fingers on a paper napkin and then took a fresh napkin from the metal holder and slipped it into her jacket pocket, for her souvenir drawer. "Very happy, thank you."

Tom paid the waitress, and as they stood up and walked to the door, the other kids watched, the older boys wondering who that girl was, out with Tom Forbes, everyone speculating. Snowy could practically feel Rita's eyes boring into her back. She walked chin up, proud.

Puddles, looking innocent, said to Rita, "They make a cute couple, don't they?"

Rita did not reply.

In the car, Tom lit a cigarette. "Sorry," he said. "Would you like one?"

She was flattered, but she didn't know how to smoke. "No, thanks."

"Gum?" He took a pack out of his jacket pocket.

"Thank you." It was only spearmint; she liked bubble gum best. She unpeeled a stick and put the wrapper in her pocket.

Tom started the car and they drove up North Main Street. Just one week ago, Snowy thought, she was walking home with Puddles from Hooper's, being passed by cars of kids going parking, and now she was in a car, with Tom.

He said, "You spend the night at Bev's a lot?"

"Well, more often she stays overnight at my house, it's handier, but we swap. Or sometimes one of us stays at Puddles' house, or all of us stay at one of our houses."

Tom grinned. "In other words, you sleep around." He glanced over at her and said, "Excuse me, forgot my manners."

She didn't understand, but she laughed bravely.

He said, "You used to date—Ed Cormier, wasn't it?"

"Yes."

"We never double-dated, did we?"

"No." Bev had suggested this, but Snowy had declined because she didn't want to have to see them necking in the front seat.

Tom said, "You're one of those girls that jump up and down during JV games?"

His irreverent tone surprised her, and she realized that with him she should speak carelessly of cheerleading, as if it were natural and not a miracle that she was a JV. "Skyrocket, skyrocket," she said, "sis boom bah, Gunthwaite Jay Vees, rah rah rah."

"Hey, you're the one they all rush in and lift up."

"Yes. I'm the skyrocket. I have to be, I weigh the least, but it scares the daylights out of me, and Puddles always threatens to tickle."

"Puddles is a JV too?"

"Yes, Puddles, too."

And they both thought of that other JV, Rita. Tom pictured

boobs nearly bursting her green corduroy vest, her green underpants flashing in a cartwheel, and he again mused on how her
ability to do a split certainly ought to be some experience in a
parked car if he could just get her to that point. But again the
question loomed: if that moment actually happened, would he
dare? He was as nervous about knocking up a girl as the girls
were about getting knocked up. It was a hell of a situation. Here
he was, he thought, almost seventeen years old and he'd only
had one piece of ass in his whole life, last summer, an unsatisfac-
tory furtive poke after fumbling on a Trojan, the girl a cheap
older broad who'd quit school, the type you took out for just
one reason, and he had been so disgusted and afraid and embarrassed he'd never taken her out another time; indeed, the very
next evening, when he'd seen her sauntering past Varney's he
had clambered hastily down into the grease pit and hidden.

He glanced at Snowy. She sat far on her own side of the car,
jacket collar turned up, looking straight ahead. A stranger.

They passed the outskirts of town, a colony of tar-paper
shacks known as Frog Hollow, and then there were woods.
Snowy suddenly remembered a game she used to play on Sunday drives with her grandparents. She had pretended that she
held a tiny fairy in her hands, a fairy no one knew about but
herself, and she was looking for a place where it could live. She
had looked out the car window into the woods, hunting for a
mossy rock, a golden-brown brook. Then she'd pretend to let
the fairy out of her hands and watch it fly there. But as the drive
continued, she would see a better place, an apple tree, a stone
wall into which a chipmunk dived, and she would pretend she
had the fairy back in her hands and would let it fly to that place.
But again as soon as she let the fairy go, she would see another
place, and again she would pretend the fairy back, over and over
until the end of the ride.

Tom said, "You have to be in at midnight?"

"Yes."

He looked at his watch and then at her, trying to judge. Eleven o'clock.

Snowy waited, taut.

Tom put out his cigarette and cleared his throat. He began clowning. "I don't suppose you're the sort of girl who goes parking."

"Never!" she said, and managed to laugh.

"Maybe," he said, "we could call it something else. How about 'nature study'?" and he turned off onto the dirt road known as the Cat Path. The white snowbanks gleamed in the headlights. The Cat Path was kept plowed because it crossed to another main road, but hardly anyone used it as such, so the town was plowing for parkers. Tom honked, and they passed Victor Andrews' car parked on the side of the road, and two heads appeared. Victor and Ellen Hatch. Tom laughed, drove on around a couple more corners, and stopped the car. He switched off the headlights but left the car running, for heat.

Snowy said, coy and scared, "I can't see any nature now."

"Okay," he said, "let's go for a nature walk," and he seized her hand and started opening the door, and Snowy laughed and struggled, and then he shut the door, and they were close in the dark.

Metal was digging into his hand. He said, "What have I here? Some charming charms?" and began to examine them, holding her wrist. "A State of New Hampshire, very patriotic. A—what the hell's this?"

"A Girl Scout trefoil."

"I've got a Girl Scout in my clutches?"

"A senior Girl Scout, I'll have you know."

"And what's this?"

"My birthstone. A bloodstone."

"That sounds pretty gory."

"Yes, why couldn't I have an emerald or a sapphire or something?"

"It sure is different."

"Yes."

He said, "You are, too," and as he took off his glasses and hung them practicedly over the sun visor and she realized that he was going to kiss her, she remembered she still had her gum in her mouth and she didn't know what to do with it. So she swallowed it.

On the radio, Al Hibbler sang: "Oh my love, my darling,/ I've hungered for your touch/A long lonely time."

The car smelled of heated White Lilac and Old Spice.

Tom said, "It's five past twelve. Are you going to change into a pumpkin?"

Both he and Snowy were breathing fast. They had kissed and kissed and kissed, and even French-kissed, which shocked Snowy because you didn't French-kiss on the first date and which gave Tom an aching hard-on. They looked at each other, self-conscious now in the transition from kisses to composure.

He said, "I wish there was no such thing as a clock."

But he reached for his glasses and put the car in gear. The Cat Path was narrow, and while he was busy backing and filling, Snowy moved to her side of the car and quickly smoothed up her nape hair wisps, hoping he wouldn't notice this personal detail. As they drove back, they passed three parked cars and their headlights flushed Gene Chabot and Nutty, Sonny Poor and Brenda Dutile, and Victor and Ellen again. Tom wondered where Wally had taken Rita parking and what he'd got.

They drove along the main road. Fields of snow were swirled frozen against snow fences.

Tom said, "Bev sure does live out in the boondocks."

"Yes."

"Her stepfather still pick her up at school or your house?"

"And he drops her off at my house in the mornings. When they moved, her mother promised it wouldn't interfere with clubs and friends and everything."

"You and Bev have been friends a long time?"

"Oh, yes. We're best friends."

So, he guessed, she must know all about him and Bev and the Getting Fresh. Had anyone ever Got Fresh with her? She'd certainly been taught to kiss; Ed Cormier? He glanced over. She was far away again, her nose and chin looking haughty. Christ, was she worth any bother? The taste of red lipstick lingered like the scent of her perfume.

The radio sang about Davy Crockett.

What Snowy was bracing herself for was the end of the evening, the end of the date, the end.

They turned up the dirt road to Bev's, and headlights came at them. Roger, in his 1941 Ford that was known as the Heap, honked, and Tom honked back as they squeezed past.

Then the dark woods enclosed them. The little road twisted uphill and down. It had been sanded, but where it crossed a brook there was an icy white sheet, and the car skidded slightly.

"Jesus," said Tom, who'd never driven this road in wintertime. "I should've put on the chains."

At the top of the next hill, the woods opened into a field, and they saw lighted windows. Tom turned up the driveway and drove between snowbanks around to the back.

Bev's house was an old low white Cape, plain and shutterless, with a gray barn behind it. People wondered how Bev's mother could stand being alone way out here all day, but the remoteness of the place appealed to Julia Miller, a solitary woman. Here she had the company she preferred, birds at the bird feeders, an occasional glimpse of fox and deer. She'd escaped the coffee-and-gossip days of residential Gunthwaite. In the mornings she wove the place mats and pocketbooks the League of Arts and Crafts sold; in the afternoons she worked in the gardens, roamed the

woods, read. She had at last returned to the life she wanted back
when, after two unhappy years of working as a secretary in Boston, she'd married Richard Colby, a hometown boy from Bed-
ford, Massachusetts, and they'd moved to Gunthwaite and
bought that Depression dream, a chicken farm. Then the war
had come, and he had been killed for an island. She'd sold the
farm and moved into town.

Tom switched off the headlights. The kitchen windows
seemed bright squares painted on the black night.

Snowy had read that a girl should not thank a boy for a date,
that the boy should thank the girl, but this was one rule she
didn't follow because she felt it was rude not to acknowledge
the money he'd spent on her. She forced herself to say the end-
of-a-date words. "Thank you very much for the evening."

Her formality was a barrier. Tom had been thinking of some
more necking; instead, he reached into the back seat and found
the overnight case. "You're very welcome. And I thank you."
He got out.

She remembered to wait and let him open her door. They
walked along the shoveled path toward the back door and
good-bye.

They were at the granite doorstep.

She looked up at him. The cold wind fanned her ponytail, and
he touched it and asked, "Do you ever wear your hair down?"

She'd learned, from Ed's perfume question, that she must fight
embarrassment and answer.

"Sometimes," she said, and then they both realized this meant
he had never noticed.

"Well," he said. He gave her the overnight case. He tilted her
chin, kissed her, and said, "Be seeing you," and turned.

She wrenched open the storm door and back door and got inside the house before the tears exploded. She dropped the overnight case and fell into a kitchen chair and sobbed.

The overhead light was harsh to the kitchen, displaying the

worn brown linoleum, the old yellow wallpaper of faded tea-pots, the yellow wooden cupboards with gray fingerprint smears around their handles.

Bev, upstairs getting ready for bed, heard the car leave and came down, buttoning her blue polka dot flannel pajamas as she walked through the night-shadowed dining room which was her mother's workroom. Silver threads glinted on the great loom, and there was a stuffy smell of fabric.

She heard, then saw in the kitchen Snowy hunched crying at the wooden table.

"Snowy, what's the matter?"

Snowy choked.

Bev grabbed a box of Kleenex off the counter, put it on the table, and sat down. "What happened?"

"He didn't ask me out again!"

Bev said, "Men."

Snowy yanked at a Kleenex. "And we had such a good time and everything and everything, I kept hoping and hoping he would—"

"Men!" Bev said. "You know what Roger did? We were watching TV after Mother and Fred went to bed, we were lying on the sofa and I thought it was all so sweet and cuddly, and then Roger let out this terrible snore. He was sound asleep, snoring like a walrus with asthma."

Snowy hiccuped.

Bev scratched at a dab of dried marmalade on the plastic place mat. "Maybe Tom has to work tomorrow night, or maybe he's tied up."

"With Rita?" Snowy blew her nose. "Oh, God, Bev, Rita was at the movies with Wally Smith—"

"Ughy-pew, she must've been desperate."

"That's what Puddles thought. Do you think she didn't have a date because Tom asked me?"

"Well, she certainly wouldn't've accepted Wally until the last minute. How about a sandwich?"

"I don't know—"

Bev stood up and opened the refrigerator and said, "Marshmallow fluff and raspberry jam?"

This was their favorite sandwich in the wintertime; tuna fish was in the summertime.

Snowy took off her jacket. "Well. Okay."

Bev dealt out four slices of Sunbeam bread onto the counter. "It's not the end of the world."

"Isn't it?" Snowy said. She spread marshmallow fluff so violently the bread tore.

"Roger brought a bottle of Moxie, there's some left."

"Okay."

Bev poured. "Were the movies any good?"

"I didn't pay much attention. He held my hand during the first. He put his arm around me in the second."

"And you must've gone parking."

"Yes, on that road I went once with you and Roger and Frankie."

"The Cat Path."

They sat down at the table and bit into their sandwiches.

Snowy said, "He wouldn't've taken me parking if he thought I was horrible, would he?"

"No. Did he get all hot and bothered?"

"Kind of. He didn't Get Fresh or anything. Do you really think maybe he has to work tomorrow night?"

Bev had forgotten that Tom used to take her out to Hooper's and parking after he got through work at Varney's. "It seems likely."

"Charl said something about a party at Sam Page's tomorrow night. A birthday party?"

Bev laughed. "A beer party, Snowy. The junior gang."

"Oh."

"Okay, so maybe he has a date for it with Rita, but maybe it'll be his last. They *aren't* going steady. When I told Roger you had a date with Tom tonight, he said Tom likes to be footloose and fancy-free, that's why he won't go steady with Rita."

Snowy licked jam oozing out of the edge of the sandwich. "He went steady with you."

"I probably made him a confirmed bachelor."

"Did Roger say anything else?"

"Well, he said that going steady or not, Tom no doubt was getting all he could."

"Getting Fresh?"

"Um, yes. Boys will be boys."

A silence. Bev remembered how Tom used to unhook her bra one-handed. Tom had been the first and only boy except for Roger she'd allowed to Get Fresh. Snowy remembered Ed's large soft hand on her blouse, the hand she kept pushing away, and she thought of Tom's hands.

Mice scurried in the walls.

Snowy said, "If Tom doesn't ask me out by Friday, I guess it's over, isn't it? There's no hope left."

Bev didn't want to agree pointblank. "Let me get Roger to arrange a double date with one of the senior guys—"

Snowy was sniffling again. "He asked me if I ever wore my hair down, does that mean he'd like to see it that way?"

"Sure. So there *is* some hope. Wear it down Monday."

"Wouldn't Monday be too obvious? Maybe later in the week? But no matter when, if I wear it down, he'll know I had to set it and everything."

"Snowy, he doesn't believe you were born with a ponytail. He knows you have to fix it. Wear it down, wear a chignon, keep him confused."

Snowy blew her nose. "I would give my right arm for naturally curly hair."

"I'd give my hair for Rita's figure. Roger practically turned pea-green thinking of what Tom was getting."

Snowy said sourly, "I've seen her changing into her uniform, honest to God her bubbies are so big it's a wonder she can stand up straight."

Bev crossed her eyes.

And at last Snowy could giggle. "Puddles was brownnosing her at Hooper's to find out why she was out with Wally, it was quite a sight."

"Was New Boy at the movies? With Linda?"

"Yes, and I thought Puddles and Linda were going to come to blows in the ladies' room."

Bev stood up and carried the glasses and plates to the sink. "What shall we do tomorrow besides Latin? Did you bring your book?"

"It's in my bag. Well, we could listen to the Radio Club show. And you wanted me to give you your cues again."

"Oh, God, yes."

The first night of *Our Town* was this coming Thursday. Bev played Emily, and Snowy and Puddles were on the publicity committee and would sell tickets at the door.

Snowy said, "Are you scared yet?"

"I'm never what you could call really scared."

But Snowy knew that although Bev was calm during rehearsals, as the first night drew nearer and nearer she went into a coma.

Bev pulled the string to turn off the overhead light, Snowy picked up her overnight case, and they went through the other doorway to the living room. Snowy liked the easeful shambles of the room, yet because of her background, she always had an urge to tidy it. The cushions in the deep chairs were squashed, the Boston *Globe* spilled across a footstool, the tables heaped with magazines and books were dusty, and there were cracker crumbs lost in the lumpy sofa. The room smelled of cigarette smoke and of woodsmoke from the fireplace where ash and wood chips littered the hearth.

In daytime, the lake could be seen out of the front window, a pool of blue far below against the mountains.

Snowy said, "Let's walk up the brook tomorrow and have a picnic. Maybe at the bog?"

Bev laughed. She could never understand why her mother and Snowy were so fond of the bog. But she said, "Okay, let's," and turned down the thermostat and switched off the lamp.

Snowy followed her out to the little front hallway and up the stairs that were scooped thin by generations of footsteps.

There were only two bedrooms, under the eaves. Bev went into the bathroom between them to brush her teeth and apply Noxzema, and Snowy went into Bev's bedroom to unpack. Bev had stripped her room of childhood; all that remained were the *Anne of Green Gables* books which she couldn't bear to put away because she and Anne had so long together suffered carroty hair before it darkened to auburn. Over the water stains on the floral wallpaper she had tacked glossy photographs from her plays and *Seventeen* magazine cover girls. White net curtains hung limp at the small-paned windows. Her schoolbooks were piled on the mahogany veneer desk that was the same as Snowy's, bought by their parents the same junior high Christmas, and on her bureau Roger's yearbook picture watched Snowy undress and put on pajamas the same as Bev's except that Snowy's had pink polka dots. They always shopped for clothes together, and although they were careful not to buy school-clothes alike—"The twins," Bev said, "are enough of a side-show"—their nightwear and underwear were apt to match. And so did their pocketbooks. Snowy and Bev still weren't too sure about those pocketbooks, but they and Puddles had got silly in the store and bought three of them, pocketbooks like plaid ice-cream buckets, with round plastic handles.

Bev came in. The slanting walls made her look even taller. "It's all yours."

In the bathroom, Snowy took down her ponytail and brushed her hair and then brushed her teeth. Her eyes were swollen from crying, and her cheeks were red from beard burn. She patted on Noxzema.

Bev's single divan-bed had been opened into a double. Snowy got in beside her. Usually they talked for ages, but tonight they lay flat on their backs and looked up at the dark.

Bev thought of her boring evening, with Roger falling asleep and not Getting Fresh or any thing, and she thought of their parking rituals, which lately led up to what she'd learned from him was called jerking him off, and she began to imagine what it would be like with someone else, Jack O'Brien or—horrified at her disloyalty to Snowy, she imagined what it would be like with Tom.

And Snowy, staring up, saw the gray days ahead. She had taught herself to get through them by thinking of the pleasures, the scheduled and unexpected glimpses of Tom, the lunchtime gossip, her favorite clothes, cheerleading, getting an algebra example or a Latin translation right, writing an article for the school newspaper, but now she saw the days as a tunnel caving in on her. "Please, God," she prayed silently, "please let him ask me out again."

They lay side by side, turmoil churning, both smelling of Noxzema.

Then Bev began to recite in her head her *Our Town* lines and fell asleep, but Snowy lay awake so long, chasing questions around and around, that at last she got out of bed, went carefully down the dark stairs, turned on a lamp in the living room, and took a pack of cards from the drawer of an end table. She sat on the carpet and played solitaire.

The room grew chilly.

Stairs creaked. Bev's mother came in, tying the belt of her old blue flannel bathrobe.

"Oh," Snowy said, starting to get up, "I'm sorry, did I wake you?"

"No. Sit still. But I saw the light on the snow, and I wondered if anything was wrong." She went to the front window and looked out, as she did every morning to inspect the lake, but she saw only her own reflection and the room behind her. Julia Miller was tall; this was all that Bev had inherited from her. Julia's brown hair had turned prematurely white, she wore it in a short straight Dutch bob, and her skin was sallow, her face sharp. Gaunt, she seemed nothing but collarbone and elbows and height.

Snowy said, "I just couldn't sleep."

"Did you have a good time with Tom? I always liked Tom, he's a charmer."

Snowy put a black seven on a red eight. "Yes. He's wonderful."

"Has he decided yet what he's going to do?"

"Do?"

"When he graduates. The last time I saw him, he was going to change to the shop course and he was thinking of cabinetmaking."

"I don't know, we didn't talk of it."

Julia's nicotine-yellow fingers searched the clutter of books and pencils and ashtrays on the lamp table and found a pack of Camels. She lit one.

Snowy said, "What's cabinetmaking?"

"Building fine things."

"Oh."

Julia asked, "Is Bev asleep?"

"Yes, she went to sleep."

"And why aren't you?"

"I don't know."

"Did he ask you out again?"

"No."

Julia looked at her sitting cross-legged on the worn carpet, in her pink polka dot pajamas, her face scaly with Noxzema, her eyes puffy, and pitied her. "What is it you're playing? Canfield?"

She took another pack of cards from the end table.

So they sat together on the floor, the woman and the girl, and played double Canfield.

There might never have been the intimacy in the car.

On Monday, Tom's hi's at his traffic post were as offhand as ever, and during lunch he stayed up on the platform, seeming as unaware of Snowy as before.

And Puddles' secret-agent work had elicited from Rita only the information that Rita was thinking of going out for majorettes instead of sticking around on JV's if she didn't make Varsity. This alternative had never occurred to Snowy and Puddles because at Gunthwaite High School the majorettes were girls outside the gangs, unknown girls or girls with reputations, and they were startled that Rita could consider it. Puddles said, "I'd rather quit JV's and be nothing."

But during Monday gossip, they learned that Rita had gone to Sam Page's party with Wally and that Tom had been there alone.

He'd stopped by the party after he got out of work at Varney's and had a few beers and watched Rita pointedly ignore him to concentrate on Wally. When Jack O'Brien passed out, Tom took him and his date home, leaving Jack off first, and asking the date at her door, "Which one are you?" "I'm Charl." "Well, Charl," he said, "since Jack wasn't able—" and because he'd never kissed a twin before, he kissed her good-night. Charl was so surprised she almost fainted.

Charl told Darl, and by lunchtime on Monday the whole Gang knew, including Snowy.

After school, when the JV's and Varsity were changing into their gym suits to teach cheering, Rita said to Snowy, "Have fun Friday night?"

Snowy said, "It was okay."

Rita said, "Got another date?"

Snowy stalled, tying her sneakers laces, and Puddles rescued her by saying, "That's for Snowy to know and you to find out."

Rita tried. She waylaid Tom before school the next day and began talking about how great *Twenty Thousand Leagues* was supposed to be, and Tom agreed but didn't ask her to it. Snowy and Bev and Puddles, on their way to the balcony to join the Gang, saw them in the corridor, Tom leaning against a locker, grinning down at vivid Rita.

So Tom strolled through the days, postponing a decision, and Snowy studied *The Merchant of Venice* and World War I and tacked up *Our Town* posters and taught cheering and helped Priscilla finish the lovelorn column and began studying for Friday's big Latin test on Caesar's Book I, and went to a Girl Scout meeting Wednesday night at Puddles' house, where they planned more rummage sales and food sales to earn the final amount the troop needed to go to Washington, D.C., during April vacation. At night she lay awake in bed, Laurie warm beside her.

She wore her hair down Thursday, hoping Thursday would be lucky, like last week, and maybe even extra-lucky because it was St. Patrick's Day. But when she and Bev were walking back from the ice-cream counter past the platform, Tom didn't speak to her; instead, he called to Bev, and Snowy put her chin up and walked on. When Bev returned to the table, Snowy asked, "What did he say?"

Bev was staring at her ice-cream sandwich as if she'd never seen one before. *Our Town* lines were pounding in her head, and she scarcely remembered talking to Tom at all. "Oh, nothing, I guess."

That evening lights glowed in the high school, and Snowy and Puddles waited at the right-hand entrance of the auditorium to sell tickets to the people who hadn't already bought them from Dramatics Club kids or in downtown stores. Puddles looked at the bare half-lighted stage disapprovingly.

"Aren't they even going to close the curtain? I mean, so they can open it when the play starts?"

"No," Snowy said. "There's not supposed to be any curtain."

"Well, I must say I don't like it. How come no scenery? A play's not a play without scenery."

Snowy had puzzled over all this when reading the play and giving Bev her cues and catching glimpses of rehearsals, and it disturbed her.

She said, "Bev said it's modern."

"Modern? I thought she said she has to wear high-button shoes or something."

"At least she does get to wear costumes."

Puddles said, "It's a wonder the actors aren't supposed to be stark naked."

What Snowy and Puddles were wearing was lucky-green, although during the day they had worn Thursday-pink. The dramatics teacher had told the ticket sellers and ushers to dress up tonight, and Snowy and Puddles kept glancing behind to make sure the seams of their nylons were straight. Puddles wore her green wool churchgoing dress and black flats. Snowy wore her black wool suit with a lime-green sweater, black flats, and her hair still down in loose curls. The girls looked dolled up but not, as they believed, grown up.

The auditorium began to fill with parents, teachers, and kids.

Snowy and Puddles were hoping for Tom and New Boy, yet they knew that the boys who mattered didn't usually come to a play unless they were dating a girl in it. Roger was here, sitting with Julia and Fred. The audience murmured, programs rustled.

Then Larry Clark, who played the Stage Manager, wandered onstage carrying a table and chair. He went back and returned with more chairs.

An usher said, "Well, I guess everyone's here who's coming," and started to shut the double doors.

Puddles clutched the money box. "Let's go upstairs, they'll leave the hall lights on." They hurried up to their locker and got out Snowy's Latin book she'd brought for Puddles, and they leaned in one of the windows overlooking the auditorium.

"God," Puddles said. "If Mrs. Moulton said there's going to be plenty of construction work, we've got to know the whole damn syntax."

"Yes," Snowy said. She was even more keyed up about the test than Puddles was. Puddles would be happy with a B. Not Snowy.

Puddles said, "Has Bev done any studying?"

"Some. I doubt if much sunk in."

"Mrs. Moulton *would* have to schedule the test for tomorrow of all days. That's life."

Down below, the Stage Manager began to speak. This bothered Snowy, too, the way he chatted with the audience. She frowned.

Puddles said, "Funny to think it's supposed to be New Hampshire. He talks awful hicky."

"It was a long time ago."

Neither Snowy nor Puddles realized that they themselves had accents, dropping and inserting *r*'s, so "modern" was "morden."

Puddles sighed and took out the rules section. Snowy waited.

"Here she comes."

Bev ran onstage carrying a pile of strapped schoolbooks and sat down at a table with the freshman boy who was playing her young brother. Snowy's hands began to sweat.

Bev spoke her first line. "I'm both, Mama; you know I am."

Her voice carried clear and self-confident up to their window.

"Whew," Snowy said. "She's going to be okay."

"She always is," Puddles said. "When do she and Dudley kiss?"

Dudley was playing George Gibbs.

"Near the end of the second act."

"That I've got to see. Miss Norton must be a terrible prude not to let them kiss during rehearsals."

"Bev said she allowed a quick peck at the dress rehearsal."

"Big thrill."

"Well," Snowy said, "Dudley claims he's going to make up for it tonight. Did you hear him at lunch telling Bev he was going to ravish her? I don't think Bev heard a word."

"Imagine getting kissed right onstage."

"I'd die," said Snowy.

But Bev had just been worried she'd start laughing.

During the first act, Puddles tried to watch the play and study Latin at the same time, and during the intermission they gave each other vocab words. When the second act began, however, Puddles closed the book, and they both watched the morning of the wedding, the flashback to the courtship, and the beginning of the wedding.

"Dudley is cute," Puddles said. "Even if he is a brain."

"This is her entrance."

"Where is she?"

"Watch. She said the dress is a dream."

"She's coming through the audience!"

They gaped.

The bride walked tall and stately up the aisle, her long white dress trailing behind her and the white veil floating.

Roger stared. Julia, telling herself she was being absurd, felt tears sting.

Bev was oblivious of the audience. She took careful hold of her skirt, lifted it slightly, and walked up the steps without tripping.

Puddles breathed, "Sheesh."

And when the wedding ceremony was over and Dudley kissed Bev, it was a very solemn embrace.

Snowy said, "Do you suppose we'll ever really get married?"

"Everybody does," Puddles said.

During the second intermission they sold coffee in the cafeteria. Cookies were free. Then they ran back upstairs to the Dramatics Office, where Miss Norton was waiting for them, and they handed over the money box. The little office was topsy-turvy with old props and costumes and smelled of makeup. Miss Norton cried, "It's going well, isn't it!" and dashed off.

Puddles said, "Our job's done. Should we stay or go home?"

Snowy didn't like the last act, all the dead people sitting in the cemetery; Bev's line, "Oh, earth, you're too wonderful for anybody to realize you," seemed the saddest thing she'd ever heard. She said, "We ought to go home and study. Want a sugar cookie? I made them."

"No, thanks. Did you try any of the oatmeal ones I brought? They were left over from the Scout meeting. Hard as rocks."

"They were good last night."

"If we go home," Puddles said, "we'll worry, not study."

They walked over to the window and looked down.

Puddles said, "Anyway, we ought to stay here to give Bev moral support."

"Mmm," Snowy said, munching a cookie.

Behind her, Tom said, "Eating again, I see."

Snowy spun around.

Tom was wearing chinos, sneakers, and the brown leather

jacket he wore when he was working at Varney's, alpaca collar turned up.

Puddles said, "Jesus Christ, Tom, you almost made me drop my book and I'd've beaned someone down below."

"*My* book," Snowy said breathlessly. "It's very precious."

"It is?" he said, wondering why she was so astonished to see him. He'd mentioned to Bev he might stop by the play after work, and he'd assumed Bev would tell Snowy. "It looks older than Moses."

She grabbed the book from Puddles. "Older than Caesar," she said, "it's my Latin, see how the vocab and stuff come out at the back," and standing near him she smelled leather and an oily gas-station maleness.

"Well," he said, handing it back, "I think you ought to give it a decent burial come June." He leaned against the window-frame. "How's the play going?"

Puddles said, "Don't ask us, we've been studying."

Snowy, to be fair, said, "It's going great, and Bev is sailing right along."

Puddles said, "Big clinch with Dudley and everything. Roger looked like he was having a conniption fit."

"I'll bet," Tom said. "Where's Bev now?"

"Offstage," Snowy said. "Dead."

"Her part's over?"

"Oh, no. That's a cemetery down there."

"What a weird play."

Tom had arrived here telling himself he would just stop by to see Bev acting, that's all, he hadn't committed himself to anything more, but Snowy's long soft hair, as well as her tight skirt, forced him into a decision.

He said, "Have you got a ride home?"

"Nope," Puddles said.

"Are you through working? Do you have to stay till the end?"

Snowy looked at him. He'd *known* she'd be here?

"No," Puddles said, "we're just giving Bev moral support."

Tom said, "Would you two like a ride home?"

"Sure," Puddles said.

So Tom didn't see Bev after all. He walked between Snowy and Puddles past the library, the English and sociology rooms, the history room, to their locker. They pulled on their boots, and as Puddles hauled out their coats, he took them and helped first Puddles and then Snowy on with them. Puddles, like many girls, wore her hair tucked inside her turned-up coat collar, but although Snowy admired the style she hated the feel; she lifted her hair free of her collar, and her hand touched his.

They went downstairs to the first floor and out the side door between the buildings. It was very cold, and there had been snow flurries.

Tom said, "I'm parked over here." He opened the passenger door, Snowy hesitated, but Puddles hung back, so she slid in, then Puddles.

He started the car and drove out the driveway to State Avenue. Snowy held her breath, waiting to see which of them he would take home first.

He asked Puddles, "Where to?"

"Tweedle," sang the radio, "tweedle dee, I'm as happy as can be!"

"Gowen Street," Puddles said. "There ought to be a law against tests on Fridays. There ought to be a law against school on Fridays. There ought to be a law against school."

Snowy said, "Think of Mr. Foster, he's something to look forward to each day, and he's in rare form on Fridays."

Mr. Foster, their English teacher, dark and lean with hollow cheeks and sunken eyes, in appearance a poet, was really a clown. He had a little white picket fence around his desk to keep kids away, and a wicked curved knife, a long pointer he used like a bayonet, a collection of extra blackboard erasers to throw, and a gas mask to put on when a kid gave a stupid answer. He both entertained and terrified his students. Today he had smeared the end of his knife with red ink—or maybe, Puddles said, blood—and during their reading of *The Merchant of Venice* he had pranced around the room preparing to cut off a pound of flesh.

Puddles said, "I must say I don't find him such a riot since he threw that eraser at me. Just because of a prepositional phrase."

Snowy giggled.

Tom said, "Bought any malt balls lately?"

Puddles said, "No, but you know what I found at Woolworth's the other afternoon? Some great big enormous underpants—"

"Puddles!" Snowy said, scarlet.

"They must've been size two hundred," Puddles said. "I told Snowy, I said to her, aren't these beautiful, and they're just your size—"

Tom started laughing.

"And I grabbed them up," Puddles said, "and Snowy was backing away, and I chased her all around the store waving them at her until she got to the door and ran outside and I couldn't go after her or I'd be shoplifting. Whoa, there's my house. On the left."

It was a brown house, its high screened front porch sticking out as if it were pregnant. In the backyard was a pine tree Puddles had taught Snowy to climb to the dizzy top of, and a sundial, and, in summer, Mrs. Pond's rock garden and a dusky grape arbor.

Puddles said, "Maybe I'll get sick and not go to school tomorrow."

Snowy said, "You'll just have to take a makeup test. And we're supposed to sell tickets again tomorrow night; it'd be kind of suspicious if you showed up then in the peak of health."

Puddles opened the door and the cold came in. "You can talk, you and your A's."

"Puddles!"

"Okay, okay. See you tomorrow. Thanks for the ride, Tom."
He backed out of the driveway.

"Someday," Snowy said, moving over so he wouldn't think
she wanted to sit close, "somebody is going to murder Miss Jean
Pond."

He grinned.

They drove past the wintery houses to Chestnut Street, and
she couldn't believe she was actually in this car with him again.

He said, "What was that about A's?"

Flustered, trying not to scare him off, she said, "Oh, I just sit
around and memorize." She had a trick memory; she would
memorize her notes and the part of the textbook they were
going to be tested on, and during the test she could picture the
pages, reading through them, turning them in her mind until she
came to the one that contained the answer. She couldn't understand why the other kids didn't use what she thought was simply
a method, and she wondered why they flapped around so hap-
hazardly memorizing, but she sensed enough about her memory
to feel guilty, as if she were cheating. She said, "Then I forget
everything right after the test."

"That's better than forgetting before, like me." He turned
onto Emery Street and drove along the river. "You have to
work at the play tomorrow night? Bev didn't say anything
about that."

Realization came to her: Bev and the coma. Good God, what
if she and Puddles hadn't stayed at the play?

He parked in her driveway.

He said, "You're wearing your hair down."

"Yes," she said.

There was a pause.

He said, "Bev did say, though, that a certain someone is turn-
ing Sweet Sixteen on Saturday. I've got to work tomorrow
night, but unless you've already got a date, maybe I could pick

you up about the same time as tonight, and we could go get something to eat, and at midnight I'll give you your First Kiss."

"Eek!" she said in mock terror. This was a noise she and Bev had long copied from comicbooks.

"In the meantime," he said, hanging his glasses over the sun visor, "let's have a rehearsal," so they kissed until, deep in the leathery smell of his jacket, she opened her eyes and saw the glow on the snow from the light over the back door, the light awaiting her as Laurie was awaiting her indoors, and tomorrow was a schoolday with a big Latin test.

"I ought to go in," she said. "Where's my precious book?"

They found it under the seat. He asked, "When's your class?"

"Second period."

"Then I'll wish you luck now, in case I don't see you before."

"Thank you," she said, although she knew she would see him before the test, going past his traffic post to and from her first period study in the cafeteria.

He stroked her hair. "I like it this way. But I like the ponytail. Two different you's."

She couldn't tell him he was two people also, the horn-rimmed one and this one.

His arm was around her shoulders as he walked her along the path to the door. Laurie began barking.

She said, "Thanks for bringing us home."

He kissed her, at the back door where she'd been kissed good-night by Ed and other boyfriends.

Indoors, she hugged Laurie. "That was Tom," she said. "That was *Tom.*"


After the test, the familiar exhaustion came, an exhaustion so total that not even Mr. Foster cavorting through *The Merchant of Venice* the next period could revive her, and during her 4AB study she sat rag-doll limp, blank, unable to do any homework.

At his traffic post, Tom gave her ponytail a tug. "Hi."

"Hi," she said.

She and Bev bought ice-cream push-ups—Snowy was still wary of sundaes—and when they returned to their table Tom was sitting on the edge of the platform. He asked, "How'd the test go?" and Bev said shortly, "It's over," and walked on to their seats, where Puddles and the rest of the College Prep part of the Gang were groaning about it and squabbling over Snowy's algebra, but Snowy, suddenly reckless, collapsed beside him on the platform.

"It was a real doozy," she said. "Did you ever take Latin?"

"No, I took Spanish my freshman year, I figured that'd be easiest." He reached for her hand and looked at the sore red groove on her middle finger from gripping the pencil so intensely. "I don't know which is worse, ink or these battle scars."

She giggled.

He said, "Think you got an A?"

"I think I flunked."

"Sure you did."

He was holding her hand. In her other, her push-up began to melt. She saw him and herself sitting here together just the way she'd always wanted, a teen-age couple, Tom in his blue V-neck sweater and his chinos, Snowy in her angora sweater and black watch plaid pleated skirt. So when he released her hand, she stayed sitting with him the rest of the period, while upperclassmen walked over to kid around with him and, because she was there, flirt with her.

But afterward, in history class, she was flabbergasted at her daring.

And that night, after the second intermission, when she and Puddles were again leaning in an upstairs window of the auditorium and he didn't come and he didn't come, she began to panic. Had her presumptuousness frightened him off? She was again dolled up, in her royal blue velveteen jumper and her white nylon blouse with puffy elbow-length sleeves so sheer her arms could be seen through them, and, following Bev's advice, her hair in a chignon to keep him confused. She'd only worn her hair this way once, for the Freshman Dance, because it was so complicated. She kept patting at it, afraid it would fall down. Here she was, on the eve of her sixteenth birthday, and would she find herself stood up?

Beside her, Puddles was watching not the play but New Boy in the audience. They had been amazed when he appeared at the door alone and bought a ticket. Puddles had asked, "Where's Linda?" and New Boy, who'd decided Linda was frigid, said, "Oh, that's over with." He was here to see Bev in the play; like all the other boys, he had an eye on her even though the gold basketball made her forbidden. When he'd taken a seat, Puddles repeated rapturously, "That's over with, that's over with. Isn't he a doll! How can I get him to give me a ride home, throw myself under his car?" During the second intermission she plied him with Toll House cookies and chattered about tonight's terrible snowstorm, but all he talked about was Bev and Dudley's clinch. And now the last act was in progress. Puddles stared down at him. She mustn't lose tonight's golden opportunity. She must be very crafty.

There were footsteps coming up the stairs and along the corridor. Snowy prayed that it was Tom.

Tom said, "Hey, Puddles, you seen Snowy anywhere?"

Puddles said, "She's probably down in the cafeteria finishing off the intermission cookies."

"Ah, well," he said. "Could you introduce me to your friend here?"

Snowy, trembling, giggled.

He wasn't in his garage jacket, but in his green football jacket, and chinos, and white bucks.

Puddles said, "She's Henrietta Einstein."

He looked at Snowy. "What do you think about pickups?"

"I don't know," she said. "I've never been picked up."

"Then it's about time," he said. "Puddles, you need a ride?"

"No, thanks, I want to see the play through."

Snowy said, "Good luck."

"Good luck?" Tom asked as he and she walked away. Snowy laughed and shrugged.

At the locker, he helped her on with her coat. Her father had given her and Puddles and Bev a ride here, so she hadn't worn boots. She considered boots unromantic.

Tom said, "I'm sorry about being late. I thought I ought to go home and clean up, and there wasn't any way I could get hold of you. I should've thought of it earlier and let you know."

She couldn't believe her ears. She'd been afraid the fabulous Tom Forbes wouldn't show up at all, and now he was apologizing to her as if she had rights.

"That's okay," she said.

They went outdoors, and while he brushed off the windshield, she sat huddled in her coat in the car, watching the snow-darkness being swept away to streetlight paleness, and she was incredibly happy.

He started the car. "Aren't you kind of far away?"

She wasn't sure she understood. "Far away?"

"It'd be warmer closer."

She slid along the seat to him.

He said, "That's some hairdo, how's it done?" His hand tilted her head as he examined it.

She blushed. "There's a doughnut thing."

"Takes a lot of bobby pins."

"Yes."

He turned on the headlights and drove down the driveway, and the tire chains rattled. The snow blew into a white funnel.

This was the first time she'd ever sat close to a boy who was driving. She had seen and envied other girls so self-assured and secure, sitting close; it was a goal like wearing his gold football and his letter sweater and carrying in her wallet his school picture with, below his chin, the word LOVABLE clipped from a Lovable Bra ad.

He said, "How about going to Jimmy's instead of Hooper's?"

"Fine," she said, awed. She had never been to Jimmy's Diner. Bev had, with Roger, and had reported it was a milestone. Bev and Snowy kept mental lists of such milestones as their first kisses and the first time they shaved their legs, and Bev said this was the first time she'd gone slumming.

Jimmy's was located in the middle of downtown, on a sinister side street which led to the river. There were dark warehouses and a sagging building whose small neon sign said CAFE, a euphemism for beer joint. Across the street, Jimmy's was a silvery railroad car.

Tom parked behind two town plows. Snowy wondered if she should wait for him to open the passenger door for her, but since she was closer to his, she got out with him on his side. Snowflakes flicked against her face.

She was scared.

Tom pulled open the door. Bright light, the smell of coffee, the oniony smell of Western sandwiches. The drivers of the plows sat drinking coffee at the counter, and they turned and looked at her.

The booths were empty. Tom said, "Here okay?" and she nodded and slid in and gingerly sat. The table and torn seats were clean but smeary, as if they'd just been wiped with a sour rag. There was a black crust of ashes in the bottom of the glass ashtray.

Tom took one of the two menus propped between the ketchup bottle and the napkin container and handed it to her. Pulling off her knit gloves, unbuttoning her coat, she read, astonished at all the things besides sandwiches, the bacon and eggs and chicken croquettes and pork chops and fried clams and breaded veal cutlets. She wondered how they could cook all that in this little place and who would come here to eat it instead of going to a real restaurant.

Tom said, "What would you like?"

"I don't know, what're you having?"

"Hamburger and French fries."

"I'll have the same."

"You don't have to."

"No, it sounds fine." It also sounded reassuringly like Hooper's or Sweetland.

The man in white, Jimmy, came over from behind the counter, bringing glasses of water. "Guess winter's still with us."

"Guess so," Tom said.

"Well, if we live here, we gotta put up with the weather. What'll it be?"

"Two hamburgers, two orders of French fries, two black coffees—" He glanced questioningly at her. She nodded.

"Onion?" Jimmy asked, looking at her.

She busied herself shrugging out of her coat. "No, thank you." Her voice was almost a whisper.

Tom said, "No onion on either."

Jimmy left, and she bunched her coat behind her.

Tom said, "You want to hang it up?"

"No, no, it's okay."

Tom lit a cigarette. Snowy read the ketchup label.

Jimmy brought the coffee.

"Sixteen," Tom said. "When are you getting your license?"

"Heaven knows. My father's given me a few lessons, he doesn't have much patience. I don't stall the car too often anymore, but I don't think I'll ever in my whole life learn to parallel-park."

"Maybe I could give you a lesson when the weather gets better," Tom said, and stopped, appalled at even vaguely committing himself to another date.

Outside the window the snow fell steadily, quiet and determined.

She smiled. "You're not afraid I'll smash up your car?"

"I'll take my chances."

Jimmy brought over the food. Snowy pulled two napkins from the holder and slipped one behind her into her coat pocket for a souvenir.

Tom rubbed out his cigarette and passed the ketchup to her. "Got ourselves a regular blizzard."

"Yes." She took a small bite of the hamburger, chewed, and swallowed. She looked at him, surprised. "It's good."

He grinned. "Think it'd be horsemeat? Jimmy makes a good hamburger. And I like straight French fries, this kind, not the crinkly kind some places make nowadays, don't you?"

Snowy had never considered the finer points of French fries; she liked them all. But she said, "Yes," and took one.

Tom said, "And you ought to see Jimmy working over there at the grill when the place is packed; his arms are going so fast he looks like he's an octopus."

She giggled and relaxed.

A milestone.

In the car, she sat next to him without his asking. The radio played "Melody of Love."

He said, "Snowstorms really make you think."

"About what?"

"About what's plowed and unplowed. Thank God you're not sleeping over at Bev's tonight."

"They always get plowed out eventually."

"They've got a Jeep, haven't they?"

"Yes, and Fred likes it so much he drives it more than the car." She didn't add that riding in the Jeep mortified Bev. She said, "Bev's sleeping over at my house tonight."

"Oh. Well, let me see." He mused on parking places as they drove up Main Street and State Avenue. "I'd say our best bet is right here." He pulled into Varney's gas station, closed now, and drove around to the back. His headlights showed junk cars padded with snow.

He had parked here during snowstorms before. It had one drawback. "Let's hope some cop doesn't think we're casing the joint. Though poor old Varney is stolen blind by the guys anyway."

She laughed, but she wished the spot were more romantic.

He switched off the headlights, kept the car running, hung his glasses over the sun visor, and turned to her.

They looked at each other in the darkness. Anticipation tingled; they waited on the brink of the necking.

Tom thought, I'm getting involved, driving lessons and birthdays, will I be getting anything else? Was she worth the bother? At the moment, what he was getting was a hard-on.

So was Snowy, but she didn't know it. She knew only an awful ache. Yet she had discovered, a few years ago when her pajama bottoms got twisted in bed, a secret she kept even from Bev, and since then when the ache became unbearable she had intentionally twisted them until the night seemed to explode, she didn't know why, she didn't know what it was all about, such pleasure and such shame.

Snowflakes slid down the windshield.

Tom said, "It isn't midnight, but—" and kissed her, and they were off.

And soon she felt his hand move inside her coat to her breast. Her instinct was to protect her reputation by pushing him away as she had pushed Ed, but she didn't, and his hand investigated the ruffles of her blouse, the velveteen jumper down to her waist and around her back and found the zipper and also, beneath velveteen and nylon, her bra hooks. When she understood that he was trying to figure out how she was dressed, she nearly screamed. Ed had never tried this. And then all at once she wanted to giggle. Tom wanted to swear. A complex problem:

the jumper zipped down the back; underneath, the blouse buttoned up the front. It could not be done subtly. But at least she
was allowing a feel, and his hand went back to her breasts, and
Snowy thought how she'd tell Bev, "A jumper outfoxed him!"
She was, however, already planning what to wear on their next
date if he really did ask her out again. Something simpler, a
blouse and slacks. To see what might happen; to learn the next
step.

Then, horrified, she realized she was letting him Get Fresh on
their third evening together, and you weren't supposed to until
you were going steady.

They French-kissed, his hand on her breast. The radio played
Dave Brubeck.

She got her breath while he was kissing her throat and asked,
"What time is it?"

"Damn," he said. They untangled themselves, and he looked
at his watch. "Quarter past twelve."

So she was sixteen.

She said, "I'd better be getting home."

Her hair had tumbled down, and as he drove she made herself
try to fix it, but she'd lost most of the bobby pins which had
now joined the other things he'd find on the floor when he next
cleaned the car out, bottle caps, matchbooks, movie stubs, pencils, candy-bar wrappers, tarnished pennies. Once he had found
one nylon, and he still speculated about to what girl, of the
many double-date couples who'd been in the back seat, it belonged.

His tires cut fresh white tracks into the snow of her driveway.
"Bev's not back yet."

"I guess not."

"I suppose you've got something planned for tomorrow
night."

"Bev's sleeping over again, and Puddles." It hadn't been much
of a prospect, to celebrate her birthday just with them and cake.

"Could you do something before?"

He was asking her out again. "Yes. Bev and Roger are going to the movies. And," she added, not underestimating Puddles, "maybe Puddles is, too."

"Why don't I get hold of Roger and see about going together?"

She would be dimmed by Bev's presence, but there wasn't anything she could say except "Fine."

"I'll phone you tomorrow."

Her first phone call from him.

He leaned across her and took a small package out of the glove compartment. She stared at it, recognizing the jewelry store's wrapping paper.

He had bought it after school today, as a continuation of one of their jokes, but now when he saw she was too surprised to reach out, and he had to put it in her hand, he was glad he'd spent more than he'd intended, so it became more than a joke.

"It's for you," he said. "Happy birthday."

She held it like an award. "Thank you."

He quickly kissed her, a horn-rimmed kiss, and opened his door, and she didn't have to worry about whether or not to unwrap the present in front of him. They got out of the car.

He said, "That dog of yours is the noisiest little thing."

"She thinks she's guarding the house. She probably thinks she could tackle any burglar."

There were two more inches of snow since the last time her father had shoveled this evening. Their shoes left tracks as they walked around to the back door.

Tom said, "See you tomorrow," and kissed her again, and indoors she gave Laurie only a brief hug before she set the package on the kitchen counter and looked at it.

She knew what it was.

And it wasn't the angora sweater she'd had to unwrap last year in the cafeteria, embarrassed, while Ed beamed at her.

So she unwrapped it slowly, savoring the happiness. She slipped off the ribbon and folded the paper, to be saved for her souvenir drawer. She opened the box. It was indeed a pen. Then she saw the brand name and realized what it had cost. It was a Parker pen.

"So I figured," Puddles said, scooping up snow, "if he was sitting on that side of the auditorium, he'd leave by the door near Mr. Clough's room, so I went into the Dramatics Office and got those extra publicity posters and went downstairs and hung around the door trying to look like I was doing something official."

Bev said, "Thank heavens I didn't know what drama was going on offstage."

Puddles threw the snowball, and it smashed satisfyingly against a stop sign.

In their matching blue wool jackets, Snowy and Bev and Puddles were walking downtown to do the Radio Club's Saturday morning show, *Teen Tunes and Topics*. The program was a confused half hour of sudden silences, cleared throats, paper shuffling, and giggles. Being underprivileged sophomores, they'd only been allowed to broadcast once before, and Bev had done the smoothest job; terror pitched Snowy's voice high and junior-miss, and Puddles read her news items as if proclaiming doomsday.

The sun glittered on the new white snow.

"I waited," Puddles said, "and I waited and I waited, all those curtain calls, Bev, you could've been more considerate, and then everyone poured out, and he didn't come. So I raced around to the other side of the aud, and there he was coming out the other door, why I'll never know. And I didn't even think, I just did it; I dropped all the posters."

"Like your hanky!" Bev said.

"And then I felt like such an idiot I almost started bawling, half the damn audience was trampling all over them, and there I was trying to pick them up, and then I saw his shoes."

Bev and Snowy collapsed against the signal light and howled with laughter.

Snowy said, "Was he in them?"

"He was. I looked up and he looked down, and he said, 'Butterfingers.'"

"Stop it," Bev cried, "I'll wet my pants."

Puddles giggled. "I don't see what's so funny."

The light changed to red-and-yellow, and they crossed Main Street and walked along it past make-believe rooms in the windows of the furniture store.

"Anyway," Puddles said, "he helped me pick them up and then asked if I was lugging them home, and I had to say yes, what else could I say, and he said he'd give me a ride. Now I've got the whole stack of them under my bed. Is it stealing?"

"Contraband!" Snowy said.

"I suppose I could lug them back Monday, but what if he saw me? Anyway, we parked in the driveway and talked and all that. He's from Massachusetts, and God, is he fast! Linda always acts so sweet and innocent, but she sure can't be if she's been going out with him. The first time he kissed me he started Getting Fresh, I had to fight him off like Wonder Woman."

Bev said, "Then how come you're going to the movies with him tonight?"

"Well, he's better than Norm Noyes, isn't he? He's a doll. Norm's a drip. And I can protect myself, I've heard a knee in the nuts stops them dead in their tracks."

"Puddles!" Snowy and Bev said.

Snowy pulled open the door between the shoe store and camera store in the stone Masonic Temple Building, and they climbed the old wide stairs to the second floor and walked down the dark corridor. They felt uncomfortable here because they didn't really belong in this place where grown-ups earned money. Names of dentists and lawyers and insurance companies were painted on the opaque glass windows of the doors.

The radio station was at the end of the corridor. Bev opened one of the doors and they went into a room that had a dusty-black smell of records, all the jacketed 78's and 45's and bound albums filed on shelves along the walls. On the table in the center was a microphone. A big window in one wall showed a carpeted room with metal chairs for the kids who would come to listen, and through another window they saw Sherman Drew, the fat, bald disc jockey, broadcasting. He waved to them, eyed Bev appreciatively, and they waved back. They wished he were more glamorous, as they'd imagined disc jockeys to be before they'd joined the Radio Club and met the ones at this station.

Bev said, "Snowy, you choose the music, it's your birthday."

"Okay."

So while Puddles and Bev sat at the table and Puddles went over with Bev the news Puddles and Snowy had written up, most of which was culled from the March issue of the *Smoke Signal*, the school newspaper, and which Bev had been too busy with the play to help write, Snowy prowled, getting jittery. She chose not the hit-parade songs she owned, but other favorites, "And the Angels Sing," "When You Wish Upon a Star," "In the Mood," and "Stardust." Kids began to come into the audience room. She'd only seen Tom here a few times, he was probably working; would he listen, though? Was there a radio at Varney's?

She took the records to Sherman Drew and then sat down at the table and folded her sweaty hands. The audience of kids grew larger. Al Hanson, the program director of the Radio Club, wandered in to make sure they'd shown up, to check their news, and to flirt with Bev. He was a National Honor Society senior, but his ears stuck out, and he managed teams instead of playing on them.

Then Gloria Taylor came in.

Gloria Taylor was Snowy's idol. She was a senior, the captain of the Varsity cheerleading squad, the editor of the yearbook, the *Totem*, she'd gone to Girls' State, she was the DAR Good Citizen, she was secretary of the senior class, the Key Club Sweetheart, and she'd been Queen of the Junior Prom.

She dazzled.

And Bev hated her guts, because Roger had gone steady with her their junior year. And although Gloria had caused the breakup by falling in love with an older man, a Gunthwaite boy now a junior at the university, Gloria hated Bev's guts, too, because she thought Roger should have remained faithful to her memory.

The power Gloria would wield at the Varsity tryouts was the reason Snowy and Puddles froze the moment she entered. Snowy wished she'd worn her newer dungarees; Puddles wondered if she'd got lipstick on her teeth. But Gloria didn't notice them at all; she zeroed in on Bev.

"Bev!" Gloria said. "I remembered I saw Al had you down for broadcasting today, so I thought I'd stop by to tell you I've been hearing marvelous things about the play."

"How nice of you," Bev said.

Gloria's dark hair fell in careful curls to her shoulders, and Bev had much to say to Snowy about what Gloria must look like in pincurls every night. Gloria's mouth was Hazel Bishop Kiss-Proof. Her eyes were large and blue, and Snowy had noticed that whenever she went past a mirror in the girls' gym office or locker room, she made a special face, not a funny one as Bev would, but a pretty one, opening her eyes wide and pouting her mouth, and then she carried the expression on with her until she forgot it. Loyalty made Snowy point this out to Bev, and Bev had practiced until she got the imitation cruelly perfect.

Gloria was wearing, over charcoal slacks and a blue sweater, her white leather jacket. The first time Snowy had seen it she'd resolved to buy one with her summer-job money.

Gloria said, "And since I'm here, I might as well give in and do my prize-speaking; Al's been hounding me to."

Gloria had won second place in the Girls' Dramatic division of the State Prize-Speaking Contest. This wasn't too surprising; Gunthwaite, famous for its speakers, usually won nearly everything. The English and Latin teachers were a press gang, and the students understood that going out for prize-speaking might help their marks, so Gunthwaite sent busloads of contestants while other schools sent carloads.

"Well, well," Al said, "at long last, that's great. Now, we can pull this news, and this, and save them in case you need to fill in at the end. Let's change the program to first some news, then a record, then Gloria—"

Bev sat, watching him scribble. Puddles and Snowy looked at each other. Roger would listen to the program, at Lambert's Market.

Gloria said, "Wait, Al, maybe they want to keep their program as is—"

Al glanced at them.

Bev adjusted the microphone. "No, of course not, Gloria. We are honored."

Puddles ran her tongue across her front teeth.

Sherman leaned in the doorway. "You kids all set?"

Gloria took off her jacket. The fraternity pin on her left breast outranked Bev's gold basketball.

"Yes," Bev said.

The audience had stopped milling around and was sitting, waiting. Snowy checked again and saw the Gang and other kids, but Tom, to her relief, wasn't here.

They went on the air. Bev read the first news, about the debaters, including Roger, who'd won the cup at the University of Maine, and she was rattled enough to stumble over two words.

Gloria, when her turn came, wasn't. She announced, " 'The White Cliffs of Dover' by Alice Duer Miller," and charged right into it.

> I have loved England, dearly and deeply,
> Since that first morning, shining and pure,
> The white cliffs of Dover, I saw rising steeply
> Out of the sea that once made her secure.

Puddles sat spellbound, recalling New Boy's English car, and Snowy was quite moved when Gloria reached:

> Bad news is not broken
>   By kind tactful word.
> The message is spoken
>   Ere the word can be heard.
> The eye and the bearing,
>   And the breath make it clear,
> And the heart is despairing
>   Before the ears hear.
> I do not remember
>   The words that they said:
> "Killed—Douai—November—"
>   I knew John was dead.
> All done and over—
>   That day long ago—
> The white cliffs of Dover—
>   Little did I know.

Bev swallowed hard, and in one hideous instant Snowy remembered her father, the dead redheaded father.

But Gloria, unknowing, continued remorselessly on to the end.

> I am American bred,
> I have seen much to hate here—much to forgive,
>   But in a world where England is finished and dead,
> I do not wish to live.

Bev, who had introduced her, should now thank her. Bev looked at Snowy imploringly. Snowy pulled the microphone over and heard herself say, "Thank you, Gloria. That was Gloria Taylor doing her prizewinning 'White Cliffs of Dover.' Now let's listen to 'Stardust,'" and when Sherman in the next room started the record and they could talk privately, she said fast, to cover for Bev, "What a swell piece and you did such a good job," gushing too much, rushing crazily on, "My dramatics piece was 'Madame Butterfly,' but I was lousy, I did better in humorous with 'The Mad Hatter's Tea Party,' I made it to semifinals—"

"Actually," Gloria said, "I think it's pretty sappy. Mrs. Moulton chose it." She looked at Bev. "Is Roger working today?"

"Yes."

"He must be working as much as possible now, for money for college. I think it's criminal the way his folks won't help, the way they want him to go work at Trask's instead of go to college."

Puddles said, speaking up for the first time, "That's just the way French Canadians are."

Snowy gasped. Gloria could very well be French herself, last names weren't always indications.

Gloria wasn't, and she laughed. "You can say that again. Well, good luck with the rest of the program."

When the door closed behind Gloria, Bev widened her eyes and pouted her mouth, and Snowy and Puddles giggled encouragingly. But they saw that Bev's clear-polished nails had dug red half-moons in her palms.

After the program, they joined the Gang and walked along Main Street, chattering and looking in windows, until they came to Dunlap's Department Store. Snowy and Bev and Puddles went inside. It was a dark heavy place, as respectable as the racks of men's suits, but it made dresses seem flimsy. They examined the spring dresses and cotton skirts and Ship and Shore blouses and spring jackets and chose what Snowy should spend her birthday money, from aunts and uncles, on: a shiny green rain slicker.

At Sweetland, Bev and Puddles took a booth behind the twins and Carol Tucker and Patty Nichols, while Snowy went to the phone and called her mother. Her mother agreed she needed a slicker, so Snowy knew her folks hadn't already bought her one.

For lunch, Snowy had a grilled cheese sandwich and a strawberry frappe, Bev had a hot dog and a black-and-white frappe, and Puddles, her mother would be relieved to learn, had a hamburger and a ginger ale. Because it was Snowy's birthday, Bev and Puddles treated.

Then they walked back to Dunlap's, and Snowy bought the slicker, and they went into Woolworth's, where Snowy bought some new ink for her new pen and Puddles bought some white shoe polish for her sneakers and they reminded Bev that she'd mentioned she was almost out of notebook paper.

Puddles left them at the Emery Street corner, to go home and wash her hair and take a bath and change. It was times like these when she was jealous of Bev and Snowy's extreme closeness, and as she walked along faster, alone and cold, she imagined their gossiping together while they too washed their hair and bathed. But when she got home, she was soon busy bossing her brothers, wrapping the present she and Bev had secretly bought, setting her hair, helping her mother get supper, and the jealousy waned.

At Snowy's house, Snowy's mother was working in the kitchen, where there was the warm smell of cake, and her father was downstairs in the cellar he'd decided to make into a rumpus room. The mail had come. "Oh, murder," Snowy said, recognizing the handwriting on an envelope addressed to her. She opened it. A flowery birthday card, and inside was written, "Have fun today. Ed." She gave the card to Bev. Bev said, "Ughy-pew."

The phone on the end table by the sofa rang.

Bev said, "Let it ring a couple more times. Mustn't act too

eager." She went upstairs, and Snowy sat down on the sofa and looked at the telephone.

She lifted the receiver. "Hello."

"Snowy?" Tom said.

"Yes."

"I got hold of Roger, and we'll be picking you and Bev up about quarter of seven, if that's okay. I guess we'll be taking my car."

His telephone voice was light and low and was almost drowned out by the pandemonium behind him, the crashes and yells and—oh, damn, she thought—the radio music.

"That's fine," she said.

"What about Puddles?"

"She's got a date with New Boy. Mike Young, I mean. He'll pick her up here."

"Okay."

Someone in the background bellowed, *"Come off of there, you son of a bitch!"*

Mad banging.

"Um, sorry," Tom said. "I'm calling from Varney's, as if you couldn't tell. Jack's trying to beat off his muffler with a cold chisel."

"Oh," Snowy said, feeling as if she'd intruded into a men's room.

He said, "Heard you on the radio this morning. It didn't sound like you."

She blushed.

He said, "But you sound like you on the phone."

She said, "The pen is beautiful."

"Well, you seemed to need one."

"It's beautiful."

"Having a happy birthday?"

"Oh, yes."

"Well. See you tonight."

"Okay."

"Good-bye."

"Good-bye."

Upstairs in the bathroom, Snowy and Bev washed their hair, and then in Snowy's bedroom they returned to the topic they'd discussed last night. They hadn't mentioned the Getting Fresh to Puddles because God only knew what Puddles might blurt out about it sometime.

"Our third date," Snowy said, sitting at her desk combing her wet hair. "No, our second real date. And I let him. He must think I'm cheap."

Bev lay on her stomach on the bed, in the midst of the toy pandas and teddy bears, and leafed through a *Seventeen.* "I don't know. I don't think Tom goes much by rules."

"I sure didn't last night."

Pages slapped slowly.

Bev said, "Here's one way to look at it. A guy takes you out and spends money on you, and if you like him a lot, why not give him something back?"

Snowy considered this, tugging her comb through a snarl. "But Tom didn't Get Fresh with you until after you were going steady. How come me? It can't be that he was driven mad by my enormous bubbies."

"He's almost a year older. And he hasn't got time," Bev sang, "for the waiting game. Roger tried to Get Fresh before we started going steady, remember."

"But you didn't let him."

"I wanted to, though."

Snowy crouched down by the register and began curling the ends of her hair with her hands. "Maybe," she said worriedly, "I'm oversexed."

As suppertime neared, they took baths and got dressed, Bev in her plaid wool slacks and white blouse, Snowy in her gray wool slacks and a blouse of little violets. Shirttails out, collars turned up. Snowy fastened the gold clamp around her ponytail elastic, and they went downstairs.

In the dining room, the maple table was set with the good china and the centerpiece of wax fruit, on a white tablecloth instead of place mats. Snowy's parents celebrated birthdays and holidays very solemnly, preserving every tradition from the Christmas-tree angel to this dinner menu: roast beef and gravy, and Snowy's favorite potatoes, peeled and cooked with the roast, and her favorite vegetable, broccoli.

Puddles arrived, wearing brown wool slacks and her tight brown sweater, snailcurls bouncing fresh from pincurls, just in time for dessert. Chocolate was permitted on Snowy's birthday because chocolate cake had been the tradition since childhood. Her mother brought it in, chocolate cake with white seven-minute frosting, and sixteen pink candles, flames trembling.

Puddles said, "Bet I know what you're going to wish for."

Varsity. But Snowy was torn between that and Tom's love. She took a deep breath. She could wish for fame, wish she would never die. She was frightened, though, of learning the answer to any of these, so she wished to herself, "I wish I'll get an A on the Latin test," and blew out all the candles.

Her mother cried, "It'll come true!" and Bev helped her bring in the vanilla-strawberry-chocolate brick ice cream.

Puddles studied Snowy. "What did you wish for?"

"I can't tell."

"Varsity?"

"Well. No."

"Oh."

After the cake and ice cream, there were presents. Snowy dreaded this, the striving to appreciate them enough to please her parents. Her mother brought them forth, Puddles added another, and Snowy sat shy and embarrassed.

"Go ahead, go ahead," her mother said, always as excited about presents as a child, "open the one from Gram first."

It was a big box, but not the crate of oranges and grapefruit her grandmother had sent at Christmas. When her grandfather died last year, her grandmother moved to Florida near a son and daughter-in-law. Snowy hoped she and her folks might go visit her sometime, but her father said it cost too much, and besides, just what he'd heard from his in-laws about Florida weather and orange trees right in the yard was enough to last him a lifetime.

Snowy opened the box. A wealth of bright cotton colors. As she took out one skirt after another, she couldn't believe how many there were, she started counting, and when she got to twelve, while Bev and Puddles exclaimed and pawed, she knew what her grandmother had done. Sixteen summer skirts for her sixteenth birthday.

She looked wonderingly at her mother, who said, "Gram's been working on them since Christmas," and Snowy wanted to cry.

From Kit the cat: razor blades.

From Laurie: bubble bath.

From Bev and Puddles: a bateau-necked Italian jersey, gray and black horizontal stripes on white.

"Wow!" she said.

From her parents: a white slip, socks, a gold charm which said SWEET 16, and a sleeveless full-skirted aqua summer dress with a Peter Pan collar.

"It's lovely," she said. Whenever her parents bought her any clothes, she felt that she was being dressed like a paper doll. "It must be the loveliest dress in the whole town."

Her mother said, "Well, we looked in Dunlap's and in Yvonne's and we couldn't decide and we couldn't decide, we thought of a slicker, as a matter of fact, or a new spring jacket but yours ought to go another season, and you don't have a nice summer dress and your father saw this and said he liked it and—"

Snowy's parents had no hobbies; the house was a passion; their only recreation was shopping. They would get all dressed up and go downtown and stroll around looking at things, consulting each other, and they brought home with them as well as their purchase a tale of the stores they had visited, what the clerks had said, how they had decided, and the tale was repeated many times. Snowy could almost recite the saga of the television set.

"—and you don't have anything aqua," her mother said, "it ought to make your eyes bluer—"

Her father said, "Now, Charlotte, her eyes are a fine blue," and got up from the table and went into the living room. Snowy braced herself. He came back carrying a beribboned box, and she knew that this was, though it wasn't a big package, the big deal present.

"What on earth," she said, holding it, admiring the wrapping, shaking it gently, "what on earth—"

Her father, trying to appear nonchalant, as he always did at these moments, said, "If you opened it, you might find out," and lit a cigarette, but she fussed with it some more, prolonging, and Bev and Puddles twittered.

Then she opened it.

Her father said, "We thought you might need something better than that old Brownie to take pictures of Washington. It's a Kodak Pony One Thirty-five."

Her mother said, "At the camera store, they told us it'd be perfect—"

"Thank you," Snowy said, "thank you so much, it's wonderful."

Her father said, "There's instructions, I'll show you how to work the settings."

"At the store," her mother began again, but Laurie started barking, and Puddles cried, "Help, we've got to brush our teeth!" and ran for her overnight case, and the girls raced upstairs. They brushed their teeth and reapplied lipstick. When they came back down, Snowy's parents, as Snowy feared, were showing Tom and Roger the camera and telling the story. Laurie was in another frenzy of barking, this time at the front door, Snowy yanked the door open, and New Boy was standing on the steps.

Tall and fair and slim, Mike Young had blank dark eyes that Julia would call bedroom eyes. He said, "Does it bite?"

"No, no," she said, grabbing up Laurie, "come in, *shush*, Laurie," but Laurie, overwrought by all this company, squirmed in her arms and kept on barking.

Tom said, "Calm down, pups," and masterfully took Laurie. "Thatsagirl, calm down." Laurie did. He grinned at Snowy. "Dogs like me. So do old ladies."

"Have you got a dog?"

"I used to. He was run over."

"Oh, God. I'm sorry."

"Yes, it was pretty terrible. But it was years ago."

Puddles, pulling on her jacket, introduced Mike to Snowy's parents, while behind their backs Bev paraded around the dining room for Roger, holding Snowy's new slip in front of her. "Note," she said, "the shadow panel."

Roger said, "I'm noting."

Snowy said to her mother, "Please don't do the dishes, leave them, we'll do them when we get home."

"I'll do them," her mother said. "It's your birthday."

Snowy said, "Thank you. Thank you for everything. Everything was wonderful."

Her mother smiled and kissed her. "It was a nice birthday, wasn't it? Have a good time."

Sitting together on the fashionable side of the theater, they watched *Twenty Thousand Leagues Under the Sea*. Snowy knew that Rita, with Wally two rows behind, would see that Tom had his arm along the back of her seat. Bev and Roger watched cheek to cheek; Mike put his arm around Puddles, and

Puddles spent the rest of the movie pushing one of his hands away from her breasts and the other off her thigh. Then Tom slid his hand down around Snowy, pulling her to him. There they were, three double-heads deep down in the seats.

After Hooper's, Mike and Puddles whisked off in Mike's car to go parking, and Tom belatedly realized how awkward he might feel parking with Snowy while Bev was in the back seat. He asked Snowy, "Would it be okay if you and I went back to your house and I'll let Roger have the car?" Snowy said yes, although she preferred the car, even with Bev in it, to the house.

Her folks had gone to bed, but she could still sense their presence in the crisp empty downstairs. She and Tom wandered into the living room.

He said, "Do you play the piano?"

"Some. I stopped taking lessons awhile back, I hated recitals."

Tom sat down on the sofa and lit a cigarette. Snowy, uncomfortable, turned off one lamp and turned on the television, low.

He said, "I think someone's come between us."

Panic whirled her around.

He was smiling at Laurie, who had jumped up on the sofa and settled against him.

"Oh," she said. "Oh, Laurie." She picked her up and dropped her on the braided rug, and Laurie went into the kitchen and barked at the door. Snowy let her out.

In the living room, she sat down at the other end of the sofa. "Thank you again for the pen."

"You're welcome. That's a nice camera you got."

"Yes."

"Your father work at Trask's?"

"Yes."

He leaned forward to put out his cigarette in the beanbag ashtray. "So does my old man."

But she didn't want to talk about her family or learn that he had one, and she reacted with the same method she'd used to distract Ed: she dived across the sofa and started tickling Tom.

"Cut it out," he said, laughing, "cut it out, you're asking for it," and he tickled her, she wriggled in his arms, and they rolled off the sofa, nearly knocking over the coffee table, and wrestled on the rug. Tom wasn't so afraid of hurting her as big Ed had been, and she lost. Tom lay on her, pinning her shoulders down, and she felt something hard pressed against her, something she knew must be It. Her heart beat wildly.

Tom said, "Aren't you the wise guy!" and kissed her.

Then he picked her up and carried her back to the sofa and took off his glasses. Before he kissed her again, she saw by the lamplight that his eyelashes were long and straight.

And eventually, there on the sofa, she learned what the next step was. His hand slid across her breast and began unbuttoning her blouse.

She snatched at his hand, tried to push him away.

He held her firmly and kept right on unbuttoning.

"*No!*" she said.

He stopped. He sat up and lit a cigarette. His profile was taut with anger.

Laurie barked to come in, and Snowy dashed out to the kitchen, let her in, scooped her up, and buried her face in the soft golden fur.

Tom took fast, furious drags of his cigarette. What the hell, he thought, was he bothering with this for, why not give in and go steady with Rita? And he answered himself, damned if I know. He put on his glasses, ground out the cigarette, and walked to the kitchen.

He said, "I'm sorry."

She looked up. Laurie, anxious, licked tears.

She said, "There's some birthday cake left. Would you like some birthday cake?"

"Okay."

As she set Laurie down, Tom saw a glimpse of white bra, and she realized she'd forgotten to rebutton her blouse. Tom stepped forward and buttoned it slowly, then kissed the tip of her nose.

He said, "You got any coffee?"

So for the first time she served him food and timidly made two cups of instant coffee, and they sat at the dining-room table.

He said, "I have to work till nine Friday night, could you go out afterwards, to Hooper's or something?"

"I think so."

Bev and Roger arrived then. Like Snowy's, Bev's face was aflame with beard burn. When Tom and Roger left, Bev said, "Have you been crying? Did Tom behave himself tonight?"

"He Got Fresh, but I stopped him." Snowy put the cake plates in the sink and turned to Bev. "And he asked me out again!"

"That proves it. He's not just after your body."

Snowy looked doubtful.

Bev didn't dare tell Snowy that when she and Roger were fooling around in Tom's car they had discovered a pack of Trojans in the glove compartment. Roger had laughed and said, "His emergency kit," and Bev had said, "I'd better start checking *your* glove compartment," but later, when they were naked and sweaty, the titillating thought of those contraceptives so handy led them on farther, and this was the other thing Bev didn't dare mention, what Bev had learned tonight: a blow job.

Snowy said, "Want some cake?"

Bev swallowed. "No, thanks."

Laurie started barking. Snowy said, "Here comes Puddles," and opened the door. "Did you have a fight? Why didn't he walk you to the door?"

Puddles' lipstick was gone, and her pale face was scuffed red. "He just doesn't, I'm going to have to teach him some manners, that's all." She took off her jacket. "God, what a time. We went to the sandpit. Wally's car was there, incidentally, Snowy, but I didn't see anyone in it, they must've been going great guns." She pulled at the neck of her sweater. "I swear I've got twenty hickeys, he really gets carried away. And I used to think keeping track of Norm's hands was a chore. God! I mean, it's not just bubbies, Mike tries for your crotch and everything!"

Snowy stared, scandalized.

Puddles said, "So I let him Get Fresh. I figured that that was the least of the evils."

Snowy said, "Did he ask you out again?"

"Yup, the movies Friday night."

Snowy said, "Well, what's going to happen next time you go parking?"

"I'll cross that bridge," Puddles said, "when I come to it."

Upstairs, Snowy's presents had been arranged by her mother in her bedroom, the new dress and jersey and skirts draped across the bed to be admired again. Laurie jumped onto the bed and curled up in the middle of them. The girls tiptoed into the spare room. Kit, asleep on the bed, awoke and stalked out, very dignified. Her parents had redone the room after the other rooms were finished, choosing daisy wallpaper and yellow curtains and bedspread and a green-and-yellow braided rug, but when Bev wasn't here, it remained just a bleak spare room. Now Bev's clothes dangled from her overnight case and were tossed over the rocking chair, and the room was a mess which Snowy's mother tried to ignore.

They took off their clothes and put on their pajamas. Puddles examined her throat in the bureau mirror.

"Only two," she reported. "I could've sworn I was getting chewed to bits."

Bev and Snowy sprawled on the double bed, and Snowy brushed the elastic kink out of her hair while Puddles put her hair up in pincurls. Puddles said, "How'd things go with Tom?"

"Okay," Snowy said. "We're going out Friday, when he gets

through work. If Mother and Daddy let me. Where do I tell them we're going at nine o'clock at night?"

Bev did remember this time. "You're going to Hooper's."

"For three hours?"

"Well, you know my mother. I didn't have to spell it out."

"With my folks," Snowy said, "I'd better have an ironclad alibi. Though at least they don't say I have to be home by eleven, like Betty Jane's folks, so I wonder what they think we're doing."

Puddles said, "Holding hands."

They giggled.

Bev said, "You could say you're going over to that dairy bar in Leicester. Or you're going to catch the rest of the second feature."

"But what if he asks me to the movies Saturday night? We could be going to see the movie we missed, but will we sit through the second feature again, and if not, how come I'm not home early?"

Puddles said, "This is why she gets A's."

They pondered.

"The Carnival!" Snowy cried. "The National Honor Society Spring Carnival is Saturday night!"

Bev said, "Oh, God, I'd forgotten. Roger is running the penny toss, seems like the president could give himself a better job. There's a dance afterwards."

Puddles stabbed in the last bobby pin. "Spring? If a robin showed up now, he'd die of frostbite."

They went into the bathroom and brushed their teeth and Noxzemaed. Bev said, "I hope spring never comes." Spring meant June and graduation, after which she wouldn't see Roger in school every day ever again. The prestige of going steady with a college boy would be some compensation, but she could not picture herself sitting home weekends, waiting for his vacations, and she was disturbed that the prospect of new boys kept teasing her.

In the bedroom, Snowy turned off the light, and they groped for the bed.

As usual, when all three of them slept together, Snowy was awakened during the night by too many elbows and knees, and she crawled over Bev, wrapped herself in the puff, and lay down on the rug. She preferred this to sleeping alone in her room with Laurie. She thought of her sixteenth birthday, the only one she'd ever have, and of how close it had come to ruin. She shivered. But he had asked her out again. Laurie, lonesome, scratched at the door, and she got up and let her in. They slept, curled up together.

One week left until tryouts.

On Monday, the Latin tests were given back. Snowy and Dudley got A's. Bev got a C+ and Puddles a B. After school, Snowy and Puddles taught cheering.

Tuesday, in history, Snowy was called on to give her oral report about the most important event of the past week. To her, it had been her birthday, but she chose the publication of the Yalta papers. She stood scared in front of the class and talked from notes that became soggy in her sweaty hands, and she couldn't answer a question the teacher asked her afterward.

Wednesday, during English, a home ec girl tapped on the classroom door and looked in and said to Mr. Foster, "We've made some doughnuts, would you like one?" He said, "Why, certainly," took the doughnut, produced a thermos of coffee from a desk drawer, and tormented the class, who couldn't even chew gum in school, by sitting on his desk and having a coffee break right in front of them. Dudley called out, "May I come grovel for the crumbs?" and Mr. Foster threw an eraser at him.

Snowy and Puddles taught cheering after school on Thursday.

Friday, they had an algebra test. Mr. Dodge stopped by Snowy's desk while she was struggling with one example:

$$X^2 + 7X + 3 = 0$$

He suggested she try the quadratic formula. Mike Young, behind Puddles beside her, said, "Yes, Henrietta, give that a try, where are your brains today?" and Snowy, frantic, spun around and screamed at him, "*Will you shut up!*" After a stunned moment, the class whooped with laughter. Snowy looked up in terror at Mr. Dodge. He just said lightly, "Don't have a nervous breakdown this year, Henrietta. Save it for next year."

And during the days in the dark school there was Tom, Tom walking along the corridors carrying sometimes only one book, sometimes carrying none, there was Tom standing very solid at his traffic post, and there was Tom stepping off his proctor's platform to sit with Snowy and look through her pile of books and her notebook and discovering, jolted, while she blushed, that all her doodles were:

She told her parents she was going to the second feature with him Friday night, but she and Tom went to Hooper's and then parked at the snow-covered sandpit. What Snowy learned this time was he could do a good imitation of George Gobel. Tom, having decided on stealth, spent most of the time joking, and when at last they settled down to necking he did not Get Fresh. Snowy was both relieved and disappointed.

In her driveway, he asked her to the movies Saturday night, so she had to explain about her lie to her folks.

"Jesus," he said, "isn't it one hell of a note we have to put up with all this? I wish I was a twenty-five-year-old playboy."

"Eek!" she said.

He said, "Let's go to the first feature and then go to the Carnival, that ought to make us look good and busy."

Snowy prayed her folks wouldn't ask her about the second feature, and they didn't.

Saturday night she and Tom saw Grace Kelly and Bing Crosby and William Holden in *The Country Girl*, which they liked after they had recovered from the shock of a dowdy Grace Kelly, and then they drove to the high school.

The National Honor Society was twelve seniors. Four of them, the elite, Roger Lambert and Gloria Taylor and Kathy McKenna and Al Hanson, had been chosen the spring of their junior year, and the rest during their senior. They were selected for their Scholarship, Character, Service, and Leadership, but despite these qualities the only things the society did were give awards and hold this annual carnival to earn money to buy the awards, the Freshman Plaque, the Sophomore Trophy, the Good Citizenship Junior Award. To reign and bestow were, evidently, sufficient.

Snowy had never been to the Carnival before; she was surprised that the place was so mobbed. The NHS had not exactly succeeded in transforming the cafeteria with the balloons and crepe paper, and there was still the smell of Friday's macaroni and cheese, yet nobody seemed to mind. Even the kids who'd come here determined to sneer had lost their sophistication, and at the booths and at the cafeteria tables, now game tables, the crowds yelled and laughed and applauded in a happy uproar. Snowy and Tom pushed through them past the miniature golf, the GUESS HOW MANY BEANS IN THIS JAR, the pin-the-tail-on-the-donkey, past Gloria Taylor turbaned and earringed telling fortunes, past the curtain that hid the fashion show of senior boys dressed up in rummage sale gowns, past the refreshment booth and the weight lifting, to the penny toss, where, outside a roped-off square, kids skimmed pennies at a saucer floating in a bucket of water inside. Roger and Bev were inside, too.

Tom reached into his pocket. "Want to try?"

"No, thanks," Snowy said. "With my aim, they could just call it a wishing well."

Tom said to Roger, "What're the prizes? I'm going to wipe you out."

Roger said, "Puddles and Mike already did. Puddles has a wicked aim."

While Tom played, Bev whispered to Snowy, "Rita's here with Sonny Poor; Wally's lost another one."

Snowy considered the implications. Sonny was a senior and quite a catch, but he wasn't so handsome as Tom. She said, "I'll bet she hasn't given up on Tom, though."

"Seems like Tom's given up on her."

Snowy brightened. "Really?"

"Well, she's not here with him, is she?"

Tom won a red balloon and presented it to Snowy.

The dance was announced, the Carnival was over except for cleaning up, and they went down to the gym. Al Hanson put a bunny hop record on the record player. The bunny hop was last year's fad, and usually they would have scorned it as old-fashioned, but they all were still in high spirits. Tom grabbed Snowy's waist from behind, Adele Roberge grabbed his waist, and Sam Page grabbed Adele's, and they began to bunny hop, and the entire crowd milling about latched on, a long chain of kids hopping two-footed around the gym. One hop forward, one hop back, three hops forward, right kick, left kick, three hops forward. The hops thundered; the floor shook. Snowy was laughing so hard she didn't realize until she was halfway down the gym that for the first time in her life she was the leader. Hop, hop; hop hop hop. She hopped, holding the red balloon by its string.

The bunny hop exhausted everyone. They broke into couples and danced close in the dark as the record player sang: "Take me in your arms, dear,/Dream with me. . . ."

Snowy and Tom left and went to Hooper's for sustenance, English muffins and coffee, and then they again went parking at the sandpit. When this time during a kiss Tom started unbuttoning her blouse, she didn't stop him. He prided himself on his trick of unhooking a bra one-handed, and he got Snowy's unhooked before she knew what was happening, but then her worries dissolved in the wonder of his mouth on her breast. The freed balloon bumped gently against the roof of the car.

Sunday mornings, Gunthwaite sounded like a cathedral town, the steeples of all the churches cascading chimes. Snowy awoke at nine, very late for her. As usual, she went to her bedroom window and looked out at the river and the ducks, unconsciously copying Julia's inspection of the lake. She was startled to see the cream-colored convertible parked at the side of the street. Without thinking how she was dressed, she ran downstairs, Laurie racing behind her, pulled on her jacket over her pajamas and her boots over her bare feet, and ran outdoors. A note under a windshield wiper said, "Battery Dead." She slid it out and rushed back indoors and upstairs and told her parents, who were just getting up. She placed this sample of his handwriting in her souvenir drawer and washed and hastily dressed in her gray sweat shirt and best dungarees. She'd just finished twisting her hair into a ponytail when Laurie started barking.

She looked out the window. Roger's car now faced Tom's, and both hoods were up, so the cars appeared to be trying to devour each other. Roger and Tom leaned into the insides.

She applied lipstick, trying to decide what she should do. Tom probably didn't need any more help than Roger, but it would be impolite not to go out, and anyway, it was a chance to see him. She could use the ducks as an excuse.

She went downstairs to the kitchen. There wasn't any stale bread in the breadbox, and she took four slices of fresh, hoping her mother wouldn't notice. She let Laurie out and followed her slowly as she ran barking at the boys. They were rigging jumper cables from Roger's car to Tom's. She'd always thought it must be dangerous to lean into a car under a hood that might come crashing down, and she admired their nonchalance.

Tom straightened. "Hi. We wake you?"

"No. The battery's dead?" She tore the bread and began to throw pieces across the safety rail into the river. The ducks, quacking harshly, battled.

Tom said, "I shouldn't've come in for that coffee." He knelt and patted Laurie. "When I came out, she wouldn't start, I rolled her down the driveway and tried to jump-start her, but no luck, so I walked home. And there was my father waiting up ready to chew my ass out for being late, so it was a good thing I had an excuse."

Roger said, "And it's a damn good thing I'm bighearted enough to come to the rescue after all the wisecracks about the Heap."

Snowy giggled, suddenly no longer afraid of him. "Did you make lots of money last night?"

"That's Kathy's job to figure out, but it sure looked like we did."

Tom said, "What you ought to do is embezzle it and take off for Hawaii. No snow, and think of the hula dancers."

Roger said, "Bev's walk is all the hula I can stand."

"I'll say it is," Tom said.

Snowy, jealous, turned and threw the last piece of bread.

Tom asked, "Do you always feed the ducks?"

"On weekends. I don't have time before school."

She and the boys looked down at the ducks paddling in the slate gray river.

"Well," Tom said, "let's give her a try."

Holding Laurie for warmth, Snowy watched them get into their cars. Roger started his car, and Tom's starter ground, then the engine caught, and he got out and unclipped the cables and slammed down the hood. "I'm taking her to Varney's now," he said, "but how about a driving lesson this afternoon?"

"I've got tons of homework," she lied. "Thank you, though."

"Okay."

He and Roger drove off, and she thought how strange it had been to see Tom in the white sunlight.

After the ceremony of Sunday breakfast, bacon and eggs and cornbread which was always baked in ear-of-corn molds, Snowy mopped and dusted her room, ironed enough starched blouses for the coming week and ironed her starched gym suit for tomorrow, and then rolled up the braided rugs in the living room and spent the rest of the day, with time out for the ceremony of Sunday dinner, practicing cartwheels, jumps, and cheers.

She expected Puddles to phone, but Puddles didn't and she didn't phone Puddles because talking about the tryouts was unbearable.

In the evening, sitting on the sofa with Kit and Laurie, she watched *Range Rider*. She couldn't concentrate. With her folks, she watched Ed Sullivan's *Toast of the Town*, and she looked at the performers and thought of the competition they too faced and wondered if competition ever ended.

And in bed that night she wished impossible things. She wished Rita could not do a split; she wished Nutty were not such an athletic teacher's pet of Gilly and Jonesy's. She wished Linda were not so sweetly pretty. She wished that the twins had been born one person, to take up only one place on the squad. And she wished Puddles' cartwheels and jumps were not so effortless.

She hated them all, even Puddles. She wished them all dead.

The JV's sat together in the first row on the right-hand side of the auditorium. Across the aisle on the other side sat Gilly and Jonesy and the Varsity cheerleaders.

Puddles kept fussing with the collar of her gym suit. Gilly and Jonesy disapproved of wearing gym collars turned up, but Puddles had another hickey and she couldn't decide which was worse, to wear her collar up to hide it or to let it show. Snowy also had a hickey from Saturday night; hers, however, was hidden beneath her bra.

Linda said, "Why is it at times like these I always have to go to the bathroom?"

Puddles snapped, "You're not so special. Everyone does."

Behind them sat the other girls trying out, freshmen, sophomores, a few juniors making one last attempt, and behind these quiet girls was a noisy audience of kids. Bev and those in the Gang not trying out sat in the balcony.

Gilly blew her whistle.

Suddenly the auditorium was more silent than during any study hall.

The first tryouts had begun.

The JV's were to go up before the others did. Seven now, without Maureen, they couldn't all go up by twos, so they had scrapped their height-partner arrangement, except for the twins', and decided that Rita and Nutty, the juniors, would try out together, and Puddles and Linda and Snowy together. Snowy found a tiny bit of relief in not having to be judged beside Rita's vividness.

She folded her clammy hands on her knees.

Rita and Nutty ran up the steps to the stage. They were very good and very serious. Rita did her split, which was not required.

"Showoff," Puddles muttered. "I hope she got floor burn."

They ran down off the stage and sat in a back row.

Gilly called, "Next!"

The twins turned to Puddles and Snowy and Linda and clutched.

Puddles said, "Go on, get it over with."

Charl said, "Look at how my hands are shaking, look at them."

The twins ran up.

They were cute.

Puddles put her collar down. "Maybe Gilly won't see the hickey, but she'll sure see the collar up."

Linda said, "Shouldn't you have thought of this Saturday night?"

"Don't fight," Snowy begged. "Don't fight. It'll be bad luck."

"Next!"

The three girls rose uncertainly.

Then their training took over, and they ran for the stage as they had run out onto the gym floor, and stood in the stance, fist on hip, Snowy between Puddles and Linda. Megaphones weren't used at tryouts. They cupped their hands and yelled, announcing the first cheer, "T-E-A-M!"

Gilly and Jonesy wanted loud yells and lots of pep.

Instead of doing the "Gunthwaite Jay Vees" introductory moves, a jerk of both fists, then hands on hip, then a clap, they had to do the more difficult Varsity introduction, three outward thrusts of the right fist.

"G-H-S!"

And then came the cheer:

"T"—arms straight out in front, hands clenched in fists; "E" —fists brought back to chests; "A"—arms straight out at the sides; "M"—fists to chests; "Yay"—they jumped down, right feet kicking out, arms sweeping back in a circle; "Team!" and they jumped back up, fists to chests, and then they repeated it all twice, and with the last "Team!" they did a big jump, Puddles' hair flying, Snowy's ponytail swinging, Linda's ponytail jouncing.

Back in the stance, they cupped their hands and yelled, "Go, Gunthwaite, Go!"

It was a fast, energetic cheer. "Go, Gunthwaite, Go!" they shouted, their arms straight in front of them, wrists jerking fists in time to the words, as they lowered themselves, right feet out, to their left knees; "Go, Gunthwaite, Go!" they shouted again, raising themselves, fists still jerking; "Smash 'em, bust 'em!" was two snaps of their right fists, "That's our custom!" a little kick and a jump down to touch the floor with their fingertips; and as they shouted, "Go, Gunthwaite, Go!" they thrust themselves up into a jump, arms in V's above their heads, clenched their right fists and jammed their left fists on their hips and came down to a kneeling position, left knees on the floor, right arms straight out in front, fists aggressive.

But they had jumped unevenly.

They yelled, "C'mon and Beat!" and stood with their legs far apart and lowered themselves onto their right feet, balancing by swinging their hands, until they were kneeling with their left legs stretched straight out to the side, thigh muscles showing taut. They swung themselves back upright and did it again, to the other side. A dribble motion with their hands, a jitterbug step with their feet, and then a jump down and they came up standing, arms outspread.

> C'mon and beat Concord!
> Get hep to the jive!
> C'mon and beat Concord!
> Man alive!
> So make with your hands, boys,
> And make with your feet,
> 'Cause GHS is out to beat!

Gloria Taylor jotted in her notebook and leaned over to speak to Gilly.

Puddles and Snowy and Linda ran to the side of the stage and stood in the stance.

Puddles ran forward into a perfect cartwheel.

Then Snowy. Hers was crooked.

So was Linda's.

They ran down off the stage and up the aisle to the back row, where the rest of the JV's were. Snowy sat and listened to her heart pounding. As the other kids went up in twos, Rita and Nutty and Charl and Darl whispered about them, but Snowy and Linda just sat, and Puddles cracked her knuckles.

After the others had tried out, Gilly consulted her clipboard and called, "Okay, we'd like to see again—"

Tense silence.

"Rita, Nutty, and Charl and Darl."

The twins didn't do any clutching this time, they ran for the stage.

Puddles said, "I think I'm going to throw up. I mean it."

They did "Abnaki Locomotive." Everyone tried to picture them in Varsity uniforms and succeeded.

Gilly called, "Puddles, Linda, and Snowy."

Linda breathed, "Thank God."

They passed the other JV's running back as they ran up.

They stood sideways on the stage, looking at the audience over their right shoulders, first their left hands on the shoulder of the girl in front while their right arms moved, then their right hands on the shoulder of the girl in front while their left arms moved, then both arms moving, back and forth like the shafts of a train.

> A-B-N-A-K-I-S, rah rah rah!
> (faster) A-B-N-A-K-I-S, rah rah rah!
> (and faster) A-B-N-A-K-I-S, rah *rah RAH!*
> Abnakis! Abnakis! Yay!

"All right," Gilly said, "that's it, no use hanging around, we won't be posting the list until tomorrow."

As Puddles and Snowy and Bev walked home, Puddles said, "I'll bet Gilly used to pull the wings off flies."

They said good-bye to Puddles at the Gowen Street corner and walked on. "Remember," Snowy said, "I told my folks the tryouts were at the end of the week, so don't say anything if they get home before Fred picks you up."

"Okay, but why?"

"They would fret. That's all I need."

Although the girls had the house to themselves, they went up-stairs to Snowy's room, Bev carrying a glass of milk and their schoolbooks, Snowy carrying a glass of milk and a handful of gingersnaps. Bev lay on the bed, and Snowy sat at her desk looking down at the river, and they ate.

"Snowy," Bev said finally. "Remember when I decided not to go out for cheering?"

"Yes. You said you couldn't stand being lame."

"Did I? Well, that wasn't the reason. I absolutely couldn't face the tryouts. What if I didn't make it? Everyone would know I'd tried out and hadn't made it. So if I never tried out, maybe I could seem above it all. I'm not. Nobody is."

Snowy turned and gazed at her.

Bev untied a panda's pink ribbon. "I guess what I mean is, I know how much you want it." She retied the ribbon.

Snowy said, "Puddles wants it just as much."

"Yes."

"And Linda."

"With plays," Bev said, "if you don't get the part, there's always another play. Another chance. You're braver than I am."

"No," Snowy said. "I don't know how I'm going to live if I don't make it."

A honk outdoors.

"Fred," Bev said. "That horrible Jeep." She sat up. "You did fine this afternoon."

"Except for the cartwheel."

"Well."

After supper, Snowy finished her algebra. She'd done the rest of her homework in study halls, working hard to keep from thinking. She searched her bookcase for something to reread and chose an Agatha Christie and lay down on the bed. But she already knew whodunit, and she could not tonight enjoy rereading to follow the sleight of hand. She chewed the tip of her ponytail and looked blindly at the page.

Downstairs the phone rang; her mother answered it and called, "Henrietta!"

Laurie followed her down the stairs. Her father was reading the Manchester *Union*, and her mother was opening the Gunthwaite *Herald*. To her, they could have been on the moon.

Her mother said, "It's Julia, something about what Bev wants for her birthday."

"Oh." She sat down beside Kit on the sofa and picked up the receiver. "Hello?"

Julia said, "I suspect that what you need right now is a large scotch to help you go to sleep."

"Does it really help? I'd probably need a gallon."

But they both knew there was no booze in the house. Her father bought a bottle only at Christmastime. Four Roses.

"Look," Julia said. "I won't say making Varsity won't seem important twenty years from now because I know damn well if you don't make it you'll never feel right about yourself. I just wanted to tell you I saw the deer tonight."

So Snowy saw them too, dark silhouettes against the birches, as they came down from the woods to the old apple trees at dusk.

Julia said, "I guess we'd better mention Bev's birthday. She wants that dress in the Lana Lobell catalog?"

"Yes, the mattress-ticking dress."

"Okay. Snowy, be of good cheer. Oh, Lord, that's a pun, isn't it?"

Snowy laughed for her. "It was awful nice of you to call. Thank you."

When she'd hung up, her mother said, "Have you finished your homework?"

"Yes, I'm going to take my bath." She went upstairs. On the hallway wall hung her school pictures, all of them since first grade. There were pigtails, there were frizzy-permanent curls, big bows, French braids, Brownie Scout uniform, grandmother-made dresses, Girl Scout uniform, the junior-high style of a small scarf knotted at the side of the throat, and last year's, her ponytail shorter, her bangs peroxide-bleached. Snowy hardly ever noticed the pictures, but tonight she studied every one.

She bathed and put on pajamas and Noxzema and lay on her bed looking at the book, seeing the deer.

She and Bev walked to school together the next morning and met Puddles at the Gowen Street corner. The sun was out, the weatherman had said the day would be warmer, and spring at last was on its way.

Snowy tried to make a joke. "The day of the execution dawned bright and clear."

"Hmpf," Puddles said. She had dark circles under her eyes. She too had been unable to sleep, and she had stayed up very late, lengthening cotton skirts while sitting on her bed listening to radio programs that kept fading into static.

They walked without talking, past the whistles of Varney's, to the high school, and they didn't go to their lockers to put away their coats; they went directly downstairs. A cluster of girls stood in front of the semifinals list on the gym office door.

Someone called, "You all made it!"

They pushed through. Yes, all the JV's had made semifinals.

Pond, Jean
Snow, Henrietta

Snowy remembered last year, when her name hadn't been on it.

"Whew," Puddles said weakly. "Whew. One down, one to go."

Linda said, "I do not know how I am going to get through this day."

The only good things about the day for Snowy were that she didn't have her period, so she wouldn't have to try to cheer while knotted up with cramps, and that there wasn't a test in any of her classes. Going down the tunnel steps to lunch, she stumbled and nearly fell, and Tom noticed. Tom had wondered why she was so distracted yesterday when they talked at lunch, he'd wondered if she was being hard to get after Saturday night, and he decided two could play the game, glad he hadn't yet asked her out for this weekend. So during this lunch he didn't step down from the platform, and he flirted with Diane Morrissette when she put some paper in the wastebasket.

After school, when Snowy and Puddles were on their way to the locker room, they saw him leaning against the wall near a drinking fountain, talking to Rita.

"Oh, no," Snowy said, "I can't take any more, I can't."

Puddles said, "Forget about him, concentrate on the cheering."

In the locker room, the semifinals girls talked nervously as they put on their gym suits, but Snowy and Linda and Puddles changed silently, then stood in front of the mirror fixing their hair. Rita came running in, gave Snowy a smug glance, and began to change, plotting how to break her Friday night date with Sonny Poor if Tom, who'd kidded around like old times, asked her out.

"Eight cheerleaders," Linda said. "Maybe they'll change their minds and make it nine this year."

Snowy's hands were trembling, and she dropped one of the bobby pins she always used when she was cheering to ensure that her nape hairs would stay up.

"They won't," Puddles said. "You can't enter the cheerleading tournament if you've got more than eight."

And this year the Gunthwaite Varsity cheerleaders had won second place in the tournament, and Gilly was determined to win first place next year.

Once again they sat in the front row of the auditorium. Snowy remembered last year, watching from the balcony the chosen girls.

Rita and Nutty went up.

Charl and Darl went up.

And then Snowy found herself on the stage, between Puddles and Linda, fist on hip.

"T-E-A-M."

"Go, Gunthwaite, Go."

"C'mon and Beat."

As Snowy came up from her jump down, arms outspread, she saw Tom sitting beside Bev in the balcony.

Oh, God, she thought. Oh, God, oh, God, Bev, tell him he must go away, tell him.

Tom had been enjoying himself hugely, listening to Bev being catty about everyone except Snowy and Puddles, watching all the legs, the glimpses of green gym-suit bloomers. He admired Rita's split. But when Snowy ran up on stage, her intensity was so visible that he began to realize this was important to her and might be why she'd seemed upset. He had never paid any attention to cheerleading tryouts; if he'd thought about them he would have figured they were as natural as football was to him, you played football, you made the JV team, you made Varsity, nothing to it, and he'd only stopped in here because he'd seen Bev and thought talking with her would be a pleasanter way of killing time than hanging around Varney's. He watched Snowy run with Puddles and Linda to the side of the stage and saw her await the last and worst ordeal.

Hands up, Puddles ran out into another perfect cartwheel.

Snowy's turn. And she would fall, she knew she would fall. She didn't.

Fist on hip, she stood beside Puddles and looked back at Linda and saw something glint on the floor.

Linda ran forward, flipped, her hand skidded, and she fell.

Linda's face was scarlet as they ran down the stairs, and when they reached the back row, she burst into tears. The twins clutched, and Puddles, Mike completely forgotten, hugged her and said, "You must've done a hundred cartwheels at the games, they know you can do one, you did one yesterday," but Linda sobbed and sobbed. Snowy sat terrified.

After the other girls had finished, the two Varsity girls from the junior class, Joanne Carter and Adele Roberge, who had been judging, went up on stage in their school clothes.

Gilly called, "Rita, Nutty, Charl and Darl!"

They ran up.

Puddles said, "They're figuring out about heights."

"Puddles!" Gilly called.

"Oh, my God," Puddles said, and ran.

Snowy and Linda sat and watched them do "Abnaki Locomotive."

"Okay," Gilly said, "let's try Rita, Puddles, Linda, Snowy, and Diane."

Down front, Diane yelped in surprise.

Snowy and Linda ran for the stage.

Gilly said, "Snowy, you beside Rita, then Diane—"

Snowy stood on the stage, fist on hip, beside Rita, and she could not look up to see Tom judging them.

He automatically, and regretfully, observed the difference in boobs, but then he saw that Snowy's legs were better than Rita's, something he hadn't noticed at JV games and couldn't tell in school clothes, when socks nearly met hems. Maybe, he thought, he could become a leg-man. Or an ass-man? He glanced at his watch.

"Snowy," Gilly said, "try the other end, you and Rita on each end. Okay, 'Abnaki Locomotive.' "

And then Carol Tucker and Nancy Gordon were called up to join the girls on the stage, and Gilly and the Varsity cheerleaders suggested combinations, consulted, tried some more. And then they withdrew to the gym office.

Snowy looked up. Tom was gone.

Darl said, "Do we wait?"

"You bet your life," Puddles said.

So they waited. Bev and the balcony Gang came down, and Snowy took Bev aside, while Rita, who'd also seen Tom, watched. Snowy asked, "Did Tom say anything about me?"

"Well, no, all we did was kid around. About how to tell the twins apart and stuff like that."

Gradually the other girls began to leave, and Bev walked to Snowy's house to get a ride with Fred and inform Snowy's mother Snowy would be late, but the JV's and Diane and Nancy and Carol waited. They sat on the edge of the stage, legs dangling. Puddles asked Snowy to play something on the auditorium piano, and she did a shaky job of one of her recital pieces, the minuet from *Don Juan*. Linda, who played popular, had recovered enough to take over, and she played "Nola" and dimpled when they applauded.

They waited.

Rita said, "We've got to stick it out. If we hang around long enough, *maybe* they'll tell us."

They waited.

The twins played chopsticks.

Nutty said, "I suppose we might as well get dressed."

They went down to the locker room and changed and went back upstairs and sat again on the edge of the stage, not talking at all now, just waiting.

At six o'clock, Gilly appeared. She vaulted onto the stage. "I see," she said, "you waited."

Nobody laughed.

Gilly said, "It's been a difficult decision."

Puddles muttered, "Stop hemming and hawing."

Gilly said, "And we feel every one of you did very well." She studied her clipboard. "It was, as I say, a difficult decision." She cleared her throat. "The Varsity cheerleading squad will be made up of: Rita Beaupre, Joanne Carter—" She looked up. "Oh, these are in alphabetical order. Charlene Fecteau, Darlene Fecteau"—two identical squeaks from the twins—"Marjorie Nutter, Jean Pond, Adele Roberge, and"—Snowy thought she was going to die—"Henrietta Snow."

She went insane, screaming and screaming.

Puddles was hugging her, the chosen girls were shrieking, it was the wildest moment of her life.

Then they realized what the list meant. Linda was the JV who hadn't made it. Linda ran crying from the auditorium, and Charl began to whimper.

Snowy walked with Puddles to the Gowen Street corner. Puddles kept saying, "We're going to have such fun. We're going to have such fun."

As Snowy walked on alone, a cream-colored convertible came toward her down the street. She was so dazed she thought it was an hallucination until Tom stopped and leaned across to open the door for her. He said, clowning, "Going my way, baby?"

She got in.

He said, "I was at the tryouts, but I had to leave, my old man thinks the world will end if we don't have supper on time, but then I called your house, and your mother said you weren't home yet. She was getting worried."

"She knew I'd be late."

"She thought you were at some club meeting, so I told her you were at tryouts and she kind of went ape, and then I came looking for you."

There was a pause. Remembering Snowy's intensity, he didn't dare ask.

Snowy said the words. "I made it."

"My God," he said, "I'm giving a Varsity cheerleader a ride home?"

"Idiot," she said, laughing. She was on his level now.

"Who else made it?" he asked, turning in a driveway and driving back along Chestnut Street.

She told him. There was Rita, there was Puddles, there was Charl, but she was the one he'd phoned and come looking for.

In her driveway, he said, "I don't have to work Friday night. How about the movies?"

"Fine."

He kissed her. "Congratulations."

That night, as she took down her ponytail, she examined the remaining bobby pin, just like the ones that had slipped out of her hair during her cartwheel. They could not possibly, she thought, have made Linda fall.

And if they had, she didn't care.

# II.

KLEENEX carnations, pink and green, were thick on the walls of the gym. The theme of the Junior Prom was Misty Gardens.

Snowy leaned back in her chair and gave a long sigh.

"Well," Tom said, "that's over with."

Puddles said, "Until next year."

"Don't be morbid," Bev told her.

Snowy had torn her favor, a paper rose, to bits. With their dates, she and Bev and Puddles sat at a card table and looked across the gym at the platform looped with pink and green crepe paper where, beneath a flowery arbor, the Queen and her court posed. Flashbulbs popped.

All the girls at the prom were wearing ballerina-length strapless gowns of net over satin taffeta, some with stiff crinoline stoles that snapped into the bodice and made them appear hunchbacked. Puddles was wearing a stole, trying to hide her gaunt shoulderblades, but Bev and Snowy weren't. Bev's gown was pale green, Puddles' was pale blue, and Snowy's was white. Snowy's parents had wanted to know why she couldn't wear her yellow gown she'd worn only once, to the Freshman Dance last year, but she'd pleaded for a new one, and they relented. The gown cost sixteen dollars and ninety-five cents at Yvonne's Apparel. She did wear the jewelry she'd bought last year,

matching gold earclips and choker. She bought new white heels.
To keep their gowns up, Snowy and Bev needed help in their
strapless bras, but they claimed they'd commit suicide if anyone
saw them buying falsies, so it was Puddles who, while Bev and
Snowy innocently drank ice-cream sodas at Sweetland, had
marched into Woolworth's and bought them two pairs of falsies,
cups of rubber breasts complete with nipples. Also under their
gowns they each were wearing a hoop and three layers of crinoline petticoats; seated, the girls were birds in nests.

Most of the boys, including Tom and Roger and Mike, wore
dinner jackets, maroon cummerbunds, and black trousers with
shiny stripes down the pant legs, rented from Dunlap's Department Store.

They watched the girls on the platform, and Puddles said,
"Judy MacGregor. That nobody."

But the boys were examining her interestedly. The selection
of Judy as a member of the court had been the biggest surprise
of the evening. Because she was such a quiet, uninvolved girl,
nobody had noticed until tonight that she was pretty. The only
thing she'd ever done was play the French horn in the marching
band. Standing there holding her gold trophy, she looked
stunned. Beside her stood Adele Roberge, the new co-captain of
the Varsity cheerleading squad; she had a pert dark DA and a
pleased red smile. Beside Adele was Ellen Hatch, the "Junior
Jive" columnist of the *Smoke Signal* and blond and wholesome.
Ellen, however, had been in Snowy and Bev's grammar school,
and they remembered her always as the girl who'd pushed
Nancy Gordon into the brook behind the school and then lied
about it. Beside Ellen stood Brenda Dutile, a popular fluffy brunette and the token General girl.

And on the Dramatics Club throne sat the Queen of the Jun-
ion Prom, Joanne Carter. The other new co-captain, she was
slender and graceful, and Snowy envied her long friendship with
Tom. Happy tears rolled down her lovely cheekbones.

Beside the platform stood the judges, businessmen and their wives, and the chaperons, the superintendent of schools and the principal and two teachers and their wives, all beaming.

And out on the dance floor, the junior girls, who'd had to dance around and around with their dates while the judges chose, were suffocated with sick disappointment.

As the lights dimmed again, and the dinner-jacketed Gunthwaite High School Dance Band pitched into "Cherry Pink and Apple Blossom White," Snowy turned to Tom and saw that he was watching Rita. Rita's date was Jack O'Brien; he and Charl had broken up this spring and Charl was here with Sonny Poor. The twins usually changed boyfriends at the same time, and Darl was now going steady with Victor Andrews. Jack stood talking to Rita. Her gown was aqua, her bare shoulders tan. Snowy and Bev and Puddles too had started sunbathing as early as possible, risking pneumonia for a good tan for the prom. Rita wasn't listening to Jack; she was looking at the platform. She had been so certain she would be on it.

Tom said, "This goddamn shindig ought to be outlawed," while admiring Rita's cleavage. Snowy, he thought, must have to stuff everything but the kitchen sink down her dress to keep it up. He gave Snowy's hair a tug. She was wearing it long and curly. "Want some more punch?"

"No, thank you," she said, jealous of his sympathy for Rita. She was almost positive Tom hadn't had a date with another girl since her birthday, although she worried there might be something she didn't know about during the week of April vacation when she was in Washington, but he still hadn't asked her to go steady. They'd been going out since March, and it was now May 21. He was playing the same game with her that he had with Rita, and Snowy still lived with the nerve-wracking question, will he ask me out again?

He said, "Then let's dance. Only a half hour left."

This was her first Junior Prom. She'd been avidly awaiting it, but now, as Tom whirled her around, she thought with dread of next year's and wished she were at a dance which was free of foreboding, like the Sophomore Dance. She hadn't gone to the Sophomore Dance because Tom had hinted he'd find it a bore and she, feeling sophisticated, agreed. Solar Serenade suddenly became a small thing, compared to a Junior Prom. Bev and Roger didn't go, either, but Mike and Puddles, who were going steady now, had gone because Puddles wanted to show off the decorations she'd helped make. Snowy and Tom had gone to the drive-in theater—The Passion Pit—and seen a Jungle Jim and *Drum Beat* with Alan Ladd. They didn't really see much of the second feature. Afterward, at Hooper's, with around them the kids from the dance all dressed up, Snowy had felt older and nicely sloppy in her blouse and dungarees. So her class dance had consisted for her of going to the school the next day, Sunday, and as a member of the clean-up committee helping to take down what Puddles' committee had put up, the crepe paper and stars and balloons and Outer Space travel posters. The project was much interrupted by Dudley Washburn's pretending to be a cheerleader, using as a megaphone a wastebasket.

They danced. The girls in their gowns were a pastel bouquet. The band played "A Blossom Fell" and "Stardust," and then it played "Goodnight, Sweetheart," and all the weeks of making paper flowers, all the choosing of gowns, all the agonizing hopes culminated and died with the syrupy saxophone.

At Snowy's house, she and Bev put their corsages in the refrigerator. They both had wrist corsages; Bev's was yellow rosebuds, and Snowy's was white carnations, pink rosebuds, and baby's breath. While Tom and Roger waited in the living room with Laurie and Kit, they went upstairs to change. In her bedroom, Snowy eased her feet out of her shoes and again wondered how her mother could wear high heels to work every day. She took off her gown and petticoats and hung them in her closet, but in the spare room Bev tossed her gown over the rocker and left her petticoats in hummocks on the floor. Thinking about next year's Junior Prom, they took off their jewelry and nylons and garter belts and bras, their breasts hot from the rubber falsies, and put on their regular bras and their socks and dungarees and white blouses, tails out, and sneakers. Snowy went into the spare room and saw Bev lift the little gold basketball off the bureau and fasten the chain around her neck.

Snowy said, "Tom went steady with you right off the bat."

"Was it?"

"Well, a couple of weeks after your first date."

"Snowy, I don't know. He's just determined to be fancy-free."

"Then why isn't he taking out other girls?" Snowy herself was determined not to let him go any farther until she had his gold football. But he hadn't tried, and she still didn't know what farther was.

Bev said, "He's going stead*ily* with you."

"Big deal," Snowy said.

They went downstairs carrying their overnight cases for Puddles' house, and Bev and Roger drove to Roger's house while he changed, and Snowy and Tom drove to Tom's.

It was on Morning Street, a narrow white clapboard house with dark-green shutters and a side porch. A tall elm loomed over the lawn. She hoped she could wait in the car, but he said, "Come on in," and so she was led along the porch to the side door and into the meat-loaf-smelling kitchen. She had never been inside the house before. The linoleum was a red-and-gray checkerboard, there was a pantry with a roller towel hanging on its open door, the curtains had a pattern of strawberries, and the refrigerator top was heaped with a clutter of *Farmer's Almanacs*, flashlights, ashtrays, and eraserless pencils. Snowy looked at the wooden table and tried to imagine Tom's eating supper with his parents and his little brother, who was ten years younger than Tom and a last try for a daughter when his father came back from the war. His older brother was away, in the Army.

They walked through the dining room into the living room. Tom said, "Have a seat," and went on into the front hall and up the stairs. Snowy sat very straight in an overstuffed chair, her hands folded. She was as motionless as, framed under glass on the wall, the blue butterfly among dried flowers against a background of milkweed fluff.

But she noted everything, from the Morris chair to the copies of *Saturday Evening Post* and *Reader's Digest* on the cobbler's bench coffee table.

Tom returned wearing chinos and a blue sweat shirt, carrying his letter sweater over his shoulder. "All set," he said.

Outdoors, he looked up at the stars. "I didn't put the top down because I figured you wouldn't want your hair to blow before the dance. Think it's still warm enough?"

"Sure," she said, delighted. She watched him unsnap the top and get in the car and pull a lever in the middle of the windshield and then start the car. The top crumpled into itself. He got out and snapped the tonneau cover over it. They drove off, and her hair blew, and she felt extremely glamorous.

The party was at Victor Andrews' grandfather's camp on the lake. Tom had been there before, but they nearly became lost in the maze of little dirt roads that twisted through the woods, and soon the Chevy was part of a string of old cars whose headlights searched the signposts nailed helter-skelter with names. Then they came around a curve into a traffic jam.

"Here we are," Tom said.

They parked at the side of the road and got out. In the darkness all the kids around them were shadows she didn't know, and she was glad when Tom took her hand as they walked down the lawn to the camp. The porch light showed kids cooking hot dogs at the stone fireplace.

"Look," Tom said, "some damn fools are swimming. Victor thought they might."

"It must be awful cold."

"It is," he said. "I always used to go in the first time on my birthday, then I started chickening out in my old age, but we were here Sunday opening up the camp and putting the raft out and stuff, so I got my birthday swim after all. Got thrown in, to be exact."

"Your birthday?" Snowy said. Bev thought his birthday was sometime in the spring but couldn't remember when; Snowy had hoped Tom would mention it and had bought him a huge funny birthday card that cost a dollar.

"The fifteenth," he said.

It had been last Sunday, and she hadn't known. She wondered what she should do with the birthday card.

"Happy birthday," she said.

"Snowy!" Puddles called from the end of the wharf. She was sitting alone holding a can of beer and a cigarette.

The main thing they learned in Washington was to inhale. They'd stayed at a Girl Scout camp; their troop had a troop house where they made breakfasts of juice, powdered scrambled eggs, burned toast, and cocoa, and prepared the sandwiches for their sight-seeing lunches, and, when they didn't have supper at a Hot Shoppe, cooked Girl Scout suppers like Rum-Tum-Tiddy, but they slept in a colony of tents, four girls to a tent. The first day of sight-seeing, Puddles slipped away and bought a pack of cigarettes, and that night in their tent she and Snowy and Bev and Nancy Gordon got sick and dizzy, but they learned to inhale. The flashbulb picture Snowy had taken of them became notorious; she did not show it to her parents.

Tom said, "You want a beer or a Coke?"

"Beer," said Snowy firmly, who had never drunk a beer in her life.

"Be right back," he said, and went up the stairs to the porch. Snowy walked out on the wharf and sat down beside Puddles. Their dungareed legs dangled above the dark water.

Puddles said, "Want a cigarette?"

"Okay," Snowy said and lit up, hoping she looked terribly old. "Where's Mike?"

"I don't know," Puddles said, "and I don't care."

But she did. Startled, Snowy saw she was on the verge of tears. "Hey, what happened?"

"He doesn't like the way I dance."

"He what?"

"When we were coming here, he said he's been wanting to tell me I shouldn't keep looking around at all the other people when we're dancing, I should just pay attention to him." Puddles' voice quavered. She threw her cigarette in the lake. "And I got mad and told him off, I mean why *can't* I look around and see what's going on, that's one reason you go to a dance! And then he got mad, and here we are, the big night, all ruined." Mike's class ring on a gold chain hung just above her breasts. She picked it up, studied it, and let it drop back.

She said, "I think I'll get drunk."

"You could apologize," Snowy said.

"Why? He's the one who's wrong, not me. I wonder how many beers it takes."

"Then don't apologize. You could just go find him and be with him like nothing had happened."

"And only last night," Puddles said, "he went out of control, and my God, you ought to've seen the mess my slacks were, I had to sneak into the house and wash them off in the bathroom, there I was scrubbing away and praying Mom wouldn't come in, the things I've gone through for him."

Snowy stared at her. "Out of control?" she asked tentatively. "Mess?"

Then she saw Tom walking toward them along the wharf. "Hi, Puddles," he said, giving Snowy a beer. "Where's Mike?"

Puddles stood up and threw her beer can into the lake and stalked off toward the camp.

Tom sat down beside Snowy. "What's the matter with her?"

"They had a fight."

"They've had fights before."

"I guess this was a real doozy."

"Oh."

Snowy took a sip of beer. It wasn't sweet, and it smelled like skunk.

Tom's arm went around her, and she forgot Puddles and snuggled against him. They sat together at the end of the wharf and looked out at the lake.

He said, "A year from now, it'll almost be over."

"Mmm."

"I keep putting off figuring out what I should do. What are you going to do?"

"After I graduate? Go to college."

"I've got the service. I can enlist, or I can get a job and wait around to be drafted."

Uniforms and guns. She shivered.

"You cold?" he asked. "Did you leave your jacket in the car?" He was wearing his letter sweater now, and he took it off and draped it over her shoulders.

He hadn't given it to her, but at least she was wearing it. "Thank you," she said. The sweater felt on her exactly as she thought it would, big and warm and secure. "How come they're still drafting guys? There's no war anymore. Even Korea's over with."

"Damned if I know. So life will be as much of a pain in the ass as possible, I guess."

They looked at the lake.

Snowy said, "Bev's mother mentioned cabinetmaking."

"She remembered that? Not much future in it nowadays. You'll be going to UNH?"

She took a deep breath and told him her goal. "I'm going to apply at Smith and Mount Holyoke."

"Where are they?"

"Down in Massachusetts."

"Not far."

"No."

Tom said, "The other day Mr. Stoddard got me into his office." Mr. Stoddard was the high school principal. "He talked to me about being a shop teacher, I guess Mr. Nelson had been talking to him."

"A shop teacher?" She didn't care that he was taking shop instead of College Prep; it didn't matter here and now. But grown-up, she thought, was different, and she was ashamed of herself for wishing he'd said English teacher or algebra or history. Then she thought how ridiculous she was to consider being married to a shop teacher when they weren't even going steady.

Tom said, "Stoddard thinks I could get in at Rumford Teachers' College. You know, over in Rumford."

"Oh."

"The trouble is money. I haven't exactly saved every cent I've ever earned. And anyway, four more years of school? Jesus."

"It's hard to believe it'll ever end."

They brooded. Suddenly running footsteps shook the wharf, and they turned and saw Roger charging at them to push them in. Snowy shrieked. Bev, running ladylikely behind him, was wringing her hands and wailing, "*Please*, Roger, I beg of you!" and he screeched to a stop and stood looking down at them.

He said, "You must admit it's a temptation."

Tom said, "How come you took so long getting here? Get lost?"

"Ha-ha," Roger said. "Let's go eat, I'm starving."

"So am I," Snowy said, standing up and slipping her arms into the sleeves of the sweater. The sleeves flapped over her hands, and as she rolled them up, Bev whispered, "You've got it!"

Snowy shook her head. "He only put it on me because he thought I was cold." She and Bev followed the boys along the wharf. "Puddles and Mike had a big fight."

"Damn. Hey, is that beer you're drinking?"

"It's vile. I can't imagine how anyone can drink enough to get drunk. That's what Puddles said she's going to do."

At the stone fireplace, Darl was overseeing the food, being very hostessy and competent, but still the hot dogs she gave them were charred on the outside and raw on the inside and tasted like all the Girl Scout hot dog cookouts Snowy and Bev had ever been to.

The banking was smooth with pine needles. They sat down, and Bev giggled. "This reminds me of Blue Island."

Snowy giggled too, egging her on. "Puddles' hot dogs or anything else?"

"Blue Island?" Tom said.

Roger said, "Here we go." He'd heard it before.

"Well," Bev said. She loved telling stories. "About this time during eighth grade the Girl Scouts, all the troops in town, had a big meeting out on Blue Island out there. It lasted three days, and we camped out in pup tents, and we were supposed to cook all kinds of things like goulash on the fires, but Puddles was going through a hot dog phase, that's all she would eat, so she brought along a supply, her pack was full of them. And of course the hot dogs were better than goulash, so we all ate them and the troop leaders were in despair." She paused for dramatic effect. "Blue Island was the time we practically got drummed out of the Girl Scouts."

"No kidding?" Tom said, looking at Snowy.

Bev said, "Puddles was going out with Ron Moore, Snowy was going out with Joe Spencer—"

Tom asked sharply, "Who's Joe Spencer?"

Snowy said, "Just a guy in our class."

"—and I," Bev said, "was going out with Frankie Richardson, whose folks have a camp and he had a little motorboat, and he and Joe and Ron were mad because we would be away those three whole days and they kept saying they were going to come out and see us, but naturally we didn't believe them, and then what happens but the second night we wake up with the tent nearly collapsing around us, and Ron and Joe and Frankie were crawling in." She took one of Roger's potato chips. "Well, the boat had made a horrible racket coming across the lake, and it woke up the troop leaders and they started a manhunt through the tents. Puddles and Snowy—sorry, Snowy, have to mention this—Snowy was wearing her hair shorter then, and she and Puddles had their hair up in pincurls, and Joe kept blinking his flashlight at them while they were desperately trying to take it down, and we were all *dying*, and Mrs. Simpson and Mrs. Cilley were getting closer and closer, and everyone was awake and wanting to know what was the matter, and then the tent fell down. There was this canvas and ropes tangling us all up and the guys trying to claw their way out and bobby pins all over the place, and they broke out and ran like mad for the boat, and we heard it go zooming across the lake, so we knew they'd got away, but there *we* were underneath the tent. Mrs. Simpson said we'd disgraced the memory of Juliette Low."

Snowy, who had been terrified at the time, was now rolling around laughing hysterically. Tom grabbed at her, shouting, "So you let men into your tent, do you?" and they rolled together, wrestling and tickling.

"Ah, me," Roger said to Bev. "Isn't it nice to see the children enjoying themselves?"

Snowy had drunk all her beer, vile though it was, and she looked out of Tom's stranglehold at Bev and said, embarrassed, "Let's go inside the camp. I'd like to see the inside."

Tom said, "Want a guided tour?"

Bev said primly, "We can manage, thank you."

It was a big old dark-green camp, with wicker chairs on the high porch. Snowy and Bev stepped into the mildewy living room. Firelight flickered, and they saw that Mike was sitting in one of the armchairs in front of the fireplace, kissing Judy MacGregor on his lap.

Snowy gasped.

Bev took her wrist and hurried her across the room to a little hall and up the stairway.

"Damn," Bev said. "Damn damn damn."

"Where's Judy's date? Who was he?"

"I don't know." Bev opened a door. "Oops," she said and hastily closed it. "A scene of mad passion, Diane and Dudley. Maybe that's the bathroom over there."

It was. Bev pulled the string that turned on the overhead light and found the hook-and-eye lock, while Snowy unzipped her dungarees. The toilet had an overhead tank, something Snowy always hated because she feared the tank would fall and crush her ludicrously dead.

She said, "What do we do?"

"Look for Puddles, I guess, and make sure she's okay. That damn Mike."

"Men," Snowy said, and wiped herself.

"Judy certainly is reaping fast rewards for the Queen's court."

"It won't be much of a reward if Puddles murders her." Snowy stood up, pulled up her underpants and dungarees, yanked the toilet chain, and jumped back. The rush of water sounded like Niagara.

Bev unzipped her dungarees. "You could forget to return Tom's sweater."

Snowy picked some pine needles off it. She inspected her face in the cloudy mirror tacked over the washbasin as she washed her hands. "That wouldn't be right, would it."

They went downstairs and peeped into the living room. Mike and Judy were still in a big clinch.

Bev said, "I hope they've come up for air. Let's check the kitchen."

Puddles wasn't there, but Tom was, talking to Charl and Sonny Poor. Drinking beer, Tom leaned against the old black iron sink that was just like the one which had been in Snowy's house when they first moved in. There was a rubble of hot dog rolls and empty beer cans and Coke bottles on the oilcloth-covered table.

Charl said anxiously, "Did you see Mike with Judy?"

"We certainly did," Bev said. "Has anyone seen Puddles?"

"No," they said, and Tom said, "Did you look upstairs?"

"Tom!" Charl said.

"Well, maybe she's getting revenge."

Bev said, "We looked in one room, that's all."

"Want a beer?"

Snowy and Bev glanced at each other. "Okay."

He got them beers out of the refrigerator. "You really worried? You and Roger could start hunting outdoors, and we'll check the camp and then join you. Where the hell did the church key get to?"

Charl said, "We'll help, we'll ask everyone."

"A posse!" Bev said.

Tom found the can opener on the table, and while his back was turned, Charl clutched at Snowy and whispered, "You've got his sweater, I'm so glad for you!"

Tom handed Snowy a beer, and she didn't have to answer. He said, "All set?"

Snowy and Tom went into the hallway and looked into the living room. More kids were kissing in the armchairs, and Mike and Judy were still at it.

Tom slid his beerless hand under Snowy's hair, holding her lightly by the neck as they went up the stairs.

She said, "That's the door Bev opened. Diane and Dudley were inside."

"Maybe there's been a turnover." He opened the door, looked in, said, "Sorry," and closed it.

She took a nervous sip of beer.

He opened the next door. Oh, shit, he thought. Rita was crying while Jack held her and swigged beer over her head. Tom quickly shut the door and crossed the hall and opened another. "Sorry," he said, closed it, and reported to Snowy, "Two sets of bunk beds and all in use."

Snowy gulped beer. Did Victor's grandparents know what would go on at his party? She imagined what her father would do if he knew.

The door at the end of the hall opened, and Adele Roberge and Sam Page came out, arms around each other. Adele's hair was mussed, her blouse was buttoned wrong, and Sam's eyes were glazed. Tom said, "Hi," and they said, "Hi," and moved on past like sleepwalkers.

Tom laughed, and he and Snowy looked at each other, and then they were wildly kissing, spilling beer all over the floor.

Snowy whispered, "We're supposed to be hunting."

"I know," Tom said. He opened the door Adele and Sam had come out of. "Just to make sure," he said, but his arm was around her waist, and she went into the room with him, and he closed the door behind them.

Nobody else was there. He took her can of beer and placed it and his on the bedside table, took off his glasses, and turned to her. She flung her arms around his neck, and while they kissed, he edged her closer and closer to the double bed until she fell backward onto it, Tom on top. She didn't have much breath left to get knocked out of her. She felt him pressed against her, and he was unbuttoning her blouse, and after the front seat of his car the lumpy old bed seemed a cloud far away in the darkness. She couldn't stop herself; as they rolled over and he kissed her breast, she reached out and put her hand on that bulge.

It was a wonder Tom didn't bite her nipple off, he was so shocked.

He'd been hoping to lead her up to this someday, the moment he could take her hand and place it on his God-awful hard-on, and she had gone and done it herself. Jesus H. Christ.

And Snowy was so petrified at what she'd done she couldn't move her hand. They lay stockstill together, amazed.

Then just when Tom recovered, teeming with mad visions of ripping her clothes off and sending her dungarees and blouse and underwear sailing around the room, she jerked her hand away. He damn near shot his load.

She said, "We've got to find Puddles."

The fucking hell with Puddles, he thought. Then reason returned. Aha, he thought, aha. But easy does it.

"Okay," he said, and kissed her nose.

She hooked her bra and tremblingly buttoned her blouse, pushed up the sleeves of the sweater, and grabbed at her beer and took a big swallow. He, behind her, adjusted things. His shorts were rather sticky.

"Well," he said, and put on his glasses. "I guess you've got the cigarettes." He slid a flattened pack of Lucky Strikes out of the sweater pocket and lit one. Over the spurt of flame Tom and Snowy looked at each other. "Oh," he said. "You want one?"

"Yes, please."

He gave her his and lit another. In the hall, even the dim light embarrassed her. He put his arm around her and they went downstairs, through the couples in the living room, out to the porch.

The night was cool now, yet still her right hand, awkwardly holding the cigarette, felt burning hot and separate, not the hand of Henrietta Snow.

More couples were necking on the porch, but when Tom and Snowy went down to the lawn, they saw horseplay on the little beach, much chasing and shouting and giggling.

"I guarantee," Tom said, "that somebody's going to get thrown in."

"I don't see Puddles anywhere, do you?"

"Could she've gotten a ride home? Or started walking?"

Snowy could picture Puddles stamping wrathfully down the dark dirt road. "Oh, God, maybe. Should we go look for her?"

Tom glanced at his watch. "It's nearly two, what time do you have to be in at Puddles'?"

"My father said two o'clock, but Puddles said her mother just said a reasonable hour."

"Whatever that is. There's Roger and Bev."

They were coming out of the woods, and they were covered with so many leaves and pine needles they might have been camouflaged.

"Hi," Tom said. "Hope you've been hunting as hard as we have."

They all heard a frail scream.

Roger said, "Somebody's getting thrown in."

"*Help!*"

Bev and Snowy said together, "That's Puddles!"

They ran down to the beach, but the kids had stopped fooling around and were looking out at the lake.

"*Help!*"

"The raft," Victor said. "Somebody's on the raft."

Snowy said, "Oh, my God."

Tom tossed away his cigarette and said, "Well, looks like I get another birthday swim," and took off his sneakers.

"Tom—" Snowy said.

He tugged off his socks, hopping. "Don't worry, I've got gills."

He had been a lifeguard at the public beach last summer, supreme above everyone on his high white platform, sometimes flirting with Bev and never noticing Snowy. Bev had suggested she pretend to drown. Snowy hadn't dared.

Roger said, "If she swam out there, why can't she swim back?"

"I don't know," Bev said, shivering, "but she must be frozen."

Snowy said, "Isn't there a rowboat or something?"

Victor said, "We took it to my house to get painted."

Roger untied his sneakers. "I'll play buddy, buddy."

Tom yanked off his sweat shirt and handed it and his glasses to Snowy, emptied his pants' pockets of wallet, coins, and car keys, and gave them to her with his watch. She hugged all these possessions of his and said, "Be careful. Puddles is crazy."

"You bet."

In his chinos and T-shirt he ran into the water, dived, and started swimming a strong Australian crawl toward the raft. Roger followed, and then the kids could see nothing but two white T-shirts moving through darkness.

"Towels," Victor said, "dry clothes," and he and Darl raced for the camp.

Bev said, "Shouldn't someone go get Mike? I mean, if this is her grandstand play, what if he misses it?"

Even in a crisis, Bev thought of strategy.

Sonny Poor said, "I'll go get the bastard."

Now they couldn't see Tom or Roger at all. But the screams had ceased. The kids stood silent, peering.

Snowy said, "There they are."

Tom swam toward the beach, towing Puddles, Roger swimming beside her.

Snowy completely forgot about her sneakers and ran into the water to Tom as he stood up with Puddles. "Oh, Tom, oh, Tom—"

"Hi," Puddles said. Her teeth chattered. "Hi there."

"Puddles!" Mike yelled, splashing up to them. "What the hell, are you all right?"

Roger said, "She's drunk out of her mind."

"I am not," Puddles said, and staggered. Mike seized her.

Necking disturbed, kids were running down to the beach from the camp. Snowy was almost incoherent. "Come on," she babbled, "come on in by the fire, come get warm," and Tom put an icy arm around her shoulders as she rushed him toward the porch. Puddles wobbled and swayed, and Mike picked her up and carried her. In the living room, Victor was prodding the fire, and Darl ran downstairs with blankets and towels. Snowy thrust her armload of Tom's belongings at him and said, "Go change. We'll get her out of those clothes upstairs."

"You ought to keep her by the fire."

"Strip her with everyone watching? Not even Puddles. She'd kill us."

Puddles lolled and giggled and then began to cry.

Mike said, "Christ, Puddles. Christ, Puddles."

"There was," Roger said, "one empty six-pack on the raft. I didn't stop for it. And there was this." He held up Puddles' sodden poplin jacket. "She must've put the beer in her jacket and tied the sleeves around her neck."

"And," Puddles sobbed, "a church key. I have to go to the bathroom."

"Six beers?" Tom said. "I bet you do."

Snowy grabbed a blanket and towels from Darl, and she and Bev maneuvered Puddles up the stairs. The bathroom door was locked. Snowy knocked, then banged.

Rita opened the door. Her eyes were swollen from crying, but she saw very clearly Tom's letter sweater on Snowy. "What happened to Puddles?"

"She went for a swim."

Rita hiccuped. "Jack's passed out."

A party wasn't considered a success unless Jack O'Brien passed out at it.

Puddles howled, "I'm going to pee my pants!"

Snowy and Bev pushed her by Rita, unzipped her dungarees and pulled her underpants down, and propped her on the toilet. Rita watched from the doorway as Snowy toweled Puddles' hair and Bev unbuttoned her blouse. Bev said, "Her underwear'd better come off too, she's soaked to the skin."

Rita said, tonight's disappointment flaring into taunts, "Haven't got his football yet, have you. How come the sweater, did you say you were cold?"

Snowy didn't reply.

"Well," Rita said, "I need a ride home, I guess maybe I'll go see if he'll give me one."

Snowy said, "You do that," and slammed the door on her.

Puddles asked, "Where's Mike?"

"Downstairs," Bev said. "He saw the end of the rescue. How did you think of swimming out there?"

Puddles sniffled. "It's so funny," she said, dragging at the toilet-paper roll, "I feel like I'm a million miles away. Or are you a million miles away? So I couldn't swim back. Where's Mike?"

"Downstairs," Bev said patiently.

There was a knock on the door, and Darl looked in. "This is all I could find," she said, handing them an old chenille bathrobe. "Will it do?"

"Yes," Snowy said, pulling off Puddles' dungarees. "Thanks."

Puddles began to cry again. "That Judy MacGregor, that stupid nobody playing her whatchamacallit in the stupid band."

Bev said, "He was just trying to make you jealous, that's all," but doubted this was true.

Puddles perked up. "I showed her, didn't I?"

They got her into the bathrobe, wrapped her in the blanket, and helped her down the stairs. In the kitchen, Tom and Roger had taken off their chinos and shorts and put on the ragged dungarees and torn chinos Victor found for them; the pants didn't fit, but, as Victor said, "It's either these or my grandmother's old bathing suit." They'd peeled off their T-shirts and Tom put his sweat shirt and Roger his sweater back on, and now in the living room they sat on the floor in front of the fire, which crackled and roared, and fortified themselves with beer. Rita knelt beside Tom, boobs against his arm, toweling his crew cut.

Snowy halted. A month ago she would have pretended not to see. She let go of Puddles so suddenly that Puddles and Bev reeled backward and she shoved her way through the crowd to the fireplace.

Tom looked up. His grin became sheepish. Rita ignored her and continued toweling.

Tom said, "How's Puddles?"

Snowy took off the letter sweater and handed it to him.

He said, "I'm okay."

"No," she said. "Put it on."

Rita said, "She's afraid you'll catch a big bad cold."

Tom said, "Snowy, your feet."

Snowy for the first time realized how squelchy her socks and sneakers were.

Tom stood. Rita rocked back on her heels.

Tom said, "Let's go," and Mike came running in from outdoors and said, "I got the cars started, the heaters are on, and I put your top up."

Snowy was too triumphant to notice, as she and Tom and Bev and Roger left with Mike carrying Puddles, Judy MacGregor crouched miserable in the porch glider, her evening of glory wrecked. Her discarded date, having got drunk with the stag boys, was vomiting in the woods.

Mike said, "If Puddles' folks are up, what do we tell them?"

Bev said, "That the kids were fooling around and she fell in."

They helped him insert Puddles into his car and watched them drive off.

"Honestly," Bev said.

Tom and Snowy got into Tom's car, and the warmth was as welcome as in winter. Tom tossed the letter sweater on the front seat and his wet clothes in the back seat. Snowy draped her jacket around her shoulders and stayed sitting on her own side, holding out her feet to the heater. All the way to Puddles' house the sweater lay between them like a question.

They parked behind Mike's car in the driveway, and Snowy led Tom through the side door and the kitchen to the living room, where they found Mike sitting on the edge of the pulled-out divan where Puddles sprawled asleep.

He said, "Nobody's awake."

Snowy said, "Go make yourselves some coffee or something," and snatched the pajamas Mrs. Pond had laid on one pillow and pulled Puddles out of the bathrobe. She had got the tops on her when Bev arrived.

Roger called from the kitchen, "Can't I come help?"

"Shh!" Bev and Snowy said, pulling up the pajama bottoms.

They tucked Puddles in and looked at each other. Around them, the familiar room of slipcovered chairs, television set, Puddles' brothers' comic books, her father's newspaper and her mother's knitting bag, seemed changed, invaded by her drunkenness.

Snowy said, "I wonder if her ring will tarnish."

Puddles snored.

Bev said, "Serve Mike right. What do we do with the bathrobe and blanket so her folks won't know?"

"Let's ask the guys."

In the kitchen, the kettle was boiling and Tom and Roger were searching cupboards for instant coffee.

Tom said, "I'll stick them in my trunk and give them back to Victor on Monday. Okay with you, Mike?"

Mike sat nervous at the table. "Sure, fine. Is she okay? Look, I've got to be going, my feet are freezing."

He fled, and Bev wrung out Puddles' bundle of clothes and hung them on the branches of the clothes-drying rack on the wall over the register. "You're the one who wakes up earliest, Snowy. If her folks aren't up yet, and these are dry, stick them in the hamper and her folks'll never know."

"Okay." Snowy reached down the instant coffee and made four cups. Bev and Roger carried theirs into the living room, supposedly to keep an eye on Puddles.

Tom said, "Your overnight thing, it's still in the car. Have you got slippers in it?"

"Um, yes," Snowy said, acknowledging she owned slippers.

He went outdoors.

She almost fell asleep in the wooden kitchen chair. The kitchen smelled of the geraniums in the window and on the kitchen table. Mrs. Pond always kept some geraniums blooming, and Puddles said she always had to pick petals out of her food.

Tom came in, and Snowy twitched awake and fumbled with her sneakers' laces. Embarrassed, she opened the overnight case; her pink polka dot pajamas and her underwear and sweat shirt for tomorrow all had to be dug up to get to her slippers at the bottom. She saw Tom looking at her bare feet. Snowy hated her feet. Puddles' feet were long and narrow, and Bev's were cute with small plump toes like a child's, but hers were just feet. She quickly put on her fuzzy blue slippers.

Tom was wearing his sweater. He picked her up and sat down in the kitchen rocker. "Some night."

"Yes," she said, her cheek against his chest. "Thank you for the corsage and everything."

There was a silence, and as it grew longer and longer, it grew tense, and instead of falling asleep Snowy became more and more alert.

Tom said, "I suppose you've guessed. I'm not much of a one for going steady."

She fairly quivered.

"It seems to me," he said, "it's just a formality, if you know what I mean. But maybe—"

She didn't say a word.

And so he had to produce it, the little gold football he'd kept in the glove compartment since April for emergencies, like the contraceptives. Getting the overnight case, he had told himself that the football, after the bedroom, might clinch matters, but now he wasn't thinking so much of the bedroom as the way she'd come splashing toward him through the lake, and he was very confused. He took the small white box out of his sweater pocket.

She opened it and saw on white cotton the little gold football. She turned it over and read his initials engraved on the back. TBF. The kitchen light shimmered in her eyes.

He put his letter sweater around her shoulders.


"And Saturday the Key Club is sponsoring a paper drive," Mrs. Moulton said, and laid the list of notices down. The Latin II and Junior English teacher and Snowy's homeroom teacher, she was also the pretty teacher, with a taste for sheer blouses through which her bra and slip straps could be seen, and a habit of sitting on the edge of her desk, skirt hitched up, one high-heeled foot on the wastebasket. The boys slavered; the girls thought her a bitch. "And, oh, yes, a note was sent to have you go down to the assembly, Henrietta. Joe, take the attendance sheet to the office."

Snowy's desk was at the back of the room, beside Dudley's. She asked him, "*Their* assembly?" The freshmen and sophomores, and the juniors and seniors, alternated using the auditorium for assemblies Wednesday mornings, and this was the juniors' and seniors' week.

"Uh-oh," he said. "I think it's some kind of awards assembly."

"NFL?" she said. "I'm supposed to get my NFL membership certificate sometime. And my *Smoke Signal* certificate. But—"

"Yes," Dudley said. "But so am I. So are a lot of us. What do you want to bet it's the Sophomore Trophy?"

She gaped. "Of course not."

"Well, I got the Freshman Plaque, they won't let me hog the show, and who else?"

"Plenty. There's Nancy and Jerry and—and—"

"Bet you ten cents."

The assembly double bell rang.

"Ten cents?" Snowy said. "All right. It'll be the easiest dime I ever made in my life."

But as she walked along the corridor, her arms feeling strangely bookless, and found herself a lone sophomore in the stream of upperclassmen, her heart began to pound. She went down the stairs, entered the auditorium, and stood uncertainly while the upperclassmen moved past.

Mr. Foster, escorting in a senior homeroom, tapped her on the shoulder. "Front row, young lady."

"Thank you."

She walked down the aisle. She had become even more adept at spotting Tom, and she saw him sitting over on the left-hand side, but he was talking to Joanne Carter and he didn't see her.

Two freshmen were sitting in the front row on the right, Becky Harris and Oliver Reynolds. Snowy sat down beside them, and their three awed faces looked up at the lectern and microphone and the National Honor Society members seated on the stage.

Roger, startled, said to himself, I'll be damned, and winked at Snowy.

She swallowed and folded her hands.

Mr. Stoddard, the principal, walked onstage and spoke solemnly of the National Honor Society's high standards, and introduced Mr. Knight, the U.S. history teacher and NHS adviser, who said, "As you know, each year the faculty chooses new members of the National Honor Society from the junior class and also the recipients of the Freshman Plaque and Sophomore Trophy."

There must, Snowy thought, be some mistake.

Mr. Knight said, "I am happy to announce that this year the new members are Larry Clark—would you please each stand up and come up to the stage—Larry Clark, Mary Clement, Ellen Hatch, and Priscilla Morgan."

Snowy watched them cross the stage, shake hands with Mr. Knight, and stand beside the other members.

Mr. Knight said, "As often happens, this year joint recipients of the Freshman Plaque were chosen. Rebecca Harris and Oliver Reynolds!"

"Oh," Becky said. "Oh."

They scurried up to the stage, and Mr. Knight gave the plaque to them and handed them two small trophy cups. "The plaque," he explained, "goes back to the trophy case, but these trophies are for you to keep."

Snowy sat alone.

"The Sophomore Trophy," Mr. Knight said, "is annually awarded to the most outstanding sophomore. This year I am very happy to present it to Henrietta Snow."

Tom nearly fell out of his seat.

Snowy walked up the stairs and across the stage. "Thank you," she said to Mr. Knight. The trophy was big and heavy, and she cradled it against her as she walked over to stand beside the freshmen, praying she wouldn't drop it. Roger came forward and announced the winner of the Good Citizenship Award, Gene Chabot, chosen by the NHS members, but Snowy didn't hear him. She read the history of the names engraved on the trophy and saw that it had been awarded jointly to Roger and Kathy McKenna two years ago and Larry Clark last year. Then her name. She looked at the little gold trophy cup she could keep. Snowy had always got 100 percents in spelling, but she was so stupefied by the award that she stared moments at the little trophy before she realized it was engraved OUTSTANDING SOPHMORE.

And suddenly as asizzle with giggles as ginger ale with bubbles, she looked directly at Tom in the audience. He grinned back, proud.

That summer Snowy learned how to make change, how to make sundaes and frappes and sodas and milk shakes and banana splits, and how to write waitress-shorthand on her order pad, ht. dg., choc. fr., hamb. w/o., ht. butsc. sund.

She and Bev worked at Sweetland, Main Street's old-fashioned restaurant of dark high-backed booths and a flashy new jukebox. They considered themselves lucky to get jobs here; it was more desirable than Hooper's because it didn't stay open late, it closed at six every night except Friday, when it closed at nine. They worked part time, from noon until six, and on Fridays from nine to two and five to nine. Snowy had Tuesdays off, and Bev Thursdays. Puddles, working as a cashier at the A&P supermarket farther along Main Street, came over to visit them at Sweetland during her breaks.

Snowy also learned that work was hell, but money was wonderful. In their white nylon aprons over white nylon short-sleeved uniforms over white shadow-proof slips, in their white socks and sneakers, Snowy and Bev padded briskly up and down the aisle when they were working on the booths and self-importantly performed their concocting show in front of the seated audience when they were working on the soda fountain, and all the while they hated every moment and loathed every customer. But they earned twenty-three dollars a week, plus nickel-and-dime tips, and before work they would check out the stores, feeling very wealthy. They bought records and summer clothes and school clothes, and Snowy bought a white leather jacket just like Gloria's that cost thirty dollars.

Tom had decided lifeguard work was boring; although the girl watching was okay, one summer was all he wanted of children watching and reading Mickey Spillanes through prescription sunglasses in the scorching sun. And he didn't want to return to his earlier working-paper jobs at the Karamel Korn stand or the bowling alley at the lake, so he took a job working construction, which was just as boring, but it got your muscles in shape for football. He and Snowy started going out every night until her father said this was too often and limited her to three nights a week. Snowy fought and won four nights, Monday and Wednesday and Friday and Saturday. Sometimes they went to the indoor movies, but mostly they went to the Passion Pit. Sometimes they went night swimming; the public beach was closed at night, but the lake's shoreline had not yet been completely bought up by summer people and developers, and they went to a neglected scrap of beach in the woods. Snowy's bathing suit that summer was a white cotton one-piece with a pattern of little blue gingerbreadmen and layers of ruffles over her bottom. The first time she had to say, "I can't go swimming tonight," she was so embarrassed she stammered. Tom only laughed and said, "You don't time things too well, do you?" Sometimes they just drove around, the top down, and bought fried onion rings and Cokes at Riley's Drive-in Restaurant near the lake.

And once they got dressed up and went to the dance hall at the lake with Bev and Roger and Puddles and Mike. The rickety old dance hall, which had barely withstood the bunny hop craze, seemed a place of fantasy to Snowy. There was a bandstand, and on the ceiling there were pink and blue and green lights blinking through gossamer bunting. Roger had wangled a pint of vodka, and they felt as grown up as the adults sitting around them at little tables, drinking booze hidden in the soft drinks the dance hall sold. The girls had two vodka and orange-ades each and became extremely silly, yet Snowy danced better than she ever had, and when toward the end of the evening the band began to play Old Favorites and everyone began singing as they danced, Tom and Snowy sang, too. "Heart of my heart," they sang, "I love that melody," and they swooped around the floor.

But Puddles and Mike's romance did not survive the summer. They had other fights, and then one night they progressed, on a blanket beside the car in the woods, from dry-humping to a blow job which convinced Mike that the ultimate was attainable, and the next night when they were baby-sitting her brothers and necking on the divan, he produced a pack of Trojans—and Puddles said no. This final fight was colossal, ending with Mike's shouting he wanted his ring back, she was nothing but a cock-teaser. Puddles threw the ring at him so hard it chipped his front tooth.

And Bev began to have more bad moods than good with Roger, irritable moods, melancholy moods, mysterious moods. Summer tugged, demanding excitement. Like Snowy, Bev spent her days off at the beach to keep up her tan, and there were summer boys who flirted, although she told them she was going steady, and one August morning a Dave Manning came along casing the beach, sat down on the sand beside her beachtowel, and Bev was so overwhelmed by his handsomeness and his line she agreed to go water skiing with him at his parents' camp that afternoon. She tried to think of it as only a lesson: a person should know how to water ski. She planned to be home before her date with Roger that evening, but of course she forgot the time, and when Dave brought her home, Roger's car was parked in the driveway. Dave said, "If not tonight, how about a date to-morrow?" Bev said, "Call me tomorrow morning." Indoors, Roger was watching television with Fred, while Julia had taken a walk to the bog to wonder how long it would be before Roger saw through the "at a friend's camp" excuse. He already had. He and Bev left, and his inquisition began in the car at Riley's Drive-in Restaurant, over hamburgers and Cokes, and continued to the Cat Path. Bev wept and confessed. Then they were kiss-ing, and she swore nothing had happened with Dave—he had, however, French-kissed her—and promised never to do such a thing again.

When Dave phoned the next morning, she whispered, and Julia at the loom in the dining room didn't hear her suggest a late-night swim at the little beach in the woods and make a date for half past midnight. Julia took Bev to Snowy's, and as the girls walked to work, Snowy said, "This Dave isn't permanent, though."

"Is Roger?" Bev asked. "He's going away next month, and what'll happen then?" Roger had got a scholarship to Dart-mouth. "And," Bev said, "what's so great about permanence, anyway?"

Snowy was sleeping over at Bev's, and she and Tom arrived there just after Roger had brought Bev home. Snowy didn't linger in the car with Tom, she came right inside, and she forgot betrayal in the thrill of intrigue. Bev undressed, put on her bath-ing suit, then put on her clothes again, and she and Snowy waited in the kitchen, whispering and giggling. But when Bev left, Snowy was suddenly scared.

Roger had sensed something was going on. He backed along the road past Bev's house, switched off his headlights, and saw Dave's car turn up the driveway and come out with Bev.

He sat there, and then he drove into town, let himself into his uncle's market, carefully paid for a six-pack of beer, and parked on a dead-end road and drank it.

The next day at lunchtime he left the market and drove to Sweetland. Bev was scooping ice cream. Snowy saw him first.

He said, "Tell Bev I want to speak to her."

Snowy, sick and ashamed, put down the water cup she was filling and went over to Bev. "Roger's here."

The restaurant was busy with hungry businessmen and clerks and Saturday shoppers, the jukebox yelled, "One two three o'clock, four o'clock rock!" and Snowy had to pick up her tray and hurry through the hubbub down the aisle, carrying toasted tuna fish sandwiches and fresh fruit cottage cheese salads, while Bev stood rigid behind the soda fountain counter.

Roger said, "Okay. That's that, it's over."

"Roger—" Bev said.

"No. No more bullshit."

Lois, the woman who was the short-order cook, said to Snowy as she snatched up a plate of chopped-ham sandwich, "Bev had better get a move on, or there'll be hell to pay."

Zoe, the snappish headwaitress, started toward Bev.

Bev lifted her hands and unfastened the gold chain.

Roger said, "I don't want the goddamn thing," and walked out.

Bev ran down the aisle to the ladies' room. It was locked; someone was using it. She wanted to hammer on the door and scream and sob, but she put the little gold basketball in her apron pocket, and, her eyes glistening, she straightened her shoulders and swung her walk back along the aisle to the soda fountain into a milky kaleidoscope of frappes.

She went out with Dave and other boys the rest of the summer. Gloria Taylor was now unpinned, and Roger returned to her.

But Snowy and Tom stayed together, and their parking sessions became very hectic. Their first date after the Junior Prom, during their necking Tom had guided her hand to his hard-on, and the next date he'd unzipped his fly and guided her hand in and unzipped and tugged down her tight little cut-off-dungaree short-shorts and her underpants. Snowy was scared to death, but, plucky, she held onto his hot throbbing, and with effort he managed to push a finger up into her.

That night at home, when she was undressing and discovered blood, she thought she was getting her period early and wondered why she didn't have cramps. She was puzzled that the period didn't continue.

And so this was what they always got around to sooner or later except for the times when Snowy would start to cry and say they shouldn't, and Tom would say resignedly, "Of course I respect you" and light a cigarette.

But at the end of the summer, just as he thought he couldn't stand only this any longer, one night Snowy couldn't stand not seeing It any longer and she pulled It out, and before she could get a good look in the darkness, Tom had grabbed her head and It was in her mouth. She choked. And Tom almost came, but yanked out in time, and they were hugging frantically until Tom stuffed himself back in, zipped his fly, and leaped out of the car to crash around on crunchy leaves and pine needles, moaning. Snowy sat still in the car and tasted her mouth. Sweetly metallic.

That was also what she learned that summer.


Beneath the September night, floodlights illuminated a field of dark grass lined off with lime. A noisy crowd was packed into the bleachers.

The Varsity cheerleaders, wearing green woolen jackets over short pleated green gabardine jumpers, one fist on their hips and the other clenching their white megaphones green-lettered GHS, marched toward the field. Ahead of them, the band was blaring and thumping the school song of war—"Onward to battle! Rah! Rah! Rah!"—and Snowy was so excited she wasn't nervous about this first game; she felt intoxicatingly confident.

The band marched onto the field, and the cheerleaders broke away and ran to the cheerleaders' bench in front of the bleachers, sat down, and looked across the field at the opposite bleachers, which were almost as full as their own because Leicester was the nearby town, the rival town. But although it was so close, the people and cheerleaders over there seemed to them from another planet.

When the band, instruments bleating now and then, began to settle into its section of the bleachers, Joanne said, "Okay!" and the cheerleaders grabbed up their megaphones and ran into their formation facing the Gunthwaite bleachers and did the first cheer. It was "Give Us an A!" and still Snowy wasn't nervous, even though she at her end of the line had to start it. She was the A. Beside her Charl was the B, Darl the N, Adele and Joanne together were the other A, Puddles the K, Nutty the I, and Rita the S. Kneeling on the cold grass, waiting for the jump when the others had finished calling out, Snowy looked up at where the Gang always sat and saw Bev with the rest of the Gang waving green-and-white paper streamers. The crowd bellowed each letter; the night was electric.

Then the football team, the Abnakis, ran onto the field, and everyone went mad. Snowy, jumping and clapping, searched and found Tom, the center, Number 38, the same number she'd followed all last fall from the bleachers. Tom didn't wear his glasses during games. The team began its exercise plays while the referees and Jack O'Brien, the captain, tossed a coin with the Leicester captain, and Leicester won the toss and elected to receive.

The teams faced each other. The band struck up "The Star-Spangled Banner," and everyone had to become very solemn and stand silently, but Puddles began giggling and nudging Snowy. Long ago Puddles had pointed out that the football teams at these moments, holding their helmets in front of them, their heads bowed, looked as if they were taking a piss in the helmets.

The anthem ended. The Catholics in the teams crossed themselves, which always unnerved Tom, and he and the other Protestants hastily put on their helmets. The game began.

Snowy didn't understand football. Gunthwaite kicked off, and nothing afterward made sense to her except Tom centering the ball. Then he would disappear into a pile of bodies, and the crowd would yell and jump up, and all she did was keep looking for him to reappear intact. Puddles had tried to explain it to her, and so had Tom, but she still didn't know a down from a touchback, and when they did their sitting chant, "Go, go, where, where, we want a touchdown over *there!*" she had to watch Charl beside her to make sure she didn't point in the wrong direction.

Leicester made the first touchdown, then Gunthwaite, and then they held. The cheerleaders led the frenzied crowd in cheers that split the night. During the half, while the band performed, the cheerleaders ran across the field to the Leicester side and did the Welcome Cheer. Leicester watched them suspiciously, these eight bouncy girls from a world in which green and white were the colors, not blue and gold. By the last quarter Snowy was so hoarse she couldn't swallow, and the score was still 6 to 6, and when at the last minute it was Gunthwaite's third down at the twenty-yard line, everyone was standing up roaring insanely.

Tom centered the ball. Sam Page, the quarterback, threw a short pass over center to Butch Knowles, the left end, who cut back to the right, but as Butch reached for the ball, a charging Leicester halfback also reached, tipped the ball, and they fell.

Tom caught it. He ran, a wild headlong sprint out of the fray and down the field to the left, away from Leicester's oncoming fullback. The fullback tackled low, and Tom sprawled rolling across the little flag at the corner of the goal line.

Trumpets squealed, the bass drum thumped as fast as Snowy's heart, and all the cheerleaders except Rita were screaming and hugging her.

Joanne shrieked, "Tom, the *center!*"

Snowy croaked, "Is he okay?"

Puddles said, "Yes, he's getting up, he's fine," and Charl, tears flowing, cried, "We've won! We've won!"

The school song burst out triumphantly. Adele called, "Come on!" and they dashed into formation. Snowy, singing at the top of her aching lungs, glanced over her shoulder and saw Tom being pounded on the back by shouting Abnakis.

Then the crowd surged onto the field. The cheerleaders ran ahead, but as they clamored and congratulated the team, Snowy stood aside, frightened of Tom. He looked much bigger in his dirty grass-stained uniform, ferocious charcoal smeared under his eyes, a hulking hero. Kids and parents jostled her and pushed past to shake his hand.

"Hell," he said, laughing, protesting, "hell—" and he spotted Snowy. "Hey, there's my girl."

And Snowy suddenly knew exactly what to do. She ran up and threw her arms around him and kissed him.

Everyone yelled.

Tom put his arm around her shoulders, and they walked in the crowd toward the high school, leaving behind them an empty field littered with ice-cream wrappers.

In the girls' gym office amid clouds of Cashmere Bouquet talcum, the cheerleaders talked excitedly as they changed, but Snowy was silent, hearing through the noise the words he'd never said before. "There's my girl."

Gilly stopped by to congratulate them on their first game. They knew, however, she was just waiting for their next practice to tell them everything they'd done wrong: their jumps were off at the end of "Abnaki Nation"; their cartwheels needed more work; Darl had automatically turned up the collar of her jacket, until Charl noticed it; Rita should have scuffed the soles of her white-and-green new saddle shoes so she wouldn't have slipped during "We've Got the Coach, We've Got the Team."

But they certainly all had been full of pep. Gilly left.

Changing gave them the status of arriving late at the dance in the gym, and the cheerleaders who had the added status of going out with football players dawdled even longer because the guys had to be untaped and take showers. Joanne, who was pinned to a Rumford Teachers' College boy, felt a sense of anticlimax as she started walking home. Charl and Nutty met their dates in the gym, and Puddles should have, too, but she stayed in the gym office with Snowy and Adele and Darl and Rita, because all that awaited her was Norm Noyes, still devoted.

Puddles was wearing tweed slacks and a pale-blue cardigan, the cardigan worn backward, buttoned up the back, as was the fashion. Combing her snailcurls before the mirror, she recited what she and Bev and Snowy had learned this first week of school in French I. "*J'entre dans la salle de classe. Je regarde autour de moi. Je vois les élèves et le professeur.*"

Snowy joined in. "*Je dis, 'Bonjour!' au professeur. Je prends ma place,*" and raised an eyebrow at her reflection in the mirror. French, she'd discovered, was much worse than Latin; you had to speak it.

Somebody tapped on the door, and Rita opened it. Bev looked in. She was wearing a black fleece jacket and black slacks, her hair intentionally the only color. Like Snowy, Bev and Puddles had decided that the time of the blue-and-gray jackets was over, and they had seen the fleece ones in *Seventeen* magazine and sent away for them. Puddles chose a patriotic green one, with a hood.

Bev said, somewhat tentatively, "I'm feeling like a street-walker hanging around waiting, may I join you?"

"Sure," Adele said. She was sitting on Gilly's desk. "Who are you waiting for?"

Bev glanced at Darl. "Um, Victor."

Victor and Darl had also broken up this summer.

Darl laughed. "V for Victory."

Tonight was Bev's first date with Victor. But he was a guard, and she intended to move on up fast, to Jack O'Brien, the captain. She said to Snowy, "Wasn't Tom wonderful!"

"Yes," Snowy said, checking herself again in the full-length mirror, her dark-blue sweater and gray slacks. She was still wearing her saddle shoes, the only part of the uniform they were allowed to wear home. Green saddles showed beneath the slacks of all the cheerleaders, badges of rank.

Adele looked at the clock on the wall. "Okay?"

They moseyed along the corridor, and they had timed it perfectly, the boys were coming out of the locker room. The girls ran up to Tom and congratulated him again. Snowy felt a keen desire to haul off and clout Rita, who'd latched onto his arm, but she was very proud.

From the cavernous gym the record player sang: "Wake the town and tell the people,/Sing it to the moon above,/Wake the town and tell the people,/Tell them that we're so in love."

Their hands were stamped at the door by an NFL boy. The National Forensic League, always raising money to go debate somewhere, was sponsoring the dance. They went down the stairs, Snowy and Tom, Bev and Victor, Adele and Sam Page, Rita and Butch Knowles, Darl and Bill LeHoullier, and Bev heard Jack O'Brien behind them kidding around with Puddles in the midst of the other guys.

Snowy remembered entering the gym at the dance after the last basketball game. The distance in time seemed farther than months.

And as they danced, she wondered where she'd be at that point of the school cycle this year. Probably, she thought, buried under an avalanche of homework. Just the first week of school had shown her how much more was expected of juniors than sophomores; the homework load was heavier, she had to work harder and longer, and she had one less study period a day because she was taking a fifth subject, Personal Typing, a course for College Prep kids, over in the Practical Arts building. Bev and Puddles were in the typing class and in her plane geometry and French I classes, but their scheduling luck had run out and they were not all together in English and U.S. history; Bev and Puddles were in the other group, and Snowy was alone. She still, though, had Dudley Washburn in all her classes. Tom drew her closer, and they danced cheek to cheek.

Jack O'Brien was here stag, to size up this year's prospects, to see how the younger girls had developed over the summer, but he got sidetracked by Puddles' sweater. Bev, alarmed, saw him dancing with her while Norm sat waiting patiently on the bleachers. Puddles didn't see anyone; she was ecstatic, yet she had learned a lesson from Mike and didn't look around for people's reactions to her glory, and she couldn't have if she tried. Crew-cut Jack was a fullback, very big, and her face was crushed into his sweater. Together, they resembled a bear dancing with a china doll.

"Then your fingers touched my silent heart/And taught it how to sing—/Oh, true love's a many-splendored thing."

Puddles realized Jack was getting a hard-on as they danced.

But the next record was a fast one, and they had to separate to jitterbug.

Tom spun Snowy, and Victor spun Bev, and both girls now could step and whirl and step with confidence, without giggles, and Puddles had become so good that tonight she and Jack were the ones everyone gradually stopped dancing to watch.

"You broke my heart!/When you said we'd part!/Ain't that a shame?"

The kids circled them, the guys shouting wisecracks to sweating Jack, the girls jealous of Puddles. Norm, on the bleachers, took a swig of Coke and waited.

Bev said, "Puddles is going to sprain her wrists if she doesn't slow down."

Snowy said, "She probably figures it'd be worth it."

"Well," Bev said, "she's not being very kind to poor Norm."

Snowy looked at her, startled.

Bev gave a short laugh. "Okay, okay, I should talk."

But this wasn't what had surprised Snowy; it was the realization that Bev wanted Jack. Oh, God, she thought.

Tom tugged her ponytail. "Let's go to Hooper's."

There he was congratulated by the other kids who'd left the dance early, and he and Snowy had black coffee and English muffins, which now to Snowy were b. cof. and Eng. muf.

Sitting close, they drove toward the sandpit. The car was their home, and they began to relax.

"Hero," Tom said. "I remember one game last year, I'd hurt my knee at practice, so they strapped it up and sat me on the bench just in case, and damned if Leon Boucher, who was replacing me, didn't get the shit kicked out of him. It was a really big moment. Coach yells at me, 'Forbes, get in there!' and I yell, 'Yes sir!' And then I jumped up and fell flat on my face."

Snowy laughed. "How come?"

"They'd strapped up my leg so tight all the circulation had gotten cut off."

"I don't remember seeing that."

"I hope to God nobody did. The team was bad enough." He turned off onto a dirt road, and they bumped through woods up to a knoll. Snowy had no idea what the sandpit looked like in daylight, the earth ripped open, the steep brown slides; to her, it was simply blackness outside the car.

Tom told another football story, about the time last year the quarterback had got mad at Tom's not handing him the ball hard enough and Tom had slammed it back to him so hard he broke the quarterback's index finger. Snowy told him about the freshman girl in her French class who always wore a shoulder pocketbook, not at all fashionable at that time, *always* wore it, even when she was sitting at her desk and when she went up to the blackboard, the strap across her chunky chest like a Sam Browne belt, and Bev and Snowy had decided that the pocketbook was a disguise for some hideous growth.

Then they were kissing, and then they were naked, Snowy giggling at his ankles which were shaven because of the tape, and then they were serious again and Snowy was whacking away at him, but this night Tom misjudged and didn't stop her in time. He exploded. Warm stickiness gushed over Snowy's hand, and she jumped back and struck the horn. It honked. She didn't know what had happened, her first thought was he'd wet himself, maybe boys' urine was different from girls', and she was horrified.

Tom lay hot and panting. Exquisite relief.

He opened his eyes and saw Snowy staring at him.

"Sorry," he said, "I'm sorry." He reached over the side of the seat and grabbed his T-shirt and mopped at himself. The goddamned stuff was everywhere. He sat up and took her hand and began wiping it, the nice-girl hand he had soiled.

Suddenly Snowy remembered Puddles' "out-of-control" remark she'd puzzled over, not quite daring to bring up the subject with Puddles, and A student that she was, Snowy made the connection. She said, "It's okay," and they were embracing, skin to skin.

And into her neck he said what she thought he would never say. "I love you."

So at last she could say, "I love you."

She was radiant as, after he kissed her good-night at the door, she went inside the house, hugged and calmed Laurie, and hung up her white leather jacket. Bev's jacket was in the closet. Snowy started upstairs, avid to tell Bev the "I love you" milestone (Ed's "I love you" didn't count), wishing she could tell Bev the rest. But she and Bev continued to avoid discussing directly the terrible things they did in cars; Bev guessed what Snowy was learning and implied that she knew, and they used vague phrases like "getting carried away." Snowy wondered if she could say "out of control" as casually as Puddles.

Laurie pranced and barked at the foot of the stairs. Snowy turned and looked at her and asked, "Where's Bev?" Laurie barked and dashed away. "Well," Snowy said, "you're better than Lassie," and followed her back into the kitchen. The cellar door was ajar. They went down the stairs.

The cellar still smelled of potatoes, although her father had almost finished transforming it into a rumpus room, and Snowy still disliked the place. She could remember how when the oil furnace had been the coal furnace, the coal man would back up his truck and the load of coal would go rumbling down through the little window into the coal bin, while she stood on the cellar stairs watching the power of the rush of coal and knowing that if she were in the bin she'd be crushed by it. Now her father had partitioned off the furnace, and the coal bin was the rumpus room with wallboard painted pale yellow. From the attic they had brought an old sofa and two chairs. Her mother wanted Snowy to put her record player down here, but Snowy wanted to keep it in her bedroom, so from the attic came the big dark wind-up Victrola Snowy had cranked when she was barely tall enough to reach the handle. Her parents were now talking about slipcovers for the furniture, and Snowy hoped they would hurry up, because this transplanted living room of her childhood confused her.

Bev sat huddled on the brown sofa, pressing Kleenex against her face and holding her breath to keep the sobs silent.

"Bev," Snowy said helplessly. "Bev."

Bev made a strangled sound, and Laurie, distressed by tears, sprang at her. Snowy seized Laurie, held her struggles, and sat down beside Bev. "Did Puddles leave the dance with Jack?"

Bev nodded. Her eyes above the Kleenex were puffy and bloodshot. Bev, who looked beautiful even when she woke up in the mornings, looked as awful as other girls when she cried.

Snowy said, "Maybe it won't amount to anything."

Bev gurgled.

Snowy said, "What about Victor?"

Bev snatched away the Kleenex and gasped, her voice too high, "He's all right."

"Did you go parking?"

"In your driveway."

"Have you got another date?"

"The movies tomorrow night. He's okay. It just always feels so funny to kiss someone who isn't Roger. *I miss Roger!*"

"Oh, Bev."

"He wasn't only a boyfriend, he was a friend, he was my *friend* and I didn't know it. I keep expecting to see him in school; it's like ghosts."

Snowy scratched Laurie behind the ear. "Why Jack? For a replacement or substitute or something?"

Bev said, "Roger and I went steady too long, that's the trouble, that's the trouble. God, I wish Puddles was sleeping over here tonight, we'd know what happened."

"It's too late to phone her."

"This year is so rotten." Bev plucked at the Kleenex. "All that wicked homework, no Roger—"

"Maybe you could write to him. You could apologize by letter."

"But he'd still be in Hanover and I'd be here."

"He'll come home sometime. Christmas. Thanksgiving, that's even earlier."

"It's forever. What do I do in the meantime, sit around and crochet doilies?"

Bev was recovering. Snowy said, "You could be chaste. Chaste around the bedroom."

Bev ignored the joke. "It's only the first week, and I'm so sick of school I could scream. There's this year and next year and then college, what's the point of it all?"

"It's what we have to do."

"*J'entre dans la salle de classe. Je regarde autour de moi.*"

"Maybe we'll go to France someday."

"Maybe."

"What I fail to see," Snowy said, "is how I am ever going to be able to prove that the bisectors of two vertical angles form a straight line."

Bev retched, a noise she'd recently perfected and Snowy and Puddles were trying to copy. "You and me both," Bev said. She stood up. "Is it true all's fair in love and war?"

Snowy, holding Laurie, sat looking up at her. "I don't know," she said. "That's what they say."

"Henrietta!" her mother called. "It's for you."

Snowy was studying in her bedroom with Bev before supper, a week later. She said, "Puddles, I bet," and ran downstairs and picked up the receiver.

Puddles said, "I passed!"

"My God," Snowy said. "Another milestone."

"It's not so bad, you'll pass, too. First you take the eye test, and then the written test—I didn't get any wrong—and then you and the Occifer go out to the car. Mom brought me and waited in the station. What're all the people in town?"

"A Shriners' convention."

"Yes, and Main Street was absolute jampacked. First the Occifer told me to turn at Woolworth's, but the traffic was so horrible he changed his mind and had me drive straight through downtown, all those fezes, it was like come-with-me-to-ze-Casbah. And you know what? He kept looking for a space for me to parallel-park, and he *couldn't find one!* So we drove straight through town and he had me stop and start on Worm Hill"—so called by the townsfolk because in front of almost all the shabby houses on it were straggly handmade signs advertising worms and night crawlers for sale—"and I nearly had heart failure, but I didn't stall. He wasn't paying much attention, I think he was pissed off at the traffic jams, and we just came back to the police station by side streets and I parked in the parking lot and that wasn't any trouble because there wasn't any curb. Mom had come outdoors by then, and when he said I'd be hearing from them, she asked right out if I'd passed, and he said yes!"

"Congratulations," Snowy said, jealous. "Was the written test hard?"

"Well, it was sort of rough, but if you study the booklet like mad, you'll be okay." Puddles laughed. "For you, it'll be easy."

"Was the eye test one of those charts?"

"Uh-huh, like the school nurse has. It always seems to me they'd be more interesting if the letters spelled something, like Fuck You."

"Puddles!"

Snowy was so nervous about the driving test that she had put off again and again mailing in the application, even though Tom figured she was ready. "I'll send in my application tomorrow."

Puddles said, "I wonder how long it'll take for my license to arrive. Today's Friday; do you suppose Monday?"

"If the mailman runs all the way to Concord and back."

Puddles giggled. "When it comes, I'll get the car, and we'll go on a solo flight!"

"Unbelievable, isn't it?"

They contemplated freedom.

Then Puddles said, "Jack mentioned Ed today, I forgot to tell you. If things go okay at the game tomorrow afternoon, he wants to give some of the second string a chance maybe, and Ed will be replacing him."

"Ughy-pew."

"I know, but isn't that nice of Jack? He's *très* sweet. Do you remember how soon he and Charl started going steady?"

"Let's see, the twins always go steady fast. The second date?"

"*Really?*" Puddles said, upset. She'd had her second date with Jack last Saturday night. They'd gone to the movies and to Hooper's and had kissed enthusiastically in his 1946 Hudson on the Cat Path.

Snowy said, "Well, maybe it was the third. I'm pretty sure it was the third."

"What's Bev wearing tonight? An evening gown?"

To get attention, Bev had been sophisticated in school, wearing nylons and flats and her dressier skirt-and-blouse outfits and jumpers. This wasn't necessary. The boys were practically queuing up to ask her out—all except Jack, who was distracted by Puddles' boobs. Bev chose Butch Knowles, because he, from the habit of double-dating with Jack and the twins, suggested a double date with Jack and Puddles. They were going to the drive-in.

Snowy yelled up the stairs, "What are you wearing tonight?"

"My birthday suit!" Bev yelled.

Snowy said, "She claims her birthday suit, but she brought her plaid slacks and green sweater."

"Oh," Puddles said. "Well, see you in the back row."

Uneasy, Snowy hung up and went slowly upstairs. In her bedroom, her record player was singing "The Yellow Rose of Texas," the Number One Hit Parade song. Bev lay reading "Thanatopsis" on the bed, surrounded by toy animals.

Snowy said, "She passed. I'm going to mail in my application, are you?"

"God, no. I still stall going into second gear, and poor Fred grits his teeth and says, 'Grind another pound.' "

"What about your mother teaching you?"

"She says just trying to teach me to weave wore her out."

"Hey, now Puddles will have her folks' car, she could teach you."

"Oh, murder. That'd be the end of a beautiful friendship."

Not looking at each other, they listened to what Bev had said.

The record player sang, "She cried so when I left her,/It like to broke my heart,/And if I ever find her,/We never more shall part!"

"Well," Bev said, "when I marry my millionaire, I'll have a chauffeur, anyway."

Snowy sat down at her desk and picked up her protractor.

Bev read to herself:

> Yet a few days, and thee
> The all-beholding sun shall see no more
> In all his course; nor yet in the cold ground,
> Where thy pale form was laid, with many tears,
> Nor in the embrace of ocean, shall exist
> Thy image.

That night Tom was late. Bev was picked up first by Jack and Puddles and Butch, so when Tom and Snowy got to the drive-in the cartoon had started, and they drove along the rows searching for Jack's car. Sure enough, it was in the back row against the woods. The back row was rakishly acceptable at the drive-in. Tom parked in the empty space beside them and rolled down his window to reach for the speaker.

Bev, in the back seat with Butch, started laughing. She and Puddles rolled down their windows and called, "You're the twentieth!"

"The twentieth what?" Tom asked.

"That speaker doesn't work," Bev said. "We have counted exactly nineteen cars who've come and gone."

"Damn," Snowy said. She wanted to be next to them, to keep an eye on Bev. Sometimes she knew Puddles could take care of herself; sometimes she knew she must protect Puddles; it was wrong of Bev to want Jack, but Jack and Puddles weren't going steady, so he was fair game. Or was he? And how in the world could she protect Puddles?

Tom found a space in the row below them, and the first movie began. It was *The Iroquois Trail*. Sitting up straight, side by side, they watched fifteen minutes of it, and then Tom turned off the speaker and turned on the radio. He hung his glasses over the sun visor and grinned at Snowy.

"Eek!" she said.

In Jack's car, Bev was being clever about the movie, egging the boys on to outdo each other in wisecracks, and Puddles had to join in. Puddles had hoped the evening would be two cozy couples separated by the barrier of the seat, but now here was Bev's personality controlling everything. Jack hadn't even put his arm around her yet.

In Tom's car, Tom was getting a grammar lesson. They'd been flat on the seat, tickling and laughing and kissing, and then he said, "Are you laying on me that way accidentally on purpose?" and Snowy gathered courage and at last corrected him, as long ago she had corrected her parents. (Her mother still forgot.) "To recline," she said, "is to lie. Lie, lay, lying, lain."

"Huh?" Tom said.

"It doesn't take an object. Lay, meaning to put or place, does. Lay, laid, laying, laid."

Tom, embarrassed, said, "I didn't bring my notebook."

Snowy was silent, hating herself.

Then Tom kissed her nose and said, "Hell, I don't even re-member what an object is. Give it to me again."

So Snowy, on top of him, lectured.

Jack still didn't have his arm around Puddles, and he was turn-ing around to the back seat, making jokes, more than he was watching the movie. Bev, past compunction, drunk on her own wit, said, "And a heroine must always twinkle at the hero, all heroines twinkle."

Jack asked, "How does anyone twinkle?"

Bev twinkled.

Snowy progressed to pronouns and objects of prepositions, correcting his "between you and I" 's she'd cringed at.

The radio sang: "Learning to love,/Be kind to me, please take it slow,/For this is my first time, you know,/I'm learning to love."

The intermission lights brightened the night, and cars that had appeared empty suddenly contained couples. On the screen, a gnome pushed the hands of a ten-minute clock while candy bars and hot dogs danced past.

Jack said, "How about some food?"

Bev said, "Butch, I would absolutely love that cute box of popcorn up there, the one tap dancing. He fills me with mad desire."

"If that's the case," Butch said, "I'll see what I can do."

When the boys left, Puddles considered all the things she wanted to say to Bev, but, uncharacteristically, she didn't say them. She said, "I have to pee. Let's stop for Snowy on the way."

Tom had gone to the refreshment stand, and Snowy was alone, craning her neck trying to see Jack's car. As Puddles and Bev approached, she got out, and Bev said, "I do believe I hear a radio."

Puddles said, "We're going to the ladies' room, want to come?"

"Okay," Snowy said, "but take a bead on where the cars are." Once this summer she and Puddles, here with Tom and Mike, had got lost in the dark when they were returning from the ladies' room after the second feature started; they stumbled against speaker cords and peered into cars at indignant couples until Tom saw them groping around and turned on his head-lights.

Snowy and Bev and Puddles walked down toward the refreshment booth, a flat-roofed cinder-block building, past cars that were each a secret little world. All at once boisterous to cover conflict, they banged on the hood of Sam Page's car, in which Adele was reapplying lipstick, and yelled at Ron Moore, who was returning to his car and Linda with popcorn. But in the glaring light of the ladies' room, in the crowd of women and girls and the wastebaskets overflowing with paper towels, in the smell of disinfectant, the brief mood soured as they stood wait-ing before the toilet doors.

Bev retched. "These places are such a horror."

Neither Puddles nor Snowy answered.

They took their turns, washed their hands, combed their hair, put on lipstick. Walking back, Snowy wished she could become invisible and waft into Jack's car to find out what was happening.

She said, "Um, did you like the movie?"

Puddles said, "I could hardly hear it."

Bev said, "Have you seen the next one? You'll enjoy it, it's very religious."

They always gently kidded Puddles because she still occasion-ally went to the Congregational church. Last Easter she'd had a cold and couldn't go, so she put on her flowery new hat and sat bolt upright in bed in her pajamas, listening to hymns on the radio.

"Yes," Puddles said, "I did see it, and it's wonderful, I hope I'll be able to see it again tonight."

Bev said, "Remember when I missed the Moulin Rouge movie and I was so excited when it came here, and then what happens but great passion and I had to keep dragging my way up to the dashboard for a peek at it—"

All three recalled at the same moment that the boy in this tale was Tom.

Bev said, "Well, now we're taking French, I can pronounce *faux pas*."

Snowy said, "There're the guys."

They were carrying armloads of food. Tom called, "Got you two hot dogs, Snowy," and said loudly to Jack and Butch, "One problem about going steady with Snowy; it's kind of difficult to make out with a girl who's always eating."

"Eating what?" Jack asked.

Tom accepted but didn't like that sort of joke, there were certain limits, and he hoped Snowy hadn't heard. She had, and she was blushing. Luckily, the lights went out.

Back in the car, Snowy sat on her own side and ate hot dog number one and sipped coffee, pretending to be enthralled by the previews. Bev and Tom, she told herself, were long ago and finished.

In Jack's car, as the second feature, *The Silver Chalice*, began, Butch's advances also began. He slid gradually closer and closer, and Bev ate her popcorn too fast. She reached the kernels at the bottom of the box, and she had nothing to do to look busy, and she couldn't continue the wisecracking because this was a religious movie. Jack crossed himself at the games, so he must be Catholic. He and Puddles, heads together, were eating their popcorn and watching intently. Butch's arm went around Bev.

In Tom's car, Tom was discussing the ethics of picnic tables.

"I'm supposed to oversee it," he said. "The park department buys the lumber, and the shop class builds thirty picnic tables for the parks next summer. But we don't get paid for the work, they're getting our work free, it doesn't seem right. They'd sure the hell have to pay plenty if they had a regular carpenter do it. And shouldn't the carpenter get the chance?"

Snowy pondered. "Does it help the guys learn anything?"

"Well, maybe the first table, but not *thirty*. An assembly line. I am going to be so goddamned sick of picnic tables."

"I'll bet."

"At least it's not thirty breadboards or birdhouses, I'd quit school." Tom paused, shy about his masterpieces. "You know that record-player-radio-cabinet in the living room?"

She visualized the room and located a big smooth dark cabinet behind the Morris chair.

"I made it," Tom said. "Now that was making something."

"You made it?" She couldn't believe he could build such an object; she thought of all furniture as being somehow born in a factory. "It's beautiful."

Tom paused again. "Sometime if I can get you upstairs, I'll show you the hope chest I made for my mother. Mahogany finish."

For his mother, not some girl. What a relief! Snowy did understand hope chests.

He grabbed her. "Guess what else I'd show you if I got you upstairs!"

Butch turned Bev's face to his and kissed her.

Puddles and Jack, in a clinch behind the steering wheel, were slowly sinking downward. Sex had won out over religion. Puddles felt Jack's hand move up under her jacket, and she thought, it's the third date, maybe he'll ask me to go steady, it's okay.

And soon Snowy was giving Tom a blow job. Last Saturday night Tom had allowed himself to come during this, and Snowy hadn't panicked but had almost choked to death on the mouthful, so tonight, resourceful, he was holding his handkerchief ready. Little starched Snowy; who'd've dreamed it? He groaned happily.

Bev was stymied, with Butch kissing her neck so frantically she knew she'd have a hickey.

Jack clasped Puddles' left breast.

Then just as Tom geysered into his handkerchief, Bev had a brainstorm. She screamed.

Butch jumped back, and Puddles' and Jack's heads popped up. Jack said, "Butch, you behave yourself."

"I—" Butch said.

Bev cried, "My appendix, I'm having an appendicitis attack!"

"Which," Puddles said grimly, "side?"

But Bev knew, having seen her mother's scar. "Here, right here, oh, what agony!"

"Jesus Christ," Jack said, hard-on now limp, and he started the car and screeched away, forgetting the speaker; the cord snapped, and the speaker banged off Puddles' knee. He remembered the headlights, and Snowy heard the noise of the car and saw the lights and said, "Was that Jack?"

"The hell with them," Tom said. "Hey, maybe they're going parking early. That sounds like a good idea."

Snowy put her arms around his neck, and they kissed.

Jack yelled, "Should we go to the hospital, or what?"

"Yes," Puddles said.

Bev said, "No, no, just take me home, my mother'll know what to do."

Puddles said, "Do you have these attacks often?"

In the Dramatics Club plays, Bev had made an important discovery: she could weep at will. She sobbed into Butch's football jacket.

Puddles said, "Aren't you sleeping over at Snowy's? What'll you do without your Noxzema?"

Jack said, "For crissakes, Puddles, this is an *emergency*."

He might as well have hit her. She hunched in her corner and listened to Bev wail.

Out on the road, Jack asked, "Where does she live?"

Puddles wanted to say wherever Benedict Arnold lived, but she said, "Take the road past the Cat Path."

Bev was really crying now, frightened at what she'd done.

They reached her house, and Butch slammed open the car door, and, with his arm around her, helped her toward the doorstep. Puddles watched her totter pathetically.

Butch said, "Should I come in, will you be all right?"

"I'll be okay," Bev said, "I just have to lie down."

"You sure?"

"Yes. Yes."

In the living room, she looked at the telephone, but Snowy wouldn't be home yet, and anyway it was too late, and she threw herself on the sofa and sobbed, a fringed cushion over her head so nobody would hear.

"My God," Jack kept saying. "My God. What a thing."

Butch said, "She said she'd be all right."

Puddles sat between them and didn't say anything.

They drove back to town and took Butch home. Jack had had great hopes for the parking session after the drive-in preliminaries, but he didn't think he should take Puddles parking when her dear friend was in agony.

"Well," he said in her driveway. "Appendicitis can be dangerous."

"It certainly can."

"Well," he said, and opened his door.

He walked her to the porch, put his hands on her shoulders and kissed her quickly.

Puddles ran upstairs to her bedroom, which was decorated with GHS pennants, and flung herself on the bed, and she too sobbed.

At the sandpit, Tom was getting his second blow job of the evening.



Snowy waited up in the spare room for Bev until one o'clock, when she fell asleep. The next morning, when she awoke and found only Laurie and Kit with her, her first thought was that there had been a car accident. She sprang out and ran downstairs to phone Puddles, and the telephone rang.

"Hi," Bev said. "Have you heard from Puddles?"

"No, what *happened?*"

"I got kind of sick, and I thought I should come home."

"All your stuff's here—"

"But I didn't tell *ma mere*, so she wouldn't worry about me being sick, I just told her I'd forgotten I was staying at your house."

This was possible.

"Oh," Snowy said. "Are you okay?"

"Well, I'm kind of queasy, and I guess I won't be going to the game. In fact, I thought at the time it was my appendix, but of course it wasn't. False alarm."

"Thank heavens."

Ruminating, Snowy let Laurie and Kit out, washed and dressed and went outdoors and fed the ducks, and she was sitting at the dining-room table drinking Postum and eating her third piece of toast when the phone rang again.

She picked up the receiver. "Puddles? Bev just called, she's okay."

"I'll bet she is," Puddles said.

"She says it isn't her appendix after all."

"Snowy—" Puddles began. And then she was crying again.

Snowy said, "Bev pulled a trick."

"Mmmff."

Snowy could have let it go at that, but something drove her toward stark truth. "Why?"

"To ruin everything, to get Jack to pay attention to *her*."

"Yes."

"He didn't ask me out again." Puddles gulped. "See you at the game," she said, and hung up.

Never, thought Snowy, will things ever be the same.

It was midmorning when Bev got the phone call she'd been hoping for.

"Hi, Bev," Jack said. "Are you okay?"

"Why, thank you for calling. Yes, I'm pretty well, a false alarm, I guess my popcorn must've been tap dancing."

"That's good."

Bev said, "I'm so sorry I spoiled everything."

"You didn't spoil anything."

They both hesitated.

Jack said, "I don't suppose you'll be coming to the game this afternoon."

"I don't think I'd better."

"How about tonight, you got a date? We could go to the movies."

Bev looked out the back window at the garden and saw Julia, in the corn, checking last night's raids by raccoons. Out the front window, Fred was raking yellow and red leaves. She thought how simple it must be to be grown-up. The lake lay blue below the mountains.

"That'd be lovely," she said.

Butch, slow off the mark, phoned five minutes later. Bev said she was recovering, and she was sorry, she already had a date.

In Snowy's bedroom, the radio played the *Teen Tunes and Topics* program, her geometry book was open beside math paper and pencils on her desk, but Snowy, sitting at the desk, was neither listening nor doing her homework. She too looked out a window, at the hazy blue river.

She sought compromise. The saying claimed all was fair in love and war, but there was also the code that said you did not steal a close friend's boyfriend. Yet did three dates make Jack Puddles' boyfriend? They had made him Charl's, and if Bev hadn't ruined last night—

She picked up a pencil and began to gnaw the eraser.

The wind blew leaves swirling down into the river. The ducks paddled and jeered.

She remembered how her role was always peacemaker in Bev and Puddles' fights. This wasn't, however, a snide crack from

Bev about Puddles' droopy socks; this wasn't Puddles' blurting out that Bev owned a pair of falsies.

She shoved back her chair, went to her bureau and got the bottle of white shoe polish, shook it, and sat down on the floor and absently polished her grass-stained saddle shoes.

The phone rang. She jumped up and dashed downstairs. Her folks had gone shopping for slipcover material.

Bev said, "Me again. Snowy, the craziest thing just happened, Jack called to find out how I was and he asked me out tonight, and I was so surprised I said yes."

"You must be feeling better then."

"Oh, yes, much."

Never before had Snowy had to keep up any such pretense with Bev.

Bev said, "Then all at once I thought of Puddles. I mean, they've just had a couple of dates—"

"Three."

"Well, you can't call the night he picked her up at the dance a real date, can you? Anyway, do you think she'll be mad?"

"Bev, what do you think?"

A silence.

Bev said, "Are *you* mad?"

Snowy didn't know what to answer.

Bev said, "They're not going steady. Oh, this is all so sordid."

Snowy said, "Look, Bev, you can get any guy you want, Puddles has more trouble. Like me," she added, intentionally very candid.

"Should I break the date?"

"How much would that solve?"

"Maybe he'd ask Puddles."

"And you'd sure as hell have to keep it a deep dark secret that he asked you first, and what if Puddles found out?"

"Damn damn damn damn."

Snowy said, "Is he worth it?"

Jack O'Brien. A substitute for Roger. Big and handsome and the captain of the football team. And an adventure. Bev said, "I guess maybe he is."

"Oh," Snowy said.

Walking back upstairs, she remembered that the homeroom teacher had asked her to take care of new-girl Puddles, but Puddles had managed just fine; it was at the Girl Scout meeting Puddles had needed her. Their troop in eighth grade had already begun planning to go to Washington, and it was understood among the girls that nobody else could join because any additions would mean they'd have to earn more money. But Puddles had heard them mention a meeting one afternoon, to be held in the basement of the Unitarian church, and hurried home and told her mother, and they drove to the church. The girls, sitting around at long tables, weren't settled down yet, they were chattering and giggling, when Puddles and Mrs. Pond entered. The troop leaders came forward to greet them. As the leaders and Mrs. Pond began talking, Puddles stood alone at the doorway of the big room, facing the now silent groups of girls. Hostility. Then she spotted Snowy, and Snowy would never forget the way she'd rushed across the room and swooped down at her, finding an ally, laughing and repeating some joke from school, while the girls looked at Snowy, transferring their hostility. Snowy had wanted to push Puddles away, she wanted to yell at the girls, "I didn't invite her here!" but she said, "Let's get you a chair." And by the time the meeting was over, the food sale posters made, Puddles was accepted.

Snowy sat down on her bed and put her face in the sleepy warmth of Kit's fur.

Then she went back downstairs. She sat on the sofa and held the phone book awhile before she even dared open it. She turned to the F's. Six Forbeses. He was the one on Morning Street, and she learned that his father's name was John.

Her hands were sweating when she picked up the receiver.

"Number, please."

"G-U four," Snowy said, and faltered. She cleared her throat. "Excuse me. G-U four, oh four seven two, please."

The phone rang.

She had never called a boy before, except Dudley to check homework.

The phone rang again.

"Hello?" A woman's voice, his mother's. Until this moment Snowy had not been able to believe he really had parents, a mother who washed and ironed his clothes, a father like hers who wanted supper on time.

"Is Tom there, please?"

"Just a minute." The phone clattered down.

He was there; she wouldn't have to call Varney's. She waited. Tom said, "Hello?"

"Hello. Tom—"

"Snowy? I'll be damned."

"I'm sorry to bother you—"

"You're really bothering me, I was thinking of you."

She interpreted this as a sexy compliment. "You were?"

"And cleaning the attic. I'm not a good son unless I clean the attic twice a year."

She didn't giggle. "Tom, do you know who's going to be captain of the basketball team? Or co-captains?"

"Sam Page and Gene Chabot. Why? You planning to change sports with the seasons?"

"Idiot." She considered Gene. He didn't play football, but he was tall and good-looking and a renowned basketball player. "Sam's out, he and Adele are practically married. Who's Gene been dating lately?"

"Nobody so far this year. He's off women. He went steady some with Brenda Dutile last year, and Nutty, and who was it this summer—"

"Carol Tucker. Do you suppose you could fix him up with Puddles for tonight?"

"Puddles? I thought—"

"Jack's got a date with Bev tonight."

"Oh, Christ. Well, I'll try. Call you back."

Her parents returned from downtown with their slipcover story, and Snowy was making peanut-butter sandwiches while her mother ladled out Campbell's Chicken-Noodle soup, when the phone rang.

Tom said, "It took some doing, but Gene's going to ask her at the game. A double date with us for the movies."

"That's absolutely wonderful. Thank you."

"And, hey, my mother wants me to ask if you can have supper here. I'd bring you after the game."

Utter shock.

Tom said, "I know it's a big ordeal, but my folks'd like to meet you. You can make up some excuse if you want."

Such as an appendicitis attack. "No, hold on, I'll ask my mother." She ran into the kitchen, telling herself she might as well get meeting them over with now instead of later, realizing she'd have to take a skirt to school to change into after the game, trying to figure out which skirt, which outfit—

Her mother said yes.

Snowy said into the phone, "Yes, I can." She didn't know the etiquette of this, so she invented one. "Tell your mother I thank her very much for inviting me."

"Will do. See you at the game. I'll be watching your cartwheels."

She lowered her voice. "Sex fiend."

He lowered his. "I love you."

At the dining-room table, Snowy ate lunch with her parents. They were also going to the game, to see her cheer. Her father talked football, her mother appeared to be listening but was worrying about their choice of slipcover material, and Snowy wondered if the status of Gene would console Puddles for the loss of Jack and help her to forgive Bev. But what if Gene didn't ask Puddles out again? Anxious, Snowy spooned soup.

It was a crisp sunny afternoon, and Gunthwaite won the game, the second string playing the last quarter.

Afterward Snowy sat at the Forbeses' dining room table and minded her manners so carefully that she ate hardly any of the New England boiled dinner, and Tom, amused, guessed this would cost him more than an English muffin at Hooper's to-night. Conversation was simple; they all discussed the game. His parents were surprised to find her so small and shy. The clues they'd extracted from Tom had made them decide that an A student Varsity cheerleader must be a good influence on him, but they'd expected a much more formidable girl. And Snowy found that his parents were indeed real; his brisk mother had Tom's blue eyes and long straight eyelashes, his father was horn-rimmed like Tom. She thought his little brother a brat.

They picked up Gene and Puddles and drove downtown to the theater. At the game, Snowy had said to Puddles, "Tom says Gene Chabot is dying to ask you out, did you know he's a co-captain of the basketball team?" "Is he?" Puddles said dully, but when Gene came over to her during the half, she agreed to go out with him. The first movie was *House of Bamboo*. Puddles, very aware of Bev and Jack sitting three rows behind, was too humbled to make an effort at attracting Gene. In the ladies' room during intermission, after the boys had left for a cigarette in Tom's car—Tom didn't dare smoke in the lobby because he was supposed to be in training—Snowy scolded, "Don't just sit there like a bump on a log!" Puddles snapped, "You want me to twinkle?" But during the second feature, *Dam Busters*, she did rouse herself, and Gene, who had admired her cheering at the game, laughed at her jokes and put his arm around her.

They went to Hooper's. Snowy ordered a BLT and a coffee frappe.

Parking at the sandpit, Snowy and Tom managed to behave themselves while Puddles and Gene got acquainted in the back seat. Snowy overheard Gene telling Puddles about the opening horrors of senior English, Beowulf and Chaucer, and wished that Tom were taking the classes she'd take next year, to give her a preview. It dawned on Puddles that she was having a better time with Gene than she'd had with Jack. Although Gene was not so spectacular as Jack or so smooth as Mike, his first name was the same as hers, which might be a sign, and she liked his tight dark crew cut and his olive skin and the solemn way he gathered her to him and kissed her.

He asked her out next Friday night, but she and the other Varsity cheerleaders were going to an away game in Rochester, so he asked her to the movies Saturday night. Gene was no longer off women.

Snowy and Bev and Puddles dreaded Monday. Puddles didn't wait for them at the Gowen Street corner but walked to school alone, and at school Bev tried to act as if nothing had happened, talking lightly of homework. Puddles, withdrawn, clammed up completely when Bev was there.

By midweek, however, flirtation with Gene began to slacken Puddles' tenseness, his flattery revived her self-respect, and by the weekend she was giggling again with Bev and Snowy.

When Gene gave Puddles his basketball a week before Jack gave Bev his football, Snowy hoped the score was even.

The junior year was a test of stamina.

Snowy learned how to say she was hungry in French, and she learned how to type "Jake had a fight. Hal asked if he had a fair fight." The history teacher said he'd give extra credit for extra projects, so Snowy researched and wrote a paper about Quetzal-coatl. She began to enjoy geometry; it was like solving an Agatha Christie. Mrs. Moulton, now their English teacher, assigned ten novels a term, which caused the kids to buy up every Classic comic book in town until Dudley Washburn broke one of the codes of the printed tests: the letter of the correct multiple choice answer was the last letter of the question. Snowy read *The Bridge of San Luis Rey*, *Wuthering Heights*, *Junior Miss*, *Our Hearts Were Young and Gay*, *Goodbye, Mr. Chips*, *My Antonia*, *So Big*, and *Alice Adams*, but she was too busy to re-read *Tom Sawyer*, and she used the code key on the test, and she didn't feel like wading through *Jane Eyre* again, so she borrowed the Classic comic from Puddles and was very startled to find in it Jane a beautiful blonde.

They were upset that they hadn't been appointed traffic officers, wondering why they weren't worthy of the honor, but there were compensations. *The Winslow Boy* was cast, and Bev got the role of the Winslow Boy's suffragette sister, Puddles was elected vice-president of Future Nurses, and Snowy was given the *Smoke Signal's* "Junior Jive" column of junior news. It, like the other class columns, had always been humdrum reporting of class meetings and projects, and Snowy decided to change it. In the *Smoke Signal* office she found a file of newspapers from other schools, studied them, and quite ruthlessly stole a style that would get herself noticed.

JUNIOR JIVE
by Snowy

Hi there!

Lost:
  one Frankie and Patty

Found:
  one Joe and Nancy

Which twin answered which question in bookkeeping?

Did:
  Puddles parallel-park?
  you memorize the Declaration yet?
  Carol tell?
  Ed flunk?

Where's the Cat Path?

Who:
  wrote "I love Mr. Foster" on her desk?
  has dimples?
  swiped the windshield of a 1949 Ford from the
      junkyard?
  does homework?

What if:
  there weren't any Classic comics?
  Bev's eyes stayed crossed?
  the Rose of Texas was Red?
  beauty wasn't its own excuse for being?

Have you heard Dudley's latest?

                                              Bye


"Junior Jive" became the most discussed column in the news-paper.

Snowy passed her driver's test, without any mistakes on the written test or eye exam. She did scrape the curb, parallel-parking in front of Woolworth's, but she didn't stall on Worm Hill. When her license came from Concord, she asked for the car and took her first drive alone, just downtown to the library to get another of Mrs. Moulton's novels, yet it seemed a trip into a new life.

The girls had begun losing interest in Girl Scouts after Washington, fewer and fewer of them attended the meetings, and now Mrs. Simpson moved away, and the troop folded.

Puddles talked Snowy and Bev into going to a Ground Observer Corps meeting at the Elliott Park Clubhouse and then talked them into joining. Snowy didn't want to, anything that didn't contribute to her success in school seemed a waste of time, but Puddles said her country needed her, and Bev said it would be an adventure. Puddles and Nancy Gordon observed on Tuesday nights, Snowy and Bev on Thursday nights from six to eight. The post was an old fire tower outside town, a snug little room reached by a zigzag metal stairway. Their first Thursday, an elderly woman joined them and, while she sat cozily braiding a rug, explained what to do and Snowy and Bev tried not to giggle. They never did get it straight how to tell a good plane from a bad plane or how to report them, so they ignored them. They brought their *Senior Scholastic* magazines to the tower to study for the *Senior Scholastic* world-events quiz Mrs. Moulton gave every Friday, and they got so silly over world affairs, shrieking, "Russia won't say hi to France anymore!" and drawing mustaches on the photographs, that New Hampshire could have been bombed into smithereens before they knew it.

Afterward, unless Bev was sleeping over, Snowy would drive her home, and on the way back to town she always had to fight a temptation to see how fast she could get her folks' 1951 green Ford going.

There were no football games on Saturday nights, so she and Tom went to the movies or sometimes baby-sat his little brother. One night Tom lured her upstairs to see the hope chest, and then of course she was shown his bedroom. It was a spartan and oddly anonymous room, with just a narrow bed under a plaid bedspread, her school picture on the bureau, and an early-shop hanging bookcase of three shelves held together by ship's line. The bookcase contained some moldy *Tom Swifts* and a stuffed owl that glassily watched Tom being blown on his bed. Tom had to use his handkerchief, a bit of a problem. Knowing it would be a disaster to put gooey handkerchiefs in the hamper, he had simply thrown them away. Then, when his mother one day commented, as she unloaded the washing machine, "Goodness, Tom, where are all your handkerchiefs going to?" Tom had dashed out and bought a box of Kleenex for the car.

They never did this in his room again—Snowy was too nervous that his parents would return or his brother would wake up —but they necked on the sofa, watched television, and raided the refrigerator. Sitting in the living room she'd once been unable to believe existed, munching a ham sandwich, Snowy felt so secure and domestic that the loss of mystery was only a wisp of regret.

James Dean, the movie star more real to them than any other, was killed in a car accident.

Snowy and the five other members of the class-ring committee visited the jewelry stores downtown and examined the rings displayed by ring salesmen. They selected three, one from each store, and in homerooms the juniors voted. Snowy and Bev wanted the modern streamlined one, but the kids chose the most traditional, gold with the school crest on an onyx stone. The next day the jeweler came to the school and took their ring sizes, and Snowy learned that hers was 4½. She half-jokingly mentioned this to Tom, who said, "For future reference?" A diamond, though, seemed an eternity away; the class ring was a present milestone. The first time Snowy wore it, with her white blazer and dark blue pullover and black watch pleated skirt and white socks and white bucks, she felt taller, and she knew she was truly an upperclassman.

And at last she knew how she was going to become famous. Reading Emily Dickinson in her American lit textbook, she decided she would be a poet. And with the resolve, the poems began. Her first poem was:

> Death:
> Save it will wait
> Until this life
> That moves so fast

Gives time
For dreams to last
And least of all
Be something more
Than merely dreams
Dreamed before.


Apple autumn dulled to gray November.

There was snow the morning of Veterans Day, and rain which stopped by late afternoon. The night was cold, the field muddy. But this was the big game, the one to decide the Class A Championship, and nothing could cancel it. Snowy jumped and clapped and screamed herself hoarse, although the big crowd didn't need any encouragement from the cheerleaders. When the third quarter ended, the score was still Gunthwaite 27, Rumford 6, and the crowd was crazy, bellowing taunts at Rumford, roaring out its glee.

Then the Abnaki coach pulled the team off the field and sent in the second string. Snowy saw one muddy first-stringer turn and run back to join the clean white-and-green second string. She gasped, "Isn't that Tom?" He was so filthy she couldn't read his number. "How come he's going back in?"

Charl said, "I don't know!"

He was going back in because his replacement, Ron Moore, disliked centering and had yelled at him as he ran past, "Stay in, ask coach, so I can go into half position!" The Rumford coach, admitting defeat, sent in his second string. Gunthwaite kicked off, and Rumford ran the ball back surprisingly well and completed a pass for a touchdown. In the huddle, Tom tried to rally the guys. "Let's stop the kick, that's all, let's stop the kick." But they didn't. The score changed to 27-13, which was not worrisome, yet the crowd quieted, intent.

Rumford kicked off, a short high kick down the middle. Full-

back Ed Cormier ran forward to take it, Tom charged toward
him, and as Tom turned to run interference for him, Ed fumbled
the ball and dropped it.

The crowd groaned.

Ed flopped crouching over the ball, and the two teams
jumped on him. Tom, in the tangle of cleats and helmets, felt the
pile begin to sink, as such piles always did. Then he heard a hollow crack. Like a gunshot. It was the most awful sound he had
ever heard in his life.

"Jesus Christ," he shouted, clawing at the guys, trying to
reach Ed, "get off him! Get the doctor!"

Ed lay broken on the muddy field.

Charl clutched at Snowy. "Ed's hurt!"

Snowy raced down the field right into the silent group of
shocked players. Tom grabbed her and hugged her against him,
rocking, saying over and over, "This fucking stupid game."

The doctor kneeling beside Ed said to the coach, "His spine.
Get the ambulance."

Snowy understood the words only when she looked up and
saw in wonderment Tom's charcoal dirty face streaked with
tears.

The next Saturday, they played a benefit game with Rumford
to raise money for Ed. He was paralyzed.

Snowy had been a patient in the hospital just once, her tonsils
and adenoids at the age of four; ginger ale and ice cream and a
new dress to wear home. She'd worked there after school during
the winter of her freshman year when the Girl Scouts had done
a nurse's aides project, but the place still frightened her. She had
not been a good nurse's aide. The first time she was asked to feed
someone, a horrible old lady with bedsores, the poor woman had
thrown up on her and she'd rushed howling out of the room.

She and Bev took to hiding in the floor kitchen, checking the nasty meals, loading them onto the trolley, and gossiping. Puddles loved the hospital and trotted around as efficiently as if she were already an RN. Snowy and Bev had to hush her descriptions of bandages and bedpans, but they did go with her into the maternity ward and stand looking through the big window at tiny red babies, who unfortunately were so swaddled that Puddles couldn't give a lesson in balls.

Puddles said, "I'm going to have six children. Three boys and three girls."

"Well," Bev said, "I guess I will too, and let the nanny take care of them."

Snowy looked at the babies, and although she couldn't believe she could produce even one, she said, "I'm going to have twins, twin girls, and name them Dawn and Dusk."

So this was the first time she had to go to the hospital to visit someone. The principal announced in assembly that Ed was now able to have visitors and wanted them.

Bev was rehearsing. Snowy went with Puddles, but at the door of Ed's room Puddles hung back. "You go in alone first. You were his girl, you're the only one he's ever gone steady with."

"Puddles—"

"Go on."

She knocked.

"Come in."

She never would have thought that hearty Ed could be so pale.

He said, "Snowy."

"Hi."

She hadn't known what to bring him, she'd left it until the last minute, and after school at the supermarket near the high school she'd almost bought him some Bazooka Bubblegum because he used to joke about how she was always blowing a bubble when he wanted to kiss her, but this seemed too frivolous, so she'd bought a small box of chocolates. She placed it on the white bedside table in the clutter of magazines, a radio, a glass with a crooked glass straw.

He said, "Thanks."

"You're welcome."

"There's a chair over there; you could bring it over."

She did and sat down, her schoolbooks on her knees. He lay in a white cocoon, and she remembered all the dances they'd gone to.

He said, "How's school?"

"Okay." She racked her brains. "Tuesday I have first period study in the caf, and all of a sudden there was this huge explosion in the kitchen, it actually jarred us, and the bells started ringing for janitors and then the fire drill bell rang and we had to go outdoors, wondering what in the world had happened, and then the bell to return to classes rang in the midst of the passing bells, we didn't know what the hell was coming off. But when we got back indoors, somehow people found out, and all along the corridors everyone was saying the pressure cooker had blown up and what would we do about lunch. Well, at the end of second period a notice came around and we skipped fourth period, we went to fifth and sixth after third, and we got out of school at one thirty."

She paused for breath, knowing that Bev would have told the story better.

But he grinned. "I wonder who monkeyed with the pressure cooker."

She smiled. "I never thought of that."

A silence. Snowy listened for Puddles, praying she'd come in before Snowy started crying.

He said, "It was just about this time of year we started going out, wasn't it?"

"The Thanksgiving Dance," she said. "The Gobble Wobble."

"Two years ago."

"Yes."

"Tom's a great guy, I like Tom."

"He'll be here to see you tonight."

"He was the one who got them off me, wasn't he?"

"I don't know."

"My dad mentioned it."

Snowy clasped her hands, which were shaking, on her books. He said, "How come we broke up?"

She didn't answer.

He said, "We broke up at that birthday party Linda had at the Yacht Club. You were wearing that stuff like towels."

"Terry cloth." Her white terry-cloth sleeveless blouse and short-shorts outfit. With black espadrilles.

He said more vaguely, "It was at the end of school," and she realized he was falling asleep.

The white room smothered her.

Puddles knocked and looked around the door.

Snowy said, "He's asleep."

"They're probably still keeping him doped up."

As they left, Snowy held her books to her chest and walked head down, her teeth gritted against tears. She watched the miracle of her legs moving.


At Christmas, Snowy gave Tom a hardback copy of *For Whom the Bell Tolls*, trying to educate him, and Tom gave her a heart-shaped gold charm engraved "I Love You."

Her parents gave her a portable Royal typewriter. They'd been trying to decide between it and a new winter coat, but when Snowy's report card showed A's in all subjects except typing, a C in typing, her first C, they concluded her coat could go another winter and she must have a typewriter so she could practice at home. She typed on it her latest poem:

Upon one foot
I've stood
In corners full of care,
And played
On wax-crayon afternoons
Alone
Beneath the stair.

The poems were still a secret, even from Bev.

The Alumni-Varsity basketball game was on New Year's Eve. Snowy never wanted to see another football game in her life, though she would have to next year, but she understood and liked basketball, and she liked the change in their cheerleading uniforms, the green jumper worn with a starched white long-sleeved blouse instead of the green jacket, and white sneakers instead of saddle shoes. They cheered for the Varsity; the JV's and some of last year's Varsity who were home, like Gloria Taylor home from Skidmore, and some who'd never left and were working in town, cheered for the Alumni. Linda had quit cheerleading after not making Varsity, so the JV's now consisted of three juniors, Diane Morrissette and Carol Tucker, co-captains, and Nancy Gordon, and five sophomores, Mary Ann Lefebvre, Becky Harris, Theresa Sullivan, Eleanor Bixby, and Gail Perkins. Bev sat with Jack in the bleachers and watched once more Roger leaping, twisting at the hoop.

She had sent him a Christmas card, writing nothing on it except "Bev." During the holidays she kept hoping he would phone. He didn't. Wearing Jack's football, she sat on the bleacher, and yells rocked the bright sweaty gym, and she watched Roger win the game for the Alumni at the last second with a fantastic shot from the far end of the court.

After the game they went to the New Year's Eve party at Sam Page's. Sam's was a new house, a ranch house in the new development of long, low pastel houses set naked on old pasture-land. The living room had knotty-pine paneling, which Snowy thought very beautiful and modern. The girls waited there, talking, and the boys hid in the kitchen telling dirty jokes and swilling beer, until Adele decided they'd had long enough and went in to fetch Sam.

The boys straggled out, and couples began to dance. The record player sang: "Well, you can cry me a river,/Cry me a river,/I cried a river over you."

Someone turned off the overhead light, but in the lamplight Bev, dancing with Jack, glimpsed Roger dancing with Gloria. Jack hummed off-key into her ear. Roger looked thinner and older. The beer can Jack held against her back sloshed.

Tom said, "Let's see if Times Square's on," and knelt down in front of the television. He'd brought Snowy a beer, and they sat cross-legged on the rug and smoked Lucky Strikes and watched the wild crowd on the television screen and Snowy told him about stopping in New York en route to Washington and seeing *The Glass Slipper* at Radio City Music Hall and the Rockettes. "One of their dances," she said, "ended in a huge *salad*." It had been as unreal as the high gray city. When they'd got back on the bus and headed for Baltimore, where they would spend the night at Mrs. Simpson's mother's house, the girls eventually fell asleep, except Snowy, who leaned against the window and looked out at the lights of the night towns they sped through and thought about all the different people who didn't live in Gunthwaite, New Hampshire.

Tennessee Ernie Ford boomed from the record player: "Y'load sixteen tons and what d'ya get?/Another day older and deeper in debt./Saint Peter, don't you call me, 'cause I can't go —/I owe my soul to the company store!"

The living room wasn't big enough for so many kids jitterbugging. The blond coffee table got knocked over, Tom caught a lamp before it fell, beer spilled, and Bev, spun by Jack, bumped into Roger.

"Excuse me!" she gasped.

More kids arrived. Sam's parents were out at another party, the kids had the house to themselves; bedrooms were busy. On Sam's bed, Gene was unhooking Puddles' bra. Jack started for the bathroom but passed out in the hall. The twins played a trick on their boyfriends, pretending to be each other, and it was as successful as when they played it on teachers. Bev located her beer behind the plastic sofa where Mike and Judy MacGregor were necking, and took a sip and gagged. Someone had put out a cigarette in it. Starving Snowy appropriated a whole box of Cheezits.

Tom yelled, "It's midnight!"

And everyone kissed. Snowy was kissed by more boys than she ever had been since spin the bottle at junior high birthday parties, but she didn't enjoy it because Tom, rather drunk and very happy, was having such a hell of a good time kissing all the girls. Bev, released by Victor Andrews, found herself in Roger's arms, once so familiar, now strange again. He tilted up her face, they looked at each other, her arms went around his neck, and as they kissed, they started to dance, circling slowly, together in the noisy gang of kids.

"You're my dream come true/My one and only you."

Tom grabbed Snowy. "I saved," he said, "the best for last."

Nineteen fifty-six had begun.

"Gilly won't be able to resist," Puddles said. She and Snowy were walking downstairs after school to the gym office one Friday in late March. "I'll bet my bottom dollar Gilly will make the twins co-captains. So cute."

"So cunning," Snowy said.

Puddles said, "Want to hear the latest song Gene taught me?"

"No!" Snowy said, but she waited, and Puddles sang to the tune of "Stormy Weather":

Don't know why
I've got lipstick on my fly,
Sloppy blow job.

"*Puddles!*" Snowy said.

The new Varsity squad, chosen Tuesday, Puddles and Snowy and Charl and Darl and Diane Morrissette, Carol Tucker, Mary Ann Lefebvre, and Gail Perkins, gathered in the gym office. Gilly sat on her desk and said, "Before we start to work out the formation, I want to say that this is the year we are going to win first place."

The girls laughed and clapped. Gunthwaite last month had again come in second at the cheerleading tournament.

Gilly said, "It's been a hard decision, but after much thought I've decided to entrust this responsibility—"

She paused. Charl crossed her fingers.

"—to the girl whose marks would indicate she's most capable of bearing it. Your captain is Snowy."

Puddles shrieked.

And as the girls hugged her, Snowy's first stunned thought was "We want a touchdown over *where?*"

The wintry year continued curving toward spring and the Junior Prom.

Snowy was in charge of the decoration committee. Because the prom was so important, the juniors had voted to have the Dennison Company plan the decorations. No Kleenex carnations for the Class of '57. One Saturday in early April, she and Carol Tucker and Dudley Washburn and Ron Moore got a bus to Concord, where they took a train to Boston. Snowy had never been on a train before, and its weary grime and cigar smoke dismayed her. They arrived at North Station. The city quenched their mission; they stood, four small-town kids, and looked at the shock of slums.

Then Dudley, who'd been here before, recovered his aplomb and said, "The only route I know to anywhere is through Scollay Square," and they walked to Dennison's insulated by the boys' wisecracks about strip shows at the Old Howard. A Dennison lady drew them designs appropriate to the *Ocean Fantasia* theme. After lunch at a Waldorf Cafeteria, Dudley led Snowy and Carol to Jordan Marsh, and the boys went off exploring on their own. The girls were so dazzled by such an enormous store that they couldn't make up their minds what to buy and finally chose only shortie nighties, which they could have bought at Dunlap's Department Store. Then they got lost. They couldn't find the entrance where they were supposed to meet the boys— "Wasn't it the one near the perfume?" "Or was it the one near the pocketbooks?"—and Snowy, beginning to panic, fearing they'd miss the train, said, "Let's go outdoors, I think I can recognize it from outside." They walked around the building, and there were Dudley and Ron waiting. "Thank God!" Snowy said, and ran up to Dudley and kissed him.

"Why, Snowy," Dudley said. "I didn't know you cared."

The rumpus room soon was a chaos of paper mermaids, baby octopuses, pastel sea horses and seashells, and the kids on the decoration committee worked there after school and in the evenings. Dudley, still the class president, overseeing all the details of the prom, stopped by to find out how they were progressing and stayed to cut out mermaids, whose long locks didn't quite cover their breasts.

"I never realized that mermaids don't have nipples."

"Dudley!"

Everything seemed happening at once. A twenty-five-page research paper was due in English the Monday after April vacation, and Snowy began writing about Edna St. Vincent Millay. Gilly noticed her ice-cream lunches and told her she must eat a hot lunch to set a good example, as a captain should, and she obeyed, but she went so broke she applied for and got her job at Sweetland and worked Friday nights and sometimes Saturdays and Sundays, while Tom worked at Varney's. She and Bev bought new gowns for the prom; Bev's was lavender and Snowy's pale pink, and they cost nineteen dollars and ninety-five cents. Before English class one day, Mrs. Moulton told Snowy she had been chosen editor of next year's *Smoke Signal*.

One Saturday she drove with her parents to Massachusetts, first to South Hadley and an interview at Mount Holyoke, then to Northampton and Smith. The pictures in the catalogs became reality, and she wasn't disappointed. Both campuses awed her. Feeling young and clumsy, she sat across a desk from a smoothly suited woman at each school and sought the right tone, not too cocky, not too timid. They spoke of her accomplishments and appeared satisfied with her. But there was still the hurdle of College Board exams next winter. And as she and her parents drove home, Snowy in the back seat didn't listen to her father's discussion of scholarships; she held Laurie and told herself that this was what she'd strived for all these years, yet she was on the brink of crying. She couldn't imagine life without Tom.

The first day of April vacation she walked to the high school and met Larry Clark, the editor of the *Smoke Signal*, in the *Smoke Signal* office. It was a tiny room lined with bookshelves of discarded English textbooks and crowded with a wooden typing desk and chairs. She remembered how frightened she'd been the first time she'd knocked and entered to face a laughing gang of upperclassmen. A sophomore, with a dumb question about a first assignment. And now the office was hers.

Larry said she might as well do the next issue, to get the hang of it, and she worked with him all day. She learned to calculate how much space a story would take up, she learned proofreading marks and headline sizes, and she learned the drudgery of typing up handwritten stories. She took them and the layout pages home, and when Tom came to pick her up for the movies, she asked her folks if he could go upstairs and see the project. It was very impressive, the big papers hanging over her desk, rulers, pencils, the stack of stories, but it was also a terrible responsibility.

Tom said, "I guess I won't be seeing much of you this week."

"I really don't know if I can get everything done."

"I could come help. Type stories or make an octopus."

"Hey, the treasure chest, could you help us with that?"

They didn't go to the movies again that week. Snowy worked on the *Smoke Signal* during the days, while down in the rumpus room the kids made Neptune and bubbles and pink fish; Tom worked at Varney's and came over in the evenings to join Snowy and the kids who'd returned after supper and he helped build the treasure chest and finish the main octopus which would be hung in the center of the gym ceiling, its tentacles swooping out. She went to visit Ed, home now, on Tuesday night as had become a habit, and brought him a mermaid. She had to work from eleven to six Wednesday at Sweetland, but she got the newspaper done by Thursday, and Larry drove her to Leicester, where she met the printer and was shown the print shop. Thursday night, she and Bev Ground-Observed before returning to the decorations. Friday, she picked up the heels she'd had dyed pink to match her gown, bought a new petticoat and a necklace-earring set, typed her research paper, and helped the kids finish the last sea horse. That evening, she sprawled limp on the rumpus-room sofa, while Tom cranked the Victrola and played an old album of Bing Crosby singing Western songs like "Don't Fence Me In" and "Pistol-Packin' Mama."

"Smile," he said. "It's over."

"No, it isn't."

"Oh, you'll get the decorations up okay tomorrow, you've got all day."

But he knew what she really meant, although she had never said a word about wanting to be Queen.

She chewed the tip of her ponytail and once again checked a mental list of her accomplishments against Bev's. She always came out ahead, until she looked in a mirror.

At seven o'clock the next morning, she loaded the decorations into the car, picked up Puddles and Carol Tucker, and drove to the high school. Bev arrived, and more and more kids came in throughout the morning, and they did not fool around as they had when decorating for the freshman and sophomore dances; they worked. They ate lunch at Hooper's. By four o'clock the big octopus was hung, the card tables were set up, the chairs had been lugged from the cafeteria and the throne from the Dramatics Office, and it was all finished. Snowy's feet hurt worse than after working at Sweetland.

She drove Bev home and drove back to her own house. She sat on the toilet and soaked her feet in a dishpan. She took a bath and washed and set her hair. Then she lay down on her bed with the hair dryer her parents had given her for her birthday, and tried to relax.

She couldn't.

At six thirty, she carefully brushed her hair out into thick curls, and began to dress. Garter belt, nylons, underpants, strapless bra and falsies, hoop, three petticoats, and the pink gown. Mascara, red lipstick. Earrings, necklace, the pink shoes. She went into her parents' bedroom and looked at herself in the full-length mirror.

Tom picked her up at seven fifteen, bringing a wrist corsage of pink rosebuds. She had to be at the dance early, because she was one of the receiving-line ushers, with Bev and Jerry Kendall and Frankie Richardson. She was so sick of the decorations she couldn't tell how the gym looked, but the chaperons and judges assembling into the receiving line were exclaiming over the big octopus, and Mr. Stoddard, the principal, complimented her. "Even a redheaded mermaid!" he said.

"Yes," she said, "Bev thought we were discriminating, with just blondes and brunettes."

He laughed.

Bev's escort was Roger, who'd come home for the dance. She had broken up with Jack on New Year's Day, and although she and Roger hadn't started going steady again because they agreed it was childish, and Bev went out with other boys and Roger with other girls, they wrote letters, and they were friends again.

The ushers took the kids through the receiving line. The chaperons were Mr. and Mrs. Stoddard, the superintendent and his wife, and Mr. and Mrs. Dodge, and the judges were a lawyer and his wife and a dentist and his wife.

And then the lights dimmed, and the prom began.

The gym smelled of perfume and corsages. The dance band played "Deep Purple," and pastel girls and dinner-jacketed boys danced slowly around the floor, and soon it was the romantic evening promised. For everyone except the junior girls. Between sets, Snowy and Bev sat with Tom and Roger at a card table and giggled together, but they were too bright and hectic, and each was thinking, "It's either her or me." Tom wondered if any junior girl had ever died here of a heart attack.

The lights went up after "I'm in the Mood for Love." Mr. Stoddard stepped onto the band platform. He looked excited. Year after year he watched this, and it never ceased to fascinate him.

His resonant schoolteacher voice didn't need a microphone. He said, "All right, will everyone except the junior girls and their escorts please sit down. The judges are ready to choose the Queen of the Junior Prom."

Snowy saw Bev make the "oh, horrors!" face at her, and tried to laugh.

The band played: "A pretty girl is like a melody/That haunts you night and day. . . ."

As Snowy danced, the gym was a blur of blue and green.

The song ended.

"I'm sorry," Mr. Stoddard said. "A decision hasn't yet been reached," and he gestured at the band. The song lilted again.

They danced.

"Hey," Tom said softly, "it's okay, it's okay."

She smiled blindly at him.

Again the song ended. Mr. Stoddard stepped down from the platform. He walked over to the Queen's platform, which was decorated with green crepe-paper seaweed. The silence was absolute.

Mr. Stoddard said what he said every year. "It's been a fine dance, and I hope you'll have happy memories of tonight all your lives." He cleared his throat and glanced at his slip of paper. "The members of the Queen's court are: Patty Nichols!"

Applause. Patty walked through the crowd, and Mr. Stoddard helped her up the steps to the platform.

"Linda Littlefield!"

Applause. Linda joined Patty, dimpling.

"Charlene Fecteau! Darlene Fecteau!"

Applause. The twins were wearing matching gowns.

Snowy and Bev didn't look at each other. They clapped, their hands cold and sweaty.

"And now," Mr. Stoddard said, and beamed, "the Queen of the Junior Prom: Beverly Colby!"

It was a nightmare, Snowy would wake up and have another chance, but her hands stung as she clapped and she knew she was awake. She hadn't even made the court.

"Jesus Christ," Tom said. "Jesus Christ, you should be up there."

She'd trained herself so well that for a second he believed her

when she turned to him and said, "Me? I couldn't care less," and
laughed.

The last of the prom was a test of her control, with every
mermaid and sea horse jeering at her. All she wanted to do was
run home and hide, but she hugged and congratulated Bev and
chatted with Gene and Puddles, who said, "The twins, the goddamned twins!" and she danced and danced and danced,
laughing so wildly at Tom's jokes that as "Goodnight, Sweetheart" began he said, "Take it easy, Snowy," and pulled her very
close to him.

She and Bev changed at her house. While the boys waited
downstairs and Bev changed in the spare room, Snowy's mother
came rushing in her bathrobe into Snowy's room. "I just
couldn't sleep, did you make Queen?"

Snowy unfastened her necklace. "Oh, no, Bev did, of course."

"Bev? The court, though, you made the court?"

Snowy took off her earrings. "No."

"Neither?"

Snowy hissed, "Will you get the hell out of here?"

"Henrietta!" Her mother slammed the door.

As they went downstairs, Bev said to Snowy, "It's such a stupid thing, really."

Snowy laughed. "No, it isn't, it's an honor, I'm so glad for
you."

At Roger's house, Bev phoned Julia while Roger changed.
Bev said, "There's royalty in the family now."

"Queen? Oh, Bev. I wish your father—"

"Yes."

There was a pause.

Julia said, "Snowy?"

"The twins got two places on the court, and Linda and
Patty."

"How is she?"

"Putting up a front."

"Damn. I don't suppose she'll ever get over it."

Bev said, "What we both should've done, we should've boy-cotted the prom, we should've gone to the movies."

"But you had fun?"

"I've got a crown of roses and a trophy and people took zillions of pictures, a newspaper guy, too."

"I can't wait to see them. Congratulations, darling. I'll go tell Fred, he'll be tickled."

They went to the party at Dudley Washburn's house. Snowy drank three vodka-and-orange-juices and dizzily kept up the gaiety, even afterward, parking with Tom, until the necking began, the undressing, and then his mouth was between her legs and she was twisting and shuddering, her moans rising to a scream, but even when she lay exhausted and felt the tears start, she held them back.

It was the green and yellow time. There were dandelions on the lawns, and when Snowy walked home from school after a spring rain, she stepped carefully over the pink squiggles of drowned worms on the sidewalk.

For Tom's birthday, she typed copies of her poems and, with the big birthday card she'd saved from last year, gave them to him, confessing her ambition. In his bedroom, Tom lay on his bed and read them, astonished and puzzled.

> Pigeons walk like
> Fat men round
> Where fountains work
> And people flutter
> Down about the circus.

Snowy and Dudley were chosen to go to the Model UN at Plymouth Teachers' College. They represented Ceylon, so it was rather uninteresting; they couldn't dramatically stalk out of the General Assembly as Russia did. They stayed in the dormitories. Snowy's roommate was a girl from Nashua. Those three days were a bleak preview of four years without Tom.

In the National Honor Society assembly, the new members were announced: Nancy Gordon, Betty Jane Owen, Henrietta Snow, and Dudley Washburn. And at their first meeting, Snowy was elected president, and she was elected general manager of the Radio Club, while Bev was elected program director, and Snowy and Nancy Gordon and Diane Morrissette and Betty Jane Owen were chosen to go to Girls' State, and sometimes Snowy could forget all about the Junior Prom. But at night, in bed with Laurie, she always remembered.

The 1956 *Totem*, the yearbook, came out, and Snowy, leafing avidly through for pictures of Tom, saw him sheepish all over the page of Superlatives. He was not the Most Likely to Succeed (Larry Clark was), but he had been voted Most Flirtatious, Best Dressed, Best Line, Friendliest, Best Dancer, and Best All-Round. He'd never mentioned this; her awe of his being such a Big Deal returned.

Tom had finally made a decision. "I figure if I can't stand it," he told Snowy, "I can quit, but I sure the hell couldn't quit the service if I wanted," and he applied at Rumford Teachers' College and was accepted into the Trades and Industry Department.

June. The tall classroom windows were open, and in drifted the warm summer breeze that disturbed both chalk dust and students. A Wednesday was the last day for the seniors. They were let out after third period, and the school shook with the stampede. Snowy and the rest of the typing class in fourth period leaned out the second-floor windows and watched the seniors run for their cars. Then the rite began. The cars sped along the street and up the driveway behind the school, circling it, horns blaring, seniors yelling, and Puddles said, "There's Tom!"

The top of the cream-colored convertible was down, and the

car was packed with kids. Snowy saw Joanne Carter crushed against him.

As the cars gradually left and the horns faded, throughout the school the juniors looked at each other. They were the seniors now.

Snowy learned what Bev meant about ghosts. It wasn't Tom; it was Joe Spencer at the tunnel traffic post, it was Frankie Richardson who was the proctor of 4C lunch.

Snowy herself had the traffic post in front of the *Smoke Signal* office. Bev's was the post in front of Mr. Foster's room, and Puddles' was downstairs on the first floor, where she had a grand time intimidating the entire junior high.

Snowy was one of the ushers at Class Day on Friday. She had to swallow back tears when she saw Tom cap-and-gowned, marching in with the other seniors. During the awards, he was given the Outstanding Traffic Officer plaque. She worked at Sweetland that night, and Tom picked her up afterward and they went parking.

He said, "I forgot to tell you. The banquet before the Senior Prom, we have to go in couples, we have to take a senior girl."

"Oh."

"I asked Joanne awhile back."

"Oh. She's going to Rumford, too, isn't she?"

"Yes, an elementary major."

"Her guy is there?"

"Well, actually, he's quitting. To get the service over with and then go back."

"Oh."

He tugged her ponytail. "Snowy, it's been a million years since I used to ride her home on my bike."

So she giggled.

She would never wear the pink gown again. She wore her white one to the Senior Prom, and then she and Tom changed and went with Puddles and Gene and Bev and Butch to the party at Victor Andrews' camp. Snowy and Tom were sitting on the wharf drinking beer when Tom suddenly grabbed her and said, "You aren't playing games, are you?"

"Games?"

"I *was*," he said. "Back at the beginning. Not any more."

On Sunday and Monday the senior boys got drunk so that they would be traditionally hung-over for graduation Monday night. Snowy watched Tom walk across the stage and accept his diploma. He gave her the tassel from his mortarboard.

The last week of school was jammed with finals for the juniors. Tom came over in the evenings and helped her study, listening to her recite her textbooks. He'd never seen her memory going full-blast before. Geometry theorems, French vocab, the Declaration of Independence, she reeled them off, and when he started testing her with spot passages from the American lit textbook, she finished the passages for him as well as identified them.

To celebrate her last day of school, Tom brought a six-pack along to the drive-in that night. The mosquitoes were out, they had to keep the windows shut, but the night was so hot that Tom took his shirt off and Snowy did more nibbling at his chest than watching the movie. They left during the second movie and went parking at the Cat Path.

Snowy said, "I don't know how I'm going to stand it next year without you."

He hugged her. "Neither do I, baby, neither do I. I wish we could get married right now, right this very night."

They clung together.

Tom started work driving a Texaco tank truck, and Snowy went to Girls' State at the university from Sunday to Saturday. He picked her up in Durham that Saturday afternoon, and she chattered so fast all the way home she didn't notice how quiet he was.

"I got assigned to the Federalist Party and in the House of Representatives, the Federalists were the minority party, and we had to keep going to these asinine meetings and there were assemblies with guys speaking about Good Citizenship, and there was a damn *flag raising*, would you believe it, at seven o'clock the first morning before breakfast, I thought I'd pass out from hunger, and the lines at meals were so long that at breakfast the second day one girl actually did pass out. I ran for Governor's Council. There was a chicken barbecue, it was *très* good, and then a rally, first the Nationalists marched around yelling, and then us Feds, with us girls who're cheerleaders leading it, and the next day, like we feared, the Nationalists won all the offices. We ran out of things to do towards the end; at committee meetings we sang. Sheesh. And wouldn't you know it, they had to go and give us an exam yesterday. After, Nancy and I were so fed up with politics we went downtown and bought love comic books to read. Did you get my letter?"

"Yes," Tom said. "Thank you."

"I kept hoping for a letter from you. I missed you awfully."

"I started one, but I'm not much of a letter writer."

"You'll have to get better this fall."

That night at the drive-in, Tom turned off the speaker and turned on the radio. Snowy, sitting close to him, waited for him to kiss her, the first kiss in a week except for a brief horn-rimmed public one when he picked her up in front of her dormitory. But he didn't take his glasses off. He sat staring straight ahead at the big faces on the screen speaking words he couldn't hear.

He said, "Do you just think of me all the time? That's everything in your world?"

"Well," she said. "Not *every*thing."

He said, "But that's the way it is with me. And it's got to stop."

Sweat sprang out. She felt it streaming down from her collarbones, between her breasts.

He said, "I thought this week'd be like when you were in Washington last year, I'd go out with the guys and drink beer and horse around."

He moved for his cigarettes, and she jumped away from him.

He said, "I didn't. I was like a zombie. I wanted to see you so bad I almost drove down and kidnapped you."

He lit a cigarette and for the first time looked at her, offering her one.

She shook her head.

"And when I saw you today," he said, "I was scared, I was *scared* at how glad I was. Say something, Snowy."

She couldn't.

He said, "We've got four years. Four goddamn years ahead of us, add in the service and it's at least six. Six years like this week?"

On the radio, Pat Boone sang, "When I lost my baby,/I almost lost my mind./When I lost my baby,/I almost lost my mind."

Tom said, "All day I've been trying to think. What we've got to do is this: we've got to go out with other people."

Snowy was a white silent scream.

He said, "It's the only sensible thing. Admit it." He jabbed his cigarette at the ashtray and seized her. "Snowy, for Christ's sake, will you help me?"

She began crying so hard he was afraid she'd strangle. "Jesus," he said into the curve of her neck. "Jesus." He gave her his handkerchief and held her tight against him as she sobbed.

Elvis Presley howled: "I want you,/I need you,/I love you,/ With all my heart."

Tom snapped off the radio, threw the speaker at its hook, and started the car. Snowy slumped nearly lifeless in her corner.

She spoke. "I don't want to go home."

"You think the fuck *I* do? Home's where they feed and clothe you and you can't talk to anyone."

But he didn't take the road to the Cat Path, he didn't take the road to the sandpit, he headed for town and Emery Street.

He said, "Snowy, maybe we can make it if we try this. Don't you understand?"

"No!"

"We can't even be off-and-on like Roger and Bev. It's like we almost ought to make a date for four years from now. But in between, we've got to get loose of each other or we'll go crazy."

"Tom, *please*—"

He drove into her driveway and immediately opened his door. She didn't get out. He walked around and opened her door and lifted her out.

She was crying weakly as he carried her to the back door and propped her up.

He said, "Do you want me to take off the football?"

She straightened, braced for a moment by a flash of pure hatred. Her fingers trembled, but she unhooked the chain and slid off the football and put it into his hand.

He said, "I love you," and walked away fast.

Indoors, she scooped up Laurie and stood looking out the window over the sink, seeing through shimmery tears Tom sitting in his car in the driveway, his forehead on the steering wheel. Behind him, the dark river swerved into trees.

Then he sat up and drove off.

Her parents were watching television in the living room.

Her father said, "You're home early."

She said, "It was a lousy movie."

Her mother said, "Where's the football?"

"Oh," she said, "the chain broke," and she and Laurie went upstairs. She automatically undressed and put on her shortie nightie. Tom's yearbook picture smiled at her from the bureau. She opened her closet and touched his letter sweater.

Then she went into the bathroom and opened the medicine cabinet and tipped iodine into a glass. It was deep red. The glass shook in her hand. She raised the glass to her mouth.

And she poured it down the drain, went back to her bedroom, where Laurie awaited her on the bed, and, between crying jags, she tried to reread an Agatha Christie. She was still awake when her parents went to bed. Their bedroom talk ceased; they were asleep. She took off her nightie and pulled on dungarees and a sweat shirt, tiptoed downstairs, found the car keys on the kitchen counter, and drove to Morning Street. His car wasn't in the driveway. She drove around downtown and at last saw it parked in front of Jimmy's Diner. So when she drove home, she knew where he was. Over there, across the river from her.

High in white gingerbread, the dance hall terrace overlooked the black lake.

Snowy walked along with Victor Andrews. They paused and leaned against the scrollwork railing, and she tried to pretend she was on a great ocean liner far away from Gunthwaite.

"Nice night," Victor said.

"Um," she said.

She was wearing a sleeveless brown linen sheath with a shoulder-to-shoulder scooped neckline of white linen, white heels, a deep bronze tan, her hair in a chignon, big feathery white earrings that covered her ears, and new perfume. She'd found she couldn't stand her White Lilac anymore, it meant Tom; she'd bought Summer Shower, which was spicy, not sweet.

Victor's hand slid up her arm. She winced. She could hear the band playing "String of Pearls," trying to sound like Glenn Miller. This was her first date with Victor.

The triumvirate had reunited to rally around Snowy. Puddles let it be known, through Gene, and Bev through Roger and her other boyfriends, that Snowy was available, and during the past three weeks she'd had dates with Ron Moore, Butch Knowles, Wally Smith, and a summer boy. And Puddles and Bev had created a network of spies. When Bev and Snowy walked to Sweetland each noon, Bev would report that Tom hadn't been seen anyplace last night with any girl, and Puddles would come in for her A&P break and confirm this. So Snowy was sure he hadn't had a date since they broke up, and she was heartened and bewildered. She drove past the Texaco plant a lot; once she saw him there, standing on the cab bumper peering under the hood, but he didn't see her. This last Tuesday, her day off, the big red Texaco truck roared toward her as she was driving home from the beach, and Tom honked the horn and waved. Snowy nearly drove off the road. All evening she waited for him to phone her. He didn't.

At Sweetland, she worked dazed. She loathed the customers even more this year, because it seemed that every goddamned one of them would put money in the jukebox and play: "When I lost my baby,/I almost lost my mind./When I lost my baby,/I almost lost my mind."

Her conscientiousness saved her from getting fired. Zoe, the headwaitress, even complimented the way she cleared off the booth tables, organizing dirty plates and silverware very neatly on her tray. She never mixed up orders, as Bev was apt to. Like a robot she worked, pausing only to lean on the counter and joke feverishly with the girls of the Gang, or boys, who'd stop in during their breaks and days off and have a frappe. She kept up the front with everyone except Bev and Puddles. Her parents thought she had caused the breakup and were rather relieved, because Snowy and Tom had seemed to be getting so serious.

On nights when Snowy and Puddles or Bev didn't have a date, they would do what was known as "broad around." Snowy's parents had traded in for a new secondhand car, a black 1955 Ford, and sometimes Snowy took it, or sometimes Puddles took her parents'. They would pick up some more of the Gang and drive to the lake and stroll around the penny arcades, bowl a few strings, play miniature golf, and flirt with the boys who were also on the prowl.

Or Snowy would go visit Ed.

The first time he'd seen her football-less, he said, "What the hell happened?"

In the dark duplex, his bedroom was so small that the hospital bed filled it. The mermaid had been tacked on the wall. He lay in heaps of magazines, and his radio played continuously.

She said, "We broke up."

"Who? You or him?"

She shrugged.

He said, "Who?"

"Well, him."

"That son of a bitch."

She sat straighter. "It's not a regular breakup. I mean, he wants us to go our own ways until we're through school."

Ed stared. "I don't get it."

Neither did Snowy, but she said, "It's quite sensible."

As Puddles had remarked, when she heard the news, "Leave it to Tom to do something weird like this."

The next time Snowy visited, Ed said, "Tom was here last night. I can't figure him out."

"Did he say anything?"

"I asked him what was going on, and he said he didn't really know."

The words chilled Snowy, each an icicle.

Ed said, "In my opinion, he's all screwed up."

She began to visit Ed more often, on the chance she might run into Tom there, but she didn't. She was too tormented to notice that the frequent visits had begun to make Ed hope.

His radio sang: "I know you belong to somebody else/But tonight you belong/To me."

And at the dance hall, the band played "String of Pearls," Victor's hand slid up Snowy's arm, and as he turned her from the lake to him, she looked at his face, his taut eyelids across his deepset eyes, getting closer and closer to her face.

She said, "Let's go inside and dance."

He froze. "Okay."

They walked back through the doorway to the dance floor.

Gossamer bunting clouded the pink and blue and green lights, as it had last summer when she'd come here with Tom. She wondered if last summer would forever be the happiest summer of her life.

And then suddenly she was angry at herself, furious that she was here at this nice place and hating it and hating Victor, who was spending money on her. His arm around her waist, he drew her in to dance. The band attempted one of the latest songs, "On the Street Where You Live," and Victor said something about UNH, where he'd be a freshman this fall. For the first time she made herself really listen to him.

She said, "Did you have senior English with Mr. Foster? What's Beowulf like?"

"I'll say I did. He calls Grendel and Grendel's mother the gruesome twosome—"

"Who's Grendel?"

"Well, he's this big monster that Beowulf fights."

"A monster with a *mother?*"

They laughed, they spun, and Snowy saw Tom dancing with Gail Perkins. Tom was looking at her.

She didn't stumble. "And Chaucer," she said, "what's Chaucer like?"

Victor said, "Foster made us memorize the Prologue from

*The Canterbury Tales*, eighteen lines of it, in Middle English."

"I bet you can't still do them!"

"What do you bet me?"

"Well," she said, and smiled up at him.

" 'Whan that Aprille with his shoures soote,' " Victor began rapidly, " 'the droghte of March hath perced to the roote'—"

Snowy gave the dance hall a quick scrutiny, hunting for Bev, who was here with a summer boy. She didn't look at Tom again.

"—'And bathed every veyne in swich licour, of which vertu engendred is the flour. Whan Zephirus'—"

The bandleader began to croon: "I have often walked/Down this street before/But the pavement always stayed/Beneath my feet before—"

"—'Hath in the Ram his halfe cours y-ronne,' " Victor said. "Give up yet?"

"Is that all of it? You've got to do all of it."

She saw Charl, here with Jack O'Brien once again, flutter her hand on his shoulder. Snowy raised a nonchalant eyebrow.

" 'The holy blisful martir for to seke, that hem hath holpen whan that they were seke,' " recited Victor, finishing triumphantly just as the song and set ended. "Okay, I did it, let's go outdoors."

"Wait, there's Bev, I've got to speak to her."

"Oh."

Bev saw Snowy and Victor coming toward her and said, "Excuse me," to her date, hurried to Snowy and said, "I've got to fix my hair, want to come?"

Bev's hair never needed fixing.

"Yes," Snowy said.

The ladies' room was the usual mess of paper towels and clogged toilets. Girls and women, some none too sober, went in and out. Snowy said, "Gail Perkins."

Bev fished a lipstick out of her bag. "I must say he's in his second childhood. JV cheerleaders again."

"She made Varsity, remember? I voted for her."

"Snowy," Bev said, and began the pep talk with which she and Puddles tried to jar Snowy out of her trance. "If he can put you through this misery, he doesn't love you, and you've got to get over him. He's not worth it. What'll he be four years from now? A shop teacher! You deserve something better."

"He's Tom," Snowy said, trembling.

"Don't cry, your mascara'll be ruined."

"Yes," Snowy said, and threw back her head, a trick that made the tears run sideways out of her eyes. Bev handed her a Kleenex.

Bev said, "How do you like Victor?"

"He can recite eighteen lines of *The Canterbury Tales.*"

"Can Tom?"

A large woman lurched against them.

Snowy said, "Bev, did you like Victor?"

"I might've, if I'd given him a chance. If I hadn't been such an idiot about Jack."

"Brace up," Snowy said fiercely to her reflection in the mirror. "Brace *up.*"

Tom, on his way to the soft-drinks counter, saw her come out of the ladies' room and thought he must be insane to be here with anyone else.

This was indeed his first date. He had worked, hung around Varney's, and slept, and then as he began to be able to think about available girls, the ones not pinned or going steady, he dismissed the ones he'd dated before Snowy, considered all the others he'd flirted with, and last night he drove to Riley's Drive-in Restaurant, went to Gail's window, ordered a frappe, kidded, and asked her out.

He knew from gossip at Varney's that Snowy had been going out. The guys thought he'd simply broken up with her, so they discussed her in front of him, Ron and Butch and Wally saying she was as cold as her name but if Tom had gone steady with her all that time there must be some hope she'd melt. Tom laughed and didn't answer. He pictured Snowy in parked cars with them, unprotected. He tried not to look for her everywhere, but always he watched for the flick of a dark-blond ponytail.

She was walking back to Victor. She seemed as aloof as when he first knew her, though he guessed it wasn't shyness now; it was a barricade of true haughtiness. He found himself walking after her. No ponytail tonight. But the white scooped neckline ended in a bow in back, with two long white linen ribbons streaming down, and he gave one a tug.

She turned, and they looked at each other.

Bev said, "Come on, Snowy, the guys await us."

Neither heard her.

Bev sighed and left them, seeing Gail watching at Tom's table.

Tom said, "How've you been?"

"Okay."

The band began to play, and they started to move into each other's arms, it was so natural.

Tom said, "You smell different."

Snowy stepped back and put her chin up. "Do I?"

Tom remembered the lifeless girl he'd carried to the door. He felt fear. He said lightly, "I hear you're giving the guys a hard time."

Then he saw that her small hands were clenched into fists at her sides.

She said, "What the fuck do you care, Thomas Brandon Forbes?"

"Snowy—"

She whirled, white ribbons flying, and walked away.

He'd never known her to say "fuck" before.

He went on to the counter for Half-and-Half mix, and returned to Gail and the gin in the paper bag under the table.

Victor was waiting at Bev and Summer Boy's table. He stood up, and Snowy said, "Let's dance."

They danced. Victor could feel her shaking.

"Look," Victor said, "you still got something going with Tom?"

The band was playing the theme from *Picnic*, which Tom had once called, when they were parking, the sexiest song ever.

"Tom?" Snowy said, and laughed. "Who's he?"

Victor began to dance her toward the terrace.

God *damn* it, Tom thought, and took a big swig of his drink, lit a cigarette, and turned to Gail, who was talking nervously about how the dishwashing machine at Riley's had broken down today. She had a short brown DA, big brown eyes, and a quirk of smiling sideways. She was stacked, and Bill LeHoullier claimed she was hot stuff.

Tom said, "It must've been some day. How about another drink?"

Out on the terrace, Snowy and Victor were kissing. She heard the band begin to play Old Favorites.

"Heart of my heart,/I love that melody."

The islands in the lake were distant and black.


Puddles said, "Joanne came to my register yesterday, and I asked her when Rumford started. For them, it's this Monday, same as us. The freshmen have to be there a week early. Funny to think they're going to be freshmen all over again, isn't it."

"*Très drôle*," Snowy said, and shifted into third. It was the Friday before school began, and they were driving to the high school for the last cheering practice before the first game. Since mid-August they had been practicing every weekday rainless morning; the girls like Puddles, who went to work at nine, had had to rearrange their hours. In the back seat were piled twelve hundred copies of the *Smoke Signal*.

Puddles said, "She was in to buy some Tampax. Remember when we couldn't use it, remember the time I tried?"

Their freshman year, they had gone giggling into the drugstore, cased the joint to make sure no boys were there, and Puddles had bought a box of Tampax while Snowy and Bev buried their heads in love comic books. At Puddles' house, Puddles sat on the toilet, and outside the bathroom door Bev declaimed the instructions, and Snowy had hysterics on the floor. Puddles had emerged and said, "Impossible." Bev had said, "No milestone?"

Snowy stopped at a stop sign. "Remember how you said we'd need the Big Milestone before we could?"

"Well, we didn't really. Just a finger."

"Puddles!"

Puddles said, "And after last night, I'll never have any trouble again."

Snowy stalled the car. She stared at Puddles. "The Big Milestone?" Puddles didn't look changed.

"Yes. Oh, it was bound to happen sometime anyway, but what with Gene leaving for UNH next week and all—you and Tom never did?"

"No," Snowy said, grinding gears, "not quite. Puddles, what if you get pregnant?"

"Well, he used two skins, poor thing, it's a wonder he could come at all."

Snowy hesitated. "What was it like?"

"It hurt like hell, but I figured after all the fuss about it, it ought to be more fun, so we went to Hooper's and had a frappe and then went back to the Cat Path and tried again. And it was."

Snowy burst out laughing.

Puddles said, "I can hardly walk," and giggled. "Oh, Tom was in Hooper's with Alice St. Pierre. He sure is back to his old ways, playing the field, Gail and Alice and Becky and Darl, keeping them all in a dither."

"Okay, Puddles," Snowy said, and flicked the directionals for the high school driveway. The long lawn was sunburned.

Puddles said, "Joanne mentioned she's getting a ride to Rumford with him Sunday."

Snowy said, "I've been thinking of cutting my hair."

"You want to set it? Just ask me, pincurls every night."

"I know, that's the drawback."

"Nobody'd recognize you without the ponytail."

"I can't wear it the rest of my life. I can't be an old gray-haired lady with a ponytail."

"You only want to shock Tom. I wouldn't cut off my hair for anyone who treated me like he has you. What did you and Victor do last night?"

"We finished folding the *Smokes*. Then we went parking up at that big old house for sale on that hill, and he told me he loved me a million times and asked me to go steady two million."

"You might as well say yes. There sure the hell aren't any new guys left in school to go out with this year, just the ones we've known since we were freshmen."

"Well, I was tempted."

"To see if you could make Tom jealous."

Snowy parked in the parking lot. "Know everything, don't you?"

Puddles giggled. "And I bet you finally let him Get Fresh after you said no. A consolation prize."

Snowy laughed and got out of the car.

September, and already the mornings were crisp, the sky a deeper blue, and she felt that she and Puddles should be wearing slacks and sweaters instead of their dungaree short-shorts and gray sweat shirts. Another September. She and Puddles loaded up with the *Smoke Signals* and walked to the school she had conquered. Another September, and the last.

Puddles said, "God. I miss Gene already, and he hasn't even left yet."

The quiet school smelled of varnish.

In the main office, Mr. Stoddard smiled at them. "Well, Snowy, just as I expected, you've got the newspaper done on time."

"Thank you. Is it all right if I leave it here and Betty Jane and I'll come in this afternoon and count out copies and take them to the homerooms?"

"Fine, just fine. Put them over there on those chairs. No one's waiting there to be called in on the carpet—yet!"

They lowered their stacks to the chairs. Snowy stood back and looked at the slick newspapers with satisfaction. Betty Jane Owen, the assistant editor, had assigned the columns and stories this summer, and Snowy had spent all her spare time in August doing the layout of the six big pages, editing and typing the stories, choosing headlines, writing editorials, then taking everything to the printer in Leicester, going back again for the proofs, correcting the proofs, returning them, and at last collecting the finished newspaper and folding the copies. When school started, the *Smoke Signal* staff would fold the next issues on the auditorium stage before homeroom. Snowy only regretted she'd had to use last year's pictures in the ads, kids posing in the downtown stores, and there was Tom with his white grin in front of a television in the furniture store. The photography staff promised new pictures this month.

She handed Mr. Stoddard a copy. "Compliments of the management."

"I'm very grateful. How's—" He noticed that she wasn't wearing Tom's football. He kept remarkable tabs on romances during the school year but always had to get his bearings again each September. So he didn't ask after Tom; he said, "How was your summer?"

"Ice-creamy. Yesterday was my last day, thank heavens."

"Well," Mr. Stoddard said, "this ought to be a good year."

"Yes," they said dutifully.

Snowy said, "We're off to cheering practice now."

They went down to the basement, and Snowy unlocked the gym office door, and they loaded up again, with eight megaphones. Out back, the rest of the Varsity squad was watching the football players charge walking dummies and blocking sleds.

Darl said, "Punctuality, Snowy, punctuality. Isn't that what you keep telling us?"

"I'm sorry, we had to deliver a mountain of *Smokes,* but that's no excuse—"

"Hey," the girls said, "the *Smokes* are out, can we see one?"

"How about after? Thank God, they're not using the field, we can try 'T-E-A-M' on the fifty-yard line. Come on."

Gail muttered, "Slave driver."

They did "T-E-A-M" twice. Snowy saw that Puddles was moving awkwardly. She shouted through her megaphone, "Okay, great, that's great, let's go back to the bench and run out into 'Abnaki Nation' formation," and as they walked back, she said in a low voice to Puddles, "Are you okay? Your cheering's rotten."

Puddles looked at her and saw Authority. "I'll restrain myself before the first game, Coach."

"You mean it wasn't just this once, you and Gene are going to do it again?"

"Why not?"

"Think of Adele and Sam."

Adele had scraped through graduation without anyone's realizing she was pregnant until she and Sam got married right afterward. Sam had planned to go to UNH; he was now working at Trask's.

Puddles said, "Two skins, remember that. I wish I could figure out how to get hold of a diaphragm."

"A what?" Snowy said.

Puddles said, "Hey, there's Joanne."

Joanne, wearing a sweater and slacks, was sitting on the cheerleaders' bench, and she was crying.

Charl rushed to her and hugged her.

Joanne whimpered, "I knew I shouldn't've come here, I knew I would cry."

Charl had already cried with Joanne and Adele and Rita and Nutty after the last basketball game, but she began to cry again now.

Joanne said, "I'm such an idiot. Such an idiot. Anyone got a Kleenex?"

No one had.

Joanne sniffled. "Snowy, the squad looks wonderful."

"Thank you," Snowy said.

Joanne stood up and took her by the arm, leading her away. "You've got a tougher job than Adele and I had, there were two of us they could get mad at, but I still think Gilly's right to have only one captain again. No one knows who's boss the other way." Then, when they were a distance from the girls, she said, "What on earth happened with you and Tom?"

Snowy shrugged.

Joanne said, "Ever since grammar school, he and I have been, well, we've been friends. Sounds funny, doesn't it, but that's what we are."

Snowy reflected that she and Dudley had been friends a long time too, but Dudley had never ridden her home on his bike.

Joanne said, "Did you break up with him?"

"I guess you could call it a mutual breakup."

"Oh. Then you don't want me to talk to him? I'm getting a ride down to Rumford with him Sunday."

"Are you?" Beneath the coolness, Snowy was begging her, *ask him to write me, ask him to write me.*

"I just thought maybe I could help."

Snowy's cynicism had sharpened during the summer. She

wondered if Joanne wanted to play matchmaker only to be able to talk very intimately with Tom about love. She studied the fraternity pin on Joanne's left breast.

She said, "Well, if he wants to write me, he knows my address," and started walking back toward the girls.

Joanne sniffled again. "Hey, everybody, see you later, alligator."

The girls clung to Joanne, wishing her luck. As she walked away, Snowy suddenly dashed after her.

"Joanne!"

Joanne turned.

"Tell him—tell him—"

Snowy stood, words welling up in her, none of them adequate. Tell him I'll love him forever and ever.

"Tell him I said good-bye."


"Look out!" Snowy yelled, and the hot test tube shattered in the beaker of cold water.

She jumped back, bumping into Dudley, who grabbed her. Dudley was her lab partner. "Jesus," he said, "you ought to *play* football instead of cheer. It's supposed to break."

Around them in the chemistry room, the kids continued the iron sulfide experiment, test tubes glowing like furnaces.

"I know," Snowy said, "but my God. I'm never going to be Madame Curie, that's for sure." She wondered why Dudley kept on holding her by the shoulders; he had his balance back.

Dudley was wondering, too. Then he saw her hanging upside down on the jungle gym, pigtails dangling, her little skirt over her head. A vision flashed in his mind of Snowy with her skirt up in a parked car, and his reaction was not brotherly.

"I'll be damned," he said.

Snowy said, "Let go, Dudley, Mr. Howe will see."

Dudley let go. "I have observed that you are not wearing a football this year, not a football or a basketball or a class ring or a fraternity pin or a chastity belt."

"Dudley!"

"Am I correct in deducing you might be free to help me at the NFL dance tonight after the game?"

"Well—" Snowy said. She'd planned on going right home after the game to finish next month's *Smoke Signal*.

Dudley said, "We might even trip the light fantastic."

Snowy giggled.

He touched the Stevenson button nearest her left breast. She was wearing her own letter sweater, the white knit covered with green letters and stars: JV cheerleading, Varsity cheerleading, GAA, NFL, Thespians, and a gallant display of Stevenson-Kefauver buttons. A Stevenson button had replaced the Awful-Awful button on the chunky beige plastic pocketbook which had replaced the plaid ice-cream bucket. Election year, and the senior sociology classes were working on a mock election, and he and Snowy and Bev, almost the only Democrats in the class, were campaigning against great odds. Snowy's parents were Republicans, and they had been horrified by her buttons. Dudley said, "We Democrats have to stick together, you know."

"Okay," Snowy said. "Politics does make strange bedfellows—"

Dudley started laughing.

"Oh, God," Snowy said. "See why I never went out for debate, only prize-speaking? Foot in my mouth."

They went back to the experiment.

Mr. Howe, the chemistry teacher, called, "All right, class, finish your notes and start cleaning up the lab area. Read the next chapter for Monday, and we'll see a film about the mining and manufacturing of potash."

"Won't that," said irrepressible Dudley, "be stimulating?"

\*     \*     \*

This year Snowy was more an executive than a student. At first she was surprised that everyone seemed a little afraid of her, even Bev, even Puddles, everyone except Dudley, and then she got used to it.

She had only four courses again, sociology, French II, chemistry, and English, and she spent her study halls in the *Smoke Signal* office, sometimes working very hard on the newspaper, but other times just sitting kidding around with members of the staff, to whom she was allowed to give excuse slips. Bev and Puddles were columnists; Bev did the "Platter Chatter" column about hit songs, and Puddles, with Darl, did the "A Senior?" column which showed a baby picture of a senior, listed the senior's traits and quotes and accomplishments, and at last revealed the senior's name. Ron Moore did the sports page. To the seniors on the staff, the office became a refuge from study halls.

Dudley was once more elected president of the class. Snowy was elected vice-president, and she and he, with Shirley Blanchard, the secretary, and Frankie Richardson, the treasurer, began to plan rummage sales and car washes and dances.

Gilly was pleased with the cheerleaders. During the summer, Snowy had finally put her mind to her father and Puddles' lessons in football, and now she understood it. But although she jumped and yelled more enthusiastically than ever, she never again enjoyed it.

Snowy even found herself teaching English. Whenever Mr. Foster was busy, he asked her to take over; so there she was in front of the class teaching the Chaucer she had feared and pretending to be exasperated at Dudley's wisecracks about the Nun's pinched wimple.

She went out with Dudley, and with Joe Spencer and Ron Moore, and when Victor came home, she went out with him. She wrote him once a week, wondering why on earth she was bothering when it was Tom she should be writing to. All day long she talked to Tom in her head, telling him her news as always.

And news of him seeped back from Rumford, mainly via letters from Joanne to Adele, who told the girls who visited her in the shabby upstairs apartment she and Sam had rented. Snowy knew that Tom had a job washing pots and pans in the college kitchen, that he went beer drinking a lot with older guys who had GI Bill money, and that he had taken Joanne to the movies three times.

Puddles said, "Platonic, my foot!"

One day Snowy learned he had taken a little blond home ec major to a party at the married students' barracks. That night, when she'd finished her homework, she looked around her room and then gathered up her dolls, leaving just the toy animals, and carried them up to the attic. She brought down some cartons and packed away her childhood books. She cleaned out her souvenir drawer, throwing away everything except the Tom souvenirs, the paper napkins and gum wrapper, the "Battery Dead" note and the Parker pen she didn't use now, a limp red balloon, the "I Love You" charm she'd broken off her bracelet, ribbons, the pink heart-shaped box which still smelled of Valentine chocolates, the figure of Laurie he had carved for her seventeenth birthday, three pressed corsages, and the tassel from his mortarboard, and these she put in another carton and laid his yearbook photograph facedown on top. She hadn't been able to decide what to do about the letter sweater; tonight she folded it neatly, went downstairs and got a brown paper bag and cut it open into wrapping paper, wrapped the sweater, tied the package, and addressed it to, "Mr. Thomas Forbes, Rumford Teachers' College, Rumford, New Hampshire."

She lay in bed, stroking Laurie, listening to her radio: "Well, I never felt more like crying all night,/'Cause everything's wrong and nothing ain't right/Without you./You've got me singing the blues."

One Sunday morning in October, when the church bells were chiming and on her desk the *Smoke Signal* layout pages awaited her, Snowy left a note for her sleeping parents, fed the ducks, and drove to Bev's.

Julia was drinking coffee and smoking her second cigarette at the kitchen table, watching a chipmunk in the bird feeder. "Hi. Bev's still asleep."

"I figured she would be. I hoped you might be up."

"What's the matter?"

Snowy said, "I think I'm suffocating."

Julia ground out her cigarette and took her jacket off a nail on the cellar door. "Let's go to the bog."

They walked past the barn into the old orchard. Julia paused and picked up a few dropped apples and tossed them at the piles she collected for the deer. Then they walked to an arch of birches curving over the path to the bog, and they entered the woods. The leaves were fading.

Julia said, "Did you know one man could build sixteen feet of stone wall in a day?"

But the fields had gone back to woods, and the work was meaningless, the stone walls lost in the oaks and maples and birches and pines. Snowy and Julia climbed up through juniper bushes and stood looking down at the bog.

In the spring and summer it whirled with birds, and frogs popped out of the scummy green water; in winter it was a white bowl. Now the chilly breeze blew a patter of falling leaves into it.

Snowy said, "Bev calls me Madame President. Puddles calls me Coach. I'm me."

Julia sat down on a rock, her thin shoulders hunched. Snowy sat down on pine needles.

At the back of the bog was a steep gray wall, a cliff man-made of scrap rocks dragged here from the fields on oxen-drawn stoneboats and dumped.

Snowy said, "And this'll happen all over again. I'll go away to school and spend the next four years trying to be a big deal and get all A's and be best."

"You've proved it once. Isn't that enough?"

"I don't want to, but I'll do it."

"Well, some of it you can't help, can you? The A's. You're a student."

"I'm not really. I've got a good memory, that's all. I don't want to spend the next four years memorizing."

Julia said, "It never ceases to amaze me that Bev is always able to remember her lines in her plays."

"Maybe she forgets everything else to save up for them."

"Most of the time I'm glad she's having fun, but sometimes I wish she wanted more. She won't consider New York and acting because it would be a grind."

"There's her millionaire."

"That's make-believe. She's never dared imagine a real marriage because she knows real men die."

Snowy picked up an acorn cap, a miniature of the berets she wore in her childhood.

Julia said, "If now she's talking about Boston and going to Katharine Gibbs and being a secretary and having fun until she's found a boss rich enough to marry, well, what I hope is, by that time Roger'll be through law school and she'll marry him. I suppose that's what I hope."

"When Tom broke up with me, he said it was almost like we ought to make a date for four years from then."

Julia turned and looked at her.

Snowy said, "Because it got too serious too early. I've figured that out."

"And you're waiting?"

"I don't know. All the girls he's—I don't know. I packed his stuff away and put it in the attic."

"You were fifteen when he was the one you wanted. When you go off to school, you'll meet boys from all over."

"Yes."

They listened to the leaves.

Julia said, "Think of everything you've accomplished. Aren't you proud of that?"

"Yes, but I don't want to do it again; it'd be going backward."

"Then what do you want?"

"To learn to write poems."

Julia always left her cigarettes at the house so she wouldn't smoke in the woods. She stood up. "You've caused a nicotine fit. Let's go back. Or would you rather stay here?"

"I guess maybe I will."

Julia walked along the path. A chipmunk fussed, and she stopped and saw it peeking at her out of a stone wall. Suddenly she turned, it disappeared, and she walked back to the bog. Snowy was sitting chin up, but a muscle was jumping wildly in her jaw.

Julia said, "I just had a thought. I've heard of a school in Vermont, Bennington College. No tests, no marks."

"*What?*"

"Why don't you send for the catalog?"

Snowy did, and applied, and one Saturday she drove with her parents over mountains to Bennington. The dormitories were white clapboard houses; classes were held in a low red clapboard building called the Barn. She saw girls wearing dungarees and sweat shirts, and she gawked at the girls walking barefoot even in autumn, wearing leotards and tights and dirndl skirts, their long hair hanging straight. At the interview, the woman smiled and said, "If you were cast away on a desert island, what one book would you like to have with you?"

"A dictionary," Snowy said.

They laughed.

On the way home, she and her parents stopped at a Vermont

roadside store, and her parents bought a wicker muffin basket and Snowy bought a maple sugar man.

She had set her hair the night before, but when she got home, she washed it again and combed it straight and looked at herself in the bathroom mirror. And as she walked around her bedroom getting out clothes for her date with Ron Moore, she kept glancing at herself in the mirror over the bureau.

Then she said to Laurie, "No, I'd better wait till I know, this might jinx everything," and her hands went up to curl the tips for her ponytail.

The Wednesday before Thanksgiving was a half day. Snowy had a study last period, but she handed in her excuse slip and got to the *Smoke* office before any of the other kids and locked herself in and sat down, hugging her stomach and crying. She had cramps, but what ached most was the foreknowledge that Tom would come home and would not call her.

Somebody knocked and tried the door, then knocked again.

"Snowy?" Dudley said. "Anybody in there?"

"Just a minute."

She blew her nose.

"Hi," she said, opening the door. "Sorry, I forgot it was locked."

"Getting yourself some peace and quiet? I wanted to check with you about the decoration committee for the Christmas Dance—hey, Snowy."

He put his arms around her.

She said, "I'm just being stupid."

"You need a vacation."

"And lots of turkey," she said.

"And pumpkin pie."

"And cranberry sauce."

"And mince pie."

"And boiled onions."

"And apple pie."

"And a ton of stuffing," she said, "that's the best part. What do you like, wet or dry stuffing?"

"Wet."

"So do I."

He kissed her. She'd never been kissed in school. He said. "You ought to requisition a sofa."

"Dudley!" she said halfheartedly.

He said, "I've got a secret that'd make you feel better."

"You have?"

"You'll have to swear you'll never tell I told you."

She drew back and looked up at him. He wasn't joking.

She said, "Of course I won't tell."

He rumpled her bangs. "I can't imagine why," he said, "but the Key Club has voted you the Key Club Sweetheart."

"Dudley."

"I didn't lobby for you, I honestly didn't. You'll be given the award in the next assembly. You'll have to practice looking flabbergasted."

"I will," she said. "Isn't that nice of them."

"I think you get a locket or something."

"Isn't that nice."

The bell rang. He'd earlier made a date with her for tonight. "I'll pick you up at quarter of seven?"

"Okay."

It was a rainy evening. They went to a war movie, Jack Palance in *Attack!*, and Snowy saw Tom two rows down, with Gail.

She didn't want to see him and Gail again at Hooper's, so after the movies she said, "I'm not hungry."

"Good God," Dudley said.

The place he always took her parking in his 1950 black Ford was a dirt road beyond the new housing development. Civilization, as Dudley pointed out, was encroaching, and where would people go parking twenty years from now?

They parked. On the radio, Johnny Cash sang: "I keep a close watch on this heart of mine./I keep my eyes wide open all the time./I keep the ends out for the tie that binds./Because you're mine, I walk the line."

Dudley said, "You got a date tomorrow night?"

"Yes."

"Victor?"

"Yes."

"Friday night?"

"Frankie," she said, a little smugly. Frankie Richardson was the captain of the football team.

Dudley said, "Frankie? I thought he was going steady with some sophomore babe."

"They broke up."

"How about Saturday night?"

"Victor."

"Christ," Dudley said. He began to pound his fist softly against the steering wheel.

She guessed what he was going to ask. The radio now was playing a Bing Crosby song from *High Society*. "Remember, Samantha," Bing sang, "I'm a one-gal guy," and she wondered, as she had when she saw the movie with Victor last summer, if that was her disease. Was she a one-guy girl?

Dudley said, "Okay, I've had enough of this. I'd break a leg if I tried to get down on bended knee here, but—let's go steady."

She regarded him. For her, the question was which might disturb Tom, going steady or keeping a stable of boyfriends. She chose what Tom was doing. "No," she said. "Thank you, though."

"Why?"

She quoted Bev. "Going steady is childish."

Dudley said, "Is getting married childish? It's going steady for good."

"That's someday."

"Damn it, I love you."

She reached over and slid a pack of Pall Malls out of his shirt pocket. She hid again in a quote. " 'What is love? 'tis not hereafter; present mirth hath present laughter.' "

"Oh, bullshit," Dudley said.

She lit a cigarette.

He said, "Is it Tom Forbes? Who broke up with whom?"

She exhaled and watched the curl of smoke.

So Dudley changed tactics, knowing she liked him funny. He tore the cigarette from her fingers, jabbed it at the ashtray, and shouted, "I'll win you yet, me proud beauty!" She started giggling, and he started kissing her.

Elvis moaned: "Love me tender, love me sweet,/Never let me go./You have made my life complete,/And I love you so."

For the first time, she let Dudley Get Fresh.

The day after Thanksgiving, the cheerleaders escorted Santa Claus downtown, and as they walked green-uniformed beside his red sleigh float, they distributed lollipops to the children in the crowds on the sidewalks. "Merry Christmas!" Snowy cried, running ahead, "Merry Christmas!" She thrust a lollipop into a small boy's hand and then recognized him. Tom's brother.

Above him, Tom said, "Hi."

Puddles raced up. "Look out," she yelled, "you'll get run down by Santa Claus!" and she grabbed Snowy's hand and yanked her along, but behind them they both heard Gail say, "Hi, Tom," and Darl call, "Want a lollipop, Tom? Want a lollipop?"

Tom sat drunk in a booth in his favorite Rumford beer joint, the Ritz Café. There were many wet circles on the table, from all the weeping beer bottles, and he drew his initials in them while he waited for his roommate to come out of the men's room. TBF. TBF. Thomas Brandon Forbes. What the fuck do you care, Thomas Brandon Forbes?

His cigarette stank in the ashtray's gray heap of butts. The jukebox sang: "Got along without you/Before I met you,/Gonna get along without you now."

The night after he'd taken Gail out, he had taken Darl with him to visit Sam and Adele and the very new baby. When he and Sam had come into the living room from the kitchen, carrying beer, he had overheard Adele asking Darl who had more boyfriends, Bev or Snowy. Darl said, "It's a toss-up." Both Gail and Darl had broken dates to be with him; parking, Gail let him Get Fresh, as she had last summer, and Darl, as last summer, didn't, still hoping to torture him into going steady. The next night, suddenly sick of these maneuvers, he had phoned Joanne, whose Chris was at the Coast Guard boot camp in New Jersey, and they went to the movies in Leicester, chummily eating popcorn and making wisecracks about the actors. But as they drove home, Joanne said, "Let's see if the Cat Path has changed any." Tom, speculating, drove there. It had not changed. Tom parked. Despite the rumors, he had never taken her parking; he had only kissed her goodnight. He looked at her. Joanne moved toward him and said, "Tom—" and then in a frantic tangle of sweaters, zippers, knees, he realized, astonished, that Joanne would let him Go All the Way. He banged open the glove compartment.

A tree branch became decorated with a teardrop Trojan thrown out the car window.

They didn't go to the movies the next night. They went parking. Tom's back still stung from last night's scratches. He touched the fraternity pin on Joanne's breast. She said, "Does it matter?" He said, "No."

Sunday they drove to Rumford together, and during the past month Tom hadn't dated any other girl except Joanne. He did feel guilty about screwing her while Chris was away learning how to guard the coast, but it was tail at last. And steady tail at that, by God.

The jukebox chanted, "Got along without you/Before I met you,/Gonna get along without you now."

Dan, his roommate, came down the dark aisle carrying a couple of beers. Standing up with a drink was as illegal in New Hampshire bars as Tom's drinking at eighteen.

Dan said, "You got the DT's already? You seeing snakes?"

Tom looked at the tabletop and saw that he had been drawing *S*'s.

He said vaguely, "This is my round. Isn't it?"

"On me. Merry Christmas." Dan sat down opposite. He was a freshman from Claremont, New Hampshire, a GI back from Germany, and a social studies major. "What we ought to do is, we ought to cut classes and head home tonight."

"I have to work breakfast."

"Well, I think I will. Supposed to snow tomorrow, anyway."

Tom pawed in the ashtray for his cigarette. He was trying to remember what Snowy looked like. He hadn't brought her school pictures or anything of hers here, and he had thrown away the brown wrapping paper with her handwriting on it, and there was only the faint scent of lilacs on his letter sweater. He thought, she'll have had her yearbook picture taken by now. He couldn't remember what she looked like.

He said, "How does a person change courses? I mean, say you wanted to change from social studies to, say, an English major, what would you do?"

"Go talk to the head of the English Department, I guess."

"Oh. Him." The head of the English Department was a sarcastic old man. The one teacher at Rumford Tom enjoyed was his freshman English teacher, Mr. Crawford, a big blustery guy belligerent with enthusiasm, who assigned not Dickens but *The Naked and the Dead* and *All the King's Men* and *A Farewell to Arms*.

Dan said, "You thinking of changing to English?"

"I'm just thinking."

Harry Belafonte called: "Day-O! Day-O!/Daylight come and I wanna go home."

Dan said, "Why the Christ do you want to change? You've got the life of Riley in shop."

Tom glugged beer. "I did not come here to learn how to plane breadboards. I know how to plane breadboards. But planing breadboards is what we have to do. Probably next semester we'll be allowed to learn how to build a bookshelf, if we get A's in breadboards."

Dan said, "What you should do is talk to Crawford. How're your marks in his class?"

"Maybe a C-plus average. I got a D on a grammar and usage test once. Why he bothers with that crap." Tom knew he would have flunked it if he hadn't been lectured so thoroughly by Snowy. "There's going to be a big grammar exam after vacation, before the end of semester. I do okay on the novels tests, though. He doesn't seem to mind my spelling."

"But, hell," Dan said, "it'd be work."

Tom said, "Maybe it's about time."

"If I wasn't all thumbs, what I'd do is change to shop. I've heard that at graduation, shop majors don't have to go chasing around hunting for jobs; the superintendents come here and the shop majors interview *them*."

"And get more money too."

"So why?" Dan asked. "Want to impress the gorgeous Joanne? Pipe and tweeds instead of coveralls?"

"Once in first grade," Tom said, pronouncing his words carefully, "I got up from my desk and went over to the window and looked out. I didn't think what I was doing, I just wanted to look out the window. But you weren't supposed to get up and look out the window. I had to be punished. The teacher got some rope and tied me to my desk. Her name was Miss Leach.

Joanne was in that first grade, too. I doubt if I could ever impress Joanne."

"I wonder. She doesn't act very pinned around you."

"She's lonesome for her guy."

"I sure would like to be the one cheering her up."

Tom lit a fresh cigarette, but its taste was dreary. The evening sagged.

He said, "Know something funny? It's a high school girl I want to impress. Isn't that a sidesplitter."

He saw her then, staring at him over her bouquet of red lollipops.

He said, "Isn't that a regular riot."


Bev said, "Snowy—"

"Hi," Snowy said into the phone and sat down on the sofa. "How does the gym look?"

"Wonderful," Bev said. She was the chairman of the decoration committee for the Christmas Dance. "The tree Jerry got is enormous."

"I hope lots of people come, we need the money."

Bev said, "Roger phoned this morning. He can't go to the dance, he has to go to Canada, his grandmother's dying. They were leaving right away."

"Oh, damn," Snowy said, "and after you've been slaving away all week making popcorn chains." Then she remembered to show sympathy for the grandmother. "I'm awfully sorry—"

"Snowy," Bev said. "Tom came into the gym while we were decorating the tree."

"Tom?"

Bev said, "He and a bunch of the old Varney's guys were just wandering around the school feeling nostalgic, I guess, and they saw us and came down and Tom helped me put the star on top.

He said he hadn't seen Roger yet this vacation, would he be at the dance, and I told him about Mémère."

Snowy was there ahead of Bev's next words.

Bev said, "So he asked me to go with him."

"Oh?"

"Well. I didn't know what to say. He asked if I had a ride home, and I said Jerry was giving me a lift, and he said he'd take me, and when we got to the house, I told him to call me after supper. I didn't tell him it was to let me have a chance to call you first."

A pause.

Bev said, "All you have to do is say no."

Snowy was silent, thinking that Bev herself could have said no.

Bev said, very tempted by Tom but cautious, "I don't want a mess like with Puddles that time. What I was wondering, though, is maybe he asked me so I can be a go-between."

"And you bought that nice dress specially for this dance, it'd be a shame to waste it."

"Are you over him? I mean, you haven't needed any pep talks for months."

Snowy's mother called, "Supper!"

Snowy said, "Did he mention me?"

"No."

"Have fun, see you there."

After she dried the supper dishes, Snowy went back to her bedroom and took down her pincurls and brushed her hair. She dabbed Wind Song behind her ears and between her breasts. Her hands nervous, she snagged a run when she put on a nylon and she had to file the fingernail and borrow a pair of stockings from her mother. She put on her new pale-blue wool sheath. And she kept thinking how she would be feeling if she were dressing not for Dudley but for Tom.

She opened her jewelry box and chose the Key Club Sweetheart locket. She didn't care, she told her mirror reflection; she just wanted Tom to see that she had been given it.

The Christmas tree in the middle of the dark gym was looped with popcorn strings and blue and red and green lights. It smelled of woods and movies. Snowy tried not to watch the doorway as she danced with Dudley, but she saw Bev and Tom come in. She looked away, into Dudley's sport jacket. When the record ended, Puddles pulled Gene over to Snowy and Dudley and drew Snowy aside and said, "What the hell is Bev doing? Where's Roger?"

Snowy said, "Roger had to go to his grandmother's. Tom asked Bev out."

"The bastard. And she said yes? The bitch."

"No, Puddles, she checked with me first."

"Don't you care? Well, I guess you're cured, all right. Look, there's Joanne and Chris talking to them, he's home. I wonder if he knows Tom's been taking her out."

Snowy glanced over and saw Tom standing between the two Junior Prom Queens, and she felt suddenly as plain as a nobody. She touched her locket.

Puddles said, "You decided whose picture to put in that yet?"

"No."

Asking Chris about boot camp, Tom was wondering too what Chris knew, and he was very relieved when the next record began.

"They call me the moonlight gambler,/I gambled for love and lost."

During intermission, the boys fetched refreshments from a cafeteria table at the back of the gym, and the girls clustered and chattered.

Bev said to Snowy, "He says school's a bore."

"Rumford? I don't doubt it."

Bev said, "I'd forgotten he was such a good dancer."

Dudley handed Snowy a paper cup of punch and a napkin

of cookies. "A toast!" he said, holding his own cup up at the Christmas tree. "God bless us every one!"

"Idiot," Snowy said, and giggled.

Dudley spread out his arms and began to serenade the tree. "*Mon beau sapin!*" he bellowed, "*Mon beau sapin!*" and Puddles and Bev and other kids from their French class joined in, and Tom walked up behind Snowy.

He said, "Eating as always, I see."

She turned and realized that he no longer had a crew cut. His hair was still cut very short, but it was brushed from a side part. Collegiate.

They both tried to think of something to say.

He said, "How's Ed?"

"Not too good," she said. "He won't do any schoolwork; he just listens to the radio and reads magazines."

Tom said, "I've been meaning to go over."

"He'll be glad to see you. I went over on Christmas, to take him his present."

"What did you get him?"

"Some paperbacks. Murder mysteries."

Not the present of love Ed kept hoping for.

Tom said, "Are you working at Sweetland?"

"No. I'm too busy, and I got a raise in my allowance."

He looked at the locket where his football had been.

Snowy said, "Just a little trinket from the Key Club."

He said, "How'd you earn it?" and then could have bitten his tongue off.

Snowy put her chin up. "Oh, I slept with them all and the entire Kiwanis Club."

Ever since last summer he had tried not to think that she might be getting laid. It didn't seem likely, she wasn't going steady and she hadn't let him even when they were, but—

"Lucky guys," he said.

He had hoped his date with Bev might make her jealous, because Bev was the only girl he had gone steady with except her. Snowy didn't look jealous. She looked distant.

He said, "Damn shame about Roger's grandmother."

"Yes."

Bev emerged from Dudley's clowning gang and said to Tom, "I'm dying of thirst, is that for me?"

He gave her the cup. "If I know punch, you'll be thirstier after than before."

Tom, smiling at Bev, giving her a cup of fruit punch. The pictures Snowy had suppressed of Tom on dates with other girls, Tom in the parked cream-colored convertible, came spinning back, kisses and whispers and flesh, and she almost fainted.

Dudley said, "I only wish Miss Hubbard were chaperoning, if she'd heard me I'd've gotten an A on the spot." He crumpled his cup. "Hi, Tom."

"Hello, Washburn," Tom said.

The lights dimmed. The record player sang: "I love my baby, /My baby loves me./Don't know nobody/As happy as we!"

Afterward, at Hooper's, Snowy saw Tom fooling around, tapping a tune on water glasses with a spoon. Bev made her Shirley Temple face at him, and Snowy remembered watching them here on their first date.

She and Dudley went parking on the dirt road past the housing development. Without the going-steady guide, she had had to invent her own code of morals: French-kissing was the limit, except with Victor and Dudley; Victor she allowed only to Get Fresh, but Dudley wasn't so easy to stop and each parking session became a contest, but because she didn't really want to stop Dudley, he kept winning, and tonight he won a blow job, while at the Cat Path Tom and Bev kissed and got reacquainted.

"Look," Tom said, lighting a cigarette for her. "What's the situation with Roger?"

"Oh, if he's home, I go out with him if I haven't got another date."

Tom lit his own cigarette. "Where are you going next year?"

"To school in Boston. Boston'll be exciting. My mother didn't like it, but I will. Puddles will be in Boston too, she's going to nursing school at Mass. General."

"And Snowy, she'll be over on the other side of Massachusetts."

"Well," Bev said, "if she gets what she wants, she'll be in Vermont with the cows, going barefoot and wearing her hair straight."

"Vermont?"

"Some school called Bennington." Bev bent her left thumb backward. "How come you broke up with her that crazy way?"

The radio was playing the theme from *Picnic.*

Tom said, "I don't know."

"I can't remember why we broke up."

"Neither can I."

"Well," Bev said, "that's all back in the Dark Ages anyway."

Tom said, "I remember the first time I saw you walking down the corridor." He put out his cigarette and reached for her. "It's a wonder you didn't get raped on the spot."

"Eek!" Bev said, just as Snowy would.


The Gang still sat gossiping in the auditorium balcony before homeroom, but they no longer were intermingled, they sat in two groups, College Prep and General.

Bev said, "There was a letter from *Tom* when I got home yesterday! He's coming home tomorrow, it's semester break." She glanced at Snowy. "He asked me out."

"Oh?" Snowy said.

"But it was an awfully short letter," Bev said, "and he didn't write about his classes and his marks, like Roger does, what he wrote about was some girl, the other night in the girls' dormitory she cut her wrists with a razor blade and then got in her bed, can you imagine, just lying there bleeding and waiting to die. But she was crying, and her roommate woke up and heard her and all, and called an ambulance. She did it because of some test, she'd flunked some test. Can you imagine?"

Snowy could.

Puddles said, "Did he sign it 'love'?"

Bev said, "Um, yes."

The homeroom bell rang.

As Snowy and Puddles walked toward their homeroom, Snowy took a deep breath and finally asked Puddles, "What's a diaphragm?"

Puddles halted, kids bumped into them, and Snowy realized, with a certain satisfaction, that for the first time in her life she had shocked Puddles.

Puddles said, "You're doing it? Who? *You're not going steady*. Dudley?"

"No, Puddles, nobody. I'm just curious."

"You're thinking about it."

"Who isn't?"

"Oh." Recovering, Puddles shifted her books from her hip to her chest and started walking again. "Well, a diaphragm, it's a sort of rubber saucer that fits over the cervix and keeps the sperm from swimming upstream."

"Puddles, how do you learn these things!"

"My mother forgot and left hers in the bathroom one time, and I asked her what it was."

"Sheesh. I can just see myself asking *my* mother. What's a cervix?"

"I'll draw you a picture in homeroom. The trouble with a diaphragm, you have to be fitted by a doctor, I haven't got the nerve. I've been trying to get up the guts to go into the drugstore and buy a douche bag, but I keep chickening out."

"You couldn't. Not even you."

"And where would I hide it? I heard at work that you can use Coke. Lie down and poke the bottle up you. Gene's stopped using two skins, he uses just one and he says one is bad enough, like taking a shower in a raincoat, so I tried Coke a couple of times, it sure feels peculiar."

"Good Lord," Snowy said, "if it's supposed to rot your teeth, what does it do to your insides?"

At Rumford, Mr. Crawford had told Tom to get a B on the grammar test. After a night of coffee and cramming, Tom passed with a B+. Mr. Crawford spoke to the head of the English Department, and when Tom came home that Wednesday for semester break, he was an English major.

He didn't tell Bev. After the movies, they went parking; the January night was cold, the car snug, and they kissed and she let him Get Fresh, but he didn't tell her.

He said at her doorstep, "Tomorrow night? We could go see Sam and Adele."

"Okay."

"Are you booked up for the weekend?"

"Well," Bev said. There was Chuck Watson Friday night and Butch Knowles Saturday night. She said, "I'll come down with the grippe," and laughed.

At lunchtime, the College Prep part of the Gang still sat at the same cafeteria table, beneath the proctor's desk, but now the General part sat at another table. Friday's 4C lunch was noisier than usual, because the week was almost over, and the College Prep gang was making most of the din, reciting at each other the sonnet they'd be tested on next period.

Dudley shouted, " 'The sea that bares her bosom to the moon'!"

Snowy said, "Honestly, Dudley. That's not the only line in the whole poem."

"It's my favorite. Or is it 'A Pagan suckled in a creed outworn'?"

"Damn," Bev said. "I keep forgetting which one's rising from the sea and which one's blowing his wreathèd horn."

Nancy Gordon said, "Proteus, then Triton. P comes before T."

" 'The sea that bares her bosom to the moon'!"

"Honestly, Dudley!"

Puddles said, "Well, well. Look who's here."

They turned and saw Tom strolling across the cafeteria. He stepped up onto the platform and spoke to Frankie Richardson.

Bev's heart began to pound.

Dudley said, "What's he doing here? Did he flunk out?"

Bev said, "It's semester break."

Dudley said, "Theworldistoomuchwithuslateandsoongetting-andspendingwelaywasteourpowers—"

Puddles giggled. She said, "Remember the frog's leg?"

Snowy put her unfinished tuna fish roll on her plate, stood up and picked up her tray, and walked along the aisle to the tray-return window.

Tom asked Frankie, "Who's got the tunnel?"

"Joe," Frankie said. "Joe Spencer."

"Oh. You guys shook up a Girl Scout camp once."

Frankie grinned, and they both looked down at Bev. Tom stepped off the platform and sat in the chair beside her. "You all set for that test?"

"Proteus," Bev said, wanting to skip school and go parking with him right now, right in broad daylight. "Proteus, then Triton."

"Adele phoned me this morning, to ask some more about what she could get for jobs in Rumford in case Sam does decide to go there. It'd be a tough time, paying for a baby-sitter and tuition and everything, but if Sam gets a job too, I guess they could manage. People do."

Bev said, "You really think he'll go?"

"He won't. It was beer talk. He can make more money at Trask's than at teaching."

"Are there married couples who don't have kids? Who both go to school?"

"Some."

Snowy, coming back along the aisle, saw Tom sitting in her chair.

Dudley said, "Hey, Snowy, you can sit in my lap."

Puddles said, "Don't, it'd be too dangerous."

Snowy hesitated, then laughed and sat down on Dudley's knees.

From the platform, Frankie called, "None of that stuff!"

"Jealousy," Dudley said, his hand on her hip.

Tom pushed back his chair and stood up. "Sorry. It's all yours." He tweaked the tip of Bev's DA. "How's your cold?"

Bev coughed. "Getting worse."

Tom surveyed the cafeteria, the green and brown walls, the green tables, the familiar faces, the unfamiliar, and thought how it went on year after year. He glanced at Snowy. "Food still as bad as ever?"

"Ghastly," she said.

He looked around the cafeteria again. "Well," he said to Bev. "Good luck on the test."

"Thanks," Bev said.

"See you," he said, and left.

Snowy, whom Bev had told about breaking her dates, knew he would see Bev tonight.

" 'A Pagan suckled in a creed outworn'!"

"Dudley!"


Snowy was chosen the DAR Good Citizen. In February, Bev won first place in Girls' Humorous at the State Prize-Speaking

Contest, doing a selection from *Pride and Prejudice*, and at the cheerleading tournament in the Leicester High School gym, against cheerleaders from the entire state, Snowy's squad won first place, to Gilly's joy.

When the other senior Varsity cheerleaders wept after the last basketball game, Snowy did not.

Puddles began crossing off the days on her calendar and announcing to everyone how many were left until graduation.

"Ninety more days."

Groans. "That many?"

Bev said, "My mother says this is a negative attitude, you should enjoy each day as it happens."

"Oh, sure," Puddles said. "I'm really going to enjoy the chemistry test tomorrow, I'm really going to hate to cross tomorrow off."

Snowy had no interest in graduation; she was waiting not for June but for May and a letter from Bennington. At night she would lie in bed and pat Laurie and recite poems in her head, but the question always broke through. *What if I don't make it?*

March 19 was a Tuesday. After the ceremony of the roast beef dinner and birthday cake, her parents gave her a set of white Skyway luggage, and Bev and Puddles gave her a travel clock. The girls did the dishes and then went upstairs to Snowy's room, and Snowy sat at her desk, and Bev and Puddles sat cross-legged on the bed, and they all opened their French books, but they didn't study and hadn't expected to.

Puddles said, "Now you can get married without your parents' permission. I wonder why boys can't until they're twenty-one, if it's eighteen for us."

Bev said, "We mature faster."

They giggled.

At Rumford, Tom was washing huge pots in the college kitchen and thinking about telephones. Her eighteenth birthday.

Puddles said, "Eighty-four more days. Sometimes it seems like it's going pell-mell, and sometimes it's just standing still. Ten more days till Gene can come home next weekend."

Bev said, "Tom won't be coming home again until April vacation." He had come home February vacation, and she had gone out with him every night.

Snowy chewed her ponytail.

Bev jumped off the bed and walked over to the bureau and looked at the birthday card from Ed and the gold diploma charm from Dudley. She didn't know how Snowy had been hoping for a birthday card from Tom, how Snowy now was hoping for a belated birthday card from him. Bev said, "It must be fun to go to school married. No more waiting. Tom says there are married students at Rumford, ones without kids."

Puddles started laughing. She lay back and threw teddy bears and pandas in the air and laughed and laughed.

Bev said, "What's so funny?"

"You at Rumford. Have you ever *been* there?"

"No."

"We've cheered at the high school. The town's just like good old Gunthwaite, except there's a bunch of crummy brick buildings and that's the college. Right, Snowy?"

Snowy thought of Main Street and the high school and the way this year she had searched from the bus window for the cream-colored convertible in front of the brick buildings. "I suppose," she said.

Puddles said, "You won't find any swan boats in Rumford."

"God," Bev said. "Isn't it awful to be in love."

"Are you?" Snowy said.

"God," Bev said.


At Puddles' door, Butch Knowles handed Snowy her overnight case and asked, "Tomorrow night?"

"I'm sorry, I've got a date."

"The next night?"

Snowy looked up at him, considering. It was the week of April vacation, and a cold damp wind blew against them, but Snowy was flushed, from beard burn and booze. This had been her first date with Butch since last summer. He worked at Trask's, and Bev said he had plenty of money, not like the guys in school, so when he took her to Hooper's after the movies she had ordered a BLT on toast (five cents extra) and a strawberry frappe. And when they went parking, he impressed her by producing a bottle of Seagram's 7, bought for him by an older brother, and a bottle of ginger ale and some paper cups. Snowy had two drinks but managed to keep pushing his hands away from her breasts.

There were shrieks of laughter in the kitchen.

"Fine," Snowy said, and opened the door. They both heard Puddles say, "By Who Flung Dung!" and Snowy said hastily, "Thank you for the evening," and hurried inside and shut the door.

"The Rooster's Mistake! By Rhoda Duck!"

Snowy giggled, wondering how Puddles' folks and brothers could sleep through this racket. Puddles had decided to have a pajama party because the Gang hadn't had a big one since their freshman year and Puddles thought there should be a last wonderful party before they graduated. She'd invited everybody, all the Gang.

"Hi, Snowy," Puddles said, shoving a pizza on a cookie sheet into the oven. "Now everyone's here, except Bev and Charl. You hungry? This'll take twenty minutes, but there's potato chips, and Mom made celery stuffed with cream cheese—hey, who the hell put them on the register?" She picked up the plate. "Want one?"

Taking off her jacket, Snowy looked at the chattering paja-maed girls and said, "Thanks, I think I'll go change first." She went through the living room, where blankets were heaped in the chairs and overnight cases were open on the floor, and up the stairs to Puddles' bedroom, which now was decorated with UNH as well as GHS pennants. She took off her clothes and put on her blue bermuda-length pajamas and her slippers and examined the pictures on Puddles' bureau, the large framed yearbook photograph of Gene, the wallet-sized unframed ones of herself and the other senior cheerleaders and Bev. She supposed that Puddles would transfer these and the pennants to her dormitory room.

She went back downstairs. Puddles was spooning tomato sauce over the next pizza and saying to Darl, as she had said through tears after the last basketball game, "It *isn't* the end, we'll be cheering at the Alumni-Varsity game at New Year's."

Darl said, "That won't be the same."

"I know."

Carol Tucker said, "And we'll probably have forgotten how to cheer by then."

"Us?" Puddles said. "The champs?" She tossed the spoon in the sink. "Go, Gunthwaite, Go! GHS!"

From the doorway, Snowy watched them.

> Go, Gunthwaite, go!
> Go, Gunthwaite, go!
> Smash 'em, bust 'em!
> That's our custom!
> Go, Gunthwaite, go!

Puddles and Darl and Carol and Diane came down from their jumps. Kneeling on the linoleum, fist thrust forward, Puddles said, "We won't ever forget."

The door flew open, and wind and Charl rushed in. She waved her left hand and gasped, "*Look!*" and burst into tears.

It was a diamond engagement ring just given her by Jack O'Brien, who was working for the Gunthwaite Fuel Oil Company cleaning furnaces.

"Oh, Charl!" Darl said and hugged her, and the girls grabbed at the hand, and Puddles said enviously, "You're the first. What a milestone!" Outside the group, Snowy glimpsed the diamond and saw the footballs, basketballs, class rings, and fraternity pins most of the other girls were wearing even with their pajamas, and she felt stark naked.

"The pizza!" Puddles said and ran to the oven.

Linda Littlefield threw up on the floor.

Charl screamed. Puddles whirled around and pushed Linda to the sink and held her head over it.

Linda whooped and spewed and gagged.

"Morning sickness?" Puddles asked. "Sorry, no time for jokes." She glanced back at the mess on the floor. "Oh, shit, the celery, I'll bet the cream cheese went bad. Who the hell put them on the register? You'll be okay, upchuck and you'll be okay."

The kitchen no longer smelled only of pizza and geraniums.

Puddles said, "Snowy, could you get the mop?" and then saw how pale Snowy was. "Somebody, Nancy, Patty, get the mop, it's behind the cellar door."

Dotty Mooney giggled. "Hasten, Jason, bring the basin—"

Puddles said, "Snowy, you get some fresh air or you'll be puking, too."

Snowy dashed outside and bumped smack into Tom and Bev, who were kissing on the doorstep.

All three stood transfixed.

Then Bev said, "What's the matter?"

"Nothing."

Tom's arms left Bev. He and she looked at Snowy standing there in her pajamas, the wind blowing her ponytail.

Bev said, "Well, isn't this cozy?" and waited for Snowy to go indoors.

Snowy didn't. And gradually Bev began to feel that she herself was the third one here, not Snowy.

Tom said, "Party getting a little rough?"

"A little," Snowy said.

He said, "What is it you girls do at pajama parties?"

"Ah," Snowy said. "That's a secret."

He said, "When I was a kid, I really believed that all the women in the world got together at meetings at midnight to decide how to make life miserable for us. Like, they would decide you couldn't listen to *House of Mystery* because it was too scary, and if they made a cake, you couldn't have any because it was for company."

Snowy said, "Maybe we do."

"Actually," Bev said, "we eat and fool around and keep each other awake, which isn't too difficult if you're sleeping on the floor." She picked up her overnight case and said to Snowy, "Coming in?"

"I'm supposed to be getting some fresh air. Orders of Nurse Puddles. Linda threw up."

"How charming," Bev said, and waited.

Someone opened a kitchen window, and they heard Puddles singing. "Here comes the bride, fair, fat, and wide!" Charl shrieked, "I'm *not!*"

Snowy said, "Charl's engaged."

"How cute," Bev said. "Coming in?"

"No," Snowy said.

Bev went inside and closed the door very carefully.

Snowy walked toward his car. Tom followed. She opened the passenger door and slid in, and he took off his jacket and handed it to her, remembering a letter sweater. She put the jacket around her shoulders.

Indoors, Puddles was waltzing with the mop. "Here comes the bride, fair, fat, and wide, see how she waddles from side to side, here comes the groom, skinny as a broom—"

Charl cried, "He's *not!*"

Bev heard the car start up. She went to the window and saw headlights backing out of the driveway.

Tom lit a cigarette and gave it to Snowy. He lit one for himself, and they drove along Gowen Street and Chestnut Street and Main Street. Beneath the streetlights, a lone policeman walked down the sidewalk. They drove up Worm Hill, out of town, through woods.

"Hi, Bev," Puddles said. "Want some pizza? Where's Snowy, is she okay?"

Bev picked a dead leaf off a windowsill geranium. "She's with Tom."

"Jesus Christ," Puddles said.

Tom parked at the sandpit. He and Snowy sat far apart and looked out at the darkness.

He said, "Why'd you do this?"

"Why did you? You could've kicked me out of the car."

"Ever since last summer, I keep finding myself staring at telephones. But I never dared call, I was afraid you'd hang up on me. And you'd have every right to."

"I wouldn't've."

"I didn't know they made pajamas like those."

"Well," she said, "since bermudas are now the thing—"

"I was stupid. It's been worse hell without you than it would've been with. I was stupid."

Then neither of them could stand the distance one more moment. They lunged at each other. And as they kissed, the long-ago ocean seemed to crash over her. They kissed, and their clothes slipped off, and she was saying, "It's all right, yes, it's all right." Tom fumbled wildly in the glove compartment. He kissed her from her lips to her loins, and she looked up at him above her and felt herself being slowly impaled. His muscles were so taut there were hollows behind his collarbones. She grabbed at his shoulders, and the waves slammed and slammed and lifted her out.

Tom came. He lay panting on her.

After a while, she said, "It's like being Siamese twins, isn't it?"

"Are you okay?"

"Yes."

"Hurt?"

"Some."

He sat up. She watched him peel off the Trojan and expertly knot it. She wondered with whom he had learned all this, and suddenly she guessed Joanne. He rolled the window down and tossed the Trojan away. He gathered her up against him, and they looked out, cooling off and smelling spring.

Then he said, "You'll freeze to death," and found her pajamas on the floor. He kissed her breasts and buttoned the pajama tops. He said, "I was so goddamn stupid. We should've been together all along."

She said, "I never told you, but I didn't drink those three Awful-Awfuls in one sitting, I threw up the first two and went back and drank the third. The reason I drank them at all, I was trying to get you to notice me."

"You certainly succeeded," he said, and reached for his shorts.

"No, that was the frog's leg. That was Bev's idea."

Tom zipped his pants.

Snowy said, "She's been talking of applying at Rumford."

"I know. She—I suppose I've been taking her out because it was a way of being near you. She'll go to Boston now."

Snowy said, "She was my best friend," and shivered.

Tom draped his jacket around her shoulders. "She mentioned you applied at another place. Over in Vermont?"

"Yes."

"You haven't heard yet?"

"It'll be May, for them and for Mount Holyoke and Smith too."

"It must be nerve-wracking, the waiting."

"It is."

He gave her a cigarette and offered her his news. "I'm an English major now."

"*English?*"

"And doing okay. You might say it's your influence. I even got an A on the King Lear test last week, though that was mostly thanks to the fraternity files."

"Fraternity?"

"My frat pin is at school. I'll mail it to you when I go back, but that'll just make it official." He put his finger on her left breast. "We're pinned. We're engaged-to-be-engaged."

She looked down and imagined a little gold pin. She would belong to someone, like the other girls. She would belong to him again at last.

She said, "It must be terribly late."

"Don't you have a watch yet?"

"You know my folks. I'll get one on the proper occasion, at graduation, not an instant before."

He laughed and started the car. He drove to town, his arm around her, and she thought of all the times they had driven home like this. She had got him back again. They drove along Main Street, but instead of seeing the stores, she saw quite clearly now how the next years would be, everything unimportant except his letters and his visits. Any school would be a prison, any school but Rumford, and she couldn't go to Rumford because she'd worked too hard for something different.

He parked at Puddles' house. The downstairs lights were still on. "Christ," he said, "I wish you didn't have to go in." His arm tightened around her and pulled her against him. He said, "We wasted almost a whole year."

Her voice was so smothered he could hardly hear her. "For the longest time, I couldn't understand why you broke up with me if you loved me like you said. Then I decided it was because we got too serious too early. But it was because you were going away to school, wasn't it, and you didn't want to be all mixed up there, you didn't want to be tied down. You wanted to see what would happen. You said we had to get loose of each other or we'd go nuts, remember?"

"I was wrong. I went nuts anyway."

"No, you were right. Where you were wrong was, it should have been final. None of that business about maybe things would work out later. I waited and waited—I couldn't do anything because I was waiting. We've got to get loose of each other for good."

"Snowy, what the hell are you talking about? After what we just did?"

She kissed his throat where the dark hairs curled over the rim of his T-shirt. She slipped her hand under the rim and touched where the hollows had been.

Then she sat up and took off the jacket and slid across the seat and opened the door.

"*Wait,*" Tom said desperately, "there's the rest of vacation, we can straighten this out, I'll pick you up here tomorrow morning, and we'll spend the day together. We could go for a drive someplace."

"No," she said, "it would be going backward." She stepped out of the car and walked into the house.

The Gang had separated, General students in the living room, College Prep in the kitchen.

Bev said, "Have fun?"

Snowy was shivering. She said, "It's all over."

When Snowy got home from school on May 15, Tom's birthday, she ran across the lawn to the front door to check the mail, as she had been doing every May afternoon.

There were three letters in the mailbox. The return addresses were Smith, Mount Holyoke, and Bennington.

She walked around to the back door. Inside, Laurie barked and wagged.

"Pray," Snowy told her. "This is it."

But Laurie wanted a dog biscuit. Snowy gave her one. Laurie barked for outdoors, and Snowy let her out and then followed her, crossing the street. Snowy sat down on the riverbank and ripped open the Bennington envelope. The letter began, "I am very happy to tell you—"

She leaned back against a tree. The letter shook in her hands, and she read it and learned that the Reduced Tuition Committee was offering her a grant. Then she opened and glanced at the other letters and saw that she had been accepted and awarded their scholarships, too.

"Well," she said to Laurie. "I did it."

Above her in the trees the buds were a pale haze thickening to green.